Irresistible Magic

Books by Deanna Chase

The Jade Calhoun Novels
Haunted on Bourbon Street
Witches of Bourbon Street
Demons of Bourbon Street
Angels of Bourbon Street
Shadows of Bourbon Street (March 2014)

The Crescent City Fae Novels
Influential Magic
Irresistible Magic
Book Three in the Crescent City Fae series (June 2014)

The Destiny Novels
Defining Destiny (Dec 2013)

Irresistible Magic

A Crescent City Fae Novel

Deanna Chase

Bayou Moon Publishing

Acknowledgments

As always, many thanks to Angie Ramey, Susan Sheehan, Lisa Liddy, Chauntelle Baughman, and Anne Victory. You're help is invaluable. A special thanks to Linda, Rachel, and Suzanna for always being there. And of course, lots of heartfelt hugs to my readers. Without you I'd be nowhere.

Chapter 1

"I look like a flying giraffe." I scowled at my roommate, Phoebe, in the three-way mirror. "What were you thinking, making me try on this travesty?"

Phoebe, dressed in a miniskirt and tight red T-shirt, rolled her eyes. "You said you'd try on anything. And look at this dress. The cut is gorgeous. It's hugging you in all the right places, girl."

I crossed my arms over my chest and flared my wings in agitation. "I look ridiculous." There was no freaking way I was wearing a formfitting giraffe-print dress on my first official date with Talisen. That was a *hell* no. "You're just trying to torture me because I wouldn't buy the last dress you decided I needed."

She placed her hands on her hips. "That dress was perfect for you and guaranteed to bring Talisen to his knees."

"It would bring the majority of the male population to their knees. I think there's more material in a toddler's outfit than that scrap of cotton."

"Whatever you say, Wil." She began digging in another rack of dresses. "Try on the hunter-green one next."

"Gladly." I wrinkled my nose at the offending animal print one more time and moved toward the dressing room.

"Hold on." Phoebe trotted over to me, holding yet another crime against fashion.

"Electric yellow with sequins? Have you lost your mind?" I laughed, wondering if she'd been dipping into a dose of Illusions, an illegal vamp-made, psychedelic street drug. They tasted like candy and were often handed out at college parties.

Not that Phoebe was in college, but she did spend time at the universities when she was on undercover missions, running down rogue vampires.

"It's perfect for you." She grabbed my arm and leaned in, almost dragging me to my dressing room. "Keep walking," she whispered.

"Phoebe?"

"Shh." With her head bent to mine, she said, "I noticed the blond guy two stores back, but I just caught him taking a picture of you with his phone. He's definitely a tail."

Crap, crap, crap! Was the vampire Asher following me again? Had he found out about my ability to turn vamps into daywalkers? Or worse, about my nephew's existence, who probably had the same skill? A ripple of panic skated through me. I jerked unconsciously, wanting to see who was behind us, but Phoebe's hand tightened on my forearm until I winced.

"Jesus, Wil. Are you an agent of the Void or what? Don't turn around." Technically I was an agent, but only because I could sense vampires. Phoebe was the badass witch who could actually run them down and neutralize them if they were tagged as a danger to society. She shoved the dress into my hands. "Take this and try it on like everything's normal. I'll see about apprehending him. Then we can have some fun interrogating his ass."

"You're just going to take him down right here in front of the shop clerk?" Goddess above, that could get messy. "What if he's a witch? A bystander could get seriously hurt."

She paused outside my dressing room door, her face contorted with mock offense as she shook her head, her hand clutching her heart. "Jeez, you have such little faith. It pains me to say it, but I don't know if we can be friends anymore. But don't worry, he's human."

I shook my head, stifling a laugh. Knowing he was human put me at ease. Phoebs could take him while blindfolded and chained to a wall. All she needed was a little witch power and he'd be no more dangerous than a two-week-old puppy. "Just don't cause a scene like last time when you spelled that poor schmuck into stripping for the entire restaurant."

Her eyes glittered with the memory. "Now that was something to see."

That guy had been sent undercover to evaluate Phoebe's performance as a Void agent. Phoebe was a vampire hunter for the Void branch of the Arcane—the government agency that oversees all supernatural activity. Void agents, such as herself, worked undercover and moved without boundaries. She'd had no way of knowing the guy tailing her was a colleague. When she failed to ditch him, she spiked his drink with an inhibition spell and then flirted with him until he did a rendition of *The Full Monty*.

"He was...uh, built in all the right places," I said.

Phoebe snickered. "Yes. Yes he was. Too bad he transferred right after that." She shrugged. "Some people are too sensitive." She held the yellow dress out to me. "Get moving while I go take the stalker down. I know he's only a human, but I'm not taking any chances. Someone sent him for a reason."

Her words sobered me. Being human didn't mean he wasn't a threat. Someone probably had sent him. I stared at the offending dress still in her hands. "I'm going, but don't think for a moment I'm putting that on."

"Fine. Just take it into the dressing room to keep up appearances."

I disappeared behind the door and grimaced at my reflection. It really was too bad the giraffe dress didn't come in another print or even a solid color, because Phoebe was right. The cut accentuated curves I hadn't even known existed. I undid the side zipper and was slipping my wings out of the back slits when the dressing room door creaked open.

"This one had better not have sequins or anything that belongs in the zoo." I turned, expecting Phoebe, and let out a gasp as I clutched the dress to my chest, covering myself.

David, my ex, moved with vampire speed and clamped his hand over my mouth. "Shh."

I glared, stepping back until I was pressed up against the mirror, half-naked in one of the ugliest dresses ever. What the hell was he doing out in the middle of the day? Stalking me? Had he put the tail on us? I grabbed his arm, trying fruitlessly to break away from his hold. Then I kicked at his shin and winced when my bare toe connected with his marble-like frame.

"Calm down," he said softly, his midnight-blue eyes locked on mine. "I'll let go if you'll be quiet. I have some news."

Even though David was a vampire, he'd never intentionally hurt me. At least not physically. Less than two weeks ago, I'd found out he'd spent the better part of a year protecting me. Reluctantly, I nodded.

His hand slid from my mouth and he took a tiny step back.

My lips tingled from his touch and I wanted to kick him all over again. I hated that his touch still had an effect on me, even when I wanted to clock him for being a dominating a-hole. I glanced in the mirror and tugged the dress higher, trying for some semblance of decency. "What are you doing in my dressing room? Couldn't you have waited outside?"

"We can't be seen together."

I sighed. Of course we couldn't. In fact, he shouldn't be seen during the day at all. If word got out he was a daywalker…"Go home, David." I nervously peeked over the dressing-room stall. "You're going to get us both killed if anyone sees you."

"No one is going to see me in here." His lips quirked up into an appreciative smile as his gaze traveled the length of my barely covered body. He glanced at the dresses hanging to the left. "What's the occasion?"

I bit back a groan and stared him down. "I have a date."

The smile vanished and he straightened, his six-foot-two frame taking up almost all my personal space. His perfect lips formed into a straight line. "I see."

I didn't know what to say to that. A week ago, David had told me he still loved me. That he'd never stopped. But he was a vampire and I was a faery. Faeries and vampires did not date. Ever. Vamps embody death while fae thrive on life. Me especially. Being around vampires could make me physically ill. Besides, he'd lied and kept vital information about my brother's death from me for months.

"It's with Talisen," I blurted, angry all over again at his betrayal.

David's eyes narrowed and he slowly backed up, finally giving me some room. The gesture only made me feel that much more exposed. After a tense moment of silence, he cut his eyes to glance over the door. "That's none of my business."

"That's right. It isn't." I clutched the dress tighter to my chest. "Now leave so I can get dressed."

"No." He met my gaze with a cold, determined stare.

"What do you mean, no? Get out."

"I came to deliver a message."

His tone sent a shiver through my wings. The kind that put me on full alert. "What's wrong?"

"Eadric wants to see you at sunset, but not at the club. We can't risk having you seen there. We'll meet you at Hotel La Blanchet."

This is what he accosted me in the dressing room for? To set up a meeting with Eadric Allcot, the master vampire and unofficial leader of New Orleans? The last time, I'd been summoned by a written letter. Now he'd sent David to demand my presence. What was next, an armed escort? "Why? What's so important?"

"It's about the Void. Eadric has information."

"What information?" I worked for the Void branch of the Arcane also, and recently I'd been target number one due to my unusual abilities.

He shrugged. "I'm not sure. Father wasn't forthcoming."

Well, crap on toast. We had a new director and I hadn't even met her yet. Was I trading one nightmare for another?

"Also, you're being watched." He jerked his head toward the front of the store.

"You don't say," I said with a fair amount of sarcasm and waved an impatient hand in front of him. "I know that already.

Phoebe spotted him. I have a phone. You could've left a message. We're not idiots."

He raised a skeptical eyebrow. "Really? Is it on you?" His gaze raked over my body once more, as if to say he highly doubted it.

Of course I didn't have my phone on me. I was barely dressed. "It's in my purse." I waved a hand toward the corner. "A text would've been just fine," I forced out through clenched teeth. "Or you could've called Phoebe."

This was ridiculous. I was starting to think he just wanted to get a peek at my faery bits. Perv.

David moved in closer, this time putting his chilled hands on my shoulders. "We both know you don't ever check your phone. But that's beside the point. Your phones might be tapped, and I couldn't risk anyone knowing we're in touch."

"Tapped?" Fear started to crawl over my skin. Why would anyone tap our phones? I frantically tried to recall if Phoebe and I had talked about anything damaging over the phone during the last week. I didn't think so. It wasn't as if I used the thing that much, but I couldn't be sure.

"Tell Phoebe to sweep your house. Father wants you at the hotel by six p.m. He'll fill you in on what he knows then. Bring *the fae* with you."

I bristled at his use of *the fae* for Talisen. There wasn't any love between vampires and fae. As far as I knew, I was the only one the vamps associated with. "I just told you I have a date with him tonight. I'm not going to bring him to the hotel to meet you and Allcot." Talk about awkward.

David's emotionless eyes softened for a moment. "If he cares for you at all, he'll understand. If not, then he doesn't deserve you."

He moved to open the door, but I clamped my hand on his rock-hard arm. "Are Carrie and Beau all right?" My nephew Beau and his mother, Carrie, lived in one of Allcot's apartments above his club on Frenchmen Street. Beau's life would be in danger if anyone found out he existed. Even though I didn't care for Allcot, I had to admit the safest place for my nephew was under his care.

"For now. We'll talk later." He glanced back at the dresses lining the wall. "Wear the blue one."

And before I could say anything else, he was gone.

Standing alone in the dressing room, a cold sweat broke out over my body, and I shivered under the air-conditioning. A harsh reality settled over me. It had been over a week since I'd seen my ex, and I'd almost convinced myself I was happy about that. Right up until the moment he'd appeared before me. Even if he had just put a major kink in my date with Tal.

Talisen. A sigh got caught in my throat. Tonight was our first date. I'd grown up with Tal. He'd been my teenage crush and was my best friend. I'd waited a long time for this night. And Eadric Allcot, master vampire, head of Cryrique, was already ruining it. *Damn vamps.*

I ditched the giraffe dress, bypassed the electric-yellow calamity, and pulled out the "blue" dress David had alluded to. Upon closer inspection, it was actually a deep plum. The perfect color to go with my auburn hair.

Still flustered, I stepped into the backless, figure-hugging dress and tied the halter-top bodice around my neck. Then I left the dressing room to inspect myself in the three-way mirror. Two steps out of the room, a startled gasp stopped me in my tracks.

On high alert, I jumped back, ready to use the door as a shield. Why did I have to be attacked while wearing a backless dress and no shoes? Talk about feeling vulnerable.

"Willow, it's amazing," Phoebe exclaimed and yanked me back out of the room.

"Phoebe!" I clutched a hand to my racing heart. "You scared the crap out of me. How long have you been standing there?"

"Long enough to know you didn't try on the yellow dress. But who cares? This one is perfect. Talisen is going to strain something just looking at you." She spun me around, pointing me at the three-way mirror.

"Whoa." The dress was…well, perfect. As if it were made for me. It was formfitting, yet not too tight. The top was a tasteful halter, but the back was jaw-dropping. My wings were on full display with the rest of my tanned flesh exposed. Sexy. I'd never felt so beautiful. "You're right. This is it."

She threaded her arm through mine. "I think our mission is complete. Unless you're dying to try on the yellow one?" She wiggled her eyebrows.

I rolled my eyes. "Not on your life."

She grinned and checked her watch. "Then get changed. We have more shopping to do."

"What happened to the stalker?"

Her grin soured. "He saw me coming and jumped into a waiting SUV. He's been spotted. If he's stupid enough to show his face again, he'll be lucky if I don't break both his arms."

Well, that was unsettling. Phoebe headed to the front of the store to keep watch while I changed as fast as I could before hightailing it to the register, more than ready to leave. The checkout clerk was busy folding cardigan sweaters and didn't even look up. "Excuse me," I said with a smile.

"Just a minute," she snapped.

My smile faltered. I bit back a snarky reply and waited. But when she pulled a phone out of her back pocket and started texting, I lost the battle. "I'm sorry, but we're in a hurry. Can I pay for this?"

"I said—" Her eyes went wide with shock as she stared over my shoulder.

I spun just in time to see a man clutching a gun reach out and wrap his arm around my neck. My left wing was smashed between us and sent a dart of pain through my left side as he pulled me tight against his body. "Come quietly and no one needs to get hurt."

I swallowed a cry of protest and met the trembling clerk's eyes. Her mouth opened in silent shock as she backed up and stumbled over her feet. She went down with a yelp of surprise at the same time Phoebe appeared in my peripheral vision and yelled, "Freeze!"

Holy fae. She had blood trickling down the side of her face. He must've attacked her first. How had a human gotten the jump on her?

"Son of a bitch," my attacker muttered and spun me around, his arm cutting off my airway. My eyes bugged out as I scrabbled at his hold.

"Let her go, or I'll be putting you in a body bag in about three seconds," Phoebe demanded, flashing her sun agate at him. What was she going to do, blind him with it?

Light flared from the agate and my attacker stumbled back. "Move, Willow!"

Oh, shit. That's exactly what she'd done. I threw myself to the right, barely avoiding a collision with a rack of accessories.

The gun went off with a *thwap* and the next moment a crackle of magic exploded, illuminating the store in a brilliant flash of blue lightning.

Trembling with delayed adrenaline, I crawled from under a garment rack and peered around. Who the hell was that guy, and what did he want? Phoebe was standing in front of our frozen attacker, rubbing her jaw thoughtfully. The gun lay at her feet. Good Goddess. That was close. He'd been stunned and wouldn't be moving another muscle until she reversed her magic.

I turned and caught sight of the clerk. She was chalk white, also frozen in place, except she had tears streaming down her face and instead of being spelled, fear had rendered her incapable of moving. She didn't even answer her ringing phone.

"Who sent him?" I asked Phoebe.

"Don't know. But since the bastard coldcocked me and tried to take you, this is Arcane business. I'll call it in."

"He coldcocked you?" My voice rose in sheer disbelief.

She nodded and touched the cut on her head. "He came out of nowhere. The bastard has some sort of training."

"What the hell is going on?"

"I don't know, but we're sure going to try to find out." She kicked our attacker. "God help him after the interrogators get to him."

Forcing myself to maintain some sort of normalcy, I turned back to the clerk. My dress was still sitting on the counter. "Can I check out now?"

She didn't appear to hear me as she started to shake and slid back down to the floor. "Dammit," I muttered. Humans. I walked around the counter. The register was almost identical to the ones we used at my shop, The Fated Cupcake. "I'm sorry. But this dress is too good to leave here. If you don't mind, I'll just check myself out."

Her vacant eyes met mine, and she gave me one tiny nod. I was certain she wasn't registering what she'd agreed to, but there was no way in hell I was leaving my perfect dress.

Chapter 2

Sitting on my bed, I leaned against my enchanted oak, holding the gorgeous plum dress. As a faery, I needed nature to recharge, and in New Orleans, a city full of concrete, that wasn't an easy task. Sure, New Orleans has lots of trees and parks, but it's not like living in a forest. When I moved to New Orleans, Phoebe spelled the magical oak into existence so I could recharge in my sleep. It was the perfect solution.

Though the oak didn't seem to be helping much now. My limbs were shaking from delayed shock. I'd almost been abducted. A gun had gone off. And then I'd bought a dress as if nothing had happened. I could've *died*. What was wrong with me? Holy crow.

A month ago, my biggest worry was running out of Molten Muse at my shop. Now I had someone gunning for me. And it wasn't the guy Phoebe had taken out. Surely he was hired muscle. No, it had to be Asher, the vampire lord who had killed my brother. Did he know I'd inherited Beau's abilities? What else would prompt him to have me kidnapped from a cute boutique on Magazine Street, of all places? Not very subtle. Was he coming after me at all costs now? I'd have to be extra cautious everywhere I went from now on.

My stomach dropped with sudden fear. *My shop*. I had to tell them. What if Asher sent another gunman there? My employees could be in danger. My wings fluttered, and despite the still-lingering pain, I flew to the floor and grabbed my phone.

For once, I'd remembered to charge the thing. Link, in wolf form, pressed against my leg in a possessive manner. The second I'd walked through the door, he'd shifted from his adorable Shih Tzu form, no doubt sensing my off-the-charts anxiety level. "Back up, Link."

He looked up at me through golden eyes but didn't move.

"Fine, but stop pressing into me. Your one hundred and fifty pounds of wolf-weight is going to knock me over."

He snorted a breath through his nose and backed off a little.

"Huh." Maybe he did understand me.

The phone buzzed just as I picked it up. *The Fated Cupcake* flashed on the screen. "Tami?"

"Willow? Oh, my God," my assistant cried. "I'm so sorry."

My heart dropped to my toes hearing the panic in her voice. *Had Asher already sent people to my shop?* "What's wrong? Is everyone all right?"

"Everyone's fine." She sucked in air as if to calm herself. "It's nothing like that."

I let out a sigh of relief. As long as my employees were okay, everything else could be dealt with. "Okay, what happened?"

"I don't know exactly. It's been swamped all morning here, so I've been chained to the front counter. It must've happened last night, otherwise we would've heard something."

"Heard what?" A small headache started to form above my left eye.

"Oh, sorry. I'm flustered. Someone broke into your office. It's been trashed."

"Just my office? Nothing else?" Why the hell would anyone break into my office? There wasn't anything there but my computer and some old files. And none of that was terribly important. Even my recipes didn't mean much without my magic to alter them.

"Everything else appears to be in order."

A feeling of utter violation took up residence in my gut and started to spread. My office was my sanctuary. A space that was all mine. "I'll be right there."

"Do you want me to call anyone? The police?"

Good question. Did I want anyone involved? "No. I'll take care of it. Thanks, Tami. See you in a few." I hit End and immediately called Phoebe.

She'd gone straight to the Arcane to start filling out paperwork. I'd stopped off at home to grab Link and collect myself. I'd needed a moment before going to the Arcane building. I'd be bombarded with questions I wasn't sure I should answer. Last week, I'd found out Felton, the director of the Void, had wanted me either dead or locked up permanently to be used as his personal weapon. But Allcot eliminated him after he'd found out the director had used his sister-in-law. The immediate threat at the Arcane was gone, but I had no idea if anyone remained loyal to Felton. Did anyone still working in the Void branch share his views? Plenty of agents had carried out his orders without so much as a murmur of protest.

Of course, they could've been Influenced. Maude, my aunt, had been. I just had too many questions and trusted no one but Phoebe and Talisen.

"Wil, are you on your way?" Phoebe's voice boomed through the phone.

"No. My freakin' office was ransacked," I huffed out in frustration. "There's no way I'm going to make it to the Arcane anytime soon."

"Your office at the shop?"

"Yes. Tami just called."

"I'll be right there." Phoebe hung up before I could protest.

My phone made a sad beeping noise and then died. Dammit, I swear I'd charged the stupid thing. Grabbing the USB cord, I gestured to Link. "Let's go, boy. Never a dull moment."

Link stayed in wolf form, and honestly, I was glad. It made getting him into the Jeep a little tougher since he practically took up the entire back seat, but his large presence made me feel safer.

Seven minutes later, I parked a few spaces down from my shop in Uptown. I watched a steady stream of customers filter in and out through the gleaming glass doors. It was just another normal Saturday, except I'd been assaulted and I was being stalked. Plus my personal sanctuary had been invaded. What the hell were they looking for?

"Let's go in, Link." I jumped out and pulled the back door open. He leaped with ease to the ground and headed for my private side entrance.

What was I walking into? My pulse quickened with something close to fear. *Get a grip, Willow. No one is in there.* Tami and the staff had already checked things out. My rationale did nothing to soothe me. As I rounded the corner, Link let out a growl and pawed at the door.

"What is it, Link?" Sweat broke out on my palms as I studied the lock. There wasn't any sign of forced entry. Not even a scratch. Had they come in through the front? Surely someone would have noticed if the glass door had been damaged. No, whoever had done this was a professional.

Link sniffed incessantly at the bottom of the door but stopped growling. It was likely he smelled the lingering scent of whoever had broken in.

Confident I wasn't walking into an ambush, I slipped my key into the lock and opened the door easily. Pushing the door open, I held my breath and then gasped at the utter catastrophe within.

Link bounded in, tearing through the office, sniffing anything and everything. He stopped behind my desk and whimpered. Torn paper, destroyed books and journals, and stuffing from Link's bed and my couch littered the floor. But the worst of it was in and around my desk. It appeared every single one of my meticulous, handwritten files had been shredded, burned, and then sprinkled on top of my desk. My whole body went cold with barely suppressed rage.

Link started to whine, and I headed his way.

"What did you find?" I peeked over my desk and started to gag. "Omigod!" Who would do such a horrible thing? "Back," I told Link and then, shaking with anger, I reached down and lightly stroked the small bluebird. He was still breathing, but barely. His wings and tail had been duct-taped to the floor, and half his feathers had ripped from his body as he struggled to break free. My insides constricted, coiling into a tight ball. The horrible display was too much for my inner fae. I had to breathe life back into the poor helpless thing. A monster had done this.

Vampire.

One of them was after me and this was a message. Hate filled my vision, but I quickly pushed it aside. The bird needed my help.

My touch seemed to calm him, but he was very weak. Carefully, I peeled back the tape, and as the last strip came free, he tucked his wings to his sides and started to shake.

"It's going to be okay, little one." I cradled him in one hand and half covered him with the other. Running two fingers along his chest, I drew in a tiny bit of his life force and, together with my magic, forced it back into his being. It was just enough to stop his shaking. Normally I didn't alter the life energy of animals, as plants were my specialty, but I had to do what I could.

I sank to the floor, holding the traumatized bird, and stared at the destruction around me. The bird had been a symbol. Whoever did this was trying to intimidate me, letting me know they'd do the same to me if I got in the way. Why else would anyone harm a poor, defenseless bird?

When Phoebe arrived five minutes later, I was still sitting on the floor, cradling the poor bird. She took one look at the office and hit a button on her phone. "Forensics." Pause. "Bring the cameras, print and motion. We're going to want more than one type of record."

The Void investigators were on their way. While Phoebe and I both worked for the Void, we were vampire hunters, not forensic investigators. Phoebe did a cursory lap around the office, taking notes, inspecting the discarded papers, and finally stopped right next to me. "Someone had a bonfire on your desk."

"A small one, it appears. Good thing they put it out." My whole store could've gone up in flames.

"What's with the bird?"

I told her what Link had found and she gasped in shock. "Damn, that's awful."

I nodded. I was more upset by what the bird had been through than the state of my office. It reminded me too much of being imprisoned at the Void not too long ago. The bird started to flap its wings, forcing me to let go. He wobbled and fluttered to the ground but stood tall, ready to move on. "Good-bye, little birdie. Have a good life." I held the door open and watched as he clumsily flew out of the office under his own steam. My magic appeared to have given him a fighting chance. I hoped so, anyway.

The door that led to the shop creaked open. "Wil?" Tami, my assistant, poked her head in.

"Yeah?"

Relief flashed over her face. "I was hoping that was you in here."

I sent her a grim smile.

"Someone is here to see you."

Before I could respond, a small-framed, frizzy-haired bundle of energy plowed through the door. Her pale blue wings flexed behind her. "Miss Rhoswen." The faery came to a stop in front of me and held out her hand.

Startled, it took me a moment to extend my own hand.

"Director Halston. I'm sorry we're meeting under such unpleasant circumstances." Her grip was firm as she pumped my hand.

"Director." I cut my eyes to Phoebe. She gave me a slight shrug. Had she known the new director was coming? "I wasn't expecting you."

She smiled. "Groundwork is often underestimated. After your earlier attack and now this, I thought it was important I see to the details personally." She glanced around my office. "Looks like whoever did this was very thorough."

"My life's work has been destroyed." My voice was flat, almost uncaring, even though I was dying inside. I'd built this store from nothing, poured my heart and soul into it, and now someone had threatened what I'd created. I had backup files for all my recipes, but that wasn't the point. These records were my originals, the ones I'd made during my creative process. This was personal.

The director swept a mass of hair out of her eyes and pulled out a leather-bound notebook. "Have you touched anything?"

I repeated the story of the bird one more time. She pushed her plastic-framed glasses on and frowned. "I'm going to do the Arcane inspection myself." Paper crinkled beneath her shoes with each step as she made her way around the room.

Phoebe and I shared a curious look. Directors didn't do routine field inspections. There was only one reason she was here—she'd taken a personal interest in me.

My blood pressure rose and my wings started to twitch. The last time I'd been on a director's radar, I'd been locked up in the basement of the Arcane building waiting to be turned into a lab rat. I left my office and headed for the storefront.

Tami rushed to my side when I stepped behind the counter. "Can I get you anything? A Calming Cupcake?"

I turned slowly, focusing on her, trying to force all the anger and sadness swirling inside me into a tightly locked box. There wasn't time to process all the emotion bursting in my chest. "Actually, yes. Should've thought of that myself."

She handed me the lavender-frosted cupcake and patted my arm. "I'm so sorry this happened. I can't imagine how violated you must feel."

I picked at the paper wrapper as I glanced around the shop and noted everything else appeared to be in place. But what about my plants? A sharp jab of fear pierced my heart. Not my plants. They were like my children, so carefully cultivated and magically altered. "Is the lab all right?" I asked, not at all sure I wanted to know the answer.

"Yeah. I checked everything after I saw your office. No one has been in there."

"Thank the Goddess," I breathed, relief flooding through me as I took a bite of the cupcake. It took a few moments, but eventually the ingredients filtered through my system, easing the tension in my shoulders. I reluctantly headed back to my office to find the director had cleared a space and was sitting behind my desk, her pen flying across her notebook pages.

"Now that you're back," the director said, "have a seat." She pierced me with a stare reminiscent of a high school principal.

I obeyed and sat stiffly next to Phoebe, fidgeting with my fingernails. Why was I so nervous? I hadn't done anything wrong.

"Let's discuss the reasons you could be a target." She scanned each of our faces, lingering just long enough to make eye contact.

Silence.

"Kilsen?" she demanded.

Phoebe raised her chin, acknowledging her. "Yes, Director?"

"Your theory, please."

Phoebe glanced at me once, then gave Halston her full attention. "Any number of reasons, I suppose. Orange Influence or the fact that Willow was recently partnered with a vampire. It could be related to her brother's death—"

Blood rushed to my head. Had she really brought my brother into this? We'd decided to keep the details of the abilities I'd inherited from Beau under wraps until we knew who we could trust.

"Her brother's death?" Halston frowned and pulled a file out of her bag. She flipped through it and scanned a sheet. "It says here in the report that the incident was a random act of violence."

Phoebe shrugged. "That's the way it was ruled at the time, but who's to say? I'm just throwing out possibilities."

"Hmm." Halston made a note and glanced at me. "Rhoswen, what do you think?"

I did my very best to appear nonplussed, but I wasn't known for my poker face. I unclenched my jaw and sent Phoebe a mental death glare. "I suppose there could be someone loyal to Felton who is trying to get revenge for his untimely disappearance. I was his target at the time." Felton was the prior Void director who'd used Orange Influence to illegally control my aunt and one of Allcot's witches. He'd been exposed after he'd tried to have me locked up and used as a lab rat. Allcot had him killed shortly after I'd escaped.

"Yes. I had that thought as well." She stood. "I have what I need here. After we interrogate your attacker, I'll be in touch. Thank you for your cooperation."

Phoebe bounced to her feet, startling Link, and he let out a tiny growl. As he scanned the room, his protective snarl turned sheepish. I couldn't help but chuckle.

I stood. "Director, I'm afraid this isn't an isolated incident. Is it possible to get a detail to watch my store? My employees are human and not equipped to deal with any Void business."

She tilted her head, regarding me. "I don't think that's necessary. You seemed to be the target, and we have the suspect in custody. For the time being, I'd rather play this close to our vest. If we send in security, questions will be asked."

Foreboding gnawed at the lining of my stomach. She'd dismissed the safety of my employees. What if she was just as bad as Felton had been? Was she the one who'd sent the gunman after me? Did the plan to utilize me run much deeper through the Void than we'd suspected? And Phoebe had put her on the trail of my brother. Jesus mother freakin' crap on toast. I'd have quit the Void right there on sheer suspicion if I wasn't magically bound to them for another two and a half years.

"So you think my attacker did this sometime last night or early this morning, then?" I waved a hand around the room.

"That's the simplest explanation. And the simplest is usually the correct one." She got to her feet. "I'll be on my way. Good luck, agents." She swept out the side door, her frizzy hair bouncing with each step.

I glared at Phoebe as Link paced around her.

"What?" she asked. "Why are you so pissed? Link looks like he's ready to tear my head off."

My one-hundred-fifty-pound wolf had his teeth bared and was eyeballing Phoebe like she was a rare piece of steak that had just been snatched from him.

"Why did you bring up Beau?" I demanded.

"Why not?" She swept a pile of paper into the trash basket beside my desk.

I crossed the room and locked the door that led into the shop. This wasn't a conversation for others' ears. Once I was settled behind my desk, I turned hard eyes on her. "You know why not. If the director goes digging around and finds out about the ability I inherited from Beau, I could be right back where I was last week. In a cage."

She frowned. "If I hadn't brought it up, she might start to think there's something to cover up. It's an unknown in your past, Wil. It's the first thing an agent would look at. That's basic Void knowledge."

"And I didn't go to the Academy, right? So I wouldn't know that? Is that what you're saying?" I kicked at the debris near my feet. My only skill was sensing vampires. It was my job to alert the agents when vampires were around, not to fight them myself. I didn't need Academy training for that.

"What?" She turned to me, shock clear in her wide blue eyes. "That is not at all what I said. I was only trying to defuse the situation and buy us more time to figure out who's behind this. There's a very good possibility she'll find out anyway once interrogations begin. Your attacker is human. If he works for Asher, he could know all the details of Beau's death. How much can he stand before he spills it all? And if we pretend there isn't anything suspicious and the Void uncovers something about him, we can't have you looking like you withheld information. That's an offense that will get you prison time. You know this."

Shit. I was way too wound up. I took a deep, steadying breath. "Sorry. You're right, of course. I might be shell-shocked. It's been a bad day."

She turned a sympathetic smile on me. "As a Void agent, it was bound to happen sometime. Just be glad you have a kickass partner."

Link's head came up and he appeared to raise one eyebrow in her direction. I couldn't help the laugh bubbling from my lips. "Very humble, Phoebs. I think Link's wondering how there's enough space in this room for all three of us with that ego of yours."

She grinned. "No one ever accused me of being modest."

Chapter 3

With my back bare and the skirt hugging my hips, the gorgeous plum dress molded to my body perfectly. I ran a hand over my long hair, smoothing it to the side as butterflies took up residence in my stomach.

Five more minutes and Talisen would arrive. Our first date. This wouldn't be any normal first date, either. We'd known each other almost our whole lives. This was the start of a whole new chapter in our relationship. How do you go from being best friends to casual dating? You don't. It's a full-on commitment.

Shoes. I needed shoes. I rarely wore heels. In my line of work, it wasn't called for. But when I did, I went all out. Four-inch stilettos in shimmery silver matched the nail polish on my toes.

"Holy fuck, Wil. What are you trying to do, kill the guy?" Phoebe leaned against my doorframe, eyeing me appreciatively. "That dress is *hot*."

A slow smile spread on my lips. "Tal has seen me dressed up before."

She snorted. "But not when you were on *his* menu."

My grin widened and heat crawled up my neck. Oh goodness, was I on his menu this evening? Would he be thinking we'd end up back at his new place? Was I ready for that? Images of his large hands skimming lightly over my skin flashed through my mind. My entire body started to tingle. It was a good thing I wasn't wearing a lot of clothing because it suddenly got very warm in my room.

"Of course, anything could happen after your meeting with Allcot," she whispered in my ear, mindful of any lingering bugs, and wrinkled her nose in disgust. Being that he was as ruthless as he was power hungry, Eadric wasn't exactly her favorite vampire.

Dammit. She had to bring that up. Talisen was going to be pissed.

On the first floor, the front door banged open with a deafening crash. "Willow!" Talisen's frantic voice floated up the stairs, followed by boots pounding on the wooden steps.

"Uh oh. He must've heard what happened." Phoebe grimaced and ducked out of my room. "Hey, Tal," I heard her say.

"Phoebe, where is she?" His voice was full of fear, and I found myself moving swiftly toward the hall in my four-inch heels.

I peeked around the doorframe. "Tal?"

The tension in his face vanished as obvious relief washed over him. He swept me in his arms and let out a barely audible sigh. "Jesus, Wil. I heard there was a shooting that involved a faery. And all the reports led back to you."

I hugged him tightly, burying my face in his shoulder. Goddess, it was good to be safe in his arms. "I'm fine. Especially now that you're here."

His hold tightened around me. "Want to tell me about it?"

I let out a humorless chuckle. "Sure. Some stalker pulled a gun. Phoebs took him out. And then I bought a dress."

"Thank you, Phoebe. Try not go anywhere without her ever again."

I smiled into his shoulder. "I had the same thought, but we might want to leave her home tonight."

"Good point. Wait, you bought a dress?" He pulled back, holding me at arm's length. His forest-green eyes darkened with desire as his gaze traveled the length of my body. He let out a slow, appreciative whistle. "Nice dress."

"You like it then?" I stared up at him, taking in his corded, muscular frame. Male fae are not blessed with wings. Instead, they are gifted with the ability to climb almost anything. His years of exploring the redwood forests helped him fill out his black sports coat and dark denim jeans better than the average guy. At six foot four with his sun-lightened auburn hair, he was gorgeous.

"Like? I'm not sure that's the word I'd use." He traced his fingers down my neck, leaving a trail of shivers in his wake. Then his fingers dug into my arms and he pulled me close, his lips inches from mine.

My breath caught and I brought my hands up to his chest, lightly running my fingers over his hard planes. "What are you waiting for?"

His gaze shifted from my lips to my eyes and then back to my mouth. Nervous anticipation made me bite down on my lower lip.

"What are you trying to do to me? I'm supposed to be taking you to dinner, and right now all I can think about is ripping that torturous dress off you and locking you in this room all night." His hands relaxed as they moved up over my bare arms.

I closed my eyes, reveling in his gentle but firm caress. Tal was a healer. His touch was more familiar to me than anyone's. But this was the first night we'd ever allowed ourselves to experience each other without friendship boundaries. I *wanted* him to lock my door, take me to bed, and spend the evening uncovering my secret desires. But he couldn't. I had an appointment at Cryrique. And if I didn't show up, I knew damn well Allcot would send someone to find us.

In my heels, all it took was the tilt of my head and my lips were on Talisen's. A tiny, strangled moan escaped from him as his tongue pressed into my mouth, barely brushing against mine.

A shiver ran down my back and straight to the tips of my wings. Long-suppressed desire consumed me, and when his arms came around me, I melted against him, our bodies so close I could feel the hard outline of his excitement. Tal's hands shifted to frame my face as he deepened the kiss, greedily taking what he'd waited so long for.

When he finally pulled back we were both breathless. He chuckled and his eyes gleamed with mischief. "Try that again and we likely won't make it to dinner."

My entire body urged me to take his lower lip between my teeth. I almost did it, too, but then took a hesitant step back.

His smile broadened. "Saving something for later?"

"I went through a lot of trouble to get this dress. It deserves to be shown off."

Stepping closer, he reached out and traced a finger along the fabric tied around my neck.

My knees wobbled and I was certain I was going to melt right there beneath his touch. *Damn that felt good.* I had to get a grip on myself.

"Off is a perfect way to describe what should come next," he said.

"Tal!" I laughed and batted his hand away. "We have somewhere to be."

"Dinner can be eaten anywhere." He glanced at my queen-sized bed nestled in my magical oak. "I'm thinking bedroom picnic."

His tone had shifted from playful to husky, and I had no doubt he was testing to see how far I'd let him go. Instead of answering, I sidestepped him, grabbed my clutch purse off the desk, and glided out the door.

His dramatic, exaggerated sigh made me giggle as I descended the stairs. We were going to have a tough time keeping our hands to ourselves. I wasn't sure how long Tal had wanted me, but the underlying passion I harbored for him had been brewing for the better part of eight years.

Just as I reached the bottom step, Link, back in Shih Tzu form, scurried out of Phoebe's room with a patent red pump clutched in his jaws.

"Goddammit, dog. Drop that right this instant!" Phoebe tore out of the room with her other shoe in her hand. As soon as she spotted him, the second pump flew and bounced off

Link's small head. He yelped and cowered behind the living room couch.

"What the hell, Phoebs?" I glared at her. "You could've put his eye out."

She stomped across the living room and grabbed both shoes. "If he steals one more thing from my room, his eyes are the last thing he'll need to worry about."

Link darted between her feet and lay down between Talisen and me.

"Hey there, buddy." Talisen bent to pick him up. My dog half-whined, half-yelped in excitement and proceeded to lap his tongue over Tal's face.

I gave Tal a pained look. "You're not helping."

He grinned and continued to let Link love him all over.

"This is so not cool." Phoebe stomped past us. "He's a year old now. He shouldn't be stealing my shit."

I closed my eyes, praying for patience. "I can't make him not steal your shoes. The best we can do is remove the temptation. Can you try keeping your door shut?" This wasn't the first time we'd had this conversation.

Phoebe paused in her doorway and glared at Talisen and Link. "I did, but the little bastard snuck in while I was going out." She glanced at me, a scowl still on her face. "That's a robe, three pairs of shoes, and one Victoria's Secret bra you owe me now."

"I'm good for it."

She took a deep breath, visibly trying to calm herself. "I know." She disappeared into her room and then popped her head back out. "Call me the moment you leave the hotel."

A slow smile spread over Tal's face. "The hotel?"

Shit. Thanks, Phoebs.

"Oh. You haven't told him yet." Phoebe grimaced. "Oops." With an apologetic glance, she closed her door on us.

Tal set Link down and straightened. His expressive eyes roamed over me once again, sparking with heat. That expression, the one of pure love and lust, just about brought me to my knees. He reached out, took my hand in his, and gently twisted me around so my back was to him. Slipping his arms around my middle, his warm lips met my neck, sending another shiver down my spine. "Do you have a surprise for me?" he whispered in my ear.

"Umm." I pulled away and turned to face him, biting my lip. "Not a good one."

His hands fell to his sides. He stared down at me with concern in his expressive eyes. "What is it?"

I let out a breath and took his hand gently in mine. "Let's go outside."

His brow furrowed.

"Trust me."

Nodding once, he snapped his fingers and Link stood at attention, ready to follow us wherever we went.

On the way out, I grabbed a light sweater to combat any overzealous air-conditioning later in the evening. The three of us walked in silence down the front path and then crossed the street to Coliseum Square Park.

Link lifted his head and sniffed deeply. He turned right then left. Satisfied there wasn't a threat, he curled up on my toes.

"Willow?" Tal stared down at me in the darkness. "What's going on?"

Just say it. "David came to see me today."

"The *vampire* wants you to meet him at a hotel?" he asked, anger vibrating in his tone. "Have you lost your mind?"

A chill swept over my body. Tal never spoke to me like that. Had he just turned into a possessive alpha male right in front of my eyes? I took a step back and placed my hands on my hips. "Could you calm down? It's not like—"

"He has no business speaking to you, and you sure as hell shouldn't be meeting him at a hotel. And tonight of all nights…" A flash of something close to pain flickered through his eyes. He blinked and the anger was back full force, but he didn't say anything else.

I gave him a moment to cool off and then in a quiet voice said, "There's concern the house is bugged. That's why I brought you out here. And I only saw David today because Allcot sent him to warn me that not only am I being followed, but it's likely I'm being watched as well. Phoebe is working on a sweep of the house, but she needs to get another witch in there to help her. If anyone managed to break in, then he or she was skilled enough they could have planted bugs Phoebe can't detect." I took a deep breath. "And the meeting is with Allcot, not David. He was just the messenger."

Tal didn't move, then he dropped his chin to his chest. "Jesus." He glanced up. "Sorry, babe. I was a dick."

I smiled because it was true. As long as Allcot was protecting my nephew, I would be in contact with him. Tal knew that and would have to be okay with it. "Trust me?"

"Yes." He pulled me into his arms.

"Then act like it."

"I'll do my best."

Located in the heart of the French Quarter, the Hotel La Blanchet had a nefarious reputation from days past. It's rumored the establishment was used for everything from a brothel to slave quarters for human women who were kept around as vamp food.

These days, vampires got their blood by frequenting food banks with willing participants or they employed private donors. No doubt Allcot had an entire team at both his personal residence and his various businesses. I glanced around, wondering if any of the high-class barflies propped up on barstools were really blood hostesses. Most likely.

It wasn't my policy to take Link on a date, but walking into vampire territory with a volatile fae was more than I thought I could handle on my own. Understandably, Talisen was not happy to be sharing me with anyone, especially not Allcot or David, who was bound to be present.

I pursed my lips and prayed Link didn't take a bite out of anyone. He was already vibrating with nervous energy. I squeezed Tal's arm. "Can you rein in your anger a little? Link is going to lose it at any moment."

Tal glanced down at the pacing Shih Tzu. "Yeah, sorry." He took a deep breath and murmured soothing words to Link. The dog froze mid-step and planted his rear between us.

David appeared and nodded for us to follow him. He led us to a quiet corner of the bar and pulled a chair out for me. "Have a seat. Eadric will call for us as soon as he's free."

I stared at the chair and then raised one eyebrow in David's direction. "I thought we had an appointment."

"You do. Have a seat and I'll get you a drink." He ignored both Talisen and Link.

I didn't sit or look at the drink menu. "I'd like a bowl of water for Link, a citrus margarita for myself and," I said, nodding at Tal, "a beer for Tal. Abita Amber, I think."

Talisen nodded and shifted into David's personal space just enough to force David to move away from me. He then positioned two chairs next to one another and nodded as if to say, "Have a seat."

I picked up Link, who was shaking from the vampire energy, and took my place next to Tal.

David studied us with his deep, midnight-blue eyes as I soothed Link with one hand and let Talisen take the other. Yes, we were a happy little family. David had no place in it. But that was his fault, really. He'd broken up with me and then chosen to turn vamp. And everyone knows faeries and vamps don't mix.

Except David and I sort of did. I'd turned him into a day-walker, after all. Every other vamp in the vicinity could bring me to my knees just by touching me for a few seconds. My vampire disability is odd. Their touch alone is like fire on my skin and leaves bruises. Some would call it a sensitivity. I'd call it a fucking nightmare. Even if I did take those self-defense classes Phoebe always harped about, they would be of no use. Not when their touch was every bit as bad as taking an unblocked blow.

There was a time when David's touch could bring me to my knees...in a good way. A tantalizing, make-my-body-turn-to-gelatin way. But that was before he'd turned vamp. Before I'd found out he'd lied to me during our entire relationship. Before I knew he was a coldhearted bastard.

I blocked the memories from my mind and met David's impenetrable stare. "We don't have all night."

David glanced once at Tal and then back to me. His gaze traveled the length of my body and paused at the hem of my skirt. "Looks like that's exactly what you have."

Heat burned my face, but I refused to look away. "We have plans. Tell Allcot we're here."

"No need for that." A slow Southern drawl I'd come to dread filtered through the jazz music. I whirled and found Eadric Allcot, David's father—both vampire and legally adoptive father—leaning against a partition, blocking us from the rest of the bar. "You can go upstairs now." He nodded at David. "Take your girlfriend to my office. I'll meet you there."

I stood. "I'm not his girlfriend. Not now. Not ever. And Talisen and Link will come with me."

He raised one amused eyebrow. "I do love a feisty fae."

Link growled and one look at Talisen told me he was moments from clocking Allcot. *Shit.*

"The dog and your fae friend will wait here." Allcot's tone was thick with finality. "Davidson," he said, "take her upstairs."

"And if I refuse?" I challenged him through clenched teeth.

Allcot pinned me with cold, hard eyes. "Do not test me. The wolf cannot come up because he's already too agitated. The fae is not welcome. You know why."

David opened a door that was concealed behind thick blue drapes and gestured for me to go first.

What did that mean? How was I supposed to know why Talisen wasn't welcome? Was it because he was fae or the fact that I obviously was on a date with Tal and David didn't like it? Either way, it was bullshit. I bit my tongue to keep from lashing out.

"Willow?" David prompted.

I glanced at Tal, my eyebrows raised. I didn't want to go with David. And I especially didn't want to go without Tal.

Talisen glared at David but reached out for Link. "Give him to me."

Link happily scooted into Tal's lap, and I couldn't help but be jealous.

"Go on. The sooner you find out what he has to say, the sooner we can get out of here."

Tal's voice was tight and I could tell it was taking all his control to stay calm. But his expression was soft, meant just for me. He wanted me to be safe, and if that meant playing Allcot's game, then that's what we'd do.

They'd spent the last year keeping me safe. They weren't likely to harm me now. "Fine." I swept past David, annoyed when my shoulder brushed his. The resulting tingle of pleasure was not welcome. Not welcome at all. I'd shut the door on that over a week ago after I'd found out David had been lying to me from the beginning.

I sure wished my body would get the memo. I steeled myself and kept walking in short strides, trying to stay upright in my heels, as if he hadn't affected me at all.

It took me a moment to realize David hadn't followed me into the corridor. Pausing, I glanced back and glimpsed Allcot shaking hands with a tall, dark-skinned man with bodybuilder-type muscles and David speaking with a shorter, wiry blond-haired man with dark brown eyes.

What? They had to be human. If they were vamp, I'd feel it. They didn't move like fae, and I couldn't sense any underlying magic, so while it wasn't impossible they were witches, I doubted it.

The dark-skinned man said something to Talisen, making him scowl. That's it. Whatever was going on, I wasn't leaving him with Allcot's lackeys. But when I started to move back into the room, Tal's eyes met mine and he gave me a tiny shake of his head. He didn't want me to interfere.

I didn't get a chance anyway, because right then, David strode into the corridor, blocking the scene from my view.

"Who are those guys with Talisen?" I demanded.

David put a hand on the small of my back and I jumped.

"Don't do that," I snapped.

"I'm being a gentleman, Willow." His tone implied he was anything but.

"Right. We broke up. We aren't even friends. I'd prefer you let me keep my personal space."

He shrugged. "You didn't seem to mind earlier today at the shop."

"You barged in on me while I was half-naked. If you hadn't been all secret agent and going on about how I was being followed, I would've thrown your ass out."

His lips turned up into a ghost of a smile. "That would've been fun to see."

"Shut up." I huffed. "Who were those men?"

"Security for your shop. Father wants insider eyes on anything that goes down during daylight hours."

My natural instinct was to decline. To tell them to stuff their security where the sun didn't shine. But the Void wasn't taking this as seriously as I wanted them to, and short of hiring a few witches to set wards that would keep more customers away than bad guys, I wasn't sure what else to do. "Why is Allcot talking to Tal about it?" It wasn't his shop, dammit. It was mine.

"They have business to discuss."

"But it's my shop. Not Tal's." If they thought for one moment they could sidestep me or coerce Talisen to get me to do something I didn't want to, they had better back their fanged asses right up. I wasn't a goddamned pushover. "Any business should be discussed with me."

David cast me a sidelong glance. "Father is discussing healer business with him. Nothing to do with your shop."

Oh. Talisen was gifted in healing, but he didn't sell his services. No wonder he'd looked pissed off. He'd spend the next hour refusing whatever it was they wanted. He didn't hesitate to use his skill when he needed to help someone, but he couldn't be bought. He had a research job at the university that paid the bills. There was no need to whore himself out to the highest bidder. Especially not to the mafia-like vamp corporation that was otherwise known as Cryrique. "Good luck to them."

We ascended the third flight of stairs and finally came to an open reception area. David crossed to the middle of the room and sat in one of four pristine white armchairs. "Have a seat while we wait for Father."

I scanned the room, thoroughly confused. Usually Allcot's offices were full of ornate, old-world, over-the-top furniture and all business was conducted behind closed doors. This was entirely too open to discuss anything of importance.

"You might want to sit down," David said.

"Why?"

A delicate clearing of the throat came from directly behind me. "Willow?"

Shock held me frozen in place for a heartbeat, then I spun. "Mom?"

Chapter 4

I ran to my mom and pulled her into a hug, then jerked back and scowled in confusion. "What are you doing here? Why are you in Allcot's hotel?"

Her amber-rimmed, hazel eyes filled with tears. "Maude called me and filled me in on a few details you neglected to mention."

Shame coiled in my gut. A week ago, I'd learned my aunt had been controlled against her will for almost three years, why my brother had been murdered, and that along with his death, I'd inherited a surprising ability to sense vamps and turn them into daywalkers. I'd sort of glossed over some of the story when I'd told Mom what happened. I hadn't wanted her to worry. Had Maude told her everything? Even the fact that I'd almost died the day I'd saved David's undead life?

"Mom, I—"

"No excuses. I know you probably have a million reasons why you kept me in the dark, but I don't want to hear them. You're in danger and I'm here to make sure you're protected." Her tears had dried and she wore her mom face.

"No excuses," I said weakly. "I'm sorry."

Mom, being Mom, smiled at me and seemed to let go of all her anger right there. She never was one for grudges unless the person in question had hurt one of her loved ones. "I know, sweetheart. You had a lot happen in a short period of time. I'm sure you're still processing."

I nodded and glanced at David. "You could say that. But why didn't you tell me you were coming? I would've picked you up at the airport. Cleared my schedule. You know, all those things normal people do."

Her pale, ice-blue wings, identical to mine, flexed. She cast a nervous glance at David. "Does she know?"

He shook his head. "Not yet. We were waiting for you."

"Mom?" What could possibly be so terrible she'd flown two thousand miles to tell me in person…and why did David know before I did? Damn them! They were all keeping things from me again. Then fear took over. What if something had gone terribly wrong? "Is it Carrie? Or Beau Junior? Did something happen to them?" Carrie had been my brother's fiancée, and unbeknownst to us, she'd been pregnant at the time of his death. Allcot had been protecting her and my nephew for the past four years from the vampire Asher. If Asher found out about Beau Junior's existence, his life would be very much on the line.

Asher was a human-loving, religious zealot of a vampire who'd made it his mission in life to track down and kill the first males of my bloodline—the ones who had the power to sense vampires and turn them into daywalkers. His sole reason was to prevent humans from being at an even bigger disadvantage. If vampires could daywalk, they would be more powerful than ever.

Mom's eyes filled with tears again, and my heart almost stopped. I took a deep breath and braced myself.

"I saw Beau today," she whispered. "He looks exactly like your brother."

The nausea that had taken up residence in my gut vanished. It was the first time she'd seen her grandson. I couldn't imagine what that must have been like for her.

As my twin, Beau's loss would never leave me, never get easier. He was my other half, the one who'd protected me, made me laugh when I was sad, and always pushed me to be better when working my spells. He'd challenged me in a way no one else could, always confident I could come up with a kickass version of whatever concoction I was working on at the time. Meeting Beau Junior had stitched back together a small piece of my heart that would always ache for my brother. I hoped Mom had experienced something similar.

"He's okay then?" I glanced around at David, but he was busy watching Mom with fascination. I settled my gaze on her.

"He's perfect," Mom said.

Thank the gods for that. "And Carrie? Is she okay?"

Mom's eyes clouded over with fear, which was then replaced by a hardness I rarely saw in her.

My heart skipped a beat and a tremor snaked down my spine. "What is it?"

Mom sucked in a steadying breath. "Sorry," she forced out.

I grabbed her hands and squeezed. Whatever had happened, I needed her to just say it. Otherwise I was going to jump right out of my skin. My wings vibrated with barely contained terror and a dark desire to unleash revenge on anyone who dared cause Carrie harm. Starting with Allcot. He was supposed to be protecting her, dammit! "Mom?"

"She's fine," David said from behind me and placed a gentle hand on my shoulder.

I jerked away and cast him a death glare, angry with his comfortable and familiar touch. "Don't do that."

He held his hands up in front of him. "Sorry. Habit."

"Break it," I snapped. Not tonight. He wasn't allowed to touch me as if we meant something to each other. We didn't. Or shouldn't. And I didn't want to. Tonight was supposed to be about Talisen and me. But if something had happened to Carrie...

"She was attacked on her way to the dentist this morning." Mom sank into one of the pristine white chairs as if it was suddenly too hard to stay upright. "He was a human, but he all but knocked out her bodyguard before he disappeared."

Bodyguard? I knew Allcot was keeping an eye on her and letting her live in a luxury apartment above his club, but I had no idea she had a personal bodyguard. I'd assumed she rarely went out. "This morning? In the sunlight?"

Mom's brows furrowed. "Yes. Why?"

I shrugged. David was a daywalking vampire now. Sure, I'd made him that way, but a few weeks ago I believed such a thing wasn't possible. Now I wasn't so sure what else was out there. What the possibilities could be. Allcot's hired guns were giants. I mean, if actual giants existed, they were the types of dudes I'd expect to be part of that race. Always over six foot tall, with enough bulk and training to take down five average men. Usually only vampires could beat them in hand-to-hand combat. "How did one random dude get the jump on Carrie's bodyguard?"

I glanced at David. He raised both his eyebrows and gave me a look, clearly waiting for me to make the connection.

Hello, lightbulb.

The attacker wasn't another supernatural—he just worked for one. Another vamp. Allcot was hardly the only vampire with hired guns. "It was one of Asher's people, wasn't it?"

"It had to be," David said and Mom nodded.

I clutched at my throat, horrified. "What happened?"

"She was leaving the dentist's office when a man jumped her. After her bodyguard barely managed to fend him off, the asshole sped off in a white SUV." A fierceness settled over Mom's features. I hadn't seen her with this much fire since before Beau died. She'd become a shadow of herself after we'd found him lifeless in her lavender fields. Now she was the strong, determined single mother I remembered from my youth. The one who'd fearlessly raised two kids on her own, without help from anyone, at the tender age of twenty-two. And had done a damn fine job. No question about it. Beau and I had enjoyed a safe, happy, loving household, and while we hadn't had luxuries, we'd had each other and had never gone hungry.

Despite the seriousness of the situation, something broke free inside me and fluttered with joy. I'd lost my brother and my mom that fateful day. Now she was back.

"It's almost exactly what happened to you today," David said, his voice full of anger.

Mom's frown deepened. "What?"

I sighed and rubbed my forehead. My wings fluttered a bit, lifting me off the ground. I forced myself to settle down. Both of them knew what the fluttering meant. I was nervous and unsure of what to say.

"Willow." Mom placed her balled fists on her hips and raised her chin. "Tell me what happened right this moment."

Shit. This wasn't the conversation I wanted to have in front of David. He wouldn't let me sugarcoat anything. Not with my life on the line. "A human tried to abduct me, as well, today. Phoebe stopped him. He's currently in lockup at the Void while they try to pump him for information."

"He won't talk," David said matter-of-factly.

"You don't know that." I glared at him and wished with everything I had he'd just go away. How was I going to reassure Mom I'd be fine if he kept this shit up?

"You have to come home," Mom said, her eyes narrowed in determination. "You're not safe here."

My chest started to ache. Mom had never wanted me to leave Eureka, the coastal town on the northern California coast I'd grown up in. It was a fae's dreamland. Lots of trees and the ocean right there, both of which were vitalizing. But after my twin's death, I couldn't breathe there. I'd had to get out. I'd moved to New Orleans two months later to live with my best friend, Phoebe. Six months later I'd opened my shop, The Fated Cupcake.

"I can't, Mom. You know that. What about my shop? Besides, the people who are after me already know where I'm from. Going back won't help."

"But I'll be there. And all the fae community. You know they'll all band together to keep you safe."

Like they'd kept Beau safe? I buried the thought. No one had known he'd been in danger. Even if they had, a master vampire had been after him. He would've found a way to get to Beau. Just like he'd find a way to get to me if he wanted. I'd be a fool to leave Allcot's protection. The only way to fight a master vampire is with another master vampire.

Before I could express those thoughts, David jumped in. "She's far safer here with Father and me to protect her than anywhere else in the world. It's the same with Carrie and Little Beau. I think you know that, Bry."

Bry? He was calling my mother by her nickname. What the…?

Mom put a soft hand on his forearm. "You're right. Of course you are. It's just a mother's nature to protect her only child." Her voice broke on the word *only*. The ache in my gut widened.

"And I have to be here to protect Little Beau," I said softly. If I ran away from this problem and anything happened to my only nephew, I'd never forgive myself.

Mom glanced at David with a calculating look, and I knew what she was thinking. Beau was our flesh and blood. She wanted Carrie to bring him back home to her. New Orleans was a terrible place for a boy who had faery blood. He needed woods and trees and Fae School to learn his skills. "He shouldn't be growing up around vampires." Mom's tone was cold and full of judgment as she stared pointedly at David. "Look at what happened to you."

Oh, holy fae. She had a point. And dammit, the thought made my blood run cold. David had asked to be turned not too long ago. As Allcot's adopted son, there was no question he'd be turned if he wanted to be. Normally fae couldn't be turned into vamps, but Beau was half-fae and half-witch. He could be turned and would be a powerful vamp if he chose that life. Like it or not, Beau Junior was related to Allcot. Sort of. Carrie was cousins with Allcot's consort. Beau wouldn't be rejected.

"Ms. Rhoswen, with respect, my life choices are mine and mine alone," David said. "I have my reasons for choosing this path. I assure you they are not what you think."

She took a step toward him, fire in her hazel gaze. "It doesn't really matter what your reasons are, does it? Being a part of Allcot's family pretty much lays the groundwork for an immortal life. Even if you feel you chose it, I can assure you that turning vampire was a foregone conclusion."

David never broke eye contact with my mother. "Everyone thinks they know my life, but I'm the only one who knows the truth."

Mom held her ground, but then after a moment she stepped back with a nod. "Fair enough. But you can't deny my nephew shouldn't be exposed to this world."

"I—" David started.

"Actually, he should be," I interjected and turned toward Mom. "If he has the same powers I inherited from Beau, he's going to need to understand the vamp world. Not only so he'll understand what his power means, but also to understand the politics of it all. I'm not saying you did anything wrong with raising Beau and me. But I can't help but think if he'd known anything about the vamp world, maybe he would have been prepared when they came for him."

Mom's mouth opened in a shocked O. "You have to under-stand, I was trying to protect you. It's not as if I didn't want to tell you about your father's abilities."

She'd known. All those years, she'd known about Dad's ability and that Beau would inherit his gifts. She'd known why they both were killed and had left me in the dark.

"Mom?" The word came out sharper, more accusatory than I'd meant. But I couldn't stop myself. Anger was boiling in my gut, rising to the surface. She'd lied to us, and no matter what her rationale was, she'd put Beau in danger by keeping the information to herself.

She brought her hand up, cupping her cheek as if I'd phys-ically slapped her. Then she crossed her arms over her chest defensively. "It was best to keep Beau out of the line of fire, and that's what I did. There was no indication any vampires even knew where we were. Up until that point, we'd never known a single day of fear. You can't ask for more than that."

I opened my mouth to argue but clamped it shut before I said something I'd regret. Then in a quiet, controlled voice, I asked, "How about honesty? Or a chance for Beau to protect himself?"

Her face crumpled into a pool of pain and guilt. "I should have told you. Your father didn't know about his ability. I found out years later when I was researching your family history." She swallowed. "He had a happy life. I wanted that for Beau. I moved us to a place where vampires don't go. I thought." Her voice cracked on the word *thought,* and she cleared her throat. "I thought we'd fly under the radar. That I'd have time to tell you both. But there weren't any warnings. After Beau's death, I couldn't bring myself to tell you because you had enough to deal with."

Righteous outrage seized me. I'd spent the last four years agonizing about what had happened to Beau, and she'd never said anything. Not once had she hinted she had a clue. How could she keep something like this from me? By not telling me, she'd put me in danger as well, though she had no way of knowing I'd inherit Beau's gifts. No one did. I cast David a death glare. He'd done the exact same thing. He'd known the whole time we'd been dating. The betrayal I'd worked so hard to overcome after I'd found out came roaring back.

My support system was truly messed up. These were two people I'd wholeheartedly trusted. Now I was just disappointed. I paced across the room and then strode toward David. "When's Allcot coming?"

Confusion flashed in David's eyes, then he shook his head "He's not."

I bit down hard on my tongue to keep from screaming and then forced out, "Then why the hell am I here?"

He nodded toward my mom. "To talk to your mom. After what happened today, Father is setting up security for you until we can track down Asher."

Wait. What? "This was all so I could speak to Mom?"

"Yes, in private. Since she's here to see Beau Junior, it's best if you're not seen together. Best if she isn't seen at all, actually. Otherwise she'll be tailed and in danger as well."

The reality that she wasn't in New Orleans to see me crashed down around me. I'd just had a bomb dropped on me, and we weren't even going to have time to work through it. I took a deep breath and focused on the other reason I was here. "Security? What does that mean? Is Allcot assigning me a bodyguard too? Because that isn't going to work for me."

David chuckled. "No bodyguard. At least not the way you're thinking. He's assigning a detail to you and to your shop to protect your employees."

I fell silent, overwhelmed that Allcot would think of the safety of my employees. I knew he wanted to keep me safe, but I'd been convinced it was only due to my ability to turn vamps into daywalkers and his desire to exploit me.

I raised a skeptical eyebrow at David. "What does he want in return?" There was a challenge in my voice.

And David heard it. He scowled. "Nothing, Willow. He's doing this because he's invested in your family now. Get used to it." David stormed off, leaving Mom and me alone in the sterile white room.

"That wasn't very polite," Mom admonished.

"I thought you didn't approve of David." Hadn't she just laid into him for his life choices?

"It's not my call that matters."

"What does that mean?"

She shrugged. "Just that he's trying to help us both and you were rude. You might want to apologize."

Yeah, that wasn't happening. I turned and headed toward the door, then paused and glanced back. "Talisen is waiting. Tell David to send for me before you leave."

Mom nodded and her eyes narrowed as if she was trying to figure something out.

I chose to ignore the look and had one foot out the door when she called, "Wil?"

"Yeah?"

"I love you."

The frustration coiled in my depths started to fade. She'd made a mistake and paid the ultimate price. She didn't need me to punish her further. "I love you, too, Mom. It's really good to see you."

Chapter 5

When I slipped back through the hidden door we'd used to head upstairs, the bar was full of patrons waiting for the adjoining restaurant. Talisen wasn't at our table. I glanced around and didn't see him anywhere. Perfect. I'd lost my date and Link. Scowling, I headed to the front entrance, scanning as I went.

Curious stares followed me, more than I usually attracted, and I had the distinct impression I was being watched. Unease quickly took over my irritation and a tremor ran through my wings. There weren't many faeries in New Orleans. Humans knew about the fae, as well as witches, and vampires of course. We weren't some secret, hidden race or anything. It was just that we spent most of our time near forests, where we thrived. Not in the concrete confines of the city.

With my senses on high alert, I did my best to appear casual and stopped at the entrance of the bar, scanning both the lobby and the restaurant entrance. No Talisen and no Link. Damn them both. Where had they gone? I couldn't go outside to look for them. I'd be too exposed.

I pulled my phone out of my small purse, tapped a message to Tal, and waited. And waited. And waited some more.

"Excuse me," a quiet, masculine voice said from behind me.

I jumped, and my wings fluttered, lifting me a few inches off the ground. I spun in the air and tilted my head to take in the human who had to be a few inches shy of seven feet.

His onyx eyes crinkled with humor. "Sorry. Didn't mean to startle you."

I forced myself to land and took a step back. "Can I help you?"

A deep chuckle escaped his lips. "Not yet."

I raised my eyebrows in slight irritation and gave him a tight smile. "If you'll excuse me." I turned to retreat back into the bar, but he grabbed my wrist. The move wasn't so much aggressive as it was a request. His touch was light and I could've easily slipped from his grasp. Instead, I stared for a moment at his fingers circled around me and then met his eyes. "You're entirely too familiar for a person I've never met before."

He released my hand instantly and backed away, holding both of his hands up. "My apologies, Ms. Rhoswen. Mr. Allcot sent me to escort you to your party."

"Allcot?" That got my attention. I studied him, taking in his dark skin; slightly-too-long, wavy black hair; the outline of bulging muscles hidden under his open sports coat, and realized I'd seen him with Tal right before David had taken me to see my mother.

My phone, still in my hand from earlier, buzzed and I read the screen. It was from Allcot himself. *I've sent Harrison to retrieve you. Do not be difficult.*

The nerve! Do not be difficult? What an ass. I eyed the man beside me. "What's your name?"

"Harrison." He wrapped an arm around me and leaned down to whisper, "I'm going to escort you upstairs, but we'll want the person watching you to think we're an item."

So my instincts were correct. Someone had been watching me.

He cast me an appreciative glance. "With that dress and your creamy white skin, no one will have trouble believing we're about to—"

A lightning-quick punch caught Harrison in the shoulder, knocking him back a few paces. His angry gaze landed on David, who'd just appeared, and he grinned, rubbing his upper arm. He placed his hand on the small of my back. "Weak, man. I thought turning vamp would help with those reflexes."

David snorted out a laugh. "Right. Talk to her that way again and you'll find out what this fist can do to your face."

"Ahem," I said loudly. "Are you two frat boys done? Because I'd really like to get on with my date."

David's face went blank and his voice came out flat, void of all humor and emotion. "Of course." He nodded at Harrison. "Get her to the fifth floor. Father's waiting." Then he stared me straight in the eye. "Do what Harrison says, otherwise someone other than you might get hurt. Got it?"

Was he threatening Talisen? Anger coiled so tight in my chest I thought I might lunge at him. If any of Allcot's people so much as breathed in Tal's direction, I'd find a way to bring hell down on the whole corrupt institution known as Cryrique.

David let out a frustrated sigh at the expression on my face. "It's not a threat. It's the truth. If Harrison fails to keep you safe, Father will punish him. Harrison's a good guy, Wil. I know you hate me right now, but you have to trust me on this."

Oh, crap on toast. He'd been talking about Harrison. My anger fled. Of course if he failed Allcot would make an example of him to the rest of the humans who worked for him. Guilt settled around my anger and ate it up. David turned to go, but I grabbed his hand. His blank eyes met mine and I knew he was hiding emotion behind that frustrating veil all vampires possessed. "I don't hate you."

His eyes searched mine with something very close to hope for just an instant. Then the cool expression returned. Nodding once, he disappeared into the crowd.

"Well," Harrison said, "that was awkward."

"Shut up." I started to move toward the elevators.

He caught up in two long strides and wrapped a possessive arm around my shoulders again.

I tensed and had to fight to keep from throwing him a death glare. I didn't want his hands on me, but I also didn't want him to suffer Allcot's wrath. Besides, we had a ruse to keep up.

As we crossed the lobby, he leaned down and brushed his lips across my cheek. I brought my hand up to smack him away, but he caught it and whispered, "Your stalker is watching. You don't want him to think we're fighting, do you?"

Did I? If this clown had been following me all night, wouldn't he know I'd arrived with Tal? I just didn't know how to play this situation.

"Make him think we're into each other and he'll assume you're staying the night. You and the fae can go out the back and ditch this loser. If we play it up now, it won't look suspicious when I'm hanging around for the foreseeable future."

I paused and glanced up at him. "I'm with Tal."

He frowned. "I know. This isn't a proposition. It's a strategy."

I took a deep breath, praying for calm. Having a fight, especially in the lobby, wasn't going to help anything. "I mean I'm with Tal. I'm not going to hide that. I don't want anyone to think I'm with you. It will be obvious who I'm with."

Harrison quirked an eyebrow. "So you're exclusive with the fae?"

What was with this guy? "Yes. Not that it's any of your business."

His hands came up to rest on my shoulders, and he turned me so we were face-to-face. Well, more like face-to-chest. I tilted my head back so I could see his eyes.

"Right behind you is one of the two men who have been tailing you for the last three days. If he finds out you're with the fae, your friend will be in just as much danger as you are, if not more. It's bad enough you're obviously close, but a romantic relationship they'll use against you to get whatever it is they want. If they think we're together, I'll be the target." His hands moved down my arms in a loving caress, supporting the illusion that we were having a moment.

And I supposed now we were. As soon as he'd said Tal would be in danger if Asher's people knew we were intimately connected, I'd made my decision. To keep Tal safe, I'd do just about anything, including pretend to be into this Harrison guy. Let him take the brunt of the fallout. I wasn't going to be able to get rid of him anyway. Not if Allcot had ordered him to keep me safe.

I reached up, cupping his cheek, and then stood on my tiptoes to whisper in his ear. From the outside looking in, it probably appeared I was making a suggestive comment, but instead I said, "Fine. We'll play this your way. But keep your hands in neutral territory and kissing is strictly off-limits. If you put your lips on me again, I'll—"

"What? Force-feed me a Truth Cluster? I assure you, I'm already in love with you. No need for such antics." Laughter bubbled out on the last word.

My anger came back full force, and it took every ounce of willpower I had to not knee him in the nuts. "Funny guy. If you ever bring up anything from my past with David again, I'll unleash my witch roommate on you. She's been experimenting a lot lately with vise-grip spells." I let my gaze wander to the fly of his dark blue jeans. "Ones that impair a person's ability to…uh, use their limbs effectively."

His face contorted with horror as my meaning sank in. He sucked in a breath. "My apologies."

I smiled sweetly and took his arm in mine. Phoebe was working on those spells, but they were for securing supernaturals when she had to bring them in. They had nothing to do with that portion of the male anatomy. Essentially they were magical manacles that not only chained captives, but also leeched power from their being, rendering them unable to escape. But Harrison didn't need to know that.

My threat didn't seem to impair his ability to play his role, however. After a few steps, his hand moved from my lower back to caress my spine and ended with him kneading the base of my neck. Everything was so wrong. What would Tal do if he saw this guy's hands on me? I didn't even want to think about it. I fought to keep the scowl off my face. I was supposed to be interested in this, not repelled. I shook my head, letting my hair form a drape to hide my expression.

His strong grip kept me firmly sealed to his side. There was no doubt what anyone watching would assume about us. It made my stomach ache. I didn't want to hide what I had with Tal, but I'd do it to keep him safe. I had to. Losing Tal wasn't an option.

Waiting for the elevator, Harrison pulled me in front of him, using his body to block me from prying eyes. "Flutter your wings."

"What?" On reflex I tucked my wings close to my back. I didn't want to be seen.

"Faeries do that when they are turned on. Give him a signal that you're into this."

"We do not flutter our wings when we're turned on." I let out an exasperated breath and kicked my wings out, only in irritation, not desire.

He laughed. "I bet you a hundred dollars you do. You're just too distracted to notice."

I opened my mouth to argue, but the elevator dinged and slid open. Harrison shuffled me into the tiny space and, without looking, hit the button to the fifth floor. As soon as the doors closed, I jumped away from him and wrapped my arms around myself, feeling trapped and slightly dirty.

His eyes twinkled with mischief, but he gave me my space right up until the elevator stopped on our floor. Then he pressed against my back and moved me forward into the empty hall.

"Let go." I pushed him away. "No one's here."

He shook his head and took his place beside me. "You never know if they are or not. It's important to keep up appearances."

"You're being an ass." I leaned against the wall as he pulled out a plastic keycard. "If you think I'm letting you manhandle me while you're part of my *detail*, you've lost your mind."

"Feisty. I like it." He used the card to unlock the door. "After you."

I slid past him and found myself in a large entry that opened into a plush, carpeted living room. Windows lined the wall, looking out over the old buildings of the French Quarter.

Ornate sixteenth-century furniture filled the space, making it almost a carbon copy of the office Allcot had over The Red Door, the club he owned on Frenchmen Street. Was he really that anal about his surroundings, or was his interior decorator just lazy? "Where are they?"

Harrison shrugged and disappeared into a galley kitchen. "Thirsty?"

"No." I paced the room. "Where are Tal and Link?" I all but shouted.

A yelp came from the next room and a door opened. Link shot out and launched himself at me. Thank goodness he was in Shih Tzu form, otherwise I would've been buried under one hundred and fifty pounds of wolf. I caught him mid-leap and buried my face in his fur. "Hey, buddy. There you are."

He licked my neck, making me laugh.

"Missed you, too. Where's Tal?"

His little body wiggled with excitement as he pressed into my shoulder.

"Okay, that's enough." I kissed the top of his head and set him back on the floor.

Harrison strode toward the door Link had shot out of but stopped in his tracks when Link growled and paced back and forth in front of the doorway. Harrison took another step and Link started to shimmer.

"I'd stop if I were you," I said. "If you get any closer, he'll shift."

Harrison froze, but it was too late. Link growled and shifted into full blown wolf. Harrison narrowed his eyes. "Call off your beast."

I could. Link would obey, but Harrison deserved a little payback for his performance downstairs. I shrugged and joined Link near the door. "Is Tal in there?"

Link rubbed his head on my leg, showing Harrison I belonged to him. I had to swallow a laugh. I wouldn't let Link hurt Harrison, but it sure was fun seeing his confidence stripped down.

I knocked once on the door that had clicked closed and then pulled it open. Inside, Allcot had his hand out and Tal was reaching for it hesitantly. The pair shook briefly, with Tal pulling his hand away first.

"Thank you for your time, Mr. Kavanagh," Allcot said. "I knew we'd come to an agreement."

I stared openmouthed at Tal, who shook his head slightly, warning me to not ask just yet. An agreement with Allcot? *Shit.* What had Tal done?

Allcot nodded once to me. "Ms. Rhoswen. I have some information for you."

I crossed my arms over my chest. "You mean other than my mother being in town?"

"She is here at Carrie's request." He was as cool as ever, irritating me to my core. We were talking about life and death and he acted like it was just another day. Maybe for him it was.

"It's good Mom has time with her and Beau," I said, happy Carrie had thought of my mom. Tal reached out and took my hand in his. I squeezed his fingers, itching to leave.

"You've had a stressful day," Allcot said.

"Is there a question in there?" I challenged. Way to state the obvious.

He cracked a smile and chuckled. "No. But you should be questioning me."

"Why? Are you behind any of it?" I was tired of his game.

His smile vanished as anger flashed in his piercing gaze. "I don't appreciate your tone, Ms. Rhoswen. Push me too far and I'll reconsider your security detail."

I shrugged but kept my mouth shut. The truth was I did want help to keep my staff safe, even if I wasn't at all interested in being followed by his henchmen.

"I see we've reached an understanding." He paced forward as if stalking me. "We have reason to believe someone at the Void is responsible for the break-in at your office."

"What? Who?" Why would they do that? They already had access to my recipes. Did they know about my abilities?

"The new director is most curious about you. We believe she's behind it." Allcot tilted his head, studying me.

"Why?" I didn't want to believe it. Didn't want to even consider that the Void might be after me again.

"We have our ways."

"And the attack today? Was that the Void too?"

He shook his head. "No. We believe the attacks on you and Carrie are both from Asher's men. I have my people working on finding him. Until then, stay near Harrison. He will keep you safe." He gestured to Harrison and said, "You may take them out the back way now."

"What about Carrie?" I called as he turned to go.

He paused and glanced back. "That is none of your concern."

Chapter 6

None of my concern? What an ass. Of course Carrie's well-being was my concern. She'd been engaged to my brother. She was the mother of my nephew. She was practically family. Effing vampire.

Tal and I followed Harrison up a flight of stairs to the roof access. Only this time, my security detail kept his hands to himself. It was a good thing, too, because I could feel the anger radiating from Tal. It was so bad, Link hadn't been able to shift back to Shih Tzu form. We were failing at being inconspicuous.

Talisen strode with purpose toward the adjoining building as if he knew exactly where we were supposed to be going.

I stopped in my tracks. "Wait a minute. If I'd been followed earlier today, my tail knows I came here with Talisen. Isn't he going to be suspicious when he doesn't see Link and Tal leaving the building?"

"It's already taken care of," Harrison said.

Tal put his arm around my waist and tugged me to him. I fit perfectly and even though I was still keyed up from my mother's revelation and the short meeting with Allcot, his presence made me calmer. Tal visibly settled, too, and Link shimmered back into Shih Tzu form at our feet. I pressed into Tal and rested my hand on his hip. He glanced down at me, his expression soft, full of all the love I knew was there.

He leaned closer and kissed my temple. "Link and I already left the hotel once. We came back in the same way we're leaving now."

"You already know about the plan then?" I glanced once at Harrison.

Tal stiffened but clamped his mouth shut and nodded.

When we got to the edge of the roof, Tal and Harrison jumped the short way over to the next building. I fluttered my way over, clutching Link to my body. Landing next to Talisen, I set Link down and glared at Harrison. "Where do you think you're going?"

He blinked. "To do my job."

"Not tonight." I placed my hands on my hips. "You can start tomorrow. I'll be at my shop by seven."

"Sorry, *Wil*." He smirked and I wanted to smack him for using my nickname. We weren't *that* familiar. "Allcot has me on duty tonight. But don't worry, you won't even notice me."

My mouth hung open in total irritation and Talisen ground his teeth together. "I don't think we have a choice," he said. "Just ignore him. Let's go." He grabbed my hand and tugged me after him through another door and down five more flights of stairs. Only the sound of shoes and paws on the wooden steps filled the narrow stairwell.

At the bottom, Harrison blocked our way through the back entrance. He stared Tal in the eye. "When we get in your car, head directly to your apartment. Don't deviate and whatever you do, do not let anyone see Rhoswen. Got it?"

"Yeah, I've got it," Tal said. "I've already been briefed." When Harrison didn't move, Tal raised both eyebrows. "Are you going to move aside, or are you going to stand there eyeballing my date all night?"

A thrill ran through me at Tal calling me his date. It was stupid because the evening had turned into a disaster. My mom, Allcot, Harrison, and David. None of them were a welcome addition. All I'd wanted to do was enjoy this night with Tal. But he hadn't forgotten our plans for the evening and neither had I. Of course, now we were banned from going anywhere accept Tal's apartment.

Oh crap. Our first date and we'd be alone at his place.

My heart started to beat erratically and my breathing turned uneven. What would he do? What would I do? Hell, I wanted him. Badly. But when we took our relationship further it would change everything. Was I ready for that? Tal gave me a worried glance. I shook my head, indicating I was fine. But I was far from it. A swarm of butterflies had taken up residence in my chest.

Harrison checked a text on his phone and then, without a word, stepped outside. The door shut silently behind us and waiting at the curb was Tal's new black truck. The four of us climbed in with me and Link sandwiched between the two of them.

"So," I said, "your place?"

Tal took off, clutching the steering wheel until his knuckles turned white. A few moments later, he purposely relaxed his grip. He reached out and placed a light hand just above my knee. "Sorry. It's not much of a date."

A smile tugged at my lips. "I'm sure we can think of something to salvage it."

He let out a surprised laugh. "You think so, huh?"

Heat crawled up my neck, but I smiled at him and tried to forget Harrison was privy to this conversation. "We'll figure something out."

"No doubt," he said in a low seductive voice. "But dinner first."

We were quiet the rest of the way to his apartment. Tal turned right off St. Charles. Another right and then a left and we were pulling into the long driveway of a large, unfamiliar French colonial home that appeared to be converted into multiple apartments. So this was where he'd chosen to live. It was gorgeous. He pulled around to the back and parked next to a red Saturn SUV.

All four of us climbed out, and without even so much as a good-night, Harrison disappeared, presumably to find a good stakeout spot. I breathed a sigh of relief.

"Fancy place," I said, glancing up at the three-story home and admiring the multitude of bay windows and intricate moldings.

"It's a one-bedroom," Tal said.

I lifted an eyebrow. "Who gets the bed?"

A gleam lit his green eyes. "We'll negotiate after dinner."

I took his hand and let him guide me to the stairs. Nervous anticipation sent blood rushing to my head. For the first time, his flirting actually meant something. When we were in the friend zone, Tal had been quick to flirt, but anything that was too overtly relationshipy, like helping me with my coat or holding my hand, had been off-limits. It had been a line we'd drawn and neither of us had dared to cross it...until last week when Tal hadn't been able to handle the thought of David and me together. Tal had finally admitted his feelings for me. Everything was new, but also familiar. It was odd. Not uncomfortable, just different.

"So," I said as we climbed the back stairs. "You said something about dinner. Does this mean you cook now? Or am I going to have a frozen dinner forced on me?"

He placed a hand on his chest and gave me a wounded look. "Ouch. If you must know, I have learned a few useful things."

"In the kitchen?" I teased.

He gave me a sly grin and stuffed a key into his door. A second later he pulled me into his kitchen, slamming the door behind us. He lifted me easily and placed me on the counter, moving to position himself between my legs. Leaning in, he brushed his lips along my jawline and trailed soft kisses to that sensitive place just beneath my ear.

"Hmm," I murmured, my skin tingling all the way to my toes. He could do that forever and I'd die a happy fae. "That's nice."

He lifted his head, his intense gaze searing into mine. Then he placed both hands on either side of my face and moved in. My nervousness came rushing back. Not from the physical act, but from the desire and intense need to belong to Talisen. To give him that part of me I'd always known was meant for him but had kept buried in the depths of my heart.

I sucked in a breath and bit my lip. Tal paused, his eyes focused on my mouth, then he met my gaze and brushed a lock of hair out of my eyes. "Is this too soon?"

I shook my head, not daring to speak, afraid I'd say too much.

"This," he said, placing a hand over my heart, "is what I've wanted for as long as I can remember. Just you and me, Wil." He brushed his lips over mine, coaxing yet another murmur of pleasure from me. He responded by darting his tongue across mine and kissed me deeply, devouring the emotion running rampant between us.

Oh God. This was really happening.

I matched his fervor and clutched at his shirt, pulling him closer so that our bodies were flush, my legs wrapped around him. His healing hands roamed over my back, under my wings, and even though he'd touched me a million times before, everything was new and different. His fingers were light, almost hesitant, but not afraid. He was taking his time. Reintroducing himself to my bare skin, knowing I wanted him to touch me intimately. To memorize the way I felt in his arms.

Shivers of anticipation crashed through me, and I pulled back, gasping for air.

His gaze went soft with undisguised desire. "Sorry."

"For what?" I leaned in and nuzzled the hollow of his neck. A faint trace of vanilla and spice filled my senses.

"Not making dinner." His fingers moved to the tips of my wings, sending a ripple of pleasure straight to my toes. It was then I noticed my wings fluttering. Dammit if Harrison hadn't been right about that little tidbit.

I sucked in a breath and gently pushed him away. "Don't think you're getting off that easy."

His eyes crinkled and then he laughed. "Easy? I was definitely going to work for it."

Heat rushed to more areas than just my face. I pushed him farther away and then hopped down off the counter. "You're a bad influence, Mr. Kavanagh. Food first, then we'll see where things go."

He took a step closer and wrapped one of his strong arms around me, gazing down at me. "I love having you here in my space."

I blinked, not expecting that. "Then why didn't you invite me over sooner?" He'd moved in a week ago and until tonight, I hadn't even known what neighborhood he'd chosen.

He shrugged. "I don't know. I guess I wanted to finish unpacking first."

I glanced around, noting a California redwoods print above his couch. The blue glazed vase I'd given him as a housewarming present sat in the center of his dining room table. He didn't have much else in the way of décor, but there weren't moving boxes lining the walls either. "Looks pretty put together already."

Shaking his head, he tucked my hand in his and led me through the kitchen to the sparsely furnished living room. He paused outside his bedroom door. "I want to show you something."

It was my turn to laugh. "Um, is this an 'I'll show you mine if you show me yours' situation?"

He stared at me with equal parts admiration and exasperation. "You *are* feisty."

I smiled up at him, noting the gleam in his eye. What was he up to?

He brushed a lock of hair out of my eyes and then pushed his bedroom door open. "Take a look."

I stepped inside and even without the light on I saw the outline of branches and leaves against the ceiling. "Tal?" I gasped out. "How?"

He grinned, clearly pleased with my reaction. "I had some help from a certain witch we know."

"Phoebs did this?" I flipped the light on and gasped at the gorgeous cypress tree and the bed nestled on the floor between its roots. If I ever stayed over, the tree would be perfect to replenish the magic I used every day at my lab creating magically enhanced treats for all my customers.

"Yeah, she worked the spell for the tree."

He pulled me to the middle of the room and turned me so I was facing him. "I want you to know I did this without expectations."

Both of my eyebrows shot to the top of my forehead. "Really? Because from here it looks like you have a whole lot of expectations for us." Tal was gifted in crystal magic. He didn't need nature to replenish. Sure, it was probably comforting, but totally unnecessary. And the tree couldn't have been easy to pull off. There was only one reason it was there. Me.

"Okay. Maybe some expectations. But future ones. The kind that I only want to happen if we're both ready for them. This"—he waved at the bed—"was more about letting you know I'm all in. What we have? It isn't going away. And I know it's new, or at least this chapter we're headed into is new, but it's real and right, and I'm in it with you. The bed? It's about letting you know that I know what you need and if I can give it to you, I will."

He stepped back, giving me some space.

I rubbed my hands over my face and when I dropped them, I found Link lying right in the middle of the bed, sprawled out as if he owned the place. "Link! Get down."

He blinked his amber eyes at me and then turned his gaze on Talisen. Damn dog. He knew who was in charge here. Tal glanced at me, then Link. "Off."

The Shih Tzu rose reluctantly but eventually did as he was told and took up residence at Talisen's feet.

I shook my head in exasperation. Tal had made him get off because he knew I didn't want Link to get in the habit of not obeying my commands. Not because he minded my dog lying in his bed. I waved a hand. "Go on, Link. It's fine. Go to bed."

Link didn't hesitate. He jumped up and a second later was curled against a pillow.

"He should be your dog," I told Talisen.

"Nah." Tal slipped his arm around my waist and pulled me back into the living room. "He adores you and if he thought I was a threat, he'd rip my face off without hesitation."

I snorted. "Not likely. He'd probably take your side in a fight."

"Good thing we'll never have to find out."

We stood in the middle of the living room and I suddenly felt awkward. Tal and I had spent countless hours together. I'd never been uncomfortable around him before, but now, on a date in his apartment, I didn't know how to act. I couldn't exactly leave and go home, in case another tail was waiting for me. We needed these people to think Harrison and I were together at the hotel. So I was stuck here. Normally this wouldn't be an issue. Tal and I would've likely even slept in the same bed. Everything would've been one hundred percent platonic. But now...

"Have a seat." Tal indicated the brown leather couch and headed to the other end of his apartment into the kitchen. "I'll work on scrounging up some dinner."

I glanced at the couch and then followed Talisen. "I'll help."

He grinned and opened a drawer full of menus. "What sounds good?"

"Takeout?"

"It's either that or a frozen veggie burger."

I wrinkled my nose. "Really? Veggie burger?"

He shrugged. "They're the fancy brand from the health-food store."

I laughed. "Since when do you shop the health-food stores? I watched you eat your weight in burgers and fries over the summer. What gives?"

Passing me a couple of menus, he leaned against the counter and crossed his feet at the ankle. "I don't know. Ever since I got down here I've been craving plant-based food. I think it's because I'm not near the forest. Sort of like how you need your tree to replenish. I think I need to digest more vegetables."

"Huh. Could be. Or maybe your body is rebelling after years of abuse."

"That's probably it."

I eyed his lanky but muscular body. Talisen had never been health conscious before and if he was craving plant-based foods, he was probably right to assume his environment was having an effect on him. And it was because of me. He wouldn't be here otherwise. I handed him back the menus. "Whatever you want to eat is cool with me."

He lifted his eyes to mine and then his gaze slowly traveled the length of my body. When our eyes met again, I swallowed the lump in my throat. "I meant food."

A slow smile spread over his handsome, tanned face. "Yeah. I know."

My pulse quickened and I shook my head. "Just order something."

He kept his eyes locked on mine as he pulled out his phone and tapped a button. A few moments later, he ordered a couple of blackened redfish dinners. "Thirty minutes," he said to me as he placed his phone on the counter.

"Sounds good." I broke my gaze from his and took up residence on his brown leather couch.

He watched me tuck my feet under myself. His light footsteps echoed in the room as he walked over to stand in front of me. He kneeled, taking my hand. "I don't want to move too fast, but dammit, Willow, I don't think I'm going to be able to keep my hands off you."

I opened my mouth, closed it, and then swallowed hard. I didn't really want him to keep his hands off me. But I also knew once we went there, we couldn't go back, and the thought terrified me. What if he decided we weren't right together?

He brought his hand up and caressed my cheek.

I closed my eyes and shivered.

"Why do you look so scared?" His voice was low, barely a whisper.

Forcing my eyes open, I met his intense stare. "I don't want things to change."

His hand tightened on mine. "I think it might be too late for that."

And wasn't that the problem. We couldn't move backward. This emotional intensity wasn't going to go away. If I stopped it now, we'd forever be left in limbo where we could never be totally honest with each other. And if we moved forward, there was potential for the heartbreak of a lifetime. "I know."

He shifted to sit next to me on the couch and wrapped both arms around me, pulling me to him.

I couldn't resist and leaned into his embrace, burying my face in his chest. "I'm sorry. I feel like an idiot. It's just that we...you're...this is important. I don't want to mess it up."

He brushed a gentle kiss over the top of my head. "You're not an idiot. This is intense and you're right, it is important. We'll take it slow. There isn't any rush here."

"No?" I knew he'd never pressure me to do anything I wasn't ready for, but the way he'd been looking at me all night, I knew exactly what he wanted. And if I was honest, it was exactly what I wanted, too.

"Of course not, Wil. I'm in this for the long haul. I'm not going anywhere. You have to know that."

The problem was I didn't believe him. It wasn't fair, but it was the truth. Tal had never been in a steady relationship longer than a few months before. Deep inside, I was afraid our relationship would suffer the same fate. I wouldn't survive losing him. It wasn't the romantic relationship I feared, though I'd wanted one with him for as long as I could remember. Wanted him so badly my fingers ached to touch him. I feared the emotional one we already shared. If anything came between us, I'd be a wreck. Tal was my oldest friend. The person who knew me best and the one I counted on above all others.

"Look at me. Hear me when I say this." He pulled away and lifted my chin with a finger. "No matter what happens, I will always be here for you. Always. Never doubt that."

A single tear ran down my cheek. He was everything I'd ever wanted. Everything I'd hoped he'd be. His words only proved he understood me all too well.

"Ah, don't cry." He brushed a gentle hand over my cheek.

"Goddess," I breathed. "I'm sorry, Tal. It's been one hell of a day. I think I'm just overwhelmed with everything that happened. The attack, seeing Mom, Allcot's directive saddling me with that Harrison guy. I don't like any of it." I placed a kiss on his cheek and ran a hand over his jaw. "All I wanted was a really good date with you, and instead I found out my mom's been keeping secrets, Carrie was attacked, the Void might be investigating me, and now Allcot's invested enough in my situation that he's assigned a security detail. It's too much to take in."

Tal's eyes narrowed at the mention of Allcot's name.

The image of Allcot and Tal shaking hands flashed through my mind. With all that had happened, I'd almost forgotten. "What understanding did you and Allcot come to?"

He sat back and ran a frustrated hand over his face.

"Tal?"

"Shit." He got up and started pacing, his limbs twitching with agitation.

I sat up on the couch, my body tense. What had Tal agreed to?

He stopped and faced me, his feet shoulder width apart. "You're not going to like this."

I got to my feet, not comfortable with the vulnerability of sitting while he stood over me. It wasn't that he scared me, it was just that I needed to not show weakness right then. I'd had enough of being taken care of. "That seems fairly obvious."

"You know that stone-based elixir I've been working on?"

I stood stock-still. "You mean the one that boosts strength and numbs the senses?"

"Yeah, that one."

Unease morphed into dread. "No, Tal. Tell me this isn't about that. Please." My voice cracked on the word *please*. Tal's magical drink was very dangerous in the wrong hands, and Allcot's were most definitely the wrong hands. It could essentially create superhumans. Ones who were extremely strong and immune to pain if enough was ingested.

He jammed his hands in his jeans pockets. "I wish I could."

"Dammit!" I'd already lived through two years of political manipulation due to the Influence drug I made. When ingested, it forced people to do whatever the administrator of the drug told them to. It was the worst kind of invasion. Cold terror washed over me. What if someone mixed the two together? Superhuman machines is what they'd be. "Whatever you agreed to, you have to back out. Allcot cannot have access to this."

"I can't." His tortured eyes met mine.

"Why?"

A muscle in his jaw twitched. "A batch went missing at the lab."

Panic started to wind through me. "When?"

"Last week."

"Talisen!" My head started to spin. "Why didn't you tell me?" Every important person in my life had been keeping information from me. The last person I'd expected that from was Tal. I'd thought he was the one I could count on to be honest.

He stepped back, clearly surprised by the intensity of my outburst. He reached out and cupped my balled fists, gently uncurling my fingers. Then he wrapped both of his hands around mine. "I'm telling you now. I never meant to keep this a secret from you." He searched my eyes. "Something else is wrong. What's going on inside that head of yours?"

I cast my eyes down and tried not to cry at the tenderness in his voice. I wanted to fight, not break down. I yanked my hands back just for some sense of control over my emotions. "Mom knew about Beau's ability. She knew a vamp killed him. She's known all along about the daywalking power and never told us."

The color drained from Tal's face. "What do you mean? Why?"

I shrugged. "To save us more pain, I guess? I don't know."

Tal's face hardened. "And in the process she put you in danger."

"Yeah, she did." If I'd known about Beau's ability sooner, I would've recognized what my vamp-sensing ability meant and maybe could've avoided being locked up in the Arcane basement where I almost spent the rest of my life under the control of a power-hungry director.

Talisen held his hand out and waited for me to take it. He was offering his support, but not forcing it on me. Something about the combination of the determination in his set jaw and the raw concern in his eyes touched me deep in my soul. Tal would be my partner in this if I let him. I took his hand.

He pulled me to him in a fierce hug. "I promise I won't keep anything important from you again. I should've told you sooner about the missing drug."

I clung to him, grateful he understood. "Damn right." I snuggled into him, soaking up his strength. But we weren't quite done. I stepped back and held him at arm's length. "Now, what agreement did you make with Allcot?"

He winced. "You're going to be pissed."

I pressed my lips into a tight line. "That was a foregone conclusion."

It was so quiet in his apartment I could hear both of our hearts beating. The tension started to get to me and my wings flexed.

Tal's gaze flickered over them. He stepped back as if to prepare for the impending storm. "In order for Allcot to keep his security assigned to you and your shop, I had to agree to supply him with my new creation."

My mouth went dry and I forced out the words. "The stone-based one? The one that just went missing? The one we both agreed was entirely too dangerous in vampire hands?" My voice rose an octave with each sentence. "The one that's just as dangerous as Influence, if not more?"

Tal stood his ground, stoically taking my wrath as I seethed in front of him.

"Well?" I ground out. "Are you actually telling me you promised your new invention to the most corrupt vampire in the city?"

He nodded slowly. "Yes."

Chapter 7

"Why?" I shouted. "Dammit, Tal, why would you do that?" A sob formed at the back of my throat, but I swallowed it and took a deep, staggering breath. "You'll be tied to him now. You know how this works. Once you're in, you're in. There's no going back." Allcot would use him in every possible way until Tal was entrenched in Allcot's illegal dealings. Then the master vampire would own him. And Tal would cease to be the good and honest man I loved so much. This couldn't happen. It was too awful.

He studied me and just as he opened his mouth to answer, a knock sounded on the door. He raised his index finger and retreated to the kitchen.

I swallowed a frustrated scream. Our dinner had shown up and I wasn't even remotely hungry. I glanced down at my gorgeous plum dress and wished for my yoga pants and a T-shirt. Any thoughts of romance had left the building.

Tal paid the delivery guy and spent a few minutes arranging our dinner on plates before he set them on his table and waved me over. "What would you like to drink?"

I ignored him and stalked to the refrigerator. Inside I found a stick of butter, ketchup, a six-pack of beer, a half-empty bottle of wine, and pomegranate juice. There was no question Tal had bought the juice for me. It was my favorite. Or had been up until someone had laced some with Cherry Bomb and Phoebe had almost died. I hadn't been able to take a drink of any since then. Angry at Tal and the fact I couldn't stomach the drink, I grabbed a beer and flopped down in my chair across from him.

He raised an eyebrow at the bottle in my hand.

I mimicked his expression in challenge. "What?"

"Nothing." He got up, grabbed a beer for himself, and rummaged around in another drawer until he came up with a bottle opener. He walked back to the table and popped the tops of both of our bottles.

I mumbled thanks, took a swig of the pale ale, and then shoveled a few bites of fish into my mouth. The food curdled in my stomach and instead of eating, I spent the next ten minutes moving the accompanying green beans around my plate.

Tal had no such problem. He finished every last bite of food on his plate and started eyeing mine.

I pushed my plate toward him and stood. "Take it. I'm not hungry." Turning on my heel, I stalked to his bedroom and slammed the door behind me. Link lifted his head and growled from his place on the bed. "You, too?" I snapped.

Link jumped down and followed me to an armchair in the corner of the room. I folded myself into it and hauled Link onto my lap. He looked up at me, his eyes flashing gold as he started to vibrate.

Shoot! I was far too upset still and Link was seconds from shifting right in my lap. I took a deep breath and stroked his fur, trying to calm us both. My rage dialed down to a simmer, replaced by fear for Talisen. Fear for what was to come.

Tal knocked on the door. When I didn't respond, he cracked it open and poked his head in. He glanced around and when he spotted me, he opened the door wider and walked in. "Can we talk now?"

"I was ready to talk earlier." I scratched under Link's ear and he started to relax by stretching out in my lap, giving me easier access.

"No, I don't think you were. I'm pretty sure you were ready to kick my ass."

I wanted to laugh but held my amusement in. I still wanted to kick his ass, but at least I didn't want to scream at him anymore. Though it wasn't off the table. "True. I was."

Kicking off his shoes, he sat on the end of the bed and faced me. "The last thing I wanted to do was team up with Allcot."

"Then why did you?"

He shook his head, not in denial, but in restrained frustration. "Because you already have."

My fingers tightened in Link's fur as anger started a slow burn in the pit of my stomach. Was he really turning this back on me? "I have *not* teamed up with him."

"Maybe not intentionally, but you're part of his circle now. Between what happened with David and the fact that he protects Beau Junior, did you really think he'd leave you alone?"

No. I'd known I was tied to Allcot. How could I not be? I'd turned his son into a daywalker and I was Beau Junior's aunt. I'd always been on his radar. But that didn't mean I'd teamed up with him. I wasn't on his payroll. "Nobody thinks he's going to ignore me. That doesn't mean I have to cooperate with him."

"Wil," Tal said with no small amount of skepticism.

"Well, I don't!"

"You already have. You've accepted a security detail. You've agreed to pretend one of them is your new boyfriend. And we're hiding out here on Allcot's orders. You're doing everything he wants you to do."

Link jumped off my lap and started to pace, a reaction to the tension in the room. "It's not like I had a choice, now is it?" I demanded. "What did you expect me to do?"

He held his hands up. "I didn't expect anything. I'm not saying you did anything wrong. I'm only saying sometimes circumstance dictates a course of action you'd rather not follow."

I slumped in the chair, suddenly feeling very exposed. I wanted to grab a blanket and wrap it around my scantily clad body. Tal was seeing straight through me, past the front I was holding tightly in place. I wasn't in control of the situation. Not even close. And Allcot did have me under his thumb. But only because I needed to protect Carrie and Beau…and Tal. I couldn't do that on my own. Not with Asher coming for us all.

"You're right," I said, my voice small. "I'm compromising my morals for protection. I don't know what else to do."

His feet hit the floor and he started to pace. Then he stopped in front of me. "Don't you think I'm in the same position?"

I didn't know how to answer that. Talisen wasn't the target. Not yet, anyway. Why did he need Allcot's protection?

"The new drug was stolen from the lab. There were only three people who even knew about it. Me. My boss. And you." He paused. "All the tests were blind, and Dawson and I ran them ourselves. That means either Dawson leaked the drug or your house was already bugged when I told you about it."

Crap, crap, crap! The hits just kept on coming. Fear and frustration fought for dominance as the two emotions weighed on my chest. Talisen had told me about his new invention about a week ago. If his boss wasn't involved, then the leak had to have come from my house. "Any idea who stole it?"

His face hardened with resolve, and I knew what he was going to say before he even opened his mouth.

"Asher's people," I said.

He nodded and sat back down on the foot of the bed. "And that's why I agreed to let Allcot's men use it. If Asher has souped-up humans coming for you, I'm going to make damned sure your security has a fighting chance."

A chill crawled over my skin, and I wrapped my arms around myself. I stared at my feet, unable to look him in the eye. "We could've found another way."

He let out an angry sigh. "Yeah. You're probably right. What do you think is better? You moving into Allcot's place with all his vamps? Or maybe David could move back into your house?" He stopped pacing and ran a frustrated hand through his sun-lightened, chestnut hair. "Witness protection maybe? You could give up everyone and everything you love: Phoebe, your shop, Carrie and Beau Junior, your mom. Of course, your wings might be a problem. It's not like there are tons of fae with ice-blue wing color."

He turned and stalked out of the room, leaving Link and me staring after him. Link lifted his head, eyeing me with confusion.

I stood, chilled to the bone by his words. None of those options were appealing and he knew it. Way to use my worst fears to scare the crap out of me. Tal knew my friends and family were everything to me, even more so after we'd lost Beau.

Shivering, I crossed the room to his small walk-in closet and rummaged around until I found a pair of sweatpants and an old T-shirt. There just wasn't enough material in my dress to keep me warm. In the adjoining bathroom I found a pair of scissors and, without asking, cut slits in his shirt for my wings. If it was that big of a deal, I'd buy him a new one. But I doubted it. Tal wasn't one to get worked up over his things.

Once I changed into his clothes, I rolled the pant legs of his sweats up so I didn't trip over them, tightened the drawstrings, and padded barefoot into his living room.

"You forgot someone," I said.

"Huh?" He sat up from his prone position on the couch, clearly startled by my silent entrance.

"You forgot someone on your rundown of people I love." I stood near his bedroom door, unable to move any closer.

His gaze traveled down my body and then seared into mine. "You look...comfortable."

"Do you mind?"

He shook his head. "But I'd be lying if I said I preferred this look to that amazing dress."

My lips twitched. "I'd be worried about you if you did."

He got to his feet and in three strides was standing in front of me. With one hand on my hip, he brushed his fingertips over my cheek and let them run down my neck.

Heat sizzled my insides and I wondered how I could have been cold only moments ago.

He gazed down at me, his conflicted eyes unreadable. Hesitation? Wariness? Fear? I wasn't sure.

Reaching up, I wrapped a hand around his neck and pulled him a little closer. "You," I whispered.

He let out a slow breath. "Yeah? What about me?"

My heart started to flutter and my breathing became shallow. "You left yourself off the list of people I love."

The conflict in his gaze shifted to something soft and tender. "You love me?"

He knew I loved him. He was my best friend, but that wasn't what he was asking and I knew it. I just didn't know if I was ready to say it. Instead I took his face in my hands and rose on my tiptoes, pressing my lips to his.

Our kiss was gentle, sweet, vulnerable. We were in uncharted territory here. Last week I would've smacked him and accused him of flattering himself while rolling my eyes at his absurd question. He would've laughed and likely swept me off my feet and thrown me on the couch in the most unromantic way possible. Later, I would've laid my head on his lap and told him matter-of-factly he was my best friend and of course I loved his ugly ass.

But today, everything was different. What we had was too new. Too intense. Just too uncertain. We'd had a fight on our first date. Was this a glimpse of what was to come? I forced the thoughts out of my mind and concentrated on his soft lips moving over mine. Our tongues met in a slow caress that almost brought tears to my eyes. This was raw tenderness underneath all the uncertainty we both were carrying around with us.

I pulled back and blinked. "I'm closer to you than anyone." My words were heartfelt but seemed to fall short to my own ears. I wasn't ready to give what he was asking.

"I know, Wil. I know." He pulled me into a hug. "Your safety is the most important thing. If protecting you means giving my elixir to human thugs that work for Allcot, then dammit, that's what I'm going to do."

Releasing me, he took me by the hand and led me to the couch. He pulled me to sit in front of him, one of his legs on either side of me. I tucked my wings in and rested my back against his chest with my legs stretched out in front of me. My nerves settled. This was where I belonged. He buried his head in my neck and pulled me tight to his body.

It was the only place I wanted to be. And even though I hated the fact that Allcot now had control over Tal and the new drug, I completely understood where Talisen was coming from. As adamant as I was about not ever using Influence or letting it into the hands of vampires, I knew if Tal's life was on the line, I wouldn't hesitate.

"Are we okay?" he asked huskily.

I twisted to look at him and placed a gentle hand on the side of his face. "More than okay."

Chapter 8

Tal and I fell asleep on the couch. At some point, I woke to him carrying me to his bed under the cypress tree. My day had caught up to me and when Tal tucked me beside him, I laid my head on his chest and instantly fell back asleep.

I awoke alone at the pulse of a blender reverberating through the apartment. After a quick trip to the bathroom to brush my teeth with the brand-new spare toothbrush I found in the medicine cabinet, I combed my hair and headed into Tal's sun-soaked apartment. The drapes were open, revealing a wall of windows. I paused to revel in the sweet warmth and let my gaze wander lazily over Tal. His back was to me as he tossed fruit into a blender, apparently whipping up breakfast smoothies.

Yum.

After not eating much the night before, my stomach was growling. But food wasn't the only thing I was hungry for. Talisen's jeans rode low on his hips, and the way the morning light cascaded over his toned, naked torso made my mouth water. After our fight, there hadn't been more than a hint of anything romantic between us. I'd been too exhausted and overwhelmed. But right now, I wanted to press myself into his gorgeous body and discover everything he had to offer.

"Good morning."

Even though I was busy staring at him...well, his body anyway, I hadn't noticed him turn his head in my direction. He wore a cocky grin that told me he understood all too well what I was thinking.

I pretended not to notice. "Morning."

"Sleep well?"

That earned him an appreciative grin. "Yes. Your tree was exactly what I needed. Thank you for thinking of me."

"Anything to get you in my bed more often."

My cheeks burned and he chuckled. All I could do was breathe a huge silent sigh of relief when he turned his attention to rummaging in the fridge. Everything was back to normal with us. Tal was once again a huge flirt and I was happy to be on the receiving end, as always.

"Phoebs dropped off some fresh clothes for you." He pulled out a basket of fresh blueberries. "Do you want me to give you a lift to your shop on my way to the university?"

Yes. I didn't want to waste one moment of this morning. Our first one together as a couple. Even though we hadn't been physical at all once we'd gone to bed, we had slept intertwined and it had felt more right than I could've ever imagined. Unfortunately, we couldn't always have what we wanted. "It's probably best if I take a cab. If anyone sees you dropping me off, they might get the wrong idea."

He crossed the kitchen, grabbed my hips, and forced me back against the wall. "They'll get the exact right impression," he said huskily as he buried his face into my neck. Then he claimed my mouth, kissing me so thoroughly that the rest of the world disappeared. The heat of his body ignited an uncontrollable fire in mine, and the faint but intoxicating scent of forest and male musk filled my senses. When he finally pulled away, my lips pulsed as if swollen, and I could barely catch my breath. He ran his hand through the slight tangles of my wavy hair. "I've wanted to hold you in my arms all night for a few years now."

I bit my lower lip and tore my gaze from his mouth. "You have?"

His soft lips brushed lightly over mine once more. "Yeah. And after living the reality, I'm going to be spending most of my waking hours figuring out how to get you back there."

I laughed and pushed him back. But only because I had to get to the shop and deal with the aftermath of yesterday's destruction. "It's time to go. Can we pick up where left off, say, seven tonight?"

Mock disappointment shone in his puppy-dog eyes. "If you say so."

Smiling, I placed a hand on that perfect chest of his and pressed a kiss to the hollow of his throat. "You'll survive. I promise."

Thirty minutes later, showered and in my own clothes, Link and I stepped out of the cab a few blocks from my shop. Announcing my arrival with a city cab was bound to raise questions.

It was still early, only just before seven, but Tami was likely already there setting up for the day.

Link ran a little ahead of me, excited to be out walking instead of cooped up in the office or the house. His tongue was out as he trotted along with a bounce in his step. I kind of knew how he felt. After the parting kiss with Talisen, I'd been almost drooling and ready to skip off to start my day, too. I chuckled. Yeah, I was doomed.

I slowed as we reached the corner. One more block and I'd have to face the destruction that had once been my sanctuary. I steeled myself. Everything could be put right. I would not let Asher and his thugs take away the one thing that was truly mine.

With much resolve, I forced myself to round the corner and strode with purpose toward the front door. The bell jingled as Link and I entered the shop.

"Morning." Tami waved and slid a tray of Molten Muse into the bakery case.

"Morning. Are Em and Georgie here yet?" I strode to the back and flipped on the lights, signaling to the world we were open.

"They're in the back preparing a fresh batch of Mocha in Motion and setting up more trays."

"Great." I snapped my fingers, and Link bounded to my side and sat obediently. "Good pup. We'll be in my office cleaning up," I told Tami.

She sent me a sympathetic smile. "Call if you need help."

"Thanks, but it's mostly trash." Taking a deep breath, I pulled my door open and strode in. Then stopped dead in my tracks. "What the hell?"

"Allcot had it taken care of."

I jumped and fluttered about three feet away. "Dammit, Harrison, you scared the bejeezus out of me." My security detail sat in my brand-new office chair at my brand-new desk, in my pristine, not-a-thing-out-of-place office. Slowly I descended and landed softly beside him. "What the hell are you doing in here?" I waved a hand indicating my office. "And how did this happen?"

He wrapped an arm around my shoulders and leaned in. "Get used to me, babe. I go where you go from here on out."

I shrugged him off and sent him a death glare. After spending the night with Tal, this guy's touch made me flinch. It was just so wrong.

"Everywhere? I don't think so. My house is off-limits."

"Careful," he warned. "If you don't let me in, the ones watching will start to get suspicious."

We stood facing each other. Harrison kept an amused expression despite his serious tone. I tried to keep the scowl from my lips. "If you know someone is watching, why don't you just go after him?"

"Because, beautiful, we're trying to turn the tables on him and track him back to Asher. It does no good to kill the messenger if we can't get to the puppet master."

I refrained from rolling my eyes at his endearment. "Don't y'all have ways of making people talk?"

"Not if they've been Influenced or had some combination of truth-blocking spells put on them. More often than not, their brains end up addled and they become totally useless."

Resentment made me tense. Something similar had happened to Pandora's sister not too long ago. With Phoebe and Tal's help, I'd been able to reverse the spells she'd been under, but that had been sheer luck. If she'd been tortured and expected to talk, she'd have ended up broken for sure. Damn it all. I still wasn't letting him in my house. I was done housing Allcot's people. No matter what anyone said.

Waving a hand around the room, I asked, "Do you know what happened here? Yesterday it was a disaster area."

"Like I said, Allcot had it taken care of."

"What?" Anger boiled up from my chest. He'd expect something in return. He always did. "Why?"

Harrison shrugged. "He's a nice guy?"

A bitter laugh escaped from the back of my throat. "Right."

Someone knocked on my door just before it opened. "Whoa." Georgie poked her head in. "Have you been here all night?"

Harrison gave her a sly smile. "Actually Willow and I—"

"Harrison came in early to clean up. I just got here," I said, glaring at Harrison. I knew he was playing the part of my human boyfriend, but I had to draw the line somewhere. Suggesting to my employees that I'd spent the night in the office with a stranger wasn't going to cut it. "Harrison managed to get me a new desk yesterday afternoon and offered to deliver it today."

"Well, aren't you a miracle worker," Em, Georgie's shorter and rounder sister, cooed as she strode in. "We'll have to keep you around for a while."

He shot me a self-satisfied grin and nodded his agreement. "That's the plan."

I rolled my eyes. "Harrison is going to be helping out with some remodeling in the back for a while. Feel free to ask him for anything." I smiled at him. If he was going to be hanging around, he could make himself useful. "Georgie, could you show him to the storage room and get him started on installing those new shelves we've been too busy to get to?"

"Sure." She smiled at Harrison. "It'd be my pleasure."

"Yes, ma'am." He saluted me and followed my employees out of the office. Link darted over to his new doggie bed. After rolling around on it, he lifted his head in sort of a nod of approval and then curled into a ball.

I grabbed the old-fashioned phone on my desk and dialed Phoebe. It went straight to voice mail. I didn't leave a message. What was the point? I couldn't say what I really wanted to. I had no idea what was bugged and what wasn't. I spent the next half hour going over paperwork and was so engrossed that when my cell phone buzzed, I actually let out a tiny yelp.

Link jumped up and started pacing. You'd think he'd be used to my overreactions by now. I was glad he wasn't. He was my first line of defense against all the crazy that seemed to follow me.

The text was from Phoebe. *I'll be there in ten minutes. The courtyard is calling.*

What the hell did that mean? We didn't have a courtyard. But the neighbors did. That was it. She wanted me to meet her outside in ten minutes.

Good. Did she have a plan of action? Asher had already come after me once. I couldn't afford to sit and wait while Allcot's people stalked his lackeys. I paced until the clock read ten minutes past the hour. Then I slipped out the side door.

Phoebe was already waiting. She grabbed my arm and pulled me back into the opening to the neighbor's courtyard, concealing us from prying eyes.

"What's going on?" I asked, rubbing my arm. Damn, the girl had a strong grip.

"What isn't?" She reached into her bag and pulled out her black stun gun. "Take this."

"Why?"

"It's yours now."

"You really think this is going to ward off vampires?" She always carried a stun gun, but they were almost useless against a vamp. Sure, it hurt, but it wouldn't slow one down. They were just too good at compartmentalizing pain.

"Yes. It's the Void's version." She held up a hand to stop my protests. I had always refused one on the premise that if a vamp got it away from me, I would be total toast. "It will work on vamps, but that's not why I brought it. It's for the souped-up humans."

I stepped back, clutching the gun. "How did you know about that?"

Her mouth opened in a surprised O. After a few beats she closed it and straightened her spine. "Sorry, Wil. I planted a silver beetle on you because of the meeting—or nonmeeting— you had with Allcot." She bit her lip, embarrassed. "I heard what you and Tal said."

Shit! Nothing was private anymore. I was even personally bugged. I started rummaging around in my pockets.

"It's not there."

"Where, then?"

"Your hairclip."

I reached up and yanked the offending accessory off my head. "This is a ladybug. Not a beetle."

She shrugged. "Either works."

I wanted to toss it to the ground and stomp on it until it was in a million pieces, but instead I handed it to her. My privacy was being invaded from all sides, but I knew Phoebs had bugged me because of Allcot. She kept tabs on me only when I was headed into dangerous territory. "You could've told me."

"With everything that was going on, I just forgot." She met my eyes and I saw sincerity there. "I should've turned it off earlier, but then you and Tal started arguing about his agreement…Well, you know me. I like to be in on the plan."

I nodded, not sure if I was pissed or not.

"But I did turn it off after I heard Tal's confession. Pretty low of Allcot to involve him, if I do say so myself."

I was suddenly emotionally exhausted. "I can't live like this." I waved to the shop, indicating Harrison, though I wasn't sure she knew what I meant. "I can't live with zero privacy, knowing someone is intent on taking me down while I sit back and do nothing. I have to take action."

Phoebe cocked her head, looking thoughtful. "I have an idea, but it isn't Void sanctioned."

"Since when has that ever stopped you?" I challenged her.

"Never. You know I'm always up for kicking some vamp ass. I just want to make sure you are."

I held up the stun gun. "As ready as I'll ever be."

Chapter 9

I opened the door to my office and whistled for Link. He shot off his doggie bed and scrambled to my side. Seconds later we were in Phoebe's car, headed toward Mid-City, New Orleans's known vampire territory. I hadn't told Harrison I was leaving. Phoebe didn't want him anywhere near her investigation. I didn't blame her.

Allcot and his people had their own way of dealing with situations. It usually involved making people disappear. Harrison would never let me go without him, if he'd let me go at all. I had Phoebe and Link. They were more than enough to battle any unexpected attacks.

"I've got the last known address of the guy who attacked you at the dress shop yesterday. The director ordered a search of the premises and I, being the fabulous manipulator that I am, managed to score the job." She grinned, clearly pleased with herself.

"Really? And how did you do that?"

She shrugged and stopped at a red light. "I may have mentioned to the agent who had the job that I'd seen him out around town with a woman about ten years younger than his wife."

"And?"

The light turned green, and Phoebe laid into the gas. "Let's just say he was willing to negotiate."

Laughing, I shook my head. Phoebe had a way of getting whatever she wanted. She could also transform into anyone she wanted. Today she was wearing a dark brown wig, carefully mussed into a carefree, college-girl style. Her tight blue jeans and formfitting T-shirt screamed student. If it weren't for Link and me, anyone who saw her would never make the Void connection.

"I thought you said the job wasn't Void sanctioned." If she was working the case, this was not only normal, but expected.

"Oh, the job is. Taking you isn't. The director ordered you benched for the time being."

"What? And she didn't tell me?" I scowled. What if Phoebe needed Link and me to go out on patrol with her?

"She left that lovely job to me." Phoebs wrinkled her perfect nose. "Sorry. I think she's off her rocker, obviously, or I wouldn't be taking you along. But to be fair, she probably doesn't want Allcot's people mixed up in any Void business."

"She knows?" Jeez. Was the Void following me, too?

Phoebe nodded slowly. "I'm sure she has informants. A good director would." Twisting, she nodded to a duffle bag in the back seat. "Find a disguise. You don't want to be spotted."

I bit my lip and rummaged around in the bag. There had to be something to hide my wings. I tugged a dark blue sweater out of her bag, tucked my wings to my back, and pulled it over my shoulders. It was late September and still far too hot for such clothing, but I had little choice.

Phoebe eyed me. "You need a wig." She pulled up in front of a shotgun double with peeling paint and grabbed a bleach-blond, shoulder-length wig from another bag.

I pinned my own hair back and turned myself into a cheap blonde. "Ready?" I asked, not daring to study myself too much.

"Let's do this."

Clutching my new stun gun, I followed Phoebs to the front door. She pulled out one of her magic-filled agates and knocked on the door. When no one answered, she peered in the window. "Looks empty."

She jumped off the porch and headed around to the back. Link and I followed, knowing this was her usual routine for breaking and entering. As a Void agent, she didn't quite have a get-out-of-jail-free card, but it was close. She was expected to go undetected, but if caught, the Void had ways of getting her off the hook. Unless the property was controlled by a vamp. Then she had to deal with him or her directly.

Before Link and I even caught up, Phoebe had the back door open and was doing a security sweep through the small house. "All clear," she called and tucked her witch agate back into her pocket.

Link and I stepped inside. I peered through the kitchen doorway to the rest of the house. Four rooms were all lined up in the shotgun-style home, each leading into the other in a straight line. The one directly off the kitchen had dirty clothes strewn all over the floor and an unmade bed.

The bedroom. I wrinkled my nose at the stale, sweaty stench. When was the last time the guy had washed his sheets?

"You start at the front of the house and I'll take the kitchen," Phoebe said.

Worked for me. If I was lucky, I wouldn't have to touch anything but the warped wood floors of the bedroom. "Sure." I snapped my fingers and Link and I hightailed it to the living room. The rancid grease stench from the abandoned fast-food bags made my stomach roll. Ick.

Link raised each paw carefully as he made his way over the debris scattered throughout the rooms. Seemed the place wasn't even fit for a dog. "We won't be long," I told him. It took me less than five minutes to determine there was nothing of informational value in the front room. Not unless you counted the stack of *Vamp* magazines towering in the corner. It was a publication devoted to humans who longed to be turned.

There were almost no accounts of wannabes of his caliber who had been turned. Vampires were very choosy about who they let into their families.

"Wil," Phoebe called excitedly from the other room. "I found something."

Link and I rushed through the dining room and bedroom to the kitchen. Phoebe was standing on the counter, holding a tattered spiral notebook. "Names and numbers. A bunch of them."

"For what?"

"It doesn't say, but some are starred. I want to start with them first to see what kind of connection there might be."

"Sounds suspicious," I said, heading for the back door.

"Where are you going?"

"To get some fresh air. This place reeks."

She nodded her agreement. "Are the rest of the rooms clean?"

I snorted. "I think clean is the last word I'd use for this place, but the living room is done. The dining room is almost empty, and you couldn't pay me to search that bedroom." I opened the back door. "I'll check the shed and then we'll wait for you on the back porch."

"Okay."

The outbuilding was about half the size of the house. I gritted my teeth at the ceiling-high cardboard boxes that blocked the windows. If it was full of storage, we'd be there all day. I glanced at Link. "This is gonna suck."

He barked.

"You can say that again."

The doorknob turned under my grip, but the door was blocked by something and wouldn't open. I glanced up and noticed the padlock slipped through a latch at the very top of the door. Better than a deadbolt.

After a quick search of the ground, I picked up a rock about the size of my fist, shed my sweater, and fluttered my wings, lifting myself off the ground. Three strikes later, the lock and the hardware had come loose. One more and the entire operation tumbled to the ground. "Termite damage," I said to Link.

He sniffed the lock and wagged his tail.

Must be nice to be a dog. The door swung open and the musty stench of mold and dirt filtered out. I fumbled around for a switch. My hand hit something cool, and fluorescent light flooded the shed. Blinking, I took a deep breath of clean air and then stepped inside.

The hair on my arms rose and I froze. A diagram of pictures was tacked to the wall with my name in the middle, surrounded by all my loved ones and a bunch of people I didn't recognize. Arrows were drawn between me and some of them, but not all, and some of the accompanying, unfamiliar names were circled and connected to other names.

I took a step closer and pressed my fingers to a picture of Talisen. He was standing on my porch in the twilight, laughing as Link bounded up to him. I recognized the shot. It was taken ten days ago. They'd been watching me for over a week and a half, at least. Asher's people, if Allcot was to be believed. Who else would be following me, unless someone in the Void had gone rogue again? But why were they making a move now?

I pulled out my iPhone and snapped about a dozen pictures of the pictorial in front of me. Phoebe and I'd have our work cut out for us figuring out who all the players were.

"Will!" Phoebe whispered harshly. "Time to go!"

I shoved my phone back in my pocket and ran out of the shed, finding her pressed against the building.

"Get over here." She indicated the space to her left as she peered around the corner.

Crouching down, I snapped my fingers and Link joined me. He was vibrating with anticipation, ready to shift if anything went down. I ran a calming hand down his back. Shifting now would guarantee we were spotted. "What's going on?" I whispered.

She waved a hand to silence me. Link pitched his ears forward as unintelligible voices floated through the yard.

Crap. Someone was here. Had the suspect been released? I tightened my grip around the stun gun and sucked in slow, calming breaths. I could do this.

"Get to the shed. All the files are in there." The deep male voice was close.

"Shit," Phoebe murmured. "They're coming. Move." She nudged my shoulder, pushing me toward the back of the structure.

But I was cemented in place. Thick honey vampire energy kept my feet glued to the ground. My wings flexed in panic and a cold sweat blossomed over my body.

"Wil," Phoebe hissed in my ear. "Move it."

I shook my head, positive my expression was frantic. "Vampire," I mouthed, knowing just how close he had to be.

Her eyes went wide with startled surprise. It was barely eleven a.m. The sun was shining full force. If there was a vampire here, that meant only one thing.

A daywalker.

And Phoebe's sun agate would mean nothing.

The energy got thicker with each passing second. The sensation pressed in on me, making it hard to breathe.

"David?" Phoebe mouthed back.

I shook my head, wishing that was the case. I'd accidently turned David into a daywalker not too long ago. One of the side effects of his transformation was that I could no longer sense him when he was around. His touch no longer caused me physical pain, either. The vamp on the other side of the shed definitely wasn't David.

"Someone's already been here," another man with a nasally voice said.

"No. They're still here," Deep Voice replied.

Phoebe sprang to her feet, her agate in one hand and something silver in the other. Link vibrated, his head morphing into a large wolf shape while his bones contorted and elongated until he was a snarling, full-fledged wolf.

Me? I was trapped in my own personal vampire hell. I'd never been affected as much by a vamp before. Normally it took prolonged exposure or a major energy depletion to cause a reaction so intense. I had no idea what was going on.

In true Phoebe fashion, she charged around the building, Link at her side, and yelled, "Siste!"

A loud chuckle came from above me. I glanced up and caught a glimpse of a medium-built man dressed in a beige seersucker suit, but his facial features were obscured by his fedora.

How old school of him. He moved away without noticing me and the vamp pressure lessened slightly, just enough that I was able to shuffle to the edge of the shed.

Halfway to the house, Phoebe tackled a thin, balding man. They went down in a tangle of limbs.

"Get off, you dumb bitch," her victim cried.

"Not likely, you sorry sack of vampire lover." She coldcocked him and he went limp.

I stumbled to Phoebe's side. The instant she touched my arm, a cool, numbing sensation filtered through me and the vampire energy no longer weighed me down. I still felt him. He hadn't left; I was just functional again.

Link stood in front of the shed, howling up at the vampire.

"Is there a reason you attacked my nephew, Agent Kilsen?" the vampire asked, more curious than angry.

Phoebe raised one eyebrow. "How do you know who I am?"

A ghost of a smile teased his lips.

"Why are you here?" Phoebe demanded with a snarl.

The vamp shifted. One second he was on the roof, the next he was standing less than a foot in front of us. He reached out and traced one finger down my cheek. A line of fire burned where he touched me and I flinched, swallowing the gasp of agony. Oh, no. I was not going to stand there and let him torment me.

I lashed the stun gun out, blindly connecting with him. My arm vibrated in time with the vampire's growl. Somehow the electric current seemed to keep us connected and as my vision cleared, we locked eyes. His angry, ice-blue ones bored into mine and fear filled my soul. Once the gun ran out of juice, I was dead. If I let go now, he'd kill me.

Another growl and Link was on him. He sank his fangs into the vamp and then let go, howling in pain. Link! Shit. He twitched, fell to the ground, and then went limp, his fur standing on end. Phoebe had moved and was now standing behind the vamp, blue witch light streaming from her fingertips.

The vampire was contained in a holding pattern of my electric current. His face contorted in obvious pain, but the gun wasn't bringing him to his knees like it should.

"Now!" Phoebe cried. I broke the connection while simultaneously thrusting my wings. I shot off the ground and flew toward Link, who was lying a few feet away. If I could get to him, my touch would help.

The vampire spun in my direction and leaped for me. "I've been waiting for this moment, Rhoswen."

Phoebe's blue magic crackled like fire over his body, stopping him. I'd seen this spell before. The second the blue flame hit the vamp, he should've started to burn from the inside out. This vampire, however, did no such thing. He writhed as if he was weighted down with chains, but clearly neither of us had caused him any damage.

"Grab Link!" Phoebe cried.

I was already on him, forcing my life magic into his battered body. He was still alive, thank the Goddess, but his breathing was shallow and his pulse was faint. "Come on, buddy."

My life magic could restore pretty much any living thing, but Link was a magical shifter and it took more than a little bit of will to force it into him. I was sweating and cursing as I waited for my power to help restore his vitals.

"Let's go," Phoebe cried.

I glanced at her. She was struggling to maintain her own power. This vamp was old. Incredibly old. That's why I'd felt him so strongly and why Phoebe was unable to contain him.

We had to get out of there. Under my touch, Link shifted suddenly to Shih Tzu form and he started taking deeper breaths. I let out a strangled sigh of relief and scooped him up into my arms, flying as fast as I could to the car.

I yanked the door open, set Link in the back, and cursed myself for not remembering my keys, which were still sitting in my desk. If I had them, I could start the car and be Phoebe's getaway driver. Instead, I rushed back to where she and the vamp were having a mental-strength showdown.

His eyes met mine and rage burned in their chilly depths. I shuddered and scanned the yard for Phoebe's pack. There. Right beside the fallen bald man. I rushed to his side and landed with an ungraceful thump. My knee gave out on impact and I went down, crashing into him. "Ouch!"

Ignoring the searing pain in my knee, I scrambled over his prone form and grabbed her pack. Reaching in the front pouch, I closed my fingers over her keys and scrambled to my feet.

A hand shot out and grabbed my ankle, pulling me back down.

"Willow!" I heard Phoebe's panicked cry and did the only thing I could think of. I elbowed the bald man in the back and then brought the stun gun down on him, ensuring he wouldn't be getting up anytime soon.

"Run!" Phoebe commanded from behind me. I'd lost sight of her while grappling with Baldy. But as I turned, I found her shaking and alone, her magic gone.

"Phoebs?"

She grabbed my arms and dragged me to the back of the car. But the vamp stood at the driver's side, glowering at both of us. If he wanted to, he could probably pick up the entire car and toss it down the street. Vamps in general were strong, but the really old ones were almost unstoppable. Especially when they couldn't be burned by the sun.

Phoebe tried to stumble past me toward the vampire but was clearly weakened from her impressive display of power. She'd never survive another full-on attack.

I pulled her back and clutched my stun gun, more than grateful Phoebe had thought to get me one. "Be ready to get the hell out of here," I ordered. I might not be trained in physical combat, but damn it, I wasn't afraid of electrocuting someone's ass. Hopefully he was drained enough that the gun would buy us a few seconds to get the hell out of there.

The vamp moved so fast, I didn't even see him coming. One second, I was headed for him, gun in hand, and the next I was lying face-first on the rough asphalt pavement. "You've messed with the wrong vampire, Rhoswen," he hissed into my ear. "Hear me? You know I can't let you live since you've learned my secret."

My world spun with equal parts agony and fear: the pain from where his hand pressed into my back, burning every last nerve ending, and the fear from not knowing how to fight such a powerful being. My gun had fallen on impact. I had no idea where it had gone. Link was out of commission in the car, and Phoebe had used up almost all her magic. I was going to die at the hand of this unknown daywalker.

The vamp brought his mouth down to my neck and whispered, "It's been two centuries since I've tasted fae."

"And it's going to be another one before you have a chance, you sick son of a bitch," Phoebe yelled.

I heard the buzz of the gun and from the corner of my eye saw Phoebe press it to the vamp's bare neck. His body started to twitch uncontrollably. The Taser was running out of juice, judging by the whining sound, and I was still trapped beneath him, every last nerve ending screaming from the vamp contact and the residual electricity streaming from him to me. My head spun and everything started to go black. I'd soon be a ball of fire. It wouldn't matter if the vamp wanted to kill me or not, I'd die from shock.

Using every ounce of strength I had left, I pushed upward, barely moving the stonelike creature sprawled over me. But when I bucked, he shifted a tiny bit and I rolled, tumbling farther into the street and over a pothole. Ouch!

I could barely get to my feet, but my adrenaline took over and I found myself in the driver's seat of Phoebe's car with the engine running. "Let's go!" I cried to Phoebe.

I had one foot on the gas and the other on the brake. As soon as her ass hit the passenger's seat and before the door was even closed, we took off, leaving a trail of rubber in our wake. I glanced in the rearview mirror as we sped down the street. The only things left of us at the house were our tire tracks, an unconscious human, and a very pissed-off, daywalking vampire.

Chapter 10

"Fuck, fuck, fuck!" Phoebe pounded her fist on her thigh and glanced behind us for the sixth time.

"Is he following us?" I checked the rearview mirror and saw nothing but midafternoon traffic. Then I eyed Link. His ears twitched, though he didn't move. He was okay. The little guy was tougher than he looked.

"No." She sucked in a staggering breath. "Not that I can tell."

I sped through my third yellow light and headed down North Broad Street. "Where to? Back to my store?"

Phoebe, visibly shaking, didn't answer.

"The Void?" We should tell them about the new daywalker. Besides, I had the pictures and we needed an analyst to track down identities.

"No. Not yet." She sat back in her seat, her eyes closed.

I gripped the steering wheel so tight my fingers started to cramp. "We need to tell someone."

"Not the Void." She twisted and peered at me. "What do you think they'll do when they find out there's another daywalker? They already want to study you and David for the effects. If they know another one exists, they won't hold back. And you won't be held in secret either. The orders will come down from the top. This is a game changer."

Son of a...shit! I ran through the possible options. We couldn't exactly go home. The vamp would track us there in no time. My shop? Harrison was there...maybe, if he hadn't taken off after I disappeared. Allcot's? I was under his protection now, but every fiber of my being screamed to stay away from him. He would protect me, but what would it cost in the long run? What would I owe him and how would he collect? Not to mention the vampires there would slowly zap my energy simply by existing. We could go to Tal's place. As far as I knew, no one knew where he lived. But if we went there, how long would it be before he became a target?

"Go to Allcot's." Phoebe slumped down in her seat and slid her sunglasses in place.

"Seriously?" That meant turning around and heading straight back into vamp territory. Was she crazy? We'd almost died. Who knew where that vampire was now?

"We need help tracking this psycho, and Allcot has the resources. Besides, there is no way he's going to let anything happen to you. You're too valuable to him." Her tone was flat, emotionless, as if she didn't care. But I knew her better. That was the tone she used when she was moments from losing control.

Her words sent a tremor of foreboding skating over my skin. She was right about Allcot. He would protect me. One day I was going to be just as tied to him as Carrie was. I shivered and focused on Phoebe. When she was like this, I followed her directions with no questions asked. Even when she was flat out blindsided, her instincts were always spot-on. I ignored the blinking warning light in my brain and made a U-turn.

"Take the side roads," Phoebe said, rummaging in her duffle bag.

I did as she said, not saying a word. She was the queen of disguise and moving places unseen.

She pulled out two new wigs and a black T-shirt.

I raised a quizzical eyebrow.

She tossed a mousy-brown wig that had been styled into a short bob in my direction. "Put it on."

I took a right onto a street filled with deserted homes that had been left in despair after Hurricane Katrina and pulled over. Phoebe changed her shirt and had her new platinum-blond wig in place before I could even remove the blond one I'd put on earlier. She used her deft fingers to help me secure the new wig in place and handed me wire-rimmed glasses. After shoving them on, I pulled out into traffic, both of us magically transformed by her bag of tricks. There wasn't anything we could do about the car, but she'd chosen a Toyota Camry for a reason. Nondescript. There were a ton of them everywhere.

We finally reached Allcot's French Colonial home after taking multiple unnecessary turns and doubling back twice. Phoebe had kept a vigilant watch but hadn't detected anyone following. My shoulders eased a bit. Phoebs excelled at her job.

I pulled the Toyota into Allcot's long driveway and parked behind the silver Mercedes I recognized as David's car. Nervous anticipation conflicted with the dread coiling through me at the thought of seeing my ex yet again. Damn. Where was the nervous anticipation coming from? Nothing had changed. I still didn't trust him. Plus, I belonged with Tal.

Phoebe jumped out of the car and cast me an irritated glance as I lingered. She wasn't waiting for anyone. Link stirred, barely lifting his head as I opened the back door. I clutched him to my chest and joined Phoebe on the front porch.

She pressed the doorbell continuously until the door finally burst open.

A short, round, middle-aged woman dressed in a black-and-white maid uniform scowled at us. "Where's the fire?"

"Get Davidson Laveaux," Phoebe demanded.

The maid's eyes narrowed and her scowl deepened. "There's no one here by that name."

"Bullshit." Phoebe stuck her foot in the door to keep it from being closed in our faces.

The unmistakable sound of a gun being cocked came from behind the maid.

"Phoebs," I said, "back off." I stepped in front of her, still clutching Link. "Tell Davidson Willow Rhoswen is here. It's an emergency."

Her face went slack and her eyes widened. "Identification?"

I set Link down while Phoebe and I handed over our licenses. The maid studied them with a careful eye, waved her backup gunman off, and opened the door in invitation.

I hadn't expected anyone to let us in without checking with David first. He must've given them a standing order concerning me. I wasn't sure if I was okay with that, but right then I was grateful.

"This way." She closed the door behind us. We followed her up the massive staircase and down the hallway toward the room I knew David inhabited. "Wait here." She knocked once before letting herself into his sitting room.

A few moments later, she pulled the door open again. "He's in his room." She waved for us to enter the sitting room and then disappeared down the hall.

Phoebe collapsed onto one of the black leather armchairs and pulled her wig off. She tucked her legs under herself and closed her eyes as if she knew this was the only moment of peace she was bound to get for the foreseeable future.

Link placed his front paws on the edge of the other chair, his legs still shaky from the aftereffects of the electrical current. I reached down and lifted him into the chair. He licked my hand and curled into a ball, tucking his head against a woven pillow.

I crossed the room, limping from the lingering pain in my knee, and knocked on his door.

"Come in," David called.

The door creaked and I poked my head in. "David?" I glanced around, not seeing him at first.

"Wil?"

I spun to my right and spotted him coming out of his giant walk-in closet. I let out an audible gasp. "Holy fae, what happened?" I ran over, inspecting his reddish-purple skin. "It looks like you've been deep-fried."

He grimaced. "Sunburn."

Phoebe stalked into the room and stopped mid-step. "Fuck, Laveaux. Did you fall into a crawfish boil?"

Ignoring her, he tugged a T-shirt over his head and winced as the fabric settled against his skin.

"How'd this happen?" I wanted to touch him, make sure he was all right and still the solid, marbled vampire he'd been the night before.

"I told you, it's just a little sunburn." He peered at me. "Why are you here and where's Harrison?"

"We ditched him," Phoebe mumbled.

"Why?"

"We were doing our jobs," I said. "Investigating for the Void."

"That sounds like Phoebe's job."

"You're right," I said. "But I couldn't sit back and wait for whatever comes next. I can't be a sitting target."

"So you ditched your security?" The muscle in his jaw pulsed. "What the hell were you thinking?"

"Leave her alone, David. It's been a clusterfuck of a day." Phoebe ran a hand through her dark, spiky hair. "All we were doing was investigating the man who attacked her. Since he's locked up at the Arcane, no one was supposed to be there. We were caught off guard. The only consolation is, we're pretty sure our attacker was, too."

"You were attacked?" he asked, his face tight with irritation and worry.

I nodded, avoiding his gaze.

He turned to Phoebe and started punching in a message on his cell phone. "This is how you keep your partner safe?"

"She's alive, isn't she?"

David glared at her

Phoebe pasted a bored smile on her face, but I knew she was putting on a show for David. She'd never let a vamp know when she was off her game. "I need a computer."

"Why?"

"To keep Willow safe," she parroted his words back to him.

"And you can't use your own because?"

"I don't have it with me." She retreated to the doorway. "Just point me to a laptop. You've got to have at least one or two around here."

He clenched his teeth and then jerked his head toward an armoire. "There's one in there. You can sign on as Guest, password Cryrique."

She chuckled to herself as she retrieved the sleek black machine. "You realize of course, that if I wanted to break into this, no password would stop me."

He turned to me and lifted a lock of my fake brown hair. One eyebrow arched in question.

"We weren't sure if we were being followed." I pulled the wig off and unpinned my hair, letting it fall around my shoulders.

"Yo. Laveaux. Did you hear me?" Phoebe asked, heading for the sitting room.

"I heard you," he said, still looking at me. His intense eyes were making me squirm. "And you know our computers are heavily monitored. If you break into my private files, that's grounds for detainment. And not the short-lived kind."

I sighed. "Can you two play nice for once?"

David shrugged. "I've got no problem with the witch."

Phoebe scoffed and I knew she was going to go on a vamp tirade. She didn't care for David at all. He hadn't been her favorite person when he'd been human, but since the day he'd dumped me by text message, she'd considered him a first-class jackass. His whole turning vamp situation hadn't helped matters.

"Phoebs." I sent her a pleading look. "Fighting isn't going to help."

"Who's fighting?" She strode through the door and kicked it closed, leaving David and me alone in his bedroom.

His phone buzzed. "Harrison," he said into the phone and paused. "Yeah, I've got her. Call Xavier in and get to the house ASAP." Irritation rippled over his face. "No. Don't tell the fae anything. We don't know what we're dealing with."

"Talisen?" I asked. "Is he with him? I need to talk to him."

David shook his head and pressed the End button on his phone.

"What the hell, David!" I backed away, clenching my fingers into fists. "He needs to know where I am."

"No. He doesn't. Not right now." He retreated to his massive king-sized bed and sat at the end. "Want to tell me exactly what happened?"

Not especially, after that display of dominance. "Want to tell me how you ended up so sunburned?"

He shrugged, clearly trying to be nonchalant, but his movements were forced, almost as if he were guilty of something. "Too much time out in the sun."

"David!" I cried. "Too much time in the sun? You weren't like this yesterday." I would've noticed, right? He'd been wearing a long-sleeved shirt the night before, though. I scanned the skin of his exposed areas. His face was as pale as ever. But his neck and the back of his hands were as red as the rest of him. "This happened today. How?"

"I already told you."

It was a few minutes past one p.m. Even if he'd spent all morning lying in the sun, he couldn't have been that bad off, could he? Vamps had super-healing properties. Wouldn't that apply to a sunburn, too? *Shit!* Was whatever I'd done to him wearing off? "So you're saying you lounged in the sun too long this morning and this is what happened?" I waved a hand impatiently. "And that either your vampire healing abilities have failed you or you looked way worse before I got here?"

He narrowed his eyes. "It's just an experiment to see how long I can stay in the sun without any harmful effects. All right? Let it go, Wil."

"That's one hell of an effect," I mumbled.

"I know." He got up and stood in front of me, gently taking my hand. "Don't worry about me. I'm fine."

"I'm not worried," I lied, yanking my hand back.

"Good." He grabbed my hand again and tugged me forward to the edge of the bed. "Sit."

I did as I was told, but instead of giving him my attention, I stared at my feet. The last time I'd been on this bed, I'd been wearing his pajamas and Allcot had just interrupted the start of a pretty intense make-out session. My gaze traveled to the wall near his door. The one he'd had me pinned to. Heat gathered at my center and started to spread.

Dammit. I did not want him to have this effect on me. I was with Talisen now.

"Wil?"

"Huh?"

"Tell me exactly what happened today." He shifted, pulling his knee on the bed to get a better look at me. "Who are you so afraid of?"

I swallowed and met his worried expression. He had a right to know he wasn't the only one. "We were ambushed by another daywalker."

Chapter 11

David was silent for a long moment after I finished relaying the day's events, including the evidence we'd found. His eyes darkened and his face turned stony. What was he thinking? Did he want to talk to the other daywalker? Did he have questions? Up until an hour ago, we'd thought David was the only daywalker in existence.

He stood and started pacing. While he wore a trail into his plush white carpet, he pulled his phone out of his pocket and hit a button. "Stevens, there's a green Camry in the driveway. Take it to Willow Rhoswen's house in the lower Garden District right away. This is sensitive. Make sure you aren't detected."

"Phoebe's car? How will we leave?"

His head snapped up as he slipped the phone back into his pocket. "You won't." He strode toward his door. "Wait here. I have to inform Father."

"No!" I jumped up and grabbed his arm.

He sucked in a gasp of pain.

Right. His sunburn. "Sorry." I loosened my grip but didn't let go. Something still didn't sit right about his sunburn. Since he was a vamp, it shouldn't hurt that much. But we had a bigger problem right then. "What will he do?"

"Father?"

"Yes, Allcot. What can he do? And what is this going to cost me?"

David's brow furrowed. "You're connected to this family now, Wil. When are you going to accept that? You're Beau's aunt. Father isn't going to let anything happen to your neph-ew's family."

Yeah. Somehow I didn't believe that was the answer.

"And as far as what he'll do, I don't know. But if I were him, I'd find out as much information from you and Phoebe as possible and then put a team out there to track that vamp. Find out what he wants. He can also put a team on researching the people in those photos you took."

"I'm going with you," I said.

"Fine. I'm sure Father will want to speak to you."

I followed David out of the room. We passed Phoebe, who had her head buried in the laptop as she typed furiously. "Phoebs?"

She waved a hand, indicating she didn't want to be interrupted.

"We're going to see Allcot," I said.

The typing stopped but she didn't look up. Then she nodded and her fingers started to fly again. "I'll be here."

As David swept me into the hallway, my phone started playing "Glad You Came" by The Wanted. *Talisen.* I yanked my phone out of my back pocket, but before I could answer it, David plucked it out of my hand and turned the phone off.

"Hey!" I reached for it.

"Your phone calls are likely being tracked or tapped. You can't use this phone." He tossed it to the floor and smashed it with his heavy boot.

I stopped mid-step and gaped. "What the...? Jesus, David. You didn't need to do that. What's wrong with you?"

He glanced at me, his face unreadable. "I'll get you a new one."

Red-hot anger started to simmer beneath my skin. How dare he? "You could've asked me to not answer it."

Something in my tone must've tipped him off that I wasn't just irritated, but upset as well, because he turned to me and in a soft voice said, "Hey, I'm sorry. I'm only trying to protect you. If it's being tracked, it's a danger. I didn't think you liked the phone that much. I mean, you never charge it." His lips quirked up in a small smile. "I'll send someone to get you another right now."

"It's not that, you idiot." An angry tear I couldn't hold back fell unchecked down my cheek. "I had pictures on that phone that weren't backed up on a cloud or computer." Mostly pictures of him before he turned vamp, but I'd walk over cut glass before I'd tell him that.

"Oh. Son of a bitch," he said under his breath. "I'm sorry. Did you have pictures of Beau on there?"

"No," I said quietly. "These were more recent."

"I'll have one of our techs try to recover them." He bent to retrieve the scattered pieces.

I said nothing, just watched him straighten and pocket the dead phone.

Silence stretched between us, becoming uncomfortable. I cleared my throat. "Can we go see Allcot now?"

"Of course." He took off down the stairs and led me to the back door.

"Wait. Isn't he here?"

David shook his head. "No. He's at Cryrique."

David inserted a key into what appeared to be a service elevator and a button lit up. I glanced around the parking garage, feeling more than a little vulnerable. David was with me, but Link and Phoebe were back at his house. All I had was my life magic. I could alter plants and change vamps into daywalkers. Not much to work with on the defense front. Hell, I'd even left my stun gun in Phoebe's car. It hadn't seemed like a good idea to bring it into Allcot's home.

The light went out on the button and the elevator doors opened. David placed a hand on the small of my back and guided me in.

Everything about the situation screamed that I should run. If Allcot wanted to, he could lock me up in this building and

I'd never be heard from again. No one knew where we were. Not even Phoebe.

The doors closed and seemed to suck all the air out of the tiny space. I concentrated on breathing, but my heart sped up and it wasn't long before I was almost hyperventilating.

"Willow?" David put his strong arm around me. "What is it? What's happening?"

"Claustrophobia," I forced out, though I'd never had that problem before. No, I was having a panic attack.

David pulled me into his arms and pressed my head to his chest. "Close your eyes," he soothed. "We'll be there in a second."

I did as he asked and tried to convince myself he was just a friend helping me get through a crisis. But deep down I knew it was a lie. David loved me. And even though I didn't want to admit it to even myself, I still had lingering feelings for him.

The elevator came to an abrupt stop, followed by a ding. The doors swept open and I launched myself out of David's arms. I clutched the hallway wall, working to get my breathing under control. David stood a few feet from me, waiting.

"Better?" he asked when my chest stopped heaving.

"Yeah." Though I certainly wasn't fine. The place was eerie. No one graced the sterile corridor, despite what appeared to be a long line of offices. There wasn't any office noise. No phones ringing. No footsteps. No voices. The place was a tomb. "Where is everyone?"

"This is Father's private floor." He headed to the end of the corridor to a nondescript white door and knocked. The door opened on its own, exactly like the door to Allcot's private office at The Red Door. Nicola, Allcot's sister-in-law, had likely spelled them. She was his resident witch, though not nearly as powerful as Phoebe.

We entered the sleek, deserted office. The brushed aluminum fixtures cast soft light over the gleaming black desk and silver, fabric-covered chairs. The desk was cleared, not one thing out of place, as if he hadn't even been in yet that day. I turned my attention to David. "He's not here."

"He is. We just need to wait." David sat in one of the plush chairs.

I eyed the phone. With a glance back at David, I strode over and picked it up. "Do I need to dial nine or anything for an outside line?"

I suppose I was mostly asking to see if he was going to give me a hard time. He only shook his head. I punched in six of Tal's numbers and paused, almost daring David to stop me. He didn't. I punched the last number and waited.

He answered on the third ring, almost out of breath. "Hello?"

"Tal, thank goodness."

"Willow!" His voice turned frantic, laced with fear. "Where are you?"

"I…" Should I say? What if his phone was tapped? I couldn't know. "I'm safe."

He let out a sigh of relief. "Good, I've been—" A clatter sounded over the line, followed by a grunt.

"Tal?"

"Get up." A harsh male voice filtered through the line.

"Talisen!" I cried, my heart trying to pound right out of my chest.

"Worthless fae." Another grunt, followed by a moan. "Who did you tell?"

"No one." I heard Tal say from far away. The tiny bit of relief at hearing his voice did nothing to calm the frantic haze of panic filling my senses. "Put Talisen on the phone!"

The person on the other end ignored my demand and yelled at Talisen instead. "Don't lie to me. Someone knows." Footsteps clattered on a hard floor, followed by the harsh reality of some sort of contact and the unmistakable sound of bones cracking.

The blood drained from my head and I went dizzy. "Tal," I whispered, clutching the phone.

"Who is this?" the stranger barked into the phone.

My throat closed. David pried the phone from my hand, holding me up with one arm. "This is Davidson Laveaux. Who is this?"

I pressed my ear close to David's, determined to be kept in the loop.

"None of your fucking business. I've got the fae now. If you want to see him alive again, find the energy-booster drug he's been working on. You have until tomorrow morning."

I heard the line go dead and lost the ability to stay standing. "No!" I cried into David's chest. "This can't happen. Not Tal. Not now."

A sharp pain hit me right in the chest and I was certain my heart was breaking in half. I couldn't lose Tal, my best friend, Beau's best friend, the man I loved. I held on to David, unaware of him except for his solid mass giving me something to cling to. *Not Tal!* I silently chanted over and over.

"Willow?" David's voice brought me back to myself and my mind raced. I had to do something. Where would he keep his new elixir? The university? That was the obvious guess. And where would I take it if I did find it? I'd worry about that later. Yanking myself out of David's arms, I headed for the door.

"Ms. Rhoswen." Allcot's smooth, Southern gentleman drawl sounded behind me. I instantly tensed as his sticky vampire energy wrapped around me and vaguely noted I should have felt him earlier. "I think you'd better have a seat."

I turned around, my hands balled at my sides. "I'm going to find Talisen. He's hurt."

The teenage look-alike leveled me with his uncaring gaze. "I can't let you do that."

"Oh? Watch me." In two steps I had my hand on the door-knob, but David came out of nowhere and wrapped his arms around my waist, pulling be back into the room. "Let me go!" I struggled, kicking and clawing, determined to make my way to Talisen, wherever he was. Nothing would stop me from getting to him. Not even David.

David just held on, his unbreakable embrace never once giving me an opening.

"Goddammit, David! This is more important than whatever your father has to say. Put me down!"

"I can't. Talisen wouldn't want you running into a situation unprepared and without backup. You know that. Calm down and we'll make a plan."

I stopped struggling as his words sank in. He'd said we. He'd help me find Tal.

"All right?" he asked.

"Yeah." I sucked in a breath. "Okay."

"Davidson, if you're done manhandling her, maybe you both would like to take a seat."

Gently, David lowered me to my feet. He clasped my hand in his and led me to the chairs directly in front of Allcot's desk. The Plexiglas surface gleamed under the office lights. There was nothing about this room that said Allcot, except that it was clearly expensive.

"Father. Willow and Phoebe learned something of importance today that you need to know." David inclined his head in Allcot's direction.

Learned something of importance. I snorted out a frustrated laugh, on the brink of losing my mind. Daywalking vamp, Link electrocuted, Phoebe and me almost killed, and now something terrible had happened to Tal and these two assholes wanted to sit here and make polite conversation.

I turned and found Allcot's dark gray eyes focused on me. "Harrison says he lost track of you today."

He was asking why I'd taken off. I scowled. "I hardly think that's the most pressing matter at the moment."

Allcot gave me a hard, cold stare and when I didn't react, he nodded to David. "Why did you bring her here if she doesn't want to cooperate with us? I've pledged my protection and she's done nothing but throw it away."

I clutched the armrest of the chair, ready to bolt. Was he seriously chastising me now? We didn't have time for this.

"Father," David warned.

And that one word made my head snap up. I'd never heard him challenge his father before. No one ever challenged Allcot.

The master vampire stood and walked around the desk to stare at us. He cast David a curious glance before turning his attention once more to me.

"It seems you have something to tell me." He leaned back against the desk and crossed his ankles.

I had a bit of déjà vu from the first time I'd met him. This was his way of seeming inviting to get one to talk to him. My preference was to march out of his office and slam the door in his face, but Tal and I were both in serious trouble here. I needed him. "Phoebe and I were attacked by a daywalker."

Allcot straightened and snapped his attention to David. "Another daywalker?"

David nodded. "They came straight to me after the incident."

"A daywalker," he said to himself.

I stood, impatient. "Phoebe is researching what she can. The problem is we can't go home or anywhere else. I'm too recognizable. The vamp wanted to kill us, and I'm certain he won't stop until he finds us." I forced myself to keep my voice strong and steady. "If I'm not mistaken, he won't stand for anyone knowing he exists."

He rubbed his smooth chin. "You're asking for my protection?"

"No." I stood taller. "I'm asking for David's."

David met my imploring gaze. "You don't have to ask."

"Thank you." His easy acceptance sparked a fire in my chest, fueling my need to get to Tal. I turned to Allcot once more. "Not five minutes ago, Talisen was attacked. I need you to send someone to his lab or else I'll be going myself."

He narrowed his eyes, anger shooting from their clear depths. "You dare make demands, Ms. Rhoswen?"

"I dare, Allcot," I said, my head spinning with all the anguish and fear coursing through my system. "Talisen is my family. I think you, of all people, would understand the need to protect family." If I hadn't known one or both of them would physically stop me from leaving, I would've bolted for the door right then.

A slow smile spread over Allcot's lips, and he leaned once again against his desk. "You've got balls, Rhoswen."

His unconcerned attitude made me bristle. "This is bullshit. I'm not playing games anymore." Without even glancing at David, I stalked toward the door.

Just as I knew he would, David jumped out of his chair with lightning speed and blocked my way. "You can't go. It's not safe."

"Someone I love is in trouble! I have to go."

Emotion rolled through those deep, midnight-blue eyes before he could blink the pain away. I'd just told him I loved Talisen.

I reached for the door, but he put his hand out, blocking it from opening. "No," he said again. "You're too valuable."

"So is he!" Argh! I couldn't even fight back. Not against vamps. This had been a terrible idea.

"She's correct," Allcot said in that smooth voice. "He is valuable and is under my protection."

I spun to stare at him, my mouth hanging open.

"Your fae and I came to an agreement. You'll know I honor my commitments, Rhoswen." He reached into his pocket and pulled out a black iPhone and held it out to me.

My hand shook as I took it from him.

"Read the last two messages."

I glanced down and my heart all but stopped.

Allcot: *The fae has been attacked. Find him ASAP.*

Harrison: *Yes, sir.*

Hope crashed through me, followed by all-encompassing rage. Allcot had been playing me the whole time.

Chapter 12

That bastard Allcot. Who played games with people when they were clearly in distress? Maybe I could get Phoebe to dust him when this was all over.

David studied my reflection in the rearview mirror. "Are you okay?"

"Just peachy." I stared out the privacy-tinted window from the back seat and willed David's phone to buzz.

We were headed back to the house to wait for news from Harrison and to form a plan for meeting Tal's attacker if Harrison came up empty. Allcot, thank the Goddess, was stuck at Cryrique until the sun went down. He was an old vampire who didn't have to sleep during the day, but he couldn't go out in the sunlight.

"Harrison will find him," David said.

David's confidence did little to reassure me. How would he even know where to start looking? The houses and trees went by in a blur. I didn't want to think about what Harrison would find if he did manage to find Tal. David pulled the car into the long driveway of Allcot's house and parked, but he didn't get out. He sat there, the muscle in his jaw pulsing. "I'm sorry for Father's behavior."

I met his conflicted eyes in the rearview mirror. "He's a controlling, egotistical douche."

He grimaced. "Yes, I suppose that's what you'd see."

"It's what everyone sees." I pushed the door open and ran in the house, straight for David's sitting room where I'd last left

Phoebe and Link. She was sitting cross-legged on his couch, the laptop closed.

I sank to my knees on the floor in front of her. "Tal's been hurt." My voice wobbled.

Her head snapped up. "What do you mean?"

I couldn't stop the tears. They fell in a hot stream as I forced out, "I called him...someone...I heard the attack."

"Son of a bitch! What are you doing *here*?" She jumped to her feet, ready to take action.

"Harrison went after him." I sniffed. "If we go we could bring even greater danger to him."

She huffed. "Not if I have ten minutes to make us over."

I shook my head sadly. "Phoebs, we got our asses kicked today. I don't know who's after Tal. All I know is I was at Allcot's office when it happened. I had no way to get to him."

She put a comforting arm around my shoulder and squeezed. "Any word from Harrison?"

I shook my head. "What if he can't find him?"

"He will." She crossed the room to where her duffle bag of disguises sat. In three minutes flat, she was made up into a college-girl research assistant. "I'm going anyway. Harrison is only one guy. He's going to need backup if there are more than two people who took Tal. You coming with?"

"Yes." There was no question. If she was going, I was going. Danger be damned. I couldn't sit here and do nothing while Talisen suffered. I opened David's door and whistled. Link bounded out in Shih Tzu form, appearing as good as new. "Am I glad to see you, bud." He wiggled and pressed against me.

The three of us headed downstairs. I paused, poking my head into the kitchen. The maid from earlier was standing next to the house chef, discussing the schedule. "Have you seen Davidson?"

"He's in Allcot's study."

I took off at a run, no longer willing to wait for anyone. I burst through the door and found David behind his father's desk, his fingers flying over a keyboard. "Phoebe and I are going after him. I can't wait here. I won't. I know you said it's dangerous if we go, but it's too dangerous for Talisen if we don't."

David studied me. "There's no talking you out of this?"

I shook my head stubbornly. "I'm going wherever Phoebe goes."

He pursed his lips in thought, then stood. "I'll drive."

Something constricted in my chest and I was pretty sure it was my heart exploding. No matter what the deal was with Allcot, David was on my side, even when it came to Talisen.

Link and I piled into the back of his car while Phoebe took the front seat. Her straight blond hair, studious-looking glasses, and professional makeup made it hard even for me to tell it was her without looking twice. I put on my mousy-brown wig and the wire-rimmed glasses once again. I'd lost the sweater earlier, but Phoebe had found another one. I'd tied the arms around my shoulders to hide my wings. It would be easy to discard if I needed to fly.

David took off, speeding his way toward the university. Minutes later, he pulled up in front of the science building Talisen worked in.

"Have you heard from Harrison yet?" I asked as Phoebe and I got out of the car. Link was staying with David for now. Hopefully they both behaved and I didn't come back to a vamp-wolf smackdown. Wolves don't care much for vamps and vice versa.

He pursed his lips and shook his head.

Phoebe leaned in his window, waving her hands animatedly as if she were telling him a story. But what she really said was: "If you don't see us back here in five minutes, come in after us and bring Link."

"Got it." David nodded and pulled away to park in the student lot. Idling at the curb would draw too much attention.

"Ready?" Phoebe asked me.

No. My palms were slick with sweat and my heart was beating erratically to the point I thought it might explode into a million pieces. But nothing was going to stop me from going in that building. Not if Talisen was in there. "Ready," I said, my voice thick with emotion.

She straightened, clearly steeling herself as she eyed me. "You sure you're up for this?"

"Yes," I said defensively and then swallowed my fear. *Please Goddess, give me strength.* "I'm fine. Let's do this."

She gave me a curt nod and led me to the front of the building. Our timing was perfect. Phoebe caught the door as a student strolled out, saving us from having to produce a campus keycard we didn't have.

I cleared my throat and forced myself to recite the script she'd made me memorize. "How long will the study take?"

"Not long. Thirty minutes or so." She smiled at some passing students, playing her role to the hilt. When we got near the lab I knew Talisen worked in, I paused to tie my shoe and gave her a slight nod. The laces slipped from my shaking fingers. I stood, pressing my hands to my thighs, trying for some semblance of control.

"Here we are, Ms. Roberts." She clutched the knob and turned. A slight frown tugged at her lips. Locked.

I shifted to block her from prying eyes. Then she whispered, "*Invado.*" Brilliant white light shot from her fingertips, surrounding the knob. She gave me a triumphant smile and pushed the door open.

It was handy to have a witch around. The reality of what we could be walking into made my limbs heavy, and I forced myself to move forward. Talisen was still alive. He had to be. Images of Beau lying lifeless in my mother's lavender fields flooded my memories. Squeezing my eyes tight as if that would shut them out, I clutched the edge of the door until my hand cramped.

"Ms. Roberts?" Phoebe asked, still in character. My eyes flew open and I realized I was still holding the door ajar. "Are you ready?"

"Umm, yeah. Sorry." I released the door. It closed with a soft click.

Phoebe zapped it with her magic once more, probably fixing the lock she'd manipulated, and then flipped the deadbolt.

Grabbing my hand, she squeezed. "We're going to find him." Magic crackled in her palms as she scanned the room. "Check the office."

Without hesitation, I spun and headed to the small room in the corner a few feet from the door. No light shone through the small office window. I knocked. No answer.

"Professor?" I said as I opened the door.

The small office was in disarray. Paperwork, books, and binders were scattered everywhere, but no one was inside.

"Empty," I called as I headed into the main workroom and whipped off the sweater I'd worn to hide my wings. I fluttered a few feet off the floor for a better view.

"Tal? You here?" Phoebe called out. I held my breath, but there wasn't an answer.

The lab was set up with four rows of workstations. Phoebe pointed to the one closest to the windows. "You start there." Then she nodded to the row in front of her. "I'll check this one out. We'll meet in the middle."

I nodded, thrusting my wings. A sense of control washed over me. Flying always gave me strength.

Ambient light filtered through the windows, bouncing off the white countertops. In sharp contrast to the office, everything gleamed, not a beaker out of place. Had Talisen been somewhere else when I'd called?

"Anything?" I asked Phoebe, who was moving slower, more meticulously, than I was. She was looking for clues. I was looking for Talisen.

"Not yet." She bent down, her head disappearing behind the counter, and I thought I heard her mutter something to herself.

Frowning, I rounded the corner and worked my way through the next row, and then the next, my wings fluttering faster and more frantically with each stroke. "He's not in here." A physical pain tore through my chest with the realization.

She popped up from where she'd been crouching down. "I've found something."

I froze, my mind racing. "What?"

Her eyes went soft with pity.

"Phoebs? What is it?" I'd forgotten to keep myself elevated My feet touched the floor and I started to run. When I got to her side, she held me back.

"It's nothing conclusive. He may have accidentally cut himself."

I glanced at the cabinet and my stomach rolled. Blood was smeared across the white doors. The thick crimson fluid had dripped down to form a small pool on the tile. This was no small cut. I reached out to touch it, but she grabbed my hand.

"No, Wil. It's evidence."

"But I'll be able to tell if it's his." My tone was low, tormented, filled with anguish. Just one touch and I'd know for sure. Pure frustration had me clenching my fists as I glared at Phoebe for standing in my way.

She held her hand up, pulled out her phone, and tapped a message. Then she hit another button and pressed the phone to her ear. "I need an investigation team....Yes....Suspected fae attack."

The Arcane. She'd called them. Of course she had. We were obligated to. Fear and relief warred inside me. The Arcane had the best trackers, the best undercover agents, and the most resources. If they decided Tal was worth it, they'd stop at nothing to find him. Unless he did something to piss them off. And giving away his new drug to Allcot would not be well received. Through my haze of disbelief, I stared at the drying blood and kneeled.

Phoebe put her hand on my shoulder, warning me back.

"I won't touch anything," I said, taking deep breaths. I had to get it together for Tal. Peering around, I checked for a trail of blood droplets. He could have walked himself out of this place. But there wasn't any, just the blood smear and the pool. A glimmer of something caught my eye from beneath the lab table, and I bent down to investigate. Broken glass? Maybe there had been a struggle.

"Yes. At the university. I'll meet you here.…No, I'm alone."
She hit the End button and put her phone back in her pocket.
"You need to go."

"Why?"

"Because if you're still around when the task team gets here,
they're going to demand you go back to headquarters. And
you'll be interrogated. After everything that happened today, we
can't risk them finding out there's another daywalking vampire,
and they will if they start asking you questions." She grimaced.
"Sorry, Wil. But you aren't trained in undercover ops."

She didn't trust me to keep my mouth shut. I glared at her.
It was true I hadn't gone through the academy and didn't have
the special training she did. But I wasn't an idiot. I could hold
my tongue. With another daywalker on the loose, I'd be forced
into study after study until they had miles of data and perhaps
a few freshly turned daywalkers working for them.

"Fine." I turned to leave and then called over my shoulder,
"Check under the counter. There's a broken beaker. It could
be from the struggle I heard over the phone." The adrenaline
coursing through me made my limbs and wings shake. With
effort, I wrapped the sweater around my shoulders, clutched the
knotted sleeves, and stalked to the door. Once the Arcane was
on the case, I'd be left out of the loop unless Phoebe managed
to get the assignment. That wasn't likely, though, since she was
a vamp hunter. Maybe Maude would know something.

I reached for the deadbolt, but Phoebe called, "Wil?"

"Yeah?"

"I'm sorry we didn't find him."

I stared at the floor. When I glanced back, she was clutching
the counter, holding herself upright. It had been a bad day for
her, too. "Me, too."

"Take me to Tal's house," I demanded as I slipped into the back
seat of David's car.

He started the car without saying a word and sped off down the street.

I sat stiff and numb as Link pressed one small paw on my thigh. That one tiny movement made my heart almost burst with emotion. I pulled him into my lap and hugged him close.

David glanced at me in the rearview mirror, but I averted my eyes, not wanting to talk. I wasn't in on the investigation. I'd been attacked, and my office had been trashed. What if the person who'd been after me had attacked Tal? What if I'd put him on their radar? It was the logical conclusion. This was my fault. Even if they hadn't caught on to the fact that Tal and I were together, anyone who knew anything about us would know he was my best friend. The plan to have Harrison pose as my boyfriend had been a stupid one.

David slowed and made a tight turn heading the opposite direction of Tal's apartment.

"You need to go the other way," I said.

He ignored me.

"David?" I sat up, pressing my body between the seats. "He lives a few blocks the other direction."

"I know."

"Then where are you going?"

He glanced over his shoulder, meeting my eyes. "My house."

"What? Why? I told you to go to Tal's. I have to find out if he's okay."

His jaw tensed and he ground out, "I'm not your god-damned chauffeur, Willow."

I jerked back as if I'd been slapped. "I never said you were."

He shrugged, clamping his mouth shut.

What in the name of asshole vampires everywhere was his problem? I was seconds from crawling into the front seat and strangling him. "Jesus, David. Now isn't the time for this. You can be mad later after we check on him."

"No, we're not going to your friend's house." His hands tightened on the wheel as he took another turn.

My pulse picked up and anger pushed all my other thoughts aside. When the car came to a stop at the next light, I placed my hand on the door handle. "Turn this car around, or Link and I will jump out right here." Tal's place was more than a dozen blocks away now, but I'd be damned if he was going to hold me hostage in his car. Especially considering he was doing his best to convince me he really was a coldhearted bastard.

He reached back with lightning speed and clasped my arm. "You will do no such thing."

"Hey!" I yanked back but couldn't break his iron-grip hold.

Link growled and started vibrating.

"Link's going to lose his shit again if you don't let go." A few weeks ago Link had shifted and attacked David while we'd been in my Jeep. I wasn't looking forward to a repeat performance, but it would mean I'd get to escape the car.

David scowled and let go. "Stay put. I'll go by your friend's place. Just promise you won't go barging in without me."

If Tal was home, bringing David would likely cause a scene. They hated each other. Well, Tal hated David. I wasn't so sure how David felt about Tal. I doubted it was warm and fuzzy. Still, if there was trouble, David would come in handy.

"Fine. But hurry."

Five minutes later, David came to a stop a few houses down from Tal's apartment. I straightened my sweater and adjusted my wig.

"Leave Link here," David said.

"Hell no. It's eighty-five degrees out. He can't stay in a hot car." I jumped out and Link followed.

"Fuck," I heard David mutter.

I almost laughed. Vamps weren't used to being told no. Especially ones as connected as David. The street was quiet with the exception of a neighbor's dog complaining about Link's presence. It should have comforted me. Instead, a shiver crawled down my spine despite the September heat.

It took all my willpower to not break into a run and head straight for Tal's door. Being casual enough to not draw attention sucked in an emergency situation. I kept a steady pace with Link, pretending we were out on a walk. David was behind me, no doubt scanning for any sign of trouble.

But none came.

I strolled up the driveway of Tal's house and rounded the back. Once out of view of the street, I sprinted, taking the stairs two at a time. Link bounded ahead of me and, without resistance, barged through the door.

My world slowed down and a soft buzz filled my ears as blood rushed to my head. Tal's front door had been cracked open. My feet seemed heavy and unresponsive. My wings ached to carry me, but my sweater was still restricting them.

Just move, Willow.

Forcing myself up the last few steps, I gasped when I caught a glimpse into Tal's apartment. I stood there, unable to move as I took in the scene in front of me.

"Damn," David whispered behind me.

The place had been trashed. All the cupboards had been emptied. Broken ceramic and glass littered the floor. The furniture had been shredded, paintings ripped apart, and books destroyed. But worst of all, right in the middle of the room, there was one of his white chairs, a message drawn in blood over its once pristine fabric.

It read *Answer it.*

Then a phone started to ring.

Chapter 13

The song "Radioactive" from Imagine Dragons filled the room. It was Tal's current ringtone of choice. I spun, following the sound. There. On the coffee table. The black iPhone lit up with the notification Unknown Caller.

I snatched the phone and hit Accept. "Where's Talisen?" I demanded.

"Willow Rhoswen?" a pleasant female asked, road noise filling the background.

"Who is this?" Was this some sort of sick joke?

"Is this Ms. Rhoswen?"

"Yes, dammit. Put Talisen on the line."

"You can find him in the penthouse suite of the 1788 Hotel tomorrow at nine a.m."

Fear and hope raged a war in my heart. "Is he alive?" I whispered.

"For now. Bring the daywalker." The line went dead.

Shit. She knew about David. Who the hell was she?

"You can't go," David commanded.

I glared at him. Obviously he'd overheard the conversation using his super-hearing vamp skills. "I have to go. And you're going with me." Shaking, I stuffed Tal's phone in my pocket just in case they called again and moved to the chair. I had to make sure that blood was Tal's.

David started pacing the room. I sank to my knees and brushed my hand over the chair. The fresh blood tingled on my fingertips. I took a deep breath and let the life force flow into my system. Hints of cinnamon and redwood permeated my senses as warmth and familiarity washed over me.

My gut ached and my heart felt like it was breaking in two. I'd known what I'd find, but I hadn't wanted to believe it. Now I had proof. The blood was definitely Tal's.

"Let's go." David grabbed my hand and tugged.

I didn't move. I didn't want to leave Tal's space. Glaring at David, I ripped my hand from his grip. If I could, I'd crawl into Tal's bed and stay there until the next day. But that wouldn't help me find him or his elixir. I needed a plan.

"Willow," David said more kindly. "We have to move. They're watching this place. How else do you explain the phone call?"

"Well they can just come for us, can't they?" My wings tensed under my sweater with irritation and dominance. If they wanted me they could damn well come get me. At least then I'd know who had Tal.

David reached for me, both hands grabbing for my waist as if he was going to physically remove me from the premises.

I held up a hand and strode away. "I'm not leaving until we look for the elixir."

The wood floor creaked under David's footsteps as he turned and headed for the door.

"What are you doing?"

Letting out an audible sigh, he glanced back at me. "Keeping an eye out for any threats. Do what you have to do, just be quick about it."

I spun and ran to the bedroom, coming to an abrupt stop just inside the door. Holy fae. The bed had been shredded to a pile of foam and fabric. But worse than that, the limbs of the lovely cypress tree he'd planted for me had been hacked off and were now lying on the floor and across various pieces of broken furniture.

The gravity of the situation hit me square in the solar plexus. The breath left my lungs as I sank to the floor, landing on my knees. There was something about the ruined tree that brought everything crashing down around me. Visions of Beau lying in the lavender fields filled my head, only this time Tal was with him. Both gone. Lost to this terrible world of power and destruction. I shook my head, dislodging the awful visions. I couldn't go there. Not now. Not today.

Whoever did this had done it for pure entertainment. They couldn't have thought Tal hid his creation in the tree. No, they'd done this only because they could. What would it mean for Talisen if we couldn't make a successful trade?

I stood on wobbly legs and systematically sifted through every ransacked drawer, his closet, the bathroom. Next was the living room and kitchen. I came up empty. I'd known I would. Clearly if the drug had been in the apartment, they would've already found it.

Clutching Link, I joined David on the front landing. "Nothing. We need to go back to the lab."

He shook his head. "I already put Phoebe on it. She didn't find anything. The experiment cooler has been trashed."

Shit! "And his boss?"

"I have someone working on finding his identity. As soon as we do, we'll have him picked up." David held out his hand. "It's time to go home, Wil. We can't do anything else right now."

I stared at his hand. I didn't want to leave Tal's place. I wanted to clean up the broken dishes, throw out the damaged furniture, and make his new home cozy again. But I knew I had to leave. It wasn't safe here. I wasn't safe much of anywhere. Except with the vampires.

Ugh.

Ignoring David's still-outstretched hand, I strode past him and said, "Fine. But make sure Phoebe knows where I am."

We argued the entire car ride back to vamp territory. David pulled into the driveway of Allcot's French Colonial.

"Take me to The Red Door to see my mother," I demanded.

"No," David said with finality. "It's too dangerous. There are far too many people there who might see you."

"The possibility of being spotted didn't stop you from roaming around today," I countered. He was a daywalker now. If anyone noticed him walking around in the sun, he'd be a red-hot target.

"And look at what happened? They know about me now." His tone was full of impatience.

I sat back in my seat and stared straight ahead, too overwhelmed to even process that new bit of information. "I want to see my mother," I said quietly, conceding he had a valid point. With Tal gone, there were only two people who I could count on unconditionally. My mom and Phoebe. Thank the gods Mom was under Allcot's protection. No one would harm her there. And I knew from experience Phoebe would be out working every angle she could until she either had Talisen in custody or the intel to find him.

David placed a light hand over mine and squeezed. The tender gesture sent a ripple of warmth through me. It was the comfort I wanted from Mom, or better yet, Tal. Instead, I was getting it from my ex.

A low growl came from the back seat. Link. He was lying down, eyeing David's hand on mine. I chuckled and pulled my hand free. "Looks like Tal has someone keeping an eye on me."

David's expression turned blank. He opened the driver's side door and glanced at me. "I'll see about getting your mother here."

Our eyes met and some of the ice around my heart started to melt. This was the David I'd known before he turned vamp. He was still in there somewhere, underneath his obedience to Allcot. "Thank you."

Once inside, the maid from earlier in the day immediately ushered us into a study that housed floor-to-ceiling books, rich mahogany-wood furniture, and elaborate glass chandeliers. "This is Allcot's private study, isn't it?"

David nodded and took a seat in one of the leather armchairs near the fireplace.

I stood in the doorway. Link snarled, his nose twitching in frantic curiosity. The place must've had Allcot's scent all over it. The skies had already started to darken. Allcot would be here any minute. "My mother?" I prompted.

David didn't look up. He just pulled out his phone and tapped a message. The phone beeped with an incoming message almost immediately. "She'll be here in five minutes."

"Good." I took a seat on the loveseat and held Link back. Otherwise he might start marking the place. Though on second thought…No. I couldn't encourage that sort of behavior, even if it would put a thorn in the side of my least-favorite vamp.

We sat in silence, and I racked my brain for where Talisen could've hidden his new elixir. I could only think of two places: his apartment or his lab. Besides Phoebe and his boss, he didn't really know anyone. Did he? Irrational jealousy consumed me as I imagined a few coeds vying for Tal's attention. What if he'd befriended someone on campus? Would he tell me?

Link jumped off the loveseat and started to pace, his nose pressed to the ground.

Tal could have made a few new friends. Maybe he'd done it on purpose so he had a backup plan to hide his new drug if anything went wrong. No one would question him hanging with a couple of twenty-year-olds. Hell, it was likely he had more than two. Probably a dozen. Tal was an equal-opportunity flirt. I wasn't naïve enough to believe he'd stopped just because we'd decided to finally be together. A man doesn't change that much.

I pulled out Tal's phone and started scrolling through his contacts, immediately ruling out any numbers with a Eureka area code. There were five that were local. My cell number, my shop, Phoebe's phone, someone named Elissa, and some dude that went by Wolfman. How original.

There was no time like the present. I tried Elissa first.

"Hello! This is Elissa. I'm screening, so if I didn't pick up, I likely don't want to talk to you."

Charming. Since I was using Tal's phone, it was entirely possible he'd done something to piss her off. Or she wasn't answering for a million other benign reasons.

Next up, Wolfman. No doubt he was a frat-douche with a name like that. The phone rang ten times before it finally disconnected. Perfect. I tossed the phone down in frustration My only clues were leading to Nowhereville.

The study door swung open and in walked Allcot. His familiar vamp signature pressed in on me, making it harder to breathe. I craned my neck, searching for my mom. "Where is she?" I asked David.

He frowned, probably at my impatient tone.

"Your mother," Allcot said, "will be here momentarily." He crossed the room to a cabinet behind his desk and pulled out a dark green glass bottle. After filling a tumbler with what appeared to be a wine-blood combination, he sat next to David and crossed his ankle over his knee.

"Good evening, Father," David said.

"Good evening," Allcot drawled, oozing Southern gentleman.

I held back a snort, rubbing my hands over my arms as if I could wipe his vampire energy off. He was anything but gentle.

"It's been quite the interesting day, hasn't it?" He swirled the red liquid, then brought the glass to his lips, sipping slowly.

"Interesting?" I sat up straight. "More like it's been a nightmare of a day." Unsatisfied with my vantage point, I stood and glared down at him. "Talisen's hurt. He's being held against his will God knows where. Phoebe and I were both attacked. Tal's attacker demanded his new elixir. Let's not even talk about what happened yesterday. And you're sitting here sipping your drink like a lounge lizard. Interesting is not the word I'd use."

David stood and reached for me, but Allcot put his hand up, stopping him. "Be seated, Davidson." Allcot turned his unflinching gaze on me. "Do not try my patience, Ms. Rhoswen. Your allies are running short these days."

I wanted to scream. That domineering tone he used made me want to scratch his eyes out. There was nothing I hated more in this world than having to count on him for help. The sad truth was, he would and could help, but his methods never failed to piss me off. And worse, he'd thrown the truth in my face. I had a select few people I could trust right now.

"Did Talisen hand over his new drug for your bodyguards yesterday?" He'd told me he'd made a deal with Allcot. If he already had some, we wouldn't need to track down his samples.

Allcot pressed his lips together in a straight line.

What did that mean? Crap! Couldn't the guy ever give a straight answer?

The master vamp nodded in the direction of my chair. "Take your seat, please."

Again with the command, but he softened it, making it sound like more of a request than it was. Still, with a fair amount of teeth grinding, I did as I was told. Antagonizing him wasn't going to get my questions answered. It was just so hard not to. The vamp had a way of crawling under my skin and festering.

"That's better." He gave me a self-satisfied smile, and I concentrated on not scowling. "To answer your question, no, I do not have any of your friend's drug. But even if I did, I would not give it to you."

With my jaw straining with the effort, I kept my mouth firmly shut. I was afraid if I opened it, I'd burn this bridge for good.

He raised a curious eyebrow. "No comment?"

Damn vampire! He was purposely baiting me. *Do not respond. Do not respond.* There was a high road here somewhere and I was determined to stay on it.

David cleared his throat. "Father…"

Allcot chuckled. "I forget your affection for her sometimes, my son. Very well, I'll make this brief."

I clasped my hands together to keep from strangling him and waited.

He took a slow sip of his drink and watched me. Was he testing what I would do? Whatever. I'd wait until my mom showed up and then I was so out of here.

Finally Allcot put his glass down and leaned forward, propping his elbows on his knees. "I wouldn't give up the elixir. It's too powerful. So instead of wasting time looking for it, we're going to utilize the remaining hours to find where your friend is being held. From there, my guys will handle getting him out."

I snorted. "Just like that? You'll find where he is and break him out?" To say I was skeptical would be an understatement.

"Just like that." Allcot got up. "You'll stay here this evening and after the fae is rescued, we'll discuss if it's safe for you to resume your regular life." He nodded to David, then started to move toward the door.

"Excuse me?" I shifted to stare at his retreating back. "Did you just order me under your care?"

He paused and turned to face me. "I'd say *order* is too harsh a word. Think of it as a request."

"No." That was a *hell no*. I had a picture diagram I needed to decipher and an elixir to search for, no matter what Allcot said. I needed a backup plan. I would not leave Talisen to die at the hands of his abductor while the twisted a-hole in front of me played mind games. And if the payment was the elixir then dammit, they could have it. Guilt coiled tight in my chest at the thought. I didn't want to, but I would…for Tal. Not that I thought that would be the end of it, but our chances were a hell of a lot better with the elixir than they were without it.

Allcot stiffened. "No?"

"I don't work for you. You can't order me to stay. And I won't." In fact, I needed to leave soon. Allcot's presence was making me weak, almost light-headed. I couldn't tell him that though. None of the vamps knew how their energy affected me. And they never would if I had anything to say about it.

"What if I don't give you a choice?" Allcot crossed his arms over his chest.

"Oh, I think you will, Eadric." A familiar female voice carried in from the open doorway.

"Mom!" I jumped up, whirling from the dizziness, and launched myself at her.

She opened her arms wide and engulfed me in a hug only a mother could give. Her lips brushed over my temple. "I'm so sorry, baby. We'll get him back, no matter what."

I sniffled into her shoulder. "You're damn right we will. I won't stand for anything else."

"That's my girl." She soothed me as she ran a soft hand over my hair. "Now, if you don't stay with Eadric, where will you go?"

I let go and stared at her. Well, shit. I didn't have an answer to that. I shrugged. "Wherever Phoebe goes?"

Mom shook her head. "Isn't she working undercover right now?"

I nodded. "Yeah. At least, I think so."

"Then it won't pay to have you and Link along, will it?"

I bit my lip and eyed Link, who was sniffing around her feet, his tail wagging with sheer joy. She was fae. He'd probably follow her every command just as he did Talisen's.

"She can come to my house," David said and got to his feet.

I studied him. "You mean the house in Mid-City?"

"Yes." He stuffed his hands in the front of his jeans pockets and hunched his shoulders slightly.

He was nervous. Why?

Allcot crossed the room to stand next to David. In a low voice he said, "I'd rather you both stay here."

Mom, who knew about my vampire allergy, shook her head. "No, I think it's best if Willow has some space. It's been a rough day and she needs to regroup before the morning. David's house will work fine."

"Mom!" I whispered harshly. I couldn't stay at David's by myself overnight. "I'd rather stay with you and Carrie."

She placed a supportive hand on my shoulder. "That would be nice, dear, but The Red Door's being heavily watched. It's been tough enough for me to go in and out unnoticed. You and Link would never make it. Besides, with Carrie, Beau Junior, and all the *vampires,* there isn't a lot of breathing room."

I frowned as I caught her inflection of the word vampires. Right. That place was crawling with them and would only make me weaker. My options for a safe house were woefully limited.

"Go with David," she said gently. "He'll keep you safe."

Her pleading eyes bored into mine and I recognized for the first time how scared she was for me. My objections didn't seem so important anymore. Mom would never survive if something happened to me. Not after losing Beau. My options were David's home, Allcot's, or my own, which was bugged and undoubtedly being watched.

"David's place it is." I turned to him. "I hope you have an extra laptop. I'm going to need one."

Chapter 14

David's two-story Victorian sat in the middle of three recently cleared lots. His house was smack in the middle of Mid-City, a section of New Orleans that had been hit pretty hard by hurricane Katrina. Shortly after the storm, vampires had taken over the area, buying up multiple lots and building on only one to ensure privacy.

No lights were on and the place had an eerie, deserted feel to it. The one and only time I'd been inside, he'd said he hadn't been there in over a week. Did he really spend most of his time at Allcot's mansion? There were a lot of pretty vamps there. An unexpected dart of jealousy sparked in my chest. Dammit, not that again. I tamped down the emotion. This was purely business.

David pulled the car into the carport at the back of the house. "Wait here. I'll do a sweep to be sure the area is clean."

I sat back and closed my eyes. "Okay."

Link stood on my lap, his ears pitched forward, on high alert. "Hear anything, buddy?"

His eyes tracked David's path, then after a moment he relaxed and settled against me.

"Guess not." His reaction was good enough for me. Without waiting for David, I pushed the door open and headed for the back door.

David caught up to me on the porch. "What happened to waiting for me in the car?" he asked with an air of irritation.

"I'm not helpless, David," I snapped. "There's a reason Link goes everywhere with me." I waved a hand at my dog, who was sitting peacefully at my feet. "He has very good hearing."

He glanced at Link, who would be in full-on wolf form if there was anything remotely resembling a threat, and inclined his head in acknowledgment. "Fair enough."

Once inside, I headed through the kitchen, down the hall, and into his book-lined study. David followed me and paused in the doorway.

I sat at his desk and lifted the cover of his laptop. "Do you mind? I want to do a reverse phone number check on the local numbers in Tal's phone."

Walking toward me, he shook his head slowly. "You'll probably want something a little more powerful than a straight Internet search."

I quirked an eyebrow.

He smiled and I stiffened. Were those…? Oh crap. His vamp fangs were poking out.

David took a step back. "What's wrong?"

I clutched the base of my neck, unconsciously covering my exposed skin. "Uh…nothing. I was wondering if you'd eaten recently."

His brow furrowed, then recognition dawned in his eyes as his tongue ran along the edge of his teeth. "Shit," he mumbled. "Sorry, it's been a few days, but nothing I can't handle." He clamped his mouth shut and reached over me to grab the laptop. A few keystrokes later, he put it back on the desk. "Try this site."

The banner read *Investigation Services after Dark*.

"A supernatural investigation agency?" I tried my best to not stare at his lips and the teeth that were poking out again.

He nodded. "They have access to private information you won't find doing a simple search. Put in however much information you have and they'll get back to you within fifteen minutes with what they know. If the information looks promising, upon your request they'll search deeper."

"And they're on Allcot's payroll?"

David sighed at the accusation in my tone. "Yes. They have a contract with Cryrique."

I shook my head. "How can I trust them as a source if they're likely to filter information?" Everyone knew anyone who worked for Cryrique stayed loyal to Cryrique. Whoever ran this investigation service wouldn't reveal anything that would be considered sensitive information concerning the vamp organization.

"Dammit, Willow!" David snagged the computer, logged on to the investigation website, and started typing. "First of all, Father isn't involved with your friend's abduction. There isn't anything to hide. Second, I'm logging you into my account. Send him whatever you want and I guarantee you'll get unfiltered results." He shoved the laptop back in my direction and then stalked toward the door. He paused, glancing back at me. Those tiny fangs were peeking out again and his eyes smoldered with something resembling dark desire.

Everything about him right at the moment unsettled me, and my wings trembled with nervous energy. "What do you want from me?"

"You could try trusting me again."

He disappeared so fast I didn't even see him move. I only heard the soft click of the door closing. My heart started to race. I wasn't sure I could ever give him what he asked for. Yet, here he was, trying to protect me and was giving me the tools to find another man and bring him home safely. I could try to be more grateful. It wasn't his fault all of this was happening.

Ugh! Why the hell had he chosen to turn vamp? It didn't make any sense to me. He was still the same person he had been, only now he had a hardness, an edge, he hadn't had before. The gentle sweetness was no longer on the surface, though it was still there, buried under his marbled persona. And the complete trust I'd had in him was gone. My heart said one thing while my brain screamed run. Run as far and as fast as possible. But to where? The Void? My mother? No. The Void couldn't be trusted either. And my mother was already under Allcot's protection. That left Phoebe, and she was already knee-deep in the middle of this nightmare. Where was she right now? Tracking down Tal's professor? Did she have a lead? She didn't know my phone was dead and I couldn't call her for fear her phone had been bugged.

She'd find me when she had news. I was sure of it. There was nothing to do but track Tal's contacts. I fished his phone out and scrolled through his numbers again. After carefully relaying the phone numbers and names, I submitted the information to David's investigator.

Less than ten minutes later, the laptop pinged with a message.

Elissa Meyers—Graduate Student—twenty-three. The message listed a last known address.

Wolfman—Phone registered to one William O'Conner. Included were his last two known addresses.

I tapped out a message asking for a more in-depth investigation, marking it Urgent—Top Priority.

"Link, let's go." I snapped my fingers and went in search of David. The house was decorated with a mix of eighteenth-century antiques and tasteful modern furniture. Despite the warmth of the Southern landscape paintings and the soft lighting, the place seemed cold, empty. More like a museum. There was no real life in the gorgeous house. The emptiness took up residence in my soul and made me shiver.

I searched the entire house for David until the last place left to look was the master bedroom. Knocking on the partially open door, I pushed it open to find him crossing the room, shirtless. "David?"

He paused, his dark blue eyes piercing me with his intense stare. "What are you doing in here?"

My mouth went dry at the sight of his plum-red chest. I forced a swallow. "Your chest is worse. How did that happen?"

He glanced down at himself and scowled. "It's not worse. I took a scalding shower." He turned his equally burnt back to me and disappeared into his closet.

My fists clenched into tight balls. He was lying. His hair wasn't damp. There wasn't any gleam of water droplets. Not to mention his defensive attitude didn't make any sense. What in the world was going on?

Something must have gone wrong with the transformation into a daywalker and he didn't want to tell me. But why?

David reappeared, wearing a long-sleeved Henley shirt, all evidence of his affliction covered.

"What's going on? Your skin isn't normal. Please, David. If something went wrong with the transformation, we have to figure out a way to fix it."

His face went blank. "The transformation?"

I huffed. "To daywalker. Your skin…it's not right. Something's wrong. When did this start? Maybe you should eat." My muscles tensed at the suggestion. The one and only time a vamp had drank from me, it had been like fire in my veins. I would not be the sacrificial blood donor. There were licensed human donors he could use if need be.

"Nothing's wrong. I told you, I spent too much time in the sun. I'm sure my skin will heal the next time I sleep. And I'm not hungry." But his eyes stayed glued to my neck.

"Don't worry about my delicate sensibilities," I said sarcastically. "We can stop at Katrina's on the way."

His eyebrows shot up. "The blood bar?"

"Yes, the blood bar. You don't think I'm going to feed you, do you?"

He started to chuckle, but the action quickly turned into outright laughter.

I placed my balled fists on my hips and glared. "What's so funny?"

"You." He cast an appreciative glance down my body, making me even more irritated. "The last thing I'd ever expect is for you to play the role of donor. Come on, Wil. You have to realize I know you better than that."

I stepped back, feeling foolish. "Of course you do."

"Besides, I already told you I don't need to eat."

Exasperated, I shook my head in disbelief. "Don't you think it might help you heal faster?"

"It might. But I'm fine. Stop worrying. Now, where do you think we're going?"

"Uptown." I waved a piece of paper containing the addresses of Elissa Meyers and William O'Conner. "Tal's contacts. We need to find out if they have the elixir."

He shoved his hands in his jeans pockets, which I'd come to recognize as a universal sign of opposition in the entire male population. "I'll contact Harrison. He can check them out."

I rolled my eyes and stalked out.

David followed, not saying a word until I entered the kitchen and headed for the back door. "What are you doing?"

"Going to check on these leads. We have about fourteen hours. I'm not wasting one more minute."

Link, sensing my urgency, shifted into wolf form. Once I had the door open, he lunged outside. "You're welcome to join us. Otherwise, we'll meet you back here."

David crossed the room and wrapped his hand around the edge of the door. "How do you think you're going to get there?"

I plucked his spare keys from where they hung on the wall. Holding them up, I smiled.

He pursed his lips and nodded. "I see."

His apparent acceptance made me nervous. This wasn't how David usually operated. He was much more brooding and bossy.

"That's it? You're not going to try to stop me?"

"No."

"Okay then." I turned to go, but the door slammed closed and David backed me up against the door, trapping me in place. "Hey!" I yelped. "You just said you weren't going to try to stop me."

"This isn't me trying." His voice was low and gravelly as he leaned in, his cool breath tickling my ear. "I get that you want to do everything possible to help your friend, but we both know he wouldn't want you to do anything to put yourself in danger on his behalf."

I turned my head and glared. "You're not doing this because of what Tal wants."

"No," he said roughly. "I'm doing this to protect you. I don't really give a damn what your friend would want. But you do."

I placed both hands on his chest and pushed him with everything I had. Surprised, he stumbled back, but quickly found his footing and once again pressed his palms to the door, using his frame to trap me within.

"I'm not your prisoner," I spat. Hot anger rushed to my head. How dare he treat me as if I was one of his minions? "Back up. Now, David."

"Or what?"

"Or whatever this is"—I waved a hand, indicating the two of us—"this partnership or questionable friendship, is over. I don't take orders from you. Or Allcot."

He straightened and stepped back, giving me the space I needed. "Questionable friendship?"

The flash of vulnerability in his eyes was so slight I almost missed it. It moved a tiny piece of me. I took a deep breath. "Look, I appreciate your help and all Allcot has done for Carrie and Beau, but I don't appreciate the orders. I can make my own decisions. And right now, my decision is to do anything in my power to help Tal. Either you're with me or you're not."

A howl came from the other side of the door, followed by scratching. Link had lost his patience. I raised an eyebrow in question. "What's it going to be, Laveaux?"

Silence stretched between us. It was only when Link howled again that David spoke. "My apologies, Ms. Rhoswen. Of course I'll help in any way I can as long as your wolf calms down."

Pleased I'd finally won an argument with him, I grinned and twisted the knob. Pulling the heavy door open, I said, "Cool it, Link. We're coming."

David followed me out, and while Link had stopped howling, it didn't stop him from snarling in David's direction. I had to stifle a laugh. It's not like he didn't deserve it with his latest display if dominance.

"Call off your wolf," David said evenly, clearly trying to keep from having an altercation.

I snapped my fingers. "Link, stop."

He snarled one last time before falling in step beside me. That was Link. He was feeding off my emotions. And while David and I had called a truce, I was still more than irritated at his behavior. I swallowed the frustration and forced myself to remain levelheaded. We had research to do.

Chapter 15

"Are you sure this is it?" I asked, peering at the darkened, run-down house. Every window and door was covered with wrought-iron bars. "The neighborhood appears to be…"

"This is Castor Price's territory." David put the car in park.

I sucked in a breath. "As in, New Orleans's most notorious human and drug trafficker?"

"Yep."

What was a college student doing living in this neighborhood? No one was safe from the crime lord within his unofficial borders.

"Let's do this." David jumped out and Link and I followed. Link kept close to me, his teeth bared. A cold stone of fear settled in the pit of my stomach. Without thinking, I reached out and clutched David's arm. Neither of us should be here. Price didn't share his territory with anyone. And if he took offense to David being here, it could cause an all-out war between his gang and Cryrique.

Darkness consumed the small house. Swallowed in shadows, I ran a hand around the edge of the door, searching until I found the smooth button of the doorbell, then pressed it twice.

"It didn't work." Due to the barred security door, David knocked on the side of the house. After a few beats he said, "There's no movement inside. She's not here."

David and Link both spun at the same time, hearing something I didn't. I jumped, startled.

"Where is she?" A gruff voice came out of the darkness.

"Who?" David asked, coolly.

"Don't fuck around, vampire. Where the hell is Elissa?" The tall, broad-shouldered man prowled forward and two shorter, beefier men joined him from the shadows.

I ran a soothing hand down Link's back to keep him from growling at the thugs in front of us and stepped forward. "I'm sorry. We don't know where Elissa is. A friend of mine is missing and I was hoping she might have some information that would help us find him."

The telltale sound of a gun being cocked echoed through the night.

"Hey. Hey, now." I raised my hands in the air. "We don't want any trouble here. If Elissa isn't here, we'll just be going."

"You're not going anywhere." The ringleader reached for me, clamping his iron grip around my wrist.

"Ouch," I cried, but my voice was drowned out by the howl of pain that came from him as Link lunged and sank his teeth into the thug's forearm. The sudden release of my arm made me stumble backward. With my wings once again covered by a sweater, I lost my balance and landed with a thud on my backside.

Two shots rang through the air, followed by a yelp and whine of pain.

"Link!" Crawling forward, I patted him down, searching for a wound. He panted heavily but let me search. Then he yelped again as I touched his back leg. Flesh wound. Relief rushed through me. He'd be okay.

David stood in front of us, wrestling the gun away from the gunman with one hand while holding the ringleader in a headlock. The third one moved in. A moment later, his fist met David's face in what sounded like a bone-crushing punch.

I cringed at the sound, my stomach rolling. "David," I cried, fear for him and for Link paralyzing me. If they overpowered David, we were dead. I had to help. But how? If I interfered now, I'd only manage to distract David.

The leader spun out of David's grasp and landed a kick in his kidney. David pitched forward with an oomph but managed to stay upright.

"Son of a bitch," David said and, with lightning speed, landed two punches and a kick of his own on each of the gang members. Blood splattered and more bones crunched under the force. Each connection was so fast and strong no human should have been able to withstand the onslaught. But all three were on their feet and circling David within seconds.

Link sprang to his feet, blood running down one leg, but he once again lunged and caught one of our attackers in the neck. Link's victim screamed, his eyes bugging out as he disappeared under Link's weight.

I ripped my sweater off and spread my wings. Just as I lifted off the ground, the ringleader recovered the gun and yelled, "One more inch, faery, and you'll have a hole in your wing."

My wings froze mid-flutter and I floated to the ground, terror making my heart almost stop. Everything going on around me faded away and my focus narrowed to the gun gleaming in the moonlight. This was it. I was going to die at the hand of some worthless scum who meant next to nothing. Images of Talisen filtered through my mind. Regret and sadness claimed me. I wouldn't even get to say good-bye.

"Call your dog off." The leader's eyes were narrow slits of rage.

"Link, come here," I ordered, my voice trembling.

His head came up, blood covering his muzzle. Oh Goddess. Was the thug lying motionless beside him dead? I didn't want to think about what would happen if he was.

"Step away from Ezra, or your girlfriend here is going to be joining me back at my hood after I put a hole in her foot."

I sucked in a breath and tucked my wings against my back in order to keep from unconsciously fluttering off the ground. Mr. Trigger-happy likely wouldn't understand my nervous tic.

David, holding his attacker by the neck, let go and took a step sideways toward me.

"How long has she been working for you?" the thug asked.

"I don't know what you're talking about." David raised his hands in front of him where they could be seen.

"Don't lie. We've seen the bite marks. Combine that with the money she found for that fancy school and the sweet ride she's been cruising around in, and only an idiot wouldn't make the connection. You're not calling me an idiot, are you?"

David only stared him down while I eyed the gun still pointed straight at my head.

"Well, motherfucker? Are you?" The thug jerked the gun and pointed it at David. That was his first mistake. The second was forgetting about Link. They both pounced. The gun went off for the third time.

"David!" I cried, clutching my chest. Blood blossomed on David's shoulder. But it didn't slow him down. He disarmed the ringleader in less than two seconds. Link growled and leaped forward, flattening the man to the ground.

"Move," David called as the other two thugs jumped him.

I didn't hesitate. My wings extended, and with two giant thrusts, I was at the car, pulling the door open. "Link! In!"

My wolf took one last swipe at the flattened gang member and bounded on three legs into the car. I jumped into the driver's seat and revved the engine. David was fighting off one thug while suffering a punch to his kidney from the other. I honked once. David swung, knocking them both out of the way long enough to dive into the passenger's side.

I hit the accelerator and the tires squealed as we sped off. "What the hell happened back there?" I stammered out a few blocks later.

"We were jumped by Price's hired guns."

"No kidding. I meant they were more than steroid-strong. Like maybe Tal's elixir-strong."

He pressed his hand to his shoulder, finally noticing the gun wound and nodded. "Yeah. You might be right. The samples did go missing."

"But how did they know about it? Elissa?"

He closed his eyes and shook his head. "Maybe."

A few blocks later, I pulled into a drugstore parking lot and twisted around to check out Link. "You okay, boy?" I ran a hand over his back haunches and legs. He whimpered but let me inspect the leg that had been grazed by the bullet. "It's not so bad, buddy."

I turned to David. "I need to run in for some first-aid supplies. Do you need anything?"

His eyes were wild and bloodshot, but he shook his head.

I frowned. Blood was still seeping from his wound. It should've closed by now. The only explanation was he hadn't fed in a while. "You need blood. Like yesterday."

"I'm fine." He closed his eyes and leaned his head back against the seat. "Get whatever it is you need. I'll watch Link."

More like Link would watch him. I stifled a worried sigh and ran into the store. Less than five minutes later, laden with gauze and antiseptic, I jumped in the car and took off once again for David's house. We couldn't check on Wolfman until David and Link were patched up. And I stopped shaking. Between Link and David, an attack led by humans should've been over in less than a minute. Instead of completely neutralizing them, we'd had to flee the scene just to get out alive.

Holy fuck. They were way too strong, too powerful. They had to be on Tal's drug.

As I pulled into the driveway, David put his hand on my knee. The foreign coolness seeped through the fabric of my jeans, and I almost jumped right out of my seat. Would I ever get used to the fact he wasn't warm-blooded anymore? "What is it?" I asked coming to a complete stop.

"Someone's here. Turn off the lights." He opened the door and disappeared across the lawn.

"Great." I killed the lights and slumped down, trying to scan the area. Nothing but bushes and leaves moved in the slight breeze. Knowing David would find anyone who might be lurking around, I climbed into the back and started administering first aid to Link's back left leg.

He whimpered as I applied the antiseptic but let me bandage the leg, despite the obvious pain. "Good boy, Link." I soothed him and snuggled against his neck. He licked my hand. "You're welcome, bud."

With Link fixed up, I started to feel like a sitting duck. "Link?"

He raised his big wolf head, gold eyes gleaming.

"You ready?"

He let out a low growl.

Good. He was feeling antsy as well. We climbed out and the pair of us headed toward the house, me fluttering and Link prowling.

"Willow!" a female voice called from across the yard.

"Phoebs?"

"Hurry up." She waved from beside David.

I shook my head and picked up the pace. When we reached them, I scowled at David. "You couldn't come back and let us know the coast was clear?"

That muscle in his jaw twitched and his eyes flashed with irritation. "I was still checking the grounds." He waved at something behind me. "Phoebe isn't our only visitor."

I spun, finding Harrison standing a few feet from me. "Where'd you come from?"

He nodded toward Phoebe. "I found that one breaking into the professor's house."

I spun back around and grabbed Phoebe's arm. "What did you find?"

"Well—"

"Let's go inside." David cut her off.

I glared, but Phoebe nodded. "That's a good idea."

Once inside David immediately pulled his shirt off and headed for the bathroom. I gaped after him.

"What's with the sunburn?" Phoebe asked.

"No idea."

"Weird." Then she smiled at me, mischief in her eyes. "Holy vampire abs. I had no idea he was so yummy underneath all that."

I snapped. "Phoebe, stop. Now isn't the time. Talisen is missing and hurt, remember?" The night had taken its toll and hot tears burned the back of my eyes. I blinked rapidly, trying to control my overwhelming emotions. David was hurt. Link was hurt. Tal was God knows where, hurt or worse, and the city's most notorious street gang had somehow gotten his new drug. Once we rescued Tal, and we *would* rescue him, he would never be safe with the powerful corruption that would follow him around.

Damn that elixir.

Phoebe sobered. "Sorry, Wil." She placed a hand on my arm. "I've been in assignment mode all day. You know how I get sometimes."

Yeah, totally obsessed with the mission and doing whatever it took to uncover the clues. She loved it, although the thrill of the chase sometimes meant she lost perspective for those involved. But at the same time, her giddy enthusiasm for her work made her one of the best agents the Void had. "I do. Just bring it down a notch. I'm not ready for jokes."

She nodded solemnly and followed me to the library.

I grabbed David's laptop once again and sat cross-legged on the leather loveseat.

She pulled out a black iPhone.

I frowned. Her phone was white. "New?"

"Yeah. I dumped the old one." She hit a button and read something. "Let me see yours. I need to see those pictures you took."

"Mine's dead." I grimaced. "David killed it."

"Dammit! Please tell me you have those photos in a cloud."

"I do." I'd emailed them to myself immediately after taking them, just in case.

She sighed in relief and her shoulders visibly relaxed. "Thank you for finally coming through on the technology end, Wil."

I chose not to respond to her jab, but only because it was true. I hated phones and all the technology I didn't understand. Powering up the laptop, I asked, "What did you find out?"

"I'm not sure yet, but I think the pictures will put some things into place."

I opened the top drawer, rummaged around, and pulled out a pen and a pad of paper. A loose sheet slipped from the legal pad as I tossed it on the desk.

Phoebe's gaze followed the paper and then her eyes widened in surprise.

"What?" I glanced at the scribble across the bottom of the paper and frowned in confusion as a ball of unease formed somewhere close to my heart. "Does that say what I think it says?"

She snatched the paper and nodded.

I leaned over her shoulder and forced myself to read the words one more time. The paper was a directive from Cryrique with a list of tasks for David to complete. And there, scrawled at the bottom, were the words: *Convince Willow to turn Father into a daywalker.*

Chapter 16

"What the fuck is this?" Phoebe waved the directive around the room. "Is this why Allcot is on his 'protect Willow' mission?"

I sat back, stunned into silence. The handwriting was David's. Was it an order, or was the mission his own idea? Righteous anger took over. I snatched the paper out of her hand and stalked out of the room.

Voices carried down the hall from David's master suite. I stomped past the four bedrooms and stormed into the suite without knocking. Three steps in, I skidded to a stop on the plush carpet. "Whoa. David, stop!"

Across the room, David had one hand clamped tightly around Harrison's neck as he suspended him a few inches off the ground. David twitched at the sound of my voice but didn't turn around. Instead, he growled and slammed Harrison against the wall.

Harrison let out a strangled groan and his eyes rolled into the back of his head.

"David!" I yelled again and ran across the room. What the hell was wrong with him? I clutched his arm, unable to move it even an inch. His shoulder was covered in a blood-soaked bandage, but the wound didn't seem to slow him down. "What are you doing? Let go. You're going to kill him."

Finally my frantic tone must have registered, and David lowered Harrison to the ground. His grip relaxed, but he didn't let go.

Harrison gasped for air, clutching at David's hand. "Fuck, dude. Let go."

A snarl curled on David's lip. "Next time, I'll rip your damn head off."

The icy calm of David's voice made Harrison's dark face turn ashen.

Even I took a step back. "David?" My tone was softer, quiet. "What's going on?" What could Harrison have done to cause such a violent reaction from David? They'd been fine five minutes ago.

David squeezed Harrison's neck for one last reminder and then let go. But before Harrison could move, David slammed his fist into Harrison's gut.

Adrenaline shot through my already-wired body as I took another step back, barely able to contain the urge to take flight out of the room.

Harrison sputtered and coughed until blood stained his lips.

David leaned in and I heard him whisper, "That's your one and only warning. No one talks about her that way."

Who? Me?

A wild, almost-crazed look flashed through Harrison's eyes. David must have seen it too because his fist flew again, but Harrison twisted and blocked the blow with his forearm at the same time.

"Stop it!" I cried, my demand falling on deaf ears.

Another fist flew and Harrison dodged, this time landing a roundhouse kick to David's torso. David grunted and paused momentarily.

Phoebe raced into the room, no doubt because she'd heard my cry and clasped her hand on my arm. "Are you okay?"

I nodded, frozen in shock. That kick had been entirely too fast and had hurt, otherwise David would've caught Harrison's leg and broken it in two before he'd ever connected. Holy shit. Could Harrison be on Tal's drug, too? There was no way to tell until the person showed their cards. Did that mean Harrison had some I could take to trade for Tal? Hope fluttered inside me.

David threw one more punch, this time an uppercut to Harrison's jaw. Then he stepped back, as if waiting to see what my supposed bodyguard would do.

"Fuck you, Laveaux." Harrison spit a mouthful of blood on David. The red saliva sprayed over David's face and chest. David's nostrils flared and surprisingly, instead of breaking Harrison's neck, he backed up slowly until the entire room separated them.

"Jesus," Phoebe muttered under her breath.

"Remember when we were friends? I do." Harrison's eyes narrowed and then he turned to me. "He didn't want to turn vamp, you know. Said he never wanted to be like his father. And now look at him. He's just like every other entitled vampire lord. And it only took three fucking months."

Didn't want to turn vamp. The words kept running through my mind in a loop. He'd told me it had been his choice. Had he lied? I turned and faced David with trepidation filling my heart. I wasn't sure I wanted to know the truth. But I had to ask. "What is he talking about? Were you forced into this life?"

David's deep blue eyes clouded with frustration as he tore them from Harrison to meet my gaze. "No. Father would never force anyone. That isn't what this is about."

Somehow I found the part about Allcot not forcing anyone very hard to believe, but I kept my thoughts to myself.

Harrison snorted his disagreement.

"Shut up, Harrison," David growled.

Harrison stood straighter, his head held high as if to let David know he wasn't afraid of him. And why should he be? In the fight they'd had, Harrison had certainly held his own. "She's going to find out the truth sooner or later."

The truth. Convince Willow to turn Father into a daywalker. That's what he didn't want me to find out. Rage filled me and everything went cold. David and Allcot were using me. Just like everyone else in this godforsaken city. I'd been fooling myself, thinking I could trust him or Allcot. What a fool I was. Damn them all. Used, betrayed, and emotionally beaten down. I had to get out of there.

David launched himself in Harrison's direction so fast I wasn't able to even process words, much less move to stop the altercation. David landed a fist in Harrison's gut, and as the guard doubled over, David twisted Harrison's left arm behind him and grasped him into a headlock.

"Whoa, boys. Maybe we should all cool down," Phoebe said, moving toward them.

They both ignored her.

"Do it," Harrison said. "Rip my head off or drain me. Go ahead. At least we'll know once and for all exactly what you've become."

David vibrated with barely contained rage. His head and fangs were so close to Harrison's neck I was certain I was about to watch the man take his last breath.

"Stop it!" I cried and ran forward.

"No." Harrison cast me a dangerous glance. "If you interrupt this, you'll never know what he's become."

David's arm tightened around Harrison's neck, cutting off the man's response. "Leave, Willow."

I stood my ground with Phoebe silently backing me up. "Let Harrison go."

Silence.

"David?" My tone was quiet, and while I was going for firm, the word came out as more of a plea.

He cut his gaze to me, and right in that moment, something shifted. He swore under his breath and pushed Harrison away. "Get out. Now," he told him.

A smug smile flashed over Harrison's face and disappeared just as fast. He glanced back at David. Some form of silent communication passed between them before he turned and nodded to me. "Good luck."

The door shut silently behind Harrison. David and I stared at each other. Finally, he ran a frustrated hand through his hair and slumped against the wall.

"I'll give you two some privacy." Phoebe squeezed my hand and then disappeared into the hall.

I fluttered forward and landed inches from him. With the paper I'd found earlier still crumpled in my fist, I placed my hands on my hips and met his troubled gaze. "What just happened here?"

He met my penetrating stare with an unflinching one of his own. "He was out of line."

I raised one eyebrow. "Out of line? Seriously, that's all you have to say?"

"It's the only thing that matters."

The rage I'd suppressed earlier came roaring back, filling up my soul and spilling into my heart. "Have you lost your fucking mind?" I raised my hand with the crumpled paper, and after taking a second to smooth it out, I smacked it to his chest and let it fall to the ground. "Everything matters. You're lying to me. How can I trust you when I have no idea what's going on?" I glanced at the discarded paper. "When I'm certain I'm being used." When he made me regret ever saving him from certain death.

I'd had feelings for this man. Had loved him enough to not let him die. Had risked my own life to keep him safe and turned him into a daywalker in the process. And what was he doing? He was trying to trick me into turning Allcot, a process that could very well kill me. And he was lying...again.

I knew my stare was cold and unfeeling. Exactly like the one David used when he was hiding his emotions. He was expert at it now that he'd turned vamp. It was part of his new personality, the one that made me want to slap the crap out of him every time he used it.

"Lying?" David asked, appearing genuinely confused. All it did was piss me off.

"Stop playing games, David! Son of a bitch. That's all you've done since we've met." I threw my hands up. "How am I ever supposed to trust you or anything you say when you have a hidden agenda?" I picked up the paper and pointed to the handwritten line at the bottom. "How do you explain this?"

A transformation came over David and I swear if it were possible for blood to drain from his face, he would've turned an even starker shade of white. He closed his eyes and let out a long breath. When he opened them, he waved a hand toward the two chairs in the adjoining sitting room. "This isn't what you think."

I ignored his invitation and crossed my arms over my chest. "From your expression, I'd say it's exactly what I think." My voice was flat, emotionless.

His piercing eyes bored into mine. "Will you sit?"

"Are you going to start talking?"

"Not right now. We have more important things to worry about."

I dug my fingernails into my palm and forced down a scream of frustration. "You're damn right we do. But I can't ignore this." I waved the paper in front of his face. "Have you lost your mind? It says here to convince me to change Allcot into a daywalker. Is that why you're helping me find Tal and why you're keeping such a close eye on me?"

He stared at me in silence for a long moment. His expression hardened. "Is that really what you think of me?"

Oh, hell no. He wasn't seriously turning this into some sort of slight on his character, was he? I shook my head in disgust. "Honestly, David? I have no idea what to think. All I know is I can't trust you. Not after the lies and finding this." Moving toward the door, I crumpled the paper into a ball and threw it at his feet. "And right now the last thing I need is one more person who's trying to use me."

Before he could stop me, I flew down the hall and back into the library. "Harrison?"

He placed a book back on a shelf as he turned toward me. "Yeah?"

"You're on Tal's drug, right?"

He glanced at the doorway, presumably looking for David. Then he focused on me again. "Yes."

"Do you have more?" I was all business now. Forget David and Allcot. I had a job to do, and no one was going to stop me.

He stuffed his hands in his pockets, pity lining his face. "No. He only supplied us with enough to last forty-eight hours. It was one dose."

Disappointment hit me hard. Was I ever going to catch a break? I nodded, acknowledging his reply and turned to my roommate. "Phoebs?"

She glanced up from the computer. "Yeah."

"Get me out of here."

Without hesitation, she jumped up, slammed the computer closed, and tucked it under her arm. "You got it."

"Let's go, Link." He sprang to his feet despite his injured leg and trotted beside us as we left without another word. Neither Harrison nor David stopped us. We climbed into Phoebe's car, and it wasn't until she turned the key that David materialized at his front door. The light from his hallway illuminated him, making him a dark shadow in the threshold. He held up a hand in a stop motion.

"Go," I told Phoebe.

"Where to?"

"Anywhere he can't find us."

"You got it." She slammed the car into gear and took off down the deserted street.

I closed my eyes and concentrated on breathing. The idea of David betraying me yet again was too much for me to process. I leaned back in the seat, wrapping my arm around Link. His familiar Shih Tzu weight comforted me and I pulled him closer. "We'll find him, boy. I promise."

Link responded by snuggling closer to my torso. He knew who I was talking about. He loved Tal more than anyone except me.

"I found something in those pictures," Phoebe said.

My entire body went rigid with a combination of hope and fear. "You know where he is?"

"Not exactly." She scanned the streets at a dark intersection and then turned down an even darker street. There wasn't a streetlamp or a light in a window anywhere. "But I recognized one of the guys in the photos, and let's just say he isn't going to be nominated for citizen of the month anytime soon."

"And you think he's holding Tal?"

"If he isn't, he'll have a good idea who is."

Ten minutes later, she pulled into a long driveway of a house obscured by trees on both sides. I peered out the window at the run-down shack that was being reclaimed by ivy. "Where are we?"

"A safe house." She jumped out of the car and headed for the back door.

I gaped. She wasn't seriously suggesting we go inside that structure, was she? It looked like one good wind would knock it down.

She paused and glanced back at me. Frowning, she headed back to the car and yanked my door open. "Come on. It's not safe out here."

I glanced around again and shivered. Yeah, there wasn't anything about the neighborhood that made me want to exit the car, much less go inside the house. "Are you crazy?"

She shook her head and laughed. "Maybe, but no one is going to look for you here."

That was true enough. And this was Phoebe. The house and property were probably protected with at least a dozen spells.

Link hunched over on full alert as we made our way to the back of the house. Paint was peeling off the porch and more than a few wooden boards on the side of the house appeared to be rotted. "Are you sure this place is stable?"

She snickered. "I'm sure." A soft glow lit up her fingers as she clamped her hand over the door handle. The lock clicked and she pulled the door open, letting me and Link into the pitch-black house. Anything could be living in the run-down place. Visions of rats scurrying to the corners made my skin crawl.

But as soon as she closed the door, she whispered, "*Illuminate.*" Candles sprang to life, casting a soft glow in the room.

My eyes widened in total shock. Inside, the place had gleaming pinewood floors, comfortable-looking overstuffed couches, and three large desks all outfitted with state-of-the-art computers. It was like the witch Bat Cave. "Holy fae, Phoebs. Is this where you go when you disappear?"

She shrugged. "Sometimes. Now come over here." She flicked one of the computers on and typed in a password. The pictures I'd taken earlier flashed on the screen. "Anything look familiar to you?"

I scanned the images and started to shake my head. But there, off to the right, the man holding a brown paper bag jumped out at me. I gasped. "He's one of the guards that held me captive last week. Pittman. Jesse Pittman."

She nodded again. "Yep. He's also trained in interrogation. And guess who he has ties to?"

I shook my head, praying she wasn't going to say Allcot. If I found out he was behind Talisen's abduction, I'd kill him.

"He was Felton's second-in-command."

Felton. The former director who had wanted me incarcerated so they could study my gifts.

"You think he's taken up Felton's cause?"

"I'd bet my life on it."

Chapter 17

I clicked on Pittman's picture, making it fill the screen. His black eyes were bottomless pools of nothing. The way his lips turned up into a private smile gave him the deranged look of a crazy person. A chill of fear swept over me and my wings twitched in agitation. "He gives me the creeps."

She nodded and clicked the mouse, bringing up another screen. "Me, too. When he's on duty he manages to appear somewhat normal, but his personality is all anger and domination. Here he gives the impression of evil incarnate."

I sank into a chair, unable to keep my eyes off the screen. "He has Tal," I said, feeling the truth of my words all the way down to my bones, the pain of the realization leaving me bereft and desolate. That psycho could have done anything to Tal by now. I steeled myself, not allowing my mind to go there. The thoughts were unacceptable.

"That's the suspicion."

Shaking my head, I turned to her. "He absolutely does. And I have no idea how I know, but I've never been so sure about anything ever before. Do you know where he lives or where he could be holding him?"

"Let's see." She pulled out the book she'd found at the vamp lover's house earlier that day and started typing in names at warp speed. After she hit enter, the computer flashed a green bar and counted down from three minutes while it calculated.

I fidgeted, picking at my fingernails, barely able to hold still. "What's it doing?"

"I've had hunches like that before. It's best to pay close attention to them, so I'm running a search on any businesses connecting Pittman and anyone on this list." She tapped the book. Another click of the mouse and a map materialized. She typed something in and three tiny stars popped on the screen.

"Hot damn!" she said, smiling.

"Whoa. There are three matches!" A tiny bit of the weight on my heart lifted. "This isn't Google Maps," I said, watching multiple routes emerge and light up the screen.

"Cool, right? This handy program gives me detailed info on which streets to take based on a number of factors: time of day, residents, crime stats, schools, businesses, and socioeconomic demographics." Another tap on the mouse and five avatars, all based on her more popular aliases, popped up. She clicked the one marked Tracker and the routes narrowed to two per location. She traced her pink fingernail over the green line. "This one is the most neutral. It's probably the safest, but it's also the one that's the most predictable if anyone is looking for me."

"So we're taking the red one," I said, realizing it would lead us right through vamp territory again. Being that it was already dark, it was the riskiest one if we had to stop for some unforeseen reason. Phoebe had over a hundred different ways to disguise herself, but all the vamps in town knew who she was and fooling them would be tricky at best.

"Was there ever any doubt?" She smirked and jumped to her feet. "Come on. We need to suit up before we go on our recon mission."

"Recon? Not rescue?" My heart sped up and my chest tightened with emotion. We had to save Tal. We just had to.

"Recon first. Then rescue." She grabbed my hand and tugged. "Trust me, Wil. The last thing we want to do is rush in unprepared."

"Right. Of course." But if it were solely up to me, I'd go in guns blazing, vampires and thugs be damned. I'd had just about as much as I could take and was ready to kick some serious ass.

She sent me a reassuring smile. "We'll bring him home. I promise."

Until we found him alive, no one could make that promise

"Trust me." Her voice went soft, as if she was speaking with a fragile victim and not another agent of the Void.

I straightened my spine, resolved. "Of course we will."

Ten minutes later we were back in the car, laden with a new stun gun, binoculars, magically enhanced voice amplifiers for eavesdropping, a collection of nasty spells originally intended to paralyze vamps and whatever else Phoebe had in her bag of tricks. The paralyzing spells were normally too potent for humans, but if the people holding Tal were hopped up on his drug, the spells might be the only thing that could give us an advantage.

I sat back in my seat, trying to compartmentalize all that had happened that day: the attack from the mysterious daywalker, Tal being abducted, David and Allcot stepping up to help.

David. What had happened to the man I'd met over a year ago in my shop? I now knew he'd been sent to watch over me. He'd been human then. And maybe he hadn't been completely honest with me, but he had been real. This new David? He acted too much like his father.

Phoebe glanced over at me. "You all right?"

I clutched Link a little tighter and nodded. "Fine." Link pressed into me, showing me support the only way he knew how

"Good. 'Cause things are about to get sticky."

"Huh?"

The car swerved right, then left, barely missing a truck that came out of nowhere.

"Who the hell was that?" I cried, holding on to the dash to keep from flying forward as she braked sharply and turned left down another darkened street. Three more turns and she popped out onto North Claiborne.

"Phoebs?"

She flew through a yellow light and let out a sigh of relief. "Sorry about that. The gang lord of that neighborhood likes to do traffic checks on unfamiliar vehicles sometimes. So far I've managed to avoid them all."

"The gang lord? Traffic checks?" What was she thinking? "And that's the neighborhood you chose for your 'safe house'?"

She smiled sheepishly. "It's the perfect hideout, right?"

"Until they find out who you are and use you against the Void," I scoffed. "If they ever catch you, you're going to be in a world of hurt."

She stopped at a red light and I stared out the window at the convenience store sign for Noble Snacks. The first three letters had been burnt out for as long as I could remember. It now read le Snacks. Classy.

"Relax, Wil. I keep my spells with me at all times. Worst case, I'd knock them out and hit them with a memory spell. They'll never see it coming."

I slumped down in the seat, unconvinced. I hated the idea of her spending time in that neighborhood by herself. I had to admit, no one would go looking for her there. But if anyone cared to take a closer look at her operation, she'd go missing in a heartbeat. Gang lords didn't take kindly to outsiders on their turf.

Phoebe reached over and pressed a button on her dashboard GPS. A moment later the same screen that had been on her computer showed up and the car calculated directions to our first stop.

"How did you choose where to go first?"

She shrugged. "Just call it a hunch."

I raised my eyebrows in question.

"It's where I'd take someone if I didn't want anyone to see or hear what I was doing."

My frown deepened. Like her fake shack house. Now I knew why she never took me on recon missions. Stalking vampires was one thing, but going into the slums was entirely another. Faeries didn't go unnoticed. I bit down on the urge to protest and braced myself for whatever came next.

Before long, we were headed over the Crescent City Connection, the bridge that spanned the Mississippi River. She took the second exit, steering us into the heart of Algiers. It was a part of town I'd never been in before. The car bounced over uneven roads through the darkened streets. Once again, there wasn't a working streetlight in sight. Parked cars lined the street, giving the illusion of inhabitants, but everything was so silent there was a feeling of desertion.

"It's creepy here," I said.

She nodded. "It really is. This neighborhood used to be a prime hunting ground for the city's vamps. Now as soon as the sun goes down, everyone disappears. There hasn't been a report of a vamp sighting in months, but people don't forget that kind of thing quickly."

No wonder she'd chosen this location first. The residential streets gradually turned into retail shops and then large commercial warehouses. Phoebe circled a few blocks. "There," she said, pointing at a darkened four-story brick building covered in ivy.

I raised my eyebrows. "Looks condemned and deserted."

"That's the point, isn't it?"

"I guess so." Link pressed his nose to the window, his tail raised in high alert. "He senses something."

A wide grin spread over her face. "I guessed correctly then." She rummaged around in her bag of tricks and pulled out two tiny earpieces. She handed me one. "Put this on."

I did as I was told.

Phoebe glanced at me, frowning. "Here." She tossed me another mousy brown wig that was shoulder length. I was already wearing jeans and running shoes. With the disguise, I'd be as nondescript as I could get except for my wings. But I had a feeling I was going to need those.

"Let's go." Phoebe hopped out of the car. Link scrambled over me, jumping out seconds before I did. He shimmered gold. His bones elongated, crackling with the shift. In full wolf form, he peered around, his eyes flashing with intelligence.

"Stay close to Willow, Link," Phoebe said. He immediately trotted to stand beside me, his large body pressing against me slightly. She patted his head. "Good dog."

I smiled. The two didn't always get along due to the shoe stealing, but when it came to hunting the bad guys, they had total respect for each other. Clutching my stun gun, I ran quietly behind her toward the warehouse. Link lifted his nose and the hair on his neck stood straight up. There was definitely trouble in that building. I didn't know how he did it, but Link seemed to have developed a supernatural sense of when someone had ill intentions.

Phoebe stepped lightly and I fluttered slightly off the ground behind her. We were silent as we made our way to the back of the building. Phoebe put her finger to her lips, unnecessarily warning us to be quiet. She touched the side of the building, a white spark spreading out in a web network under her palm, and whispered, "*Engage.*"

Static filled my left ear. She adjusted a setting on her earpiece and the static in mine faded away. Neat trick to have them connected. I turned to give her a thumbs-up but froze when faint voices filled my ear.

"Our boy isn't cooperating," an irritated voice called.

Another person grunted. "Would you? As soon as the boss gets what he wants, that one is destined for the food den."

I bristled, my wings tensed for flight. Food den was slang for forced vamp feedings. The idea of Tal being fanged by a vampire turned my stomach. Usually fae didn't have to worry about vampire bites as we take measures against that sort of thing by ingesting Sunshine. It made our blood rancid to vampires. But that didn't mean they couldn't bite or that they wouldn't. Piss one off enough and he wouldn't hesitate to rip our throats out.

Phoebe pulled out a suspiciously familiar marbled green stone. I peered at it. I'd seen that jade pendant dozens of times before. It was Tal's calming stone. She mumbled something in Latin and then pressed it into my hand. "The closer you get to him, the warmer it will get," she whispered in my ear.

"How—?"

She held up her hand, cutting me off, and shook her head. Now wasn't the time for questions. "Just follow me. If the stone gets hot, let me know."

I nodded. She clutched her own sun agate with one hand and a tranq gun in the other. A feeling of pride swelled in my chest. Phoebe was armed to the hilt and willing to do whatever it took to find Tal. All of this was for him…and me, not the Void. If the new director found out she was tracking Tal at all, she'd be in some serious shit. That job was for whomever they'd assigned his case to.

I briefly wondered if we were doing the right thing, taking this on all by ourselves. But how could I know who to trust? Besides my mom, Phoebe was the only one. Everyone else— David, Allcot, anyone at the Void—they were all suspect. Everyone had an agenda. Everyone except Phoebe. She had nothing to gain from this except trouble.

Two things happened simultaneously to pull me out of my thoughts: the stone started to burn my palm and the thick heavy sensation of vampire coated me, weighting me down until my feet touched the ground again.

"Phoebs," I whispered, but before she could turn around the earpiece buzzed and Tal's voice filled my ear.

"You might as well end this now. She'll never bring the drug to you."

End this? What did he mean? End him? A sharp pain stabbed my heart. Why was he taunting them? I grabbed Phoebe's arm.

She stared me in the eyes and then nodded to the stone in my hand. I needed to lead her to him. Shaking from the vamp energy clinging to me, I shut my eyes and concentrated. The stone was sending fire through my palm, consuming my entire hand. My reflexes begged to fling the thing from me but I clutched it tighter. The stone was my best bet to find Tal.

I stepped forward, slowly gauging the heat level of the stone. No change. A few more steps and the stone cooled. Dammit. I shuffled back and headed a few more steps in the opposite direction. It warmed and then cooled again. The spot in the middle was the most intense connection.

Glancing up, I spied a bar-covered window three stories high. Luckily I had wings. I nodded toward it and thrust through the vampire fog, fluttering to the side of the window, careful to only take a peek and not expose my presence.

My breath caught. Bright fluorescent lights illuminated a Plexiglas-enclosed lab. Tal was inside, his wrists and ankles shackled together. He was also stripped bare from the waist up with a dozen electrode wires attached to his body.

No! Dark circles lined his eyes, and his skin was so pale I could see the veins in his chest and neck.

This was not happening. It couldn't be.

But it was. They had already done considerable damage. I wanted to scream at him to just give them what they wanted. Nothing was worth what they were putting him through.

That tiny voice in the back of my head reminded me that once they got what they wanted, they'd either kill him or exploit his gifts until he was a shell of his former self. It wouldn't be the first time a vamp had turned a skilled fae into a slave.

If I wasn't careful, it was how I'd end up.

We had to get him out now.

I dropped to the ground, careful to land lightly. Any sound at all could alert the vampire within. Phoebe pressed her lips together in grim acceptance at what must have been my wild-eyed panicked look. She ran a light hand down my arm, trying to soothe me. When I opened my mouth, she shook her head violently and pointed to the roof.

Then she mouthed, "I'll meet you up there."

I nodded once and glanced at Link, who was slinking off around the side of the building. He'd catch anyone trying to flee. Steeling myself, I thrust upward and fluttered inches above the flat rooftop.

A soft light flashed, followed by Phoebe materializing out of thin air. Another neat and useful trick. Witches who could materialize were rare. The spell took an incredible amount of energy. She would likely only be able to use it once, maybe twice more before depleting her magic. She stood unmoving while we studied the building, planning our attack.

There were two chimney stacks, three air-conditioner vents, and a steel door leading into the building. The door was out. Too obvious. No way was I going to fit through the chimney, so that left the air-conditioner vents. Phoebe frowned. The only way to get through without making any noise would be to use vanishing spells. Not ideal since at this rate, she'd drain all her energy before we ever got a chance to kick some vampire ass.

I held my hand up, asking her to wait. Still flying, I searched every inch of the roof and then around the top of the building until I came to the side covered in ivy. There. Peeking out from behind the foliage was a broken window, free of the usual wrought-iron bars. Upon closer inspection, I realized all the windows on this side hadn't been barred. Someone had been too lazy to clean up the overgrown ivy.

I flew back to Phoebe and waved her over. She stepped lightly, careful to not make a sound. When we got to the edge, she knelt down and flattened out on her stomach to peer down the wall. She turned and grinned at me.

Now we were in business.

I pointed at the ivy and then myself. I was skilled with life magic and spent my days manipulating plants. Clearing the ivy was a piece of cake. I hovered near the building, letting my wings hold me steady in the air, took a deep breath, and then lightly touched my fingertips to the nearest vines.

Their life rushed into me, giving me the familiar jolt of energy, but instead of manipulating it and forcing it back into the plant, I took it and stored it away inside me and watched as the small section of the ivy wilted before my eyes. I smiled and repeated the process until enough of the plant fell away from the window, leaving us with enough room to squeeze through.

Phoebe nodded her approval and indicated she'd go first. We hadn't exactly made a plan. We didn't even know how many people were in the building. So far, I knew there were the two humans who were torturing Tal and at least one vampire who was hiding somewhere. He was close, but not so close it was affecting my ability to move. Not like what happened in Mid-City earlier in the day.

Three wasn't so bad, but it would be better if Link was inside. Phoebe could take the vampire down. But if the humans were on Tal's new drug, we could be in serious trouble.

No time to stop and worry about it now. Tal was in bad shape. I wasn't leaving without him.

Phoebe grabbed hold of the ivy I hadn't killed, climbed down the side of the building, and disappeared through the window. My pulse started to race. I gripped my stun gun tighter and fluttered to the window, squeezing my way in.

A flash of light momentarily blinded me, followed by a cry, and then a grunt of pain filled the warehouse. Footsteps echoed against the wall.

Dammit! That had to be Phoebe. What had gone so terribly wrong so fast?

There wasn't a ledge or anything to climb down on. How had she gotten to the floor? Magic? My only choice was to crawl out the window or flutter to the floor and pray no one saw me. There wasn't any contest. Phoebe and Tal needed me.

Something in the air seemed to shift. Fear gripped me as the metaphysical weight of a vampire weighed me down, forcing me to drop to the concrete below.

And before I could even blink, the form of a chiseled vampire with glowing blue eyes materialized before me.

"Willow Rhoswen," he said lightly with a smile I was sure he intended to be welcoming but came off as chilling. From his exposed fangs to the warrior stance, he was one hundred percent predator. It took all my effort to not shrink back into the shadows.

Instead, I bore the curse of his vampire weight and squared my shoulders. "Release Talisen. Now. Or this is the last moon-rise you'll ever see."

Chapter 18

The sleek, platinum-blond vampire stared at me. His lips curled as his laughter filled the warehouse.

Nervous energy mingled with my fear. Where was Phoebe? Was she hurt? I didn't dare take my eyes off the vampire in front of me. At that moment, my only defense was my stun gun, and if I didn't see him coming, I was a dead fae.

"What do you want from us?" I demanded, holding my ground. I stood with my feet apart and my finger stroking the trigger of my gun. One movement from him and I was ready to stun his ass.

He sobered and smoothed his gray silk suit. "What everyone else wants, I suppose. But that's not the question you should be asking."

I clenched my teeth, knocking back the fear threatening to immobilize me. "I'm not in the mood for games, vampire. Let Talisen go and maybe we'll talk. Until then, you'll get nothing."

Narrowing his eyes, his voice came out in a low growl. "You'll do whatever I tell you to, faery. I've got the upper hand here." He stretched his arm out and snapped his fingers.

Light filled the warehouse, making my eyes water. I blinked rapidly, trying to clear my vision. He had his attention focused off to the left and his smile was back. I glanced to the side and did a double take.

Son of a bitch! Lined up against the wall were Harrison, Phoebe, and Nicola, another witch who was Pandora's half sister. Phoebe must have been ambushed as soon as she entered the building. They'd known we were here. But how had Harrison and Nicola gotten there?

"Let them go," I said. "I'll get you what you want, but you have to let them go first."

The vampire walked casually over to Phoebe and ran a finger along the gag keeping her silent. "You'll do what I want, but there won't be any negotiating about what happens to these criminals."

Criminals? He'd lost his mind.

He turned back to me. "Breaking and entering is still a crime, you know."

"But abduction isn't?" Anger coursed through my limbs and my wings flared.

His lifted one eyebrow. "Dominance, faery?" He waved a hand to his two sidekicks. One had a needle pressed to Tal's arm. "I think we can agree who's really in charge here."

I took in a deep, ragged breath and forced my wings down. Dammit. It would be really helpful if I'd brought that sweater to keep my wings in check. At this point every movement was involuntary. I couldn't help it. "Leave him out of this."

He closed his eyes and shook his head as if he was praying for patience. "The two of you are at the center of everything I need. But I'm not unwilling to make a deal." He gestured to a metal chair a few feet from Tal's Plexiglas cage. "Have a seat and we'll see if we can come to some agreement."

Me? He'd said the two of us. What did he want with me? My Influence gift or did he want to be turned into a daywalker? How could he know about that? Forcing the panic down, I took a moment to search Phoebe's expression, but the only read I could get from her was righteous anger. If she managed to get free, he was going to pay for a long time before she dusted his ass. I didn't think I'd ever seen her look so dangerous, despite the bindings that kept her trapped against the wall. I could see it in the deep dark pools of her eyes.

The amusement on the vamp's face when he glanced at her told me he saw the same thing and welcomed the challenge. The fear coiled deeper inside me.

Nicola was struggling with her bindings, only succeeding in making them cut into her wrists. Harrison met my eyes, but I had no idea what he was trying to tell me. Maybe nothing. He couldn't do or say anything in his current state.

Without any backup other than Link waiting outside, I didn't have much of a choice. I walked slowly but with purpose to the metal chair, trying not to keep my eyes glued to Tal. Looking at him only made my heart break.

You can do this, Willow. One step at a time.

I positioned the chair so I could see Phoebe and the vamp and sat back, leaning against the cool metal. I waved a hand in the vamp's direction. "Maybe you should start by telling me who you are."

He pulled out another metal chair, positioning it backward, and straddled it when he sat. It was so out of character from his stiff demeanor that the action threw me off for a moment. This wasn't a brainstorming session. "I want to know a little more about you first."

I said nothing as my defensive walls shot up around me. Did he know who I was, besides Tal's friend?

The vampire pulled out a smart phone and tapped a button. Was he recording? "Tell me about your brother."

I jerked at the mention of Beau. "What about him?"

"Anything you want to tell me."

I tried for a normal tone, not wanting him to know how much the question bothered me, but I failed miserably as my words came out low and angry. "There isn't anything I want to tell you. This session was your idea, remember?"

He leaned forward as if my answer interested him. Of course it did. He'd chosen a topic that riled me up and I'd failed at hiding it. "How did he die?"

There was no reason to lie. His death was public record. "He was murdered. Throat cut and left to bleed out."

"Do you know why?"

I shrugged. I did know, but I sure as hell wasn't going to tell this asshole. "Random act of violence?"

He stared at me, his crazy eyes piercing me as if he could see right into my mind. Thank the Goddess vampires didn't harbor that particular gift. Then he said in a dry tone, "Don't fuck with me, Rhoswen. You'll only piss me off."

I scoffed. "If you have something you want to say, then spit it out. I don't have any information about my brother. He never hurt anyone. He led a quiet life. Then he was killed. End of story. Unless you're trying to tell me you had a hand in it. And if that's the case, then this conversation is over." I stood to make my point clear.

But before I could move, he flew out of his chair. He landed inches from me and even though he wasn't touching my skin, everything started to burn. I bit back a wince and tried to keep a neutral face. I couldn't risk letting him know how much his vampire state hurt me. I'd be tortured until every last drop of life was torn from my body.

"The reason this conversation is relevant is because I know who did kill him. He'll kill you, too, if you're not careful."

My heart skipped a couple of beats. Asher knew about my ability. He had to if he was willing to kill me. And this vamp knew it, too. "Who are you?" I breathed.

He backed up just enough that the burning eased. "The second-in-command to the vampire who killed your brother."

The second-in-command. This vampire had straight-out told me he worked for the vamp who'd killed Beau. Why? Unless he planned to kill all of us. My body tensed, on the edge of flight, but the words stirred a deep-seated promise I'd made to myself four years ago. To find and take down Beau's killer. And now his second-in-command was moments from killing Tal as well. I used my thumb to flick the stun gun on, and before I could stop myself, I jabbed it at the vamp, missing him by less than an inch.

He jumped back, eyeing the weapon in irritation. "You have to know that won't bring me down." He snapped his fingers and the two guards who had been waiting for the vamp's order to inject Tal moved forward. One of them was Pittman. The traitor. "If she tries that again, restrain her."

"Yes, sir," they said in unison as Pittman leered at me and winked. Total sociopath.

If they got anywhere near me, they'd both be in a Taser coma for days. It was the vamp-grade weapon Phoebe had stolen from the Void. The vamp would survive, but the humans wouldn't stand a chance. Doubt took up residence in my mind. What about humans on Tal's drug? It would slow them down for sure, but would it neutralize them? I could only hope.

"What's your name?" I asked the vampire through my haze. I wanted to know who I was taking out. Wanted to know that he was involved in Beau's death, but I couldn't force the words out. It was too painful.

"Sit," he ordered. When I didn't move, he growled. "Take a seat or I'll rip your arm off. The one holding the gun."

Angry vamp wasn't nearly as terrifying as calm vamp had been. I didn't care for being ordered around, and the thought of following his orders made bile rise in my throat, but I swallowed it down, refusing to let him have that power over me. The knowledge that I'd gotten under his skin was satisfying enough for now. Besides, I had no doubt he would follow through on his threat if pushed hard enough. I inched back to my chair and sat with my back straight.

He stalked to his chair and sat heavily. "Now. You can call me Von. Got it?"

I nodded. "I'm not an idiot."

"All evidence to the contrary."

I glared.

"Most faeries in your position would not challenge a vampire keeping her friends hostage," he pointed out.

"I'm not most faeries."

"No," he said softly. "You most definitely are not."

Silence stretched between us. I wanted to shout at him to let my friends go, to ask what he wanted of me, but I didn't. I just stared him down in some ridiculous mind war, waiting for him to cave.

Finally he started laughing. "Now I know why Allcot likes you so much."

"What?" I jumped, nearly falling right out of my chair. He knew about my relationship with Allcot? And he thought Allcot liked me? He couldn't be further from the truth. Allcot tolerated me because of my abilities and my ties to Beau Junior, who was, for better or worse, going to always be a part of Allcot's family. "Why do you say that?"

"You're not easily intimidated. It's rare to find anyone besides a witch who fights back."

What a sadistic bastard. He was getting off on my fight reflex. Dark, twisted piece of vamp turd. "I don't appreciate those who hurt my friends."

He sat back in his chair and crossed his arms over his chest. "Let's get down to business then, shall we?"

"Let's. How about you let my friends go and we'll let you continue to exist."

He smiled a savage grin as he shook his head at my demand. Clearly any negotiations we made would not involve us just walking out of the building. "Tempting, but I think we'll go another direction. You tell me about the abilities your brother had and which ones you inherited, get me the test samples of your friend's new superhuman drug, and then we'll see what we can do for you."

Yeah. That was closer to what I thought he'd say. I mimicked his posture. "As far as I knew, Beau never had any special abilities besides his natural fae gifts." And that was the absolute truth. I'd only learned about Beau's vampire gifts less than two weeks ago.

"But you know now." He saw right through my ploy to sidestep his question.

"So I've been told. But I never saw him use any of it, so how can I be sure this isn't all a lie?" There. That was the truth, too.

"Maybe because you have the same gifts." He kept those eyes glued to me, clearly waiting for a reaction.

I didn't give him one. The only person who'd ever seen me use my gift was Phoebe. Allcot and his people knew about it, but no one had actually seen me in action. Deny, deny, deny. If I told this vamp his mere presence sucked the life out of me and that if he touched me, it would be worse than being beaten with an iron rod, I'd be a sitting duck.

And I sure as hell wasn't going to tell him I could turn vampires into daywalkers. I didn't even know if I could repeat the experience. "I don't know what you're talking about. I'm a skilled baker who can infuse plants with magic. That's all."

He jumped to his feet and growled, "Don't lie!"

I shrank back, wishing I wasn't sitting. But if I stood, I'd have no choice but to push Von backward and I was pretty sure if I touched him, he'd snap.

"Tell me!" His face contorted as his fangs elongated and a snarl erupted from his throat. "What are your gifts? Why is Asher obsessed with you?"

I never saw him move. One minute he was glaring down at me, the controlled vampire I'd met gone, replaced by a crazed monster. The next, his hands were clutching my shoulders and my feet were dangling off the floor. The fire erupted in my arms and spread rapidly to my chest. I was going to die of shock or a heart attack if he didn't put me down.

I cried out in pure agony and reflex took over. There was so much pain I don't even know how I moved my arm, but the moment I touched him with the stun gun, the shock was so powerful it went right through him and into me through his fingertips.

We stayed locked together, frozen by the current. My synapses misfired and although my brain was screaming for me to drop the gun, I couldn't. I couldn't do anything but stand there, zapping the vampire while I screamed in pure agony until my world went black.

Chapter 19

I awoke to bright lights and shouting. Was that Tal? His voice rose above the others, calling my name. He was awake. I sat up, my head spinning and my limbs still on fire. Ugh. I'd nearly wiped myself out with my own Taser.

Blinking, I rubbed my eyes and stumbled to my feet, praying I hadn't been out for long. Across the room, Phoebe was free of her restraints and had Von shackled to the wall in her place. Harrison and Nicola were fighting both the guards who had been watching over Tal while he continued to struggle with the bindings still holding him to the chair.

How had the three of them gotten free? I shook the unimportant thought from my mind and rushed into the lab to Tal's side, half-flying, half-hobbling. My unsteady equilibrium had me tilting to the side and I lost my footing, landing face-first at Tal's feet.

"Willow. What the hell are you doing here?" His tone was full of admonishment, but when I pulled myself up, ready to give him a piece of my mind, the clear relief in his eyes stopped my verbal assault. I pressed my lips together into a thin line and shook my head, trying not to focus on the bruises marring the right side of his face. Had they broken his jaw when they'd taken him? If so, it appeared he'd managed to heal his bones already. Without speaking, I pulled a small knife from my pocket and slashed the bindings tying him to the chair. As soon as he was free, he swept me into a full body hug and walked me out of the lab backward toward what I assumed was the exit.

"Wait!" I planted my feet, prepared to fight him off if necessary, but he stopped and stared down at me.

"Why?"

"I can't leave Phoebe here." I glanced over his shoulder. The vampire was restrained, but he was conscious and struggling to get free. The chains were already showing signs of weakness. Any moment now, they'd come loose from the wall. Phoebe was chanting, spinning a binding spell that appeared to be winding around him.

Grunts and curses came from the pair fighting the guards. My eyes widened as I took in the scene. Nicola was throwing spell after spell at the tall, broad-shouldered one, but he remained unaffected, easily blocking each one. I recognized a few of the incantations from the various times I'd been on vampire patrol with Phoebe. With the amount of power she was tossing his way, he should've been dead by now.

Was he not human?

Another spell hit him and this one slammed into his nose, causing it to spurt blood. Definitely human. He lunged, catching her around the ankle, and the pair went down in a heap.

I rushed forward, pulling Tal with me, but was cut off by the shorter, black-haired guard going blow for blow with Harrison. Left punch. Right punch. Gut check. They each took their beating in stride as if the other hadn't so much as swatted at him.

Tal wrapped his arms around me, shielding me from the violence.

My insides heated with dread, making my head spin. They were all hopped up on Tal's drug. Why did they want the elixir if they already had it? Did they want to keep it out of Allcot's hands? Or the Void's?

The tall one had Nicola pinned as she squirmed beneath him. I pulled myself from Tal's grip and ran.

"Willow, no!" he called. Guilt seized my mind, but I kept going. I had to help her. Just as I reached the guard's side, he turned and knocked me halfway across the room, causing my Taser to skitter between some abandoned crates. "Shit."

Nicola was now fully restrained under the guard and Harrison was breathing heavily, his boxing match continuing with no end in sight. Phoebe was still working to hold the vampire. And where was Tal? He'd disappeared. Panic pushed away the guilt. Had they gotten him again?

"Phoebe!" I called as I sprinted to find my gun.

"Use the tranq," she called back, tossing the gun in my direction. Vampire grade. I caught it, unlatched the safety, and aimed. Right before I pulled the trigger, Link leaped out of nowhere and sank his teeth into the guard. With a vicious growl, he pulled the guard off Nicola and dragged him from her reach.

The guard screamed in blatant terror. I rolled my eyes. He'd managed to fight off a witch and yet he was afraid of the wolf? Idiot.

I glanced back at Phoebe. She was busy checking the restraints of the vamp. Then I turned my gun on the guard fighting Harrison. "Hold it," I demanded. "One more punch and I'll put you out."

The guard ignored me and landed a roundhouse kick to Harrison's kidney. Harrison grunted and fell, clutching his side.

So much for giving him a chance. Without hesitation, I squeezed the trigger and the dart landed in the middle of the guard's back. He went still and then fell face-first.

"That's one," Tal said, walking slowly across the room. He must've been the one that let Link in. He nodded to the one still struggling to get away from Link. "He doesn't know anything. Dart him."

I paused for half a moment, then let the dart fly. If Tal said he didn't know anything, then he probably didn't. No need to keep him conscious. The second guard went still in Link's jaws.

"Tie them up," Tal said, unmistakable hatred ringing from his gravelly voice.

Harrison and Nicola went to work on securing the unconscious guards.

"Hey," I said. "How did you two end up here?"

Nicola raised her eyebrows in surprise. "Phoebe sent for us."

"What?" More anger built, threatening to eat away at me from the inside out. Freaking Phoebe was keeping secrets from me again. Important ones.

Phoebe cleared her throat. "I texted them." She shrugged and sent me an apologetic look. "We needed backup and I didn't want to argue with you about it. You were pretty upset with David and there was a good chance he might find out, but I was out of options."

Oh holy mother of…crap! Not Phoebe, too. My head started to ache. I clamped my mouth shut, afraid of what I'd say. Now wasn't the time. And we'd needed Harrison and Nicola. I was glad they'd been there. But couldn't someone, anyone, just tell me the truth once in a while? I took a deep breath. "Did he? Find out I mean? Is David outside or on his way?" If he was, I just might take out my anger on him in the form of a tranq dart.

Nicola shook her head. "He was otherwise detained when I got the message."

Dammit all. The one time I actually wanted his lying ass here, he happened to be busy.

Phoebe, satisfied the vampire was secure, rummaged in her backpack and came up with a bottle of water. "Here." She handed it to Tal. "Drink slowly."

He nodded and fumbled with the cap.

"I got it." I took the bottle from him and unscrewed it. He frowned and turned away from me to sip his water. "Tal?"

"Not now, Wil."

He was naturally thin with broad, muscular shoulders, but right then he looked emaciated, as if they'd drained the life right out of him. Hot tears stung my eyes. I blinked them back, unwilling to let him see me break down after everything he'd been through.

"How much of the drug did you give them?" I asked Tal quietly.

He turned slowly and gave me an incredulous look.

"What? He demanded we bring him the extra samples. And his people are clearly drugged."

His green eyes flashed with anger. "None, Willow. Fucking none. Do you really think I'd try to save myself by risking everyone else's safety?"

"I…" *Shit.* That's exactly what I'd thought. But hell, if I'd been tortured, I might have given it up. The voice in the back of my mind whispered *No you wouldn't. And Tal knows it.*

"Never mind." Screwing the cap back on the bottle, he joined Phoebe and the vamp she'd managed to knock out with one of her spells. "He's out cold."

"Damn straight," she agreed.

Tal walked back to me and took the tranq gun from my hands. I was too stunned by his stony expression to do anything but let him. "Grab your Taser before anyone else gets it," he said.

I watched him retreat to Phoebe's side and dragged myself over to the crates to search for my stun gun. I found it lying near the wall, hidden in shadows. Was Tal really angry that I'd thought it possible he'd given his captors the drug? Well, he'd given it to Allcot. How was I supposed to know? I did know, though. He'd only given it to Allcot to help protect me. I hung my head and wandered back to him.

"I'm sorry," I whispered in his ear. "What can I do to help?"

"Stay with Link," he snapped.

I stepped back as if I'd been slapped. Granted Tal had been through a horrific ordeal, but dammit, that didn't give him license to treat me with such disdain.

"Wil," Phoebe said.

"Yeah."

"The drug was the excuse for abducting Tal, but that isn't what he was really after."

Tal snorted his agreement.

The lightbulb started flashing in my brain. Of course it wasn't. No wonder they'd been so easy to find. Von hadn't been hiding at all. "He wanted me."

Phoebe nodded. "It's why he demanded that you bring samples of Tal's drug."

I should have known as soon as he started asking questions about Beau and me. The stalking, the office break-in, and the abduction of Tal were all related to getting close to me, to find out what I knew about Beau and exactly which of his gifts I'd inherited. Did that mean Asher and company were still in the dark about me? Von had asked why Asher was so obsessed with me. Asher might know, but Von didn't seem to.

There was only one way to find out. "Wake him up," I told Phoebe.

Nicola stepped up beside me. "Can you do that?" she asked Phoebe.

Phoebe glanced at Nicola. "With your help."

"You got it." Nicola took her place beside Phoebe and the pair joined their power together. The normally bright white that pooled in their hands turned pale blue, indicating they were in sync.

Their magic melded together and shot straight at the vampire's heart. He jolted awake with a start, reflexively struggling against his restraints. With a loud roar, he jerked forward, causing one of the bolts to pop and freeing one arm.

"Hold it right there, Von," I demanded, brandishing my stun gun at him once more.

He growled, baring his fangs. Link sprang forward and latched on to Von's loose arm. The vampire roared and did his best to shake him off, but Link held on, his jaws clamped in a tight death grip. The vampire only flailed harder, this time breaking the chain holding his other arm. Before anyone could react, he clocked Link and sent him flying across the room.

"Link!" I flew to his side, running a sure hand down his still body. He blinked and looked up at me through his golden eyes. "You okay?"

His eyes closed and with effort, he stumbled to his feet.

"Willow," Phoebe called.

I jerked my head up to find the vampire laid out on the stone floor. Link and I made our way to her side. "What happened?"

"I tranq'd him." She shoved the gun into a holster on her side.

I frowned. She'd had to do something. Restraining him was proving to be impossible. But our investigation just came to a screeching halt. All our suspects were down for the count. "Gonna be hard to get our questions answered now."

"I did what I had to," Phoebe said irritably.

I took a deep breath. "I know you did."

"Come on. We have to get out of here." She nodded to Nicola and Harrison. "Help me get the vampire in the car."

"Whoa." I held my hands up. "The vampire? Where are we taking him? Shouldn't we call the Void and have them take care of these three?"

She shook her head and gave me a pointed stare. "Not unless you're prepared to tell the new director all about your family history."

I let out a suffering sigh. "No. I'm not. But can't we just tell them they violated the codes? Make up something about the vamp going after someone and the humans helping him?" There had to be something. What were we going to do with them? The restraints in the warehouse couldn't hold him. What made her think we could?

"There's no evidence. It won't stick. Besides, we need answers and if we let the Void take him, I'll be limited in what questions I can ask."

Basically, we'd be nowhere fast. And we needed information on Asher if I was going to be safe. "Then where?"

"David's house."

"What?" I straightened and shook my head. "Absolutely not. You know I don't trust him."

Tal shifted to stand closer and gently took my hand, clearly trying to soothe my agitation. It didn't work. I pulled my hand from his, even though all I wanted to do was grip it now that

I had him with me again. "Save your strength, Tal. You need it more than I do."

He let me go, moved a few feet away, and stood near Link. Link licked Tal's hand, giving him the support I seemed to be incapable of extending right at that moment. I bit down hard on my lower lip and turned my attention to Phoebe.

"He has that room, Wil. And I have a key." She patted her pocket. "I never gave it back after he offered to let me use his place when I was tracking Clea."

The sun porch. It was the perfect place to interrogate a vampire. The walls were unbreakable, reinforced glass. Left in the sun porch long enough with the threat of certain death at sunrise was the perfect way to get a vamp to talk. And David's place was safer than my shop or our home. Asher would find me in two seconds flat if we went to either one.

"And if David is there?" I asked her. "Are you willing to let him run the interrogation?" Because he would.

She grinned. "He left over an hour ago and is now at Allcot's mansion. The coast is clear."

"How do you know that?"

Holding up her phone, she let out a small bark of laughter. "I've bugged his phone with a magical tracking app."

Nicola took in a sharp breath of surprise. "He's not going to like that."

"I'm sure he won't," Phoebe agreed.

An unspoken exchange transpired between the two witches. Finally Nicola smiled. "Can you hook me up with that app?"

Chapter 20

Thankfully, the witches were able to wield a spell to carry the vampire and his two sidekicks to the cars. We'd fished the keys out of Von's pocket, and after a walk around the block clicking the unlock button, we finally had success with a beige Suburban. It was the fully loaded version, complete with drop-down movie screens and a rear full of kids' toys. Who the hell had they stolen this mom-mobile from?

Once we had the Suburban open, Harrison hauled our tranq'd victims into the back, piling them in a heap. Limbs tangled and poked into backs and ribcages. If they woke up in those positions, we were going to have some very cranky bad guys on our hands.

"I'll drive this one." Phoebe snatched the Suburban keys from me and pressed the keys to her Camry into my palm, nodding to me, Tal, and Link. "You three take my car."

Harrison and Nicola climbed into the Suburban. Phoebe waited for the rest of us to get safely to the Camry before she jumped in after them and took off.

Tal sat back in the passenger's seat and closed his eyes.

I twisted the key in the ignition and let the car idle for a moment. "Tal?"

He didn't open his eyes. "Hmm?"

I gripped his hand and squeezed, trying not to cry from the emotion swelling in my chest. "Don't ever do that again."

He opened one eye and peered at me. "Do what?"

"Get yourself abducted," I whispered. "I can't take it."

His eye closed and he sighed. "Be thankful they didn't succeed in killing me."

The statement hit me like a sucker punch to the gut. He'd just confirmed what I already knew the moment I saw him in that chair. There was no denying they'd been draining the life from him. I leaned across the car and rested my head on his leg, needing to be connected to him.

He placed his hand on my head and lightly stroked my hair. "I love you, too, Wil," he said very faintly. I sat stunned, not sure what to say. Then, as I sorted my thoughts, his shallow breathing became steady and I knew he'd fallen into an exhausted slumber.

I love you, too. The words ran through my mind over and over as I sat up and then eased the car into gear and headed back through the quiet streets. We'd never said those words to each other before. A month ago, I would've brushed them off as a brotherly type thing. But everything was different now. He'd said *the* words and I'd said nothing.

Son of a...cripes.

That was not how a declaration of love was supposed to go. I pressed my foot on the accelerator and sped the rest of the way to Mid-City. The beige Suburban was parked in David's driveway when I stopped Phoebe's car at his curb.

"Tal," I said, nudging his shoulder.

He blinked, glancing around in confusion. "Where are we?"

"David's house. Remember? We brought Von and his minions here."

"Right." He rubbed his eyes and reached for the door handle. I caught his arm. "Wait."

He glanced back at me, his face drawn with a bone-deep weariness.

"Are you up for this? I mean, all your healing crystals must be back at your apartment, right?"

He gave me a weak smile. "They are. But we both know we can't go back there right now." The door creaked as he climbed out.

Link and I followed. I clasped Tal's arm and the three of us headed into David's house uninvited. A pit formed in my stomach. What would David say when he found out we'd barged in without his permission?

Right then, I decided I didn't care. He could find a way to deal with it. David hadn't exactly been looking out for my welfare. No, he'd had his own agenda where I was concerned...again.

Inside the house, I led Tal straight to the study where I knew Phoebe would be. She was huddled around the desk with Harrison and Nicola. No one even acknowledged us. A sense of déjà vu settled over me.

Not too long ago, we'd had Clea locked in the sunroom while David and Phoebe shut me out of the interrogation process. That wouldn't be happening again. I stalked over to the desk, hands on hips. "We're here."

Phoebe glanced up. "I know. I heard you." Her gazed flicked to Tal. "You probably want to find a guest room for him."

Anger seemed to seep from my pores, but before I could argue, Tal shook his head and said, "No. I'm not the only one who was taken."

"Elissa?" I asked.

Tal gave me a confused look. "The lab assistant?"

"Yeah. She hasn't been home in days."

His brow crinkled as he frowned. "She was at work yesterday morning, but she left before the attack."

Well, that was something. "Then who?"

"My boss. Professor Dawson. They took him at the same time they got me. I saw them stuff him in another car before they knocked me out. But when I awoke in the warehouse, he wasn't there."

Phoebe sucked in a sharp breath. "Shit. We can't leave him."

I shook my head and grabbed Tal's hand. His boss was his only friend in town besides Phoebe and me. "Do you have any idea where he could be? You had multiple places to try, right?"

Phoebe bit down on her lip, thinking. With a grimace, she said, "We could check them out, but those were long shots. The warehouse was the only one that seemed plausible."

Tal's eyes narrowed. "You have other addresses to try?"

"Well, technically, yes. But I doubt we'd find anything except car parts or other petty-theft items."

"Give me the addresses. I'll go myself." Tal grabbed a pad of paper from the desk and reached for a pen.

"Wait." I wrapped my hands around his arm and gently pulled him to my side. "You can't go anywhere quite yet."

"I'm not leaving him with those monsters, Willow. You have no idea what they're capable of."

An image of Tal, white and drained of life, made me tremble with delayed shock. "I think I do," I said quietly, clutching the edge of the desk. "I know you have to do what you have to do, but please, take some time to heal first." Tal was a healer. He had the magic within himself to become whole again. He just needed to focus.

Tal sucked in a breath. "I don't have my amethyst."

"What? You always…shit. They took it from you." It wasn't a question. Tal never went anywhere without an amethyst on him. It was either in his pocket or around his neck.

Tal's lips formed a tight line. He nodded once and turned to Phoebe. "Can I borrow your car?"

"Wait." Niccla reached into her purse and rummaged around. We all stared at her while she dumped handfuls of receipts and gum wrappers on the desk. "It's in here somewhere," she said under her breath.

"What?" I asked.

She grumbled and then a smile lit her creamy features. "Aha!" She pulled out a severely knotted silver chain, but on the end dangled a wire-wrapped pale lavender stone.

Tal stepped forward and wrapped his hand around the pendant. His eyes closed and the tension instantly drained from his face. A tiny bit of pink colored his cheeks.

I sank into a chair, finally able to relax for the first time all day. He was recovering right before my eyes.

Nicola let go of the chain and stepped back.

"Thank you," Tal said.

"No. Thank you." A trace of a smile graced her lips. "Ever since you healed me last week, that amethyst seems to take away any minor ailment."

"It's a side effect," I mumbled.

"What?" She turned, glancing at me.

I cleared my throat. "After Tal touches someone with his magic, it lingers. If you keep an amethyst on your person, the magic will flair to life when you need it."

"Sort of like an energy boost?" she asked.

"Yeah." Tal's coloring was better, but the way his body swayed slightly indicated the bone-deep exhaustion was catching up to him.

I put an arm around him. "Let's go in the other room so you can concentrate." What I really wanted to do was lead him to the guest room so he could lie down. But I knew he wouldn't do that in David's house and he wasn't going to let anyone treat him like an invalid. Not that he was one. He just needed some time and space to recover. We moved into the living room where Tal took a seat on David's pin-striped settee and leaned back. His shoulders hunched forward as he clutched the amethyst.

"Tal?"

"Willow," he said, not opening his eyes. "Please. Let me be for now." His voice was strained and full of something close to desperation.

I backed up into the doorway. "Of course. I'll be with Phoebe if you need anything."

He gave me one nod and leaned forward, resting his elbows on his knees as he hung his head.

I'd give anything to be able to help him the way he'd helped me more times than I could count. The times I'd been battered and aching to the point of almost no return until his cool tingling magic took it all away. Now he'd have to use the last of his strength to heal himself. He could do it, but he wouldn't be in any shape to fight for his boss. I'd guess he'd need at least a week to fully recover. He wouldn't admit that to anyone, though. Not even himself.

"Hey," Phoebe said.

I jumped and whirled to find her standing right behind me. My heart pounded as if it were trying to beat right out of my chest. "Dammit, Phoebs. Could you have been any quieter? You scared the crap out of me."

"Sorry." She placed a gentle hand on my arm. "I need to talk to Tal for a sec."

I shook my head. "He needs some time to himself."

"Let her in," Tal said from the settee. "I'm fine."

I clamped my lips together, forcing myself to not say anything. Phoebe hurried in and sat next to Tal as I leaned against the doorframe. They weren't touching, but something about their interaction made me think Tal was more comfortable with her presence than mine. Something close to jealousy ignited inside me and I had to turn away to get a grip on myself. Absolutely nothing was going on with them. I knew that right down to my toes.

But that didn't stop the ache that formed in my chest at knowing he needed her more than me at that moment.

Stop it!

Talisen told me he loved me. He'd just been through a terrible ordeal. Whatever he needed, I'd make sure he got it. I turned back around, listening in on their conversation.

"Nicola and I think we can perform a spell to help us track your boss."

Tal raised a skeptical eyebrow. "I've never heard you talk about a tracking spell before."

She shrugged. "They're highly unpredictable and dangerous if the witch doesn't know what she's doing. I've cast a few while in Void training and Nicola was present once when her grandmother cast one, so she knows what they're supposed to feel like. We've worked together enough this past week that I think we'll be okay to at least try it. But I need something to tie us to him. Do you have anything at all that belonged to him at one point?"

Tal frowned and rubbed a hand over his face. "There are a ton of items at the lab."

Phoebe shook her head. "Can't. There's a team of at least three men watching the place in case one of us shows up looking for your new drug."

"There are?" We hadn't seen any earlier.

Phoebe cast a glance in my direction. "Yeah. I have a contact at the campus keeping me informed. They were there when we were, but thanks to our undercover mission, we went through unnoticed. It's too late for that sort of thing now. There aren't enough students to help us blend into the crowd."

Tal eyed us both and I knew he wanted to know what we'd been doing there, but he didn't ask. Instead he reached into his pocket and pulled out a worn black leather wallet. "Here." He handed Phoebe a battered business card. "He gave me this the day I interviewed."

Her eyes lit up like she'd just been presented with a new set of vampire cuffs. Or a supercharged sun agate. "Perfect. This is more than perfect. Thanks." She stood and smiled down at him. "Rest up, Talisen. We're going to need you in about thirty minutes."

"Thirty minutes!" I cried and ran forward. "No. Tal needs—"

"Willow," Tal cut me off. "I'm not broken. I just need a few minutes to myself."

I'd never seen him appear so shattered before, so depleted and on the edge of life, yet determined to force his way through whatever came next. His condition had to be hard for him to accept. I nodded once, not meeting his eyes.

"We'll be in the library if you need anything." Phoebe held the business card at the very edge with two fingers and joined me in the next room. "Try not to worry so much," she said to me.

"Easy for you to say," I grumbled.

"Actually, no. It isn't. I like Talisen. And he's important to you. So I'm worried not only about him, but you, too."

I gave her a weak smile.

"Try to remember he's in love with you. He doesn't want you nursing him or seeing him like that." Her lips quirked up into a knowing smile. "Imagine what it's doing to his ego."

I bit back a tiny surprised laugh. She was right. He was usually putting me back together, not the other way around. And to top it off, this was his skill. The thing that set him apart from everyone else. To seem so *broken* in front of everyone must be killing him inside.

"Okay. I'll stop treating him like an invalid. But I swear to the Goddess, if he rushes into something he can't handle because of what that vamp did to him, I'll kill him myself."

She laughed and shook her head. "Whatever you say, Wil."

My running shoes squeaked on the hardwood floors while Phoebe walked soundlessly. "What kind of soles are on those boots?"

"Leather. Why?"

"I don't get how you can be so quiet."

She grinned. "Silencing spell. It comes in handy for a tracker."

Witches. Was there nothing she couldn't do?

I flexed my wings, lifting myself a few inches off the ground, and flew beside her down the long corridor.

"Feel better?" she asked.

"Yes," I said smugly. I didn't have fancy spells, but I had my own talents.

Outside the library, I frowned at the raised voices inside. "What in the world is going on in there?"

"One way to find out." Phoebe yanked the door open and everyone inside turned to stare at us.

I felt the blood drain from my face as I stared right into the angry eyes of my vampire ex David.

Chapter 21

Nicola, barely five foot two, was standing between David and Harrison, her arms held out as if she could keep them from ripping each other apart.

"I told you to stay away from her," David roared. "And not only did you disobey a direct order, you almost got her abducted."

"David!" I ran forward and yanked on his arm. He didn't budge, but Harrison backed up.

"I had nothing to do with her showing up," Harrison said in a cold, hard voice. "She came after the fae all on her own."

David stared down at me. I cocked a defiant eyebrow. "Why did you go without backup?" he asked.

"Not that it's any of your business, but I had Phoebe and Link."

He glanced around the room and then fixed me once again with his intense gaze. "It's always been my business. But as soon as you brought everyone back here, you solidified that argument."

"Oh, shut up, David." I dropped his arm and backed up. Would he ever stop pretending to be a dominating asshole? Or had his vampireness really turned him into this hardened shell of his former self?

Phoebe chuckled at my response to David. "I called in Nicola and Harrison, remember? She was hardly without backup." She turned to Nicola. "Are you up for some serious spell work?"

"Absolutely." Nicola secured her wispy blond hair into a clip, left her place near the sunroom door, and joined Phoebe in the middle of the room.

I ignored everyone and headed for the glass door. Inside, the vampire sat stoically peering at the door, though I knew he couldn't see us. It was a two-way mirror and a button needed to be pushed before those in the inside could see into the study. The two humans were still knocked out. I had a moment of wondering if they'd ever recover, but then one of them twitched in his unconscious state.

They'd be fine...eventually.

"Has anyone interrogated them yet?" David said from a few feet behind me.

For the second time in ten minutes I nearly jumped out of my skin. "Don't do that."

A ghost of a smile flashed on his face but quickly disappeared. "Sorry. Vampire hazard."

Phoebe and Nicola started a low chant, something in Latin. I fixated on the pair and the business card levitating in front of them.

The longer I stood next to David, the angrier I became. The knowledge that he wanted me to turn Allcot into a daywalker had fled my mind while we were trying to find Tal, but now that he was safe, I couldn't block out the implications of what David wanted me to do. Finally I grabbed his arm. "We need to talk."

He didn't put up a fight. Why should he? I wasn't a threat to him. If he didn't want to go, all he had to do was stand there like a marbled statue. But he followed along, pretending to let me march him out of the room.

It only pissed me off more.

I avoided the living room where Tal was and instead stormed into David's bedroom. Again.

He followed and closed his door with a soft click.

I rounded on him, fluttering off the ground a few inches. "Explain yourself. What did Harrison mean you turned because of me?" Shit. Where had that come from? I'd intended to ask him about Allcot. Instead my subconscious was stuck on why he'd turned vampire. Why couldn't I let that go? I hadn't wanted him to turn vamp. Hell, I hadn't even known it was an option. I'd had no idea Allcot was his father until after he'd already turned. "I didn't have anything to do with this." I waved a hand at his solid form.

He nodded solemnly. "You're right. You didn't."

"Then why was Harrison so pissed off? Allcot coerced you, didn't he? Did he know I possessed this power?" A bolt of betrayal wound through me, and I trembled with frustrated energy.

His deep, midnight-blue eyes bored into mine and then something soft, almost tender flickered over his features. "I already told you Father didn't force me." He paused and seemed to gather his thoughts. "I'm sorry, Wil. I know I've left you in the dark for entirely too long. But believe me when I say I was only trying to protect you."

My fingers curled tightly into his crisp gray button-down shirt, my nails digging straight through the fabric and into my palm. "Stop keeping things from me." I gazed up at him, imploring him to finally let me into his secret world and all he thought he had to keep hidden.

After a long pause, he nodded. "I'll tell you as much as I can."

I shook my head. "Everything, David. I don't want to do this anymore. There are enough people trying to control me. I can't be wondering if you're one of them, too."

He raised his hand and cupped my cheek. The gesture was so tender and heartfelt that I couldn't bring myself to step away.

"Everything," he said.

I returned his intense stare. Would he really tell me the truth this time? Our entire relationship was built on lies. I was afraid that no matter what he said, I'd still be suspicious.

"Give me one more chance, Wil?"

I held back the natural inclination to cringe at his use of my nickname. He used to call me Wil all the time, but once we'd broken up and he'd turned vamp, it was too painful to hear him use the endearment. I knew it was stupid. What difference did it make if he called me Wil or Willow? After what happened, I shouldn't be talking to him at all. And yet, we were intimately connected since the night I'd turned him into a daywalker. I didn't think I could ever truly shut him out for good. Not unless he abducted me and forced me to turn his father. Then I'd probably find a way to cut his presence from my heart and soul.

"All right. But if I find out you held anything back, anything about me or my family, it's the end of whatever this is." I waved a hand between us, indicating our odd relationship. "My trust can only be stretched so far."

"That's fair," he said, his tone serious.

"Okay then." I moved across the room to a chenille armchair.

David walked slowly, keeping his gaze riveted to a spot over my head.

I glanced back, but only saw a darkened window. Was someone out there? I waited to see if he would say something before I asked. He didn't. Sitting in the chair next to mine, he leaned forward with his elbows on his knees and shifted his attention to the pristine white carpet. Then that piercing blue gaze met mine once more.

"Harrison's right. I never wanted to turn vampire."

The blunt statement made me blink. My mouth hung open in shock. Not because I was surprised by the truth behind his words, but that he'd actually come out and said it. I *had* known him. Had known he'd never wanted that life. "Then you were forced. One way or another, you were manipulated into this. I *knew* it." All the rage I'd built up throughout the day came bubbling up in my throat, and my next words were ground out with fierce venom. "Allcot's a monster. He was never your father. A father wouldn't do this to his son."

David's eyes never left mine. If they had, I would've missed the tiny hint of pity swimming in their depths.

"Don't do that," I said, my voice low. "Don't feel sorry for me because of your choices."

"I'm not."

"Then what was that look about? Do you think I don't understand politics or how ruthless your father is? Because I do. I work in a political organization, remember? I see it every freakin' day."

He pitched forward until our knees were almost touching. "No. That's not it." He cleared his throat, though I knew there was nothing to clear. It was a nervous tic I hadn't noticed before. "I already told you that I chose to become vampire. That wasn't a lie."

"No? Allcot probably gave you a choice, and turning was the lesser of two evils, right?" I didn't believe for a minute he wasn't manipulated.

He frowned. "No. That's not it at all."

"Then spit it out!"

"Dammit, Willow. I did it for you."

"What?" I sat back in the chair, stunned. "Why?"

He stood up and started to pace the room. This was an action I was familiar with. I'd seen David do this dozens of times when he was trying to find the words to tell me something. It took all my effort to hold my tongue, to not demand more answers.

I clutched my arms around my knees and waited.

David stopped abruptly and leaned against the casing of the window across from me. He crossed his feet at the ankle the exact same way Allcot had done earlier in the day. The gesture startled me. It was harmless yet stood as a stark reminder that no matter how much I wanted to believe David was different because he was adopted, he really was Allcot's son. "I already told you I'd been assigned to keep an eye on you when we first met over a year ago."

I nodded and tried to push down the hurt that pierced my heart. He'd only dated me to get close enough to protect me from Asher. It was a shitty thing to do to a girl. I'd fallen in love with him and then one day, he disappeared. Talk about a dick move. He might have protected me physically for a while, but he'd shattered my heart. If it wasn't for Talisen, I was certain I'd still be picking up the pieces.

Talisen. I took a deep breath. We were supposed to be finding his boss, not dealing with this bullshit history. But now that David was finally talking, I couldn't bring myself to walk away.

"Willow?" David's voice pulled me out of my haze.

"Yes?"

"In late spring, before you left for California, we started getting word of Asher taking an interest in you. Then the death threats surfaced. Father wanted to take me off the case and dedicate a couple of our trained guards to watch over you. But I couldn't let that happen. This was Asher's people we were talking about. I couldn't risk losing you."

"Okay. You wanted to keep looking out for me. So?"

"It wasn't enough." He took two strides and knelt down in front of me. "Don't you see? I couldn't let humans try to protect you from Asher. He's too dangerous."

"But you were human, too…" *Oh no. No, no, no.* My insides turned to ice and I shivered. "Are you saying you turned to protect me?"

"Yes."

I jumped out of the chair, my finger pointed at him. "What in the world were you thinking? How could you do such a thing?" Tears burned my eyes and I did nothing to stop them from spilling down my cheeks. "You ruined your life. For me. Why? Dammit. Why?" The words came out choked through my sobs.

Though he'd been taking pains to not touch me, he got to his feet and gently circled his fingers around my wrists. "You know why, Wil. I love you. It was the best way to keep you safe."

"Not like this." I ripped my hands from his grasp and pounded my fists on his chest. "We would've found another way. You shouldn't have sacrificed yourself for me."

"You're not hearing me," he whispered in my ear.

"I heard you," I shouted. "You turned in order to fight off a psychotic vampire who wants me dead."

"But you're not hearing why." His voice was a soft caress against my cheek.

I wiped the tears from my eyes and met his intense gaze one more time. "Why?"

"Because I knew I couldn't live without you. And I couldn't live with myself if I ever let anything harm you. This was my choice. Once I turned vampire, I could choose my own path. It gave me the freedom to work with you and protect you and myself from the most dangerous among us. As a human, Father wasn't willing to risk his only son. As a vampire, it's considered a duty to protect what is ours."

"What is ours? Do you think of me as *yours?*" I took a step back, wondering what exactly this all meant. Was I vampire property now? Never. What he did for me was incredibly unselfish, but also crazy. No one should ever turn vamp for someone else. Guilt hit me like a wave of thick summer humidity, weighing me down. All this time I'd been so angry at him, when all he'd wanted to do was keep me safe.

"Of course not. But in the vampire world, you are mine in their eyes. It's sort of like a territorial claim."

I opened my mouth to argue the ridiculousness of his point, but he held a hand up, stopping me. "You belong to no one. Never have and never will. But try to understand that by playing along this is an easy way to keep you safe from at least some of the rogues. No one wants to fight Cryrique. And everyone at Cryrique knows the boss's son will kill anyone who messes with you. Think of the situation as a friend watching over another friend."

I understood what he was saying. David had never treated me as if I belonged to him. Not while he'd been human and not while he'd been vampire either. He'd only tried to keep me safe. I owed him something for that. But still…"David, you can't imagine how incredibly overwhelmed I am. What you sacrificed for me…it's crazy. I don't think I can get over the fact that you gave up your life for mine."

"I didn't give up my life. I chose eternal life for you."

I stared up into his soft gaze and the tears started to flow silently again.

Very softly, he brushed his thumbs over my cheeks, wiping away the tears. Then he lifted my chin so our gazes met. "I have no regrets. I'd do it again today."

Then he leaned down and brushed his lips over mine.

Chapter 22

"Don't cry, Wil," David murmured against my tingling lips. The marbled softness made my toes curl with anticipation. "I won't let anything happen to you."

His words brought me back to myself and I jerked, clasping my hand over my disappointed mouth. Shame and dread made my stomach ache. What was I doing? Omigod. What would Tal do when he found out? I crossed my arms over my chest defensively. "Don't ever do that again. I'm with Talisen."

Desperate to focus on something else…anything else, I stalked across the room and picked up the crumpled paper still laying on the floor. "You have five seconds to start talking before I call Allcot myself."

David's lips quirked up into a wry twinge of a smile. "I'm sure Father would love to hear from you, but if you call him, he won't have any idea what you're talking about."

"You're saying this is your idea?" My head was spinning. Nothing was making sense. Not his words and definitely not my conflicting emotions. I wanted him. But that was wrong. I was with Talisen.

"Yes. That's exactly what I'm saying." He held out his hand for the directive. I reluctantly handed it to him and took a few steps back, putting distance between us. He smoothed the paper out and folded it over so we were only looking at the typed writing. "You see this?" He pointed to the first line.

Recruit blood donors. I shrugged. "Seems like a normal activity. Vamps need to eat."

"And you don't have a problem with it?" The skepticism in his voice wasn't lost on me.

"I'm not thrilled about it, but volunteers are better than the alternative."

"Are they?"

I sent him a flat look. "What are you trying to say?"

He held the paper out again. "Read the second line."

Retire blood donors. "Okay. So?"

"You have no idea what happens to the retirees, do you?"

I shrugged again. "I haven't really thought about it."

"Ever met anyone who was retired from the lifestyle?"

His meaning started to sink in and my heart dropped through my stomach as nausea started to take over. "You mean...?" I couldn't even say the words. It was too horrible. My voice rose to a near shout. "And that's your *job*?"

He nodded sadly. "Donors go one of two ways. They either turn or they expire."

My hand flew to my throat as I took another step back. "And you just kill them?"

He held his hands up in a horrified motion. "No! God no. I'd never do that."

"But you said..." I was more confused than ever.

"I didn't mean I killed them. Not the way you mean." He clamped his lips together in a grim line. "Fuck," he mumbled. "Vampires never talk about this, but when donors volunteer, it usually means they want to be turned. Or if they don't when they sign up, they usually do after years of service. They get used to being taken care of. And for most of them, it's the best life they've ever known. But that's not saying much, is it? Who volunteers? People who come from desperate situations. Those without resources. The ones who would otherwise end up working the streets. You can see how they'd think the life Father gives them is generous."

"Until they die." My tone was harsh and full of judgment. It wasn't directed at David, but the hurt that crossed his features told me he'd taken it that way. I bit my lip and glanced at the floor. He'd chosen this life of death. And even worse, he'd chosen it for me. I was a life faery. How could he have ever thought I'd think his decision was the right one?

"Yes. Until they die." David's voice was soft, full of regret. "The longer they serve vampires, the harder it is for their bodies to continue to recover. Often the only solution is to turn them. But you know not everyone survives the change, especially those who are weak."

"And so Cryrique uses every donor until their bodies start to give out, then they try to turn them with minimal success? That's fucked up."

David straightened and his solid take-command presence was back in full force. "You're right. And that's what I'm trying to change."

I narrowed my eyes and really studied him. I'd always known David to be empathetic, the guy who was driven to do the right thing. Was he really trying to change the course of these people's lives? "How does getting me to change Allcot into a daywalker fit into the picture?"

His blue gaze flashed with fierce conviction. "You can't possibly understand what it's like to turn vampire—"

"I think I have a pretty good idea. Vampires drain my life energy, remember? I can imagine what it's like to go through life without that inner force."

David nodded slowly. "Okay, maybe you do have an idea then. It's a lot more gradual with vampires, though. When I first turned, all the changes were physical. I was still me inside. My thoughts were still that of a human. It's one of the reasons I had to cut off our relationship so abruptly."

I froze. We'd never talked about how he'd broken up with me. After three months of no explanation, all he'd said was he had his reasons. Once I'd learned he was the adopted son of Allcot, I assumed that was as good a reason as any. I wasn't really known for my acceptance of vampires. Fae and vamps definitely did *not* get along like peas and carrots.

"I still wanted you in every way," David continued quietly, and I saw the truth shining in his tortured eyes. "But I knew I couldn't control my bloodlust, so I had to do what was best to keep you safe."

My heart was going to pound right out of my chest. Everything he'd done had been because he loved me. It was so clear and easy to see now that he'd shed his hardened shell. He took my hand and tugged me down to sit at the end of his bed. He appeared so vulnerable, staring at me with his heart in his hands. And though I wanted to wrap my arms around him, pull him close and show him that through it all, I had loved him, that I loved him still, I couldn't.

There was a hole in my chest where he'd lied to me for over a year. He hadn't just stumbled into my shop that spring day. It hadn't been an accident that we'd met or that we'd ended up dating. Everything had been calculated from the beginning. And worse, he'd known the details of my brother's death and never told me. Even though I believed he was being truthful with his confession, I didn't trust him completely. Not the way I did Talisen.

I loved Tal with everything I had. And he loved me—even if he had been a jerk after I'd done everything in my power to find him. He was just upset. Who wouldn't be after such an ordeal? I couldn't let David's confession come between us now. Not when we were just getting started. Another dart of pain stabbed me. How was Tal? Shouldn't I be checking on him?

"After a while," David continued, "that human side of me it started to fade a bit. I was still me at the core I think, but lines were starting to blur. I was…desensitized. Imagine what that would feel like for a century-old vampire, or one older?"

Desensitized. That was the exact word I would've used to describe David after I'd finally met him in his vampire form. He'd hardened. There hadn't been shades of gray in his world. Everything was black or white.

"Except now, after you turned me into a daywalker, I feel like that piece I lost is back somehow." David's lips turned up into a slight smile. "You gave me more than the ability to see the sun again. You gave me life."

His words and voice washed over me in a soft caress. I'd given him life. Of course I had. I'd given him a part of myself. But I hadn't known it would affect him on a psychological level. Emotion welled in my chest until I thought I'd burst. He given his life for me and in a way, I'd given it back to him.

"Thank you," he said.

I still couldn't form words, so I shook my head, denying his need to thank me for anything. I'd do it again. I had no regrets. Especially now that I knew why he'd turned. No matter how misguided I felt his decision was, he'd done it out of unselfish love. I placed a hand on top of his and squeezed lightly. Then I pulled away and clasped my hands in my lap, too overwhelmed to say or do anything else.

After a beat, David reached over and tilted my head up until our eyes met. "It's what I want for Father."

My mouth fell open in a shocked O. This time I had no trouble forming words. "You want me to give Allcot a piece of myself?"

He frowned. "That's not exactly what I meant, but considering that's how you changed me, I guess that is what I'm asking."

All the understanding between us fled, and I jumped to my feet, ready to stalk out of the room. When I'd turned David, it had almost cost me my life. Was his father so important he'd risk my safety? My spine tingled with the anger sparking beneath my skin. "I'm not a fucking chemistry set, David. What you're asking…it's…Well, it's dangerous. Not just for me, but for the whole city. What happens to me when people find out? Will I be hunted to turn more vamps, or will the Arcane lock me up? Or maybe the humans will come after me. If vampires are suddenly daywalkers, where does that leave the humans? Even lower on the race totem pole. They wouldn't even have the daylight to be safe from rogue vampires." He'd lost his mind. I was going to need to find a vampire psych ward and have him committed. Visions of padded walls with fang-mark punctures filled my mind.

He stood and gazed down at me, that soft understanding still shining in his eyes. "I know it sounds crazy. But can you hear me out?"

I didn't want to hear him out. I didn't want him trying to convince me of something that was so personal, that would take so much from me. But when I gazed up at him, so unvampire-like, so much like the gentleman I'd fallen for, I found it hard to form the word no.

He took it as an opening and tugged me to the far wall. Mounted and framed black-and-white pictures were staggered in a rectangular formation. "See this?" He pointed to one with a young boy of only five or six standing ankle-deep in the ocean, splashing water with a squeal of glee on his face. "And this one?" The picture to the right had the same young boy curled up on a blanket next to a woman gazing down at him with adoring eyes.

"That's you, isn't it?" I ran a finger over the frame. "Is this your mother?"

David nodded. "Look at the one to the left."

This time young David was sitting on an ornate settee, sleeping snuggled up next to a young man with light hair. The man had his arm around David and was gazing down at him with the same tender expression his mother had in the previous picture.

"And that's your father?"

David smiled, with light shining in his eyes. "You could say that. Look closer."

I frowned and leaned in. Recognition made me gasp. The clothes, the expression, the lighter hair, and the love shining through, all were so foreign from the man I knew today. There wasn't even a hint of the all-encompassing cockiness that seemed to be at the core of Allcot. This was a young man who loved his son and wanted to see him safe. "Why are you showing me this?"

David pulled another frame off the wall. This one was of David tinkering with a car. He couldn't have been more than ten. "This was the night Allcot officially became my father. My mother had died three months earlier. It was cancer. Incurable. We all knew it was coming. He'd loved her as a sister. Besides Pandora, she was his only trusted friend and in her will, she asked him to be my guardian." He stroked the edge of the frame. "He begged her to let him turn her, you know. At the time, I hated her for her decision. I hated him, too, for letting her die." Pain lined his face as the memories overtook him. "She was the only person I had in the world and he'd let her die."

I stopped breathing. David had never talked about his mother except to say she'd died when he was young and that's how he'd come to Allcot. I knew instinctively he hadn't opened up to anyone else in a very long time. "I can see how that could make a ten-year-old very angry."

David cut his gaze to mine. "I was angry for many years. You see, I didn't just lose my mother that day. I lost the only father I'd ever known."

I furrowed my brows. "You've never talked about your real father before."

He scoffed. "That's because I've never met the bastard. I'm talking about Eadric."

"What do you mean, you lost him? You've been at his side ever since."

He shook his head sadly. "In physical form yes, but the person he was with my mother died right along with her." He sat down heavily in a leather chair and glanced up at me with sad eyes. "She was his best friend. The one he counted on to keep him human. Without her, he let the darkness creep in. I didn't know it then. All I saw was an angry, unrecognizable man."

"And you want me to give him back his light." It wasn't a question. I already knew the answer, but he nodded anyway, hope clear in his pained expression. The desire to nod, to give him the answer he was desperately searching for, filled every inch of my chest. It squeezed my heart and formed a lump in my throat. How could I deny David this one request? He'd revealed more of himself to me in the last thirty minutes than he had in our yearlong relationship. And in that moment, all the pain I carried from our failed relationship fled.

He was hurting more than I was, and he'd keep on hurting for centuries for his choices. I knew rationally that I wasn't responsible for his turning, but it still weighed on me. It was because of me. I owed him something. I just didn't know if I could give him what he wanted. I cleared my throat and offered him my hands.

He grabbed them, holding me tenderly, never once breaking our gaze.

"Is it enough for me to say I'll think about it?"

A soft whoosh of air escaped from his lips and I stifled a laugh. Vamps didn't need to breathe, but he'd been holding his breath anyway. His shoulders visibly relaxed as he gently squeezed my fingers. "It's more than enough."

Chapter 23

I sat in one of the wingback chairs, studying David. Seeing him appear so *human* brought memories crashing to the forefront of my mind. And chief among them was the first day we'd met.

I'd been heading from my office to my lab when Tami, my assistant, poked her head into the hall. "Willow! Can you give me a hand for a sec?"

"Sure." I grabbed an apron, and as I entered the front of the store, I winced. A mother stood at the counter, her five kids running full tilt around the rest of the customers waiting in line.

"Where's Georgie?" I asked.

"Lunch." Tami stuffed a dozen Truth Clusters into a bag and started ringing up her customer.

I stepped around her to help the next patron and stopped in my tracks. Holy fae. The human man in front of me had the deepest midnight-blue eyes I'd ever seen, complemented by long, dark eyelashes. I licked my lips unconsciously and cleared my throat, praying he hadn't noticed my ogling.

But then his lips broke into an amused smile that reached those lovely eyes. Whoa. Dark, slightly curling hair, strong angular jaw, broad shoulders, slim through the hips, and the only flaw I could find was a small scar just below his bottom lip. Someone had superior genes.

"Good afternoon," he said in a slight Southern drawl. Local boy for sure.

"Hi," I forced out and stared. *Good God, Willow, get a grip. There's a line of people waiting.*

The cash register drawer slammed closed and I realized Tami had finished helping the mom with the hellions and had already moved on to the next customer. And I hadn't even taken this guy's order yet.

"What can I get for you today?" I smiled brightly.

His gaze flickered over the bakery case and then he pointed to what I'd named Happy Cookies. The frosting-covered sugar cookies were the only things we sold that weren't magically altered. I just thought the sprinkles and bright yellow frosting made them look happy. "Two dozen, please."

"Sure." I busied myself packing the cookies in a box, trying to keep my attention focused on the task, but my gaze kept wandering to those gorgeous eyes. It was almost cruel to bless a man with such beauty.

"Hot!" Tami whispered as she scrambled by me to the mocha machine.

I nodded, trying to keep a straight face.

"Anything else?" I asked him and placed the boxes in a two-handled bag. "Molten Muse or some Kiss Me chocolates?" *Oh crap.* Why had I offered *those*? Heat crawled up my face.

He raised his eyebrows and his lips twitched in amusement again. "Those Kiss Me chocolates, are those for me to eat or the person I wish would kiss me?"

"Uh…" I let out a nervous giggle. "The other person." My face burned hotter and I wondered how long it would be before I combusted.

He nodded thoughtfully. "Okay, then. I'll try one and see how it works out."

Of course he had someone he already wanted. I frowned. Why would *he* need Kiss Me chocolates? Whoever the woman was, she should get her head checked if she needed a nudge to lock lips with this one.

I kept the smile pasted on my face, added the Kiss Me treat to a small bag, and slid over to the register. "Ready?"

He shook his head. "Can I get a Mocha in Motion as well?"

"Sure." I spun, almost crashing right into Tami. "Sorry!"

She smirked and shook her head, obviously holding back laughter.

"Shut up," I hissed before she said anything that would make me want to hide under the counter.

"Did I say anything?"

"You were thinking it." A minute later, I handed Mr. Gorgeous Eyes his drink.

"Thank you," he said, handing me a card to pay for his purchases.

I smiled. "That's my line."

He waited patiently while I fumbled around with the credit card machine and when we were done, he tilted his head and eyed me appreciatively. "Nice wings."

I felt my wings spread with pride and knew I must be blushing again…or was it still? Faeries weren't all that common in New Orleans. We usually preferred heavily forested areas, so I was used to being stared at. But the way he studied me sent tingles to all the right places and made me squirm.

"Thanks," I said, almost shyly.

"Ahem!" the woman behind him huffed. "I'm in a hurry."

"Excuse me, I didn't mean to hold anyone up," he said to the woman in line and nodded a good-bye before he headed out the door.

I did my best to not shoot eye daggers at the woman. She was a customer, after all. But I hadn't seen such a lovely male specimen in months. It was a shame to rush him off. I sucked up my resentment and hurried to fill the woman's order.

An hour later, with the store finally empty of customers, I did a cursory sweep of the lobby and stepped outside to check the sidewalk tables.

All but one was empty.

"Hello again," Mr. Gorgeous Eyes said, leaning back in his chair.

"Oh." I sucked in a breath as my pulse quickened. He had an air of easy confidence about him. "You're still here. Enjoying the afternoon?"

He picked up the tiny bag I'd stuffed the Kiss Me chocolate in. "I was waiting for that girl."

"*Oh,*" I said again, a tremor of disappointment flashing through me.

He waved to the empty chair. "Have a seat?"

"But what about your date? Won't she be here soon?"

"No date." His eyes crinkled as he squinted into the sun. "I took a chance, hoping she'd show up here."

Poor bastard had it bad. It would be almost pathetic, except he didn't look upset in the least. I shrugged. "Sure, for a minute."

He held out his hand. "I'm David."

"Willow." Our hands met and I swear electricity jump-started my heart, making it skip a beat.

"Nice to meet you," he said.

"Likewise."

We sat in silence for a moment until he started chuckling.

"What's so funny?" I frowned, glancing around.

"Me. I was trying to figure out a way to offer you this," he said, holding up the tiny Kiss Me chocolate bag, "but I seemed to have misplaced all my moves."

"Your moves? I..." What did he just say? "You bought that chocolate to give to me?"

"Yeah." He laughed. "Any chance you'll take me up on it?"

"Um..." Heat crawled up my neck. What was I supposed to say to that?

Shaking his head in mock sorrow, he put it away. "That's what I thought. How about we try dinner instead?"

"Dinner?" I seemed to have lost my ability to form coherent sentences.

"Dinner," he said firmly. "Friday?"

For some reason, I found myself nodding. Why was I agreeing to this? I just met him. Easy answer. He was nice, too gorgeous for his own good, and I hadn't had a date in months.

"Great." He handed me a business card and a pen. "Write down your address and I'll pick you up at seven."

A moment later, I grinned and handed the card back to him. "Just so you know, my roommate is a witch. If you're a crazy stalker or serial killer, she'll find ways to make you suffer that you've never dreamed of."

"Noted." He held his hand out again. "Nice to meet you, Willow."

A spark ran through my fingers as my hand met his. "You, too. See you Friday."

"Count on it." He nodded and took off down the sidewalk. A few feet later he turned and held up the bag. "Do you think I'll need this?"

Laughing, I shook my head and disappeared back into my shop.

The sound of David moving around the room brought me back to myself. He was much more serious now that he'd turned vampire, but underneath his statuesque armor, he was still that sweet, thoughtful guy I'd met so many months before.

He hadn't turned into that douche who'd dumped me by text message. He'd been doing his best to protect me.

I stood, and feeling as if David and I had formed some sort of real connection, I walked side by side with him back to the library. He'd let me in and bared his vulnerability. A barrier had been blasted away and I finally understood the motivation behind all his recent actions.

And all the conflicting emotions running through me made me nauseated. How could I let David kiss me with Tal a few feet away in the living room, trying to recover from his horrific ordeal? David had initiated the kiss, but my entire being had responded to him. I blinked back hot, angry tears, knowing deep down I'd wanted him.

What was I doing? I was a terrible person.

I slowed, letting David go ahead of me, and trailed a few paces behind him. I needed some sort of buffer.

He paused and glanced back at me. "Everything okay?"

I nodded, not trusting myself to speak.

He didn't move. "You sure?"

"Yeah," I forced out and pointed to the restroom across the hall. "Excuse me." My shoes echoed in the silence and the click of the door closing rang in my ears. I leaned forward, pressing my hands to the marble vanity, and focused on breathing.

Okay. I could get through this. We'd had a very stressful day and David had caught me off guard by being so open with me. My emotions were running too high and too close to the surface. It was time to focus on what we needed to do. And that was to find Talisen's boss.

We should have been able to call the Void and have them deal with the abduction. Why did we have to be suspicious of everyone all the time? Would there ever be a day when I didn't have to hide what I could do?

No.

The answer was clear and definite. If the vampire world found out about my abilities, I'd be tracked by more vamps than I could imagine. Unless I wanted to be confined to a lab and strapped to electrodes indefinitely, I couldn't tell the Void either.

It meant we'd have to deal with Asher on our own. Terror edged out my guilt and the nausea intensified.

Another deep breath. My eyes were wide with dark circles lining them. I almost looked as haggard as Talisen had. Almost, but not quite. I turned the faucet on and splashed cold water on my face. It didn't do anything other than give me a little more time to myself. All I wanted to do was curl up in my bed under the oak with Link and a cup of hot chocolate laced with Soothing Peppermint.

The hot chocolate was out for now, but Link was here. I pulled the door open and whistled. Seconds later, he barreled down the hallway and then sat at attention, focusing on me.

My heart clenched, knowing I could always count on him and he never caused me any drama. "You're such a good boy, Link."

His tail thumped rhythmically against the wood floor.

I reached down and he jumped effortlessly into my arms. His warm body instantly settled me. I buried my head into his fur, grateful for his unconditional love as he pressed closer. Nothing could be more pure and uncomplicated than the love of a dog, wolf or not.

"Wil?" Tal asked from the other end of the hall.

I turned, still clutching Link. "You're up," I said, eyeing him. He still looked too thin, but the color had returned to his skin and he was standing taller, more assured than he had thirty minutes ago.

"What's wrong?" he asked.

I shook my head. I couldn't tell him about David. I would, but now wasn't the time. Not when we had a job to do. "I just needed a moment."

Yeah, a moment to wallow in self-pity. What was he going to say when he found out?

Link wiggled, trying to get to Talisen. My dog had a serious crush on Tal. I kissed the top of his head and gently placed him on the floor. He leaped and in three bounds landed in Tal's arms, his tongue lapping at Tal's cheek while his body wiggled in uncontrollable excitement.

"Looks like he's pleased you're feeling better." I stuffed my hands in my front pockets.

"He's not the only one." Tal shifted to stand next to me, letting our shoulders touch. "Are you sure there's nothing wrong? If it's the way I acted earlier, I'm sorry. I didn't mean to snap at you. You have to know that."

I sent him a too-bright smile. "I know. Don't worry. I'm just stressed about not being able to go home or to work and being stuck at a vampire's house."

He wrapped his arm around my waist and pulled me close. His familiar woodsy scent filled my senses, and I had to bite down hard on my lower lip to keep from blurting out my transgression. "We're going to get through this." He kissed the top of my head, the gesture so gentle and loving. One single tear spilled down my cheek. He gazed down at me and gently wiped the moisture with his thumb. He didn't say anything else as he embraced me, hugging me to him and Link.

Link turned his head and licked my ear.

"Hey!" I cried as I pulled back, laughing. "He gave me a wet willy."

Talisen chuckled. "Good one, Link."

"It's not funny." But I couldn't keep the smile off my face.

"Yes it is." He lifted one of Link's paws and gave him a high five. "Way to go, buddy. You broke your mom's gloomy mood."

I smirked and wiped at my ear. "Yeah, but don't get any ideas about making that a habit."

Tal whispered something to Link that made his tail wag faster.

"Stop conspiring, you two." I swatted at Tal. Link pulled back, giving me the evil doggy glare.

"Uh oh, your dog is turning on you."

I reached for Link. He shifted forward, waiting for me to take him again. "Looks like you lost, fae boy," I teased back.

Tal laughed as I hugged Link and kissed his head one last time before setting him on the floor again. My entire body relaxed. Tal was okay and we were standing in David's hallway, joking around as if nothing had happened the last twelve hours.

It gave me hope Tal would forgive me.

"Let's see if Phoebe has a line on Professor Dawson yet." Tal's fingers twined with mine and we headed back into the library. We waited near the book-lined walls, not wanting to interrupt. Phoebe and Nicola sat crossed-legged in the center of the room, their hands joined while they continued to chant. Had they been chanting this entire time? If so, their magic would be woven tightly and they'd have built a massive amount of power. I pressed closer to the bookshelf, a bit frightened of what they might be able to accomplish.

Across the room, David's stare bored into me. I did my best to ignore him, but my curiosity won out. As soon as my eyes met his, he cut his gaze to my hand, which was still twined with Talisen's. I frowned at him. What had he expected? For me to break things off with Tal just because he'd finally opened up and then kissed me?

The righteous anger I'd been carrying around ever since David had broken up with me by text came roaring back. He couldn't expect me to forgive all the ways he'd hurt me just because he'd ultimately had good intentions. Honesty would have gotten him a lot further. As it was, I was starting to trust him with my physical safety, but when it came to matters of the heart, he'd crushed mine one too many times.

I focused on Phoebe. A soft white light glowed around her, and as the pair chanted, it slowly crept its way over Nicola. I sucked in a surprised gasp.

"What?" Tal whispered.

"I think Phoebe's sharing her power with Nicola." I inclined my head. "Do you see that faint light engulfing them?"

He tilted his head and squinted. "Yeah."

"That's a magic meld. I've only ever seen it done once before. It's very invasive." I frowned. Why was Phoebe doing that? It would make them both more powerful, but was finding Tal's boss worth the risk? If Nicola wanted to, she could steal some of Phoebe's magic. And if Phoebe wasn't careful, the pair could be bound forever.

"Now!" Phoebe cried.

Nicola yanked her hands back at the same moment Phoebe raised hers skyward. Their chanting grew louder while Nicola fanned her arms to the side and slowly lifted her hands to join them once again with Phoebe's. As soon as their fingers touched, the small business card that had been sitting between them elevated and glowed with a bright white light that made me squint at its brilliance.

The card started to vibrate and then spun wildly in a circle, moving so fast it turned into a blur of white. Phoebe and Nicola lowered their arms and each scooted back, waiting to see what the card would do.

And just as suddenly as it had started spinning, it stopped. The card stayed elevated, vibrating slightly.

"It's ready." Phoebe got to her feet and smoothed her black T-shirt.

"What's it supposed to do?" Nicola asked.

"Point us to its owner."

Huh. With what? "Phoebs?"

"Yeah." She swayed on her feet.

I dropped Tal's hand and rushed to her. Placing a tentative hand on her arm, I frowned. "You used too much power already. This isn't going to work."

She shrugged me off. "I'll be all right. Trust me."

"I don't understand," Nicola said, still eyeing the business card. "How is it going to tell us where to go?"

"You'll see. Now let's get moving before it loses its juice." Phoebe strode to the door and pointed at the card. It strained to move in the opposite direction but stayed in place. "See that? It wants to go north." She snapped her fingers and the business card zoomed to her side. "Let's go."

I followed her and she paused, her head tilted to the side in contemplation.

"What?" I asked, knowing exactly what she was going to say.

"Maybe you and Tal should stay here."

"Phoebe—"

"I know. You feel obligated to go. And in your shoes, I would, too. But you're a target. We don't know who we're going to run into, wherever this trek leads us. I can't help wondering if it's safer for you to stay in David's lair while we find this guy, and then we can make a plan to get you out of this mess when we get back."

"I'm going," Tal said with grave finality.

"I'm going wherever Tal goes," I added.

He put his arm around my shoulder and as if on cue, Link sat down between our feet, facing Phoebe, his bottom teeth jutting out in defiance.

I had to stifle a laugh. Could he be any cuter?

Phoebe rolled her eyes. "Fine. But keep your heads down."

Talisen opened his mouth, probably to defend us, but I clutched his arm and shook my head. It wasn't worth arguing. We were both incredibly skilled fae, but not in combat. She had a right to be worried. Not that her fear was going to keep me locked away from the fight. I did have Link and the stun gun.

Nicola swept past us, catching up with Phoebe. She immediately started peppering Phoebe with questions about the spell they'd just completed, no doubt hoping to learn from Phoebe's superior knowledge and experience. After we'd freed Nicola from the Influence she'd been drugged with, she'd been spending every spare moment with Phoebe, learning as much as possible in an effort to never be controlled again.

Honestly, I admired her tenacity. But it scared me. She worked for Allcot. The more she learned, the more powerful she'd become, and the last thing Eadric Allcot needed was more power over the city of New Orleans.

It's not her fault she's related to him.

She was Pandora's sister. Nicola didn't have any control over that. But how loyal was she to him? At the very least she was loyal to Pandora, and that alone made her untrustworthy. I hated that feeling. I liked Nicola. She was only trying to survive in a world she'd been forced into. It wasn't her fault Allcot and his ilk were corrupt.

We all trudged outside with David and Harrison following behind us. Phoebe pointed at me. "You and Tal take my car." She gestured to the pair behind us. "And those two can ride with Nicola and me."

David stared at me, but then his gaze shifted to Tal. "Don't you think she'd be safer with us?"

Tal's hand squeezed mine, making me almost wince. I pinched his side, letting him know that wasn't okay. He immediately relaxed his hand. "She'll be fine with Link and me in the Camry."

"Yeah, David," Phoebe said dryly. "They'll be in a two-ton vehicle. If anything comes at them, running it down won't be much of an issue. Stop trying to control everything she does. It's getting annoying." She turned on her heel and stalked toward the gold Suburban we'd commandeered earlier that night. She opened the back door and waved her hand. "Now get in before I decide to leave you here."

David glared at her. Harrison chuckled, not bothering to hide his amusement.

"Shut up, Harrison," David growled.

Harrison's grin widened. "What's wrong, Laveaux? I thought you were accustomed to taking orders. Or is it the fact she's female?"

Phoebe gestured to Harrison. "I like him."

"Of course you do," I said dryly.

The muscle in David's jaw pulsed and his entire body tensed. He pulled out his phone and quickly tapped out a text.

"That had better not have been a text to Allcot. I don't need him fucking this up," Phoebe said.

David shot her an irritated look. "Someone has to interrogate the prisoners. Father has the best chance of obtaining any useful information."

"And what happens when he's done with them?" I asked. A week ago Allcot had ordered the former Void director killed without letting the Void get their hands on him first. "Kill them?"

David shrugged. "Maybe. It depends on what they say."

Fuck. Just when I thought the old David was back, the new version reared his ugly head. Goddess, that pissed me off. Through clenched teeth I said, "Please tell him to do what it takes to get information on Asher but to not kill them. I have questions of my own."

David nodded and typed out another text, then he climbed into the Suburban.

Harrison followed him while Tal and I headed for Phoebe's Camry.

"Wil?" Phoebe called.

I reached for the driver's side handle and looked up at her. "Yeah?"

"Be careful."

"She'll be fine," Talisen answered for me.

I raised my eyebrows at Phoebe and jabbed my head toward Tal as if to say, "You heard him."

She held her hands up in front of her. "Okay. I got the message. Follow me, but don't make a move until I signal."

"What's the signal?"

"When it happens, you'll know."

Chapter 24

Following the Suburban down the dark street, I turned to Tal. "Thank you."

"For?"

"Sticking up for me." Everyone else had a habit of treating me like I was a liability instead of an asset. Tal never did that.

He turned in his seat until he was giving me his full attention. The moonlight shone in through the window, illuminating one narrowed eye. "I'm not so sure you *should* be going."

"What? Then why—"

"Do you think I want you anywhere near the people who did this to me? That I won't be distracted and worried about you while trying to find Dawson? That I'm not aware I was taken in order to lure you into their hands? Damn it, Wil, if I had my way, I'd have locked you up in David's house until this is all over. Or better yet, at Allcot's with your mom and Carrie."

I stomped on the brake, jerking both of us forward. Pain seared through my chest from the bite of the seatbelt. "Did you just say that I should put my lot in with Allcot?"

A horn blew from behind us. I ignored it.

"Hell no. I said I'd prefer it if you were locked away under his protection, because I know you. You're not going to sit back and let everyone fight your battles for you. Especially if those people are Phoebe and me."

"What does that mean, especially you and Phoebe?" I eased back onto the road, scanning ahead for the giant Suburban I was supposed to be following.

"You're not going to step aside while the people you care about are in danger."

Oh. Well, he had a point. "Neither would you." Ahead, the gold Suburban made a sharp right turn and I sped up to follow.

"No, but a lot of people would."

"Not everyone was cut out to wear a superhero cape," I joked.

He smiled and rested his foot across his knee. The casual posture turned him back into the laid-back Talisen I'd known my whole life. "Do you wear anything under that cape?"

My lips twitched. "Did you have something in mind?"

His low chuckle reverberated through me and went straight to my heart. "I think black lace has some possibilities."

My mouth went dry from the husky desire suddenly lacing his tone. I cleared my throat. "I'll take that under consideration."

We turned right again and stopped under a streetlamp. His emerald-green eyes sparkled with mischief. "On second thought, forget the cape. Just wear the lace."

Laughter bubbled from deep in my throat. "Are you implying I should fight the bad guys in my underwear?"

He reached over and smoothed my hair back, caressing my cheek in the process. "No, love. I'm imagining what it might be like if we ever find more than a few moments alone together."

A shiver ran down my spine and spread to my wings. I arched my neck, pressing into his fingers, reveling in his touch.

This was who I was meant to be with. Our connection, the way we understood each other, our history, the attraction. The shiver turned to chills as I realized what I'd be giving up if I let things get out of hand with David again. I'd have to tell Tal about that kiss if I wanted us to have a real chance at a relationship, but this wasn't the time. We were headed into unknown enemy territory and I couldn't have him distracted.

"We'll find out who's targeting you, Wil," Tal said, dropping the innuendo and staring at me with concern. "And we'll do whatever it takes to stop them."

I clamped my hand over his and squeezed. There weren't enough words to express exactly how I felt about him. Tal was my person. And no matter what, I wasn't going to lose him.

The lights on the Suburban went out half a block ahead of us. "We're here," I said.

Tal pulled Nicola's amethyst out of his pocket and slipped the chain over his neck.

I patted my pocket to ensure I still had my stun gun. A fleeting desire for a batch of Orange Influence seized me. It was my one edible that could help me in battle. I shook my head, trying to dislodge the horrible thought. The only time I'd ever willfully used Orange Influence on anyone had been when I'd been locked in the basement of the Arcane, destined to be a lab rat. I'd used it to save myself. But it was a dangerous drug. One that I wished I could go back and never invent.

I eased the Camry past the Suburban and parked in front of a large truck, hoping it was enough to keep the car at least partially hidden.

"Ready?" Tal asked.

I glanced back at Link. He took one look at me and started vibrating. A moment later, my white-and-gray wolf filled the back seat.

"Now I am." I climbed out of the car and let Link out. The pair of us waited in silence for Tal.

He moved slowly, taking careful steps.

"Tal?"

"I'm fine." His gait evened out as he led the way toward Phoebe.

I kept a critical eye on him, but he took long, purposeful strides, appearing as right as rain. I didn't buy it for a second. He had one tell. If he hadn't put the amethyst on, I might not have noticed his neck muscles flexing and pulsing with tension beneath the silver chain.

Nothing I could say would stop him, though. I suspected part of the mission had something to do with the fact we'd lost Beau. That neither of us had been there to help him after he'd been left for dead in my mother's lavender fields. I felt the ache of total helplessness deep down and although we'd never talked about it, I knew he felt the same way. It wasn't that either of us blamed ourselves, but we had that awful vulnerability that doesn't go away, that makes one question everything they did right up until their life changed forever.

And that's why Talisen wouldn't let another friend go without a fight. And exactly why I'd battle right alongside him.

A slight whistle sounded from the shadows. I couldn't see her, but I knew it was Phoebe. Link put his nose to the ground and headed in her general direction. Tal fell in step beside me and we followed him to Phoebe's side.

She was busy clasping a silver locket around her neck when she finally came into focus. I eyed the locket, then noticed the silver cuff and the four rings adorning her slender fingers. "Where's Nicola?" I whispered.

"With David and Harrison. They're scoping out the building."

I eyed her locket and rings. "How dangerous are those?"

She ran a light hand over the round locket. "More dangerous than the death spell Nicola was carrying around last week."

Whoa. I took a small step back. Nicola had almost killed Phoebe with that death spell. "I didn't know there was such a thing."

Phoebe nodded once. "Just make sure you're well out of the way if I have to use one."

"Got it."

One of her rings started to glow blue. I jumped back, pulling Tal with me.

She reached out and grabbed me by the shirt. "No. Don't move," she whispered harshly. "This one detects threats. Light blue, like what you just saw, means someone with ill intent is in the vicinity. If it starts to turn green, then you can run."

I glanced around. "Is the threat out here?"

"Unlikely. It's too faint."

That made me breathe a little easier.

Phoebe adjusted an earpiece in her right ear, cocking her head to hear whoever was speaking to her. "Okay, let's move," she told Tal and me.

"Coast clear?" I asked her.

She put her finger to her lips, indicating now wasn't the time to ask questions. It drove me insane, but I'd been on enough vampire hunts with her to understand how she worked. Tal on the other hand, was new to all this.

"Phoebe," he said, impatience in his tone, "what exactly is the plan?"

She glared at him with her narrowed eyes. This time she reached out and covered his mouth with her hand and shook her head violently. If he didn't get the picture after that, she was likely to spell him into silence. If she had any power left after the locator spell.

I grabbed Tal's hand and traced what I hoped was a soothing circle over his knuckles. He didn't pull back, so I decided to go with it. Link flanked him on the other side, occasionally leaning in to nuzzle Tal's leg.

He was picking up on my worry for Talisen. The knowledge that Link would protect Tal the same way he protected me eased some of my anxiety.

"Here." Phoebe pressed one of her rings into my hand.

I held it with the tips of my thumb and forefinger, inspecting it. "What does it do?"

"It's a protection ring. It won't stop an attacker, but it will slow them down. Just put it on. It'll help."

"But won't it affect anyone fighting alongside me?" I asked as Nicola, David, and Harrison returned.

She shook her head. "Only someone who is directly attacking you." She glanced at our entourage. "And if any one of them ends up attacking you, then this will be the least of their worries after I get done with them."

I slipped the ring over my middle finger and inclined my head in thanks "This is new?"

"Sort of. It's a variation on a binding spell. But it's the ring itself that makes it work. The metal specifically."

I eyed the ring. "Silver?"

"Witch's silver."

Oh, very rare indeed. This was a family heirloom. I pulled it off and stuffed it back into her hand. "I can't take this."

"You can and you will." She held her hand palm up, the silver ring appearing as harmless as could be.

"Phoebs. It holds your family's power. It's too risky for you to give it away."

"I'm not giving it away to a random stranger. You're my family." With that, she grabbed my hand and forced the ring back on my finger. "You know my family history. This is not only encouraged, but expected."

Of course I knew about her family. She had a brother. But no one else. She'd never known her father, and both her mother and grandmother had died well before their time. She had an uncle she only saw once a year and that was only to go over family business. She'd told me once she was expected to adopt friends as family, but I'd always assumed she meant other witches. In fact, I'd been sure that was what her time with Nicola was about. Witches could feed off power from other witches, but not with fae.

"When you put it that way, I accept," I said, trying to choke back the unexpected emotion clogging my throat.

She reached out and pulled me to her in a fierce hug. I returned the embrace, pouring everything I had into the brief contact.

When we pulled apart, her eyes were brighter than usual. "Now be careful, dammit."

I chuckled. "You, too."

Harrison stepped between us. "If the love fest is over, maybe we should get on with it."

"Shut up, Harrison," David and Tal said at the same time.

Harrison rolled his eyes. "Somebody has to get this show moving."

David scowled and yanked Harrison back. Harrison sent him a bland smile and stood with his thumbs in the belt loops of his jeans.

"The plan?" I asked Phoebe.

"We break up into groups. Nicola will go with Tal, Harrison with me, and you and Link with David."

I glanced at Tal's tense stance and David's casual one and then gaped at Phoebe. "Wait, what? Why am I with David? You're my partner."

Phoebe glanced over my head at David. "Told ya."

David shrugged.

"I think it's a good plan," Talisen said quietly.

I spun. "What?"

Tal took my hand in his. I could almost feel David's stare burning into our connection. But I knew Tal wasn't doing it to show dominance. It was just a natural gesture. One he'd done a thousand times before. "The vampire is the strongest and quickest. If anyone can keep you safe, it's him."

"Phoebe and Link have kept me safe hundreds of times before," I argued.

"Not against superhumans. And what if there's a bunch of vampires in there?"

"There isn't—" I cut myself off, almost revealing to Harrison that I could sense vamps. "I mean, we don't have any reason to believe there is."

Harrison gave me an odd look.

"Either way, I'll feel better if David's watching your back." Tal dropped my hand and moved to stand next to Nicola.

Not wanting to hold the rescue mission up any longer, I reluctantly agreed. "All right. I'll partner with David."

"Good." Phoebe glanced around at all of us. "Now, here's the plan."

Chapter 25

The white antebellum home took up half a city block in the Lake Vista neighborhood and was surrounded by a black wrought-iron fence. The entire place was dark except for one light shining from the far upper right-hand window.

David pointed to a balcony on the left side. "That's where we'll enter."

"Right." Out of the six of us, it was easiest for David and me to deal with second floors.

I turned to Tal, who was standing behind me. There was no way I was getting Link up there with me. "Link is too charged to change into puppy form. Take him with you."

Talisen put his hand out to Link. The wolf nudged Tal's palm with his nose. The tight ball in my chest loosened a tiny bit. Not that I didn't have confidence in Talisen and Nicola's abilities, but they were the weakest pair. Tal was very gifted in healing…not fighting. He could hold his own in a brawl, but dealing with superhumans was another matter. And while Nicola was powerful, she wasn't very experienced.

They needed Link more than I did. Because let's face it, I had David, badass vampire, on my team. As long as I didn't get in the way, he would be able to protect me from almost anyone. Hopefully.

"Go," Phoebe said. "We'll be right behind you."

David glanced down at me. "I'll meet you up there."

I took a deep breath, shrugged off the sweater I'd borrowed

from Phoebe, and fluttered my wings, instantly feeling more in control.

I hovered under a tree and watched Phoebe and Harrison jump the iron fence. Phoebe paused at the front gate. A faint light glowed from her palm and a second later, the gate swung open. Link bounded in and she closed it.

Phoebe joined Harrison near the front door of the house. Below me, Talisen scaled the large oak with Nicola right behind him. They were headed for the backyard. Once Phoebe was in and disarmed the alarm, they would sneak in through the back door.

I kept one eye on Phoebe's progress and the other on the shadows of the balcony. David was already there, waiting for me.

Phoebe waved in my direction, giving me the signal. Time to get this party started. I flew soundlessly to the balcony and landed beside David, catching a glimpse of Link as he followed on Talisen's heels and disappeared into the backyard.

Everyone was in place. David had his hand on the knob of the French door and as soon as Phoebe had the front door open, he twisted his wrist. The flimsy lock broke easily and David ushered me inside the dark room.

This was it. Our job was to clear the way for Tal and Nicola to get Dawson out. But first, we needed to find whoever was here without tipping them off. We had the best advantage coming in from the second floor. And that meant we had no time to waste.

The more individuals we could neutralize, the easier it would be for the rest of the team. A dark walnut canopy bed took up almost the entire room. With super vampire speed, David maneuvered to the other side and checked the closet. Empty.

He cracked open the door, poked his head out, and waved me forward. We needed to check every room.

I stayed a half step behind him, listening carefully for sounds below. The house was pin-drop silent right up until I stepped on a creaky floorboard. Shit. I froze, but David grabbed my arm and yanked me into a room to the left.

My breathing quickened and sweat broke out on my neck. He pulled me to the far corner of the room and did his cursory check, then he swept a glance over me and raised one quizzical eyebrow.

His question was clear. Was I okay to continue? I mouthed *I'm fine* and smoothed my shirt. We hadn't even seen anyone yet and I was ready to jump right out of my skin. He paused by the door, listening. I wasn't sure if he was giving me another moment or if he actually heard something. But I wasn't going to ask.

We made our way down the hall and were almost to the stairs separating the west and east wings when we heard a loud crash followed by a vicious growl.

"Fuck!" Phoebe's angry voice floated up the stairs. "Resist and you'll end up six feet under, dirtbag."

Another crash, this time sounding like glass on tile.

"Move!" David ushered me down the hall. He only paused momentarily at each door, listening briefly. It appeared no one was upstairs at all…except that room at the end with the light shining from beneath the door.

When we reached the end of the hall, David pressed me against the door with one arm and listened. After a brief moment he nodded. Someone was in there.

He glanced at the door handle and then back at me to ask if I was ready. I wasn't, but we couldn't wait. If Dawson was in there, this could be our only chance to save him.

The clatter of heavy boots sounded on the stairwell and David spun.

So much for ending this mission early. I pulled the stun gun out of my pocket and held it with the hand wearing Phoebe's ring. If anyone lunged for me, vampire or superhuman, hopefully the ring's magic would slow them down.

A wiry guy with shockingly white-blond hair bounded up the stairs and into the hallway, followed closely by a stocky bodybuilder type.

David pushed me behind him and grabbed the first guy, barely catching him by his bloody T-shirt.

Where'd all that blood come from? Someone was seriously wounded. What if it was Tal? No! I refused to believe it. I hadn't heard Link and surely if Tal had been hurt, Link would've lost his shit.

Bloody T-shirt twisted at the last moment and kicked out, hitting David in the knee. My vampire crumpled but brought Bloody T-shirt down with him. David's hand wrapped around his attacker's neck and the muscles in his forearm flexed as he squeezed. Bloody's eyes started to bug out.

I took another step back, but then the bodybuilder lunged and he lost his balance, crashing into me. His heavy weight slammed us both into the wall. A sharp pain shot through my left wing, but I bit back a cry and ignored it. The bodybuilder's beady gray eyes leered into mine. He snarled and said, "Pretty. Too bad I'm going to have to crush your throat."

Was that the standard operating procedure for these fights? Because that's exactly what it looked like David was doing to the bloody guy. My attacker was too busy ogling me to notice me shift to stand on the balls of my feet, bracing myself. The stun gun hit him in the ribs and a zap of electricity shot into my shoulder where his hand still clutched me. My body spasmed, but I didn't let go.

He jerked backward with fire in his eyes. "Stupid bitch."

I smirked. "I'm not the one with a two-inch burn mark on my torso."

"You're gonna—argh!" Link lunged from the top of the stairs and sank his teeth into the man's thigh. He shook his head with enough violence that I was almost certain my wolf was trying to rip Bodybuilder's leg right off.

Someone shouted from below. An explosion ripped through the air. "Talisen," I cried and on pure reflex ran for the stairs. Was the place booby-trapped? "Phoebe!"

Talisen and Nicola rushed up the stairs, almost colliding with me.

"Willow," Talisen said. "Are you all right?"

"Yes. What the hell was that?" I clutched at his good arm and let out a sigh of relief.

"A spell Phoebe and Nicola threw. They took out a half dozen guards." He pulled me back down the hall, away from the brawls David and Link were still engaged in.

"Did you find Dawson?"

Nicola shook her head and glanced over her shoulder. "No. There's a small army of superhuman guards. Phoebe and I cast a holding spell over the rest. They're trapped in an invisible bubble right now, but it won't last."

"We've checked everywhere except there." I pointed to the room behind me.

"Come on." Tal dragged me forward, desperate to search that room.

"But—"

"Move," Nicola gasped as blue magic sprang from her hands and collided with the guard who had dislodged Link.

Talisen pressed me into the wall, shielding me with his body. I clung to his arms, staring wide-eyed over his shoulder.

Link was back on his feet, stalking the guard and waiting for his opening. As soon as Nicola's spell dissipated, Link lunged, this time mauling the guard until he crashed to the floor.

"Willow, go with Talisen," David huffed out. His guard had gotten away from his death grip, and the pair were going blow for blow with one another.

Link's maw was full of blood, but the guard he'd bitten just kept coming back for more. My stomach rolled. This was a literal bloodbath. One of them should've been knocked out by now. Tal's drug was even more dangerous than I'd first imagined.

Tal, who'd left my side, yanked open the last bedroom door and stood inside the doorframe.

What in the world was he doing? I ran. If anyone wanted to ambush him, he was a sitting duck standing there like that. But right before I reached his side, his shoulders relaxed slightly and he strode into the room.

Crack!

Behind me, a piece of the railing from the banister slammed into the wall and stuck out like an arrow. It had landed two inches from Nicola's skull.

"Goddammit!" Nicola cried. "Willow, go with Tal. The bubble burst. Phoebe needs my help." She dodged another piece of debris, launched herself over Link, and hurried down the stairs.

I didn't hesitate. There wasn't anything flying from that bedroom. Surely it was safer than the hallway.

The door had closed behind Tal. I forced myself to slow down, pay attention to my surroundings, and carefully turned the knob. Locked. What the hell?

I yanked and kicked the door with everything I had. When that didn't work, I started to bang on the door. "Tal! Open up. What's going on it there?"

Nothing. Dead silence.

"Talisen!"

The door swung open with gusto, pulling me into the room. As soon as I stumbled over the threshold, I fell to my knees, nearly crushed by the thick weight of vampire energy. I raised my gaze, the only part of me that I could move, to meet the gleeful expression of a vampire I knew.

The other daywalker.

I sucked in a painful gasp, almost unable to even fill my lungs. Everything hurt as if I were being stabbed with a thousand needles from every angle. My skin burned and my muscles ached, all while I was trapped in my own personal prison.

The vampire closed the door with a soft click. He pressed his fingers to his lips, indicating I should stay quiet.

Fear-driven adrenaline rushed through me. I scanned the empty room for Talisen, wanted to scream for him. To find out if he was all right. But I could barely breathe, let alone form words.

"That's a good faery," he crowed. "Stay quiet and your fae won't suffer as terrible a death as your brother."

Ice crawled up my spine and entered my heart. *Asher.* He had to be. He knew about Beau and he knew me. And he was a daywalker! How long had he had the ability? Had Beau turned him? Holy crow. Was that why he was eliminating all the fae with the ability to change vampires?

My throat started to close and I had to choke down the sob threatening to suffocate me. I couldn't do anything to help Tal. I was a prisoner in the vampire's presence. Where *was* Tal? Had Asher already killed him? Pure hatred fueled a bolt of determination, forcing out a cry, "Tal!"

Rage boiled in Asher's eyes as his arm moved, lashing out at me with vampire speed. But suddenly his hand slowed and I was forced to watch the blow coming in slow motion.

Phoebe's ring. It worked. I squeezed the stun gun, willing my arm to lift it, to connect with the vampire, but nothing happened. My arm stayed at my side, a traitor to my commands as the vampire's fist inched toward me one agonizing moment at a time. His hand connected, rattling my teeth, but if he'd hit me with a full blow he could've taken my entire head off. Or at the very least, knocked me unconscious.

"Willow," Tal called, panic and worry lacing his voice.

I opened my mouth but no sound came out. What had the vampire done to Tal? And where was the professor?

"I've found her," Asher called, using a slight Southern accent. "Don't worry, she's safe."

There was a pause, then Tal called, "What happened to the guard who ambushed me?"

"He's been taken care of." Asher never took his gaze from me as he walked backward toward the sound of Tal's voice. A tiny bit of his vampire pressure lifted, but I didn't dare move. I didn't know how much he knew of my abilities.

"Professor?" Tal called.

Asher's lips curled into a satisfied smile. "Yes, Mr. Kavanagh."

I let out a startled gasp.

The vampire's smile turned cold and menacing.

"I could use a hand. We really need to get out of here as soon as possible."

It was obvious to me Talisen was trying to be patient, but there was an edge of frustrated exasperation in his tone.

"We have time," Asher said.

"You don't understand—"

"Actually, it's you who doesn't understand. But everything will be clear soon enough." Asher abandoned the smooth southern gent act and spoke using an English accent. I assumed it was his regular speech because he dropped all pretense of behaving like the professor he was supposed to be. "Just as soon as your girlfriend here tells me what I need to know."

"Professor?"

I didn't know where exactly Tal was, but it was clear he was restrained and more than a little confused. My thoughts jumbled. How could I help Tal and get out of here? And why was Asher posing as a professor at the university? Why had Tal thought Asher had been abducted from the lab if he was running the show?

"Tell you what?" I spat through the vampire haze still pressing against me.

His cocky facial expression morphed to one of pure hatred as he turned back to me and all but whispered, "You're going to bring me that nephew of yours or I'm going to torture your fae lover until every last bit of his blood is sucked dry. And then I'm going to move on to your aunt, your mother, and that bitch of a witch you live with. And once I finish them off, you'll belong to me. You'll produce whatever magic edible I desire and you'll do it without complaint."

My mouth hung open in stunned silence. He knew about Beau Junior. Nothing else mattered. No one else mattered. I'd die where I stood before I'd ever hint I had a clue what he was talking about. "Is that why you broke into my office? To find out about Beau?"

His eyes narrowed. "That and other things. Elissa, my assistant, tells me you have some very unusual talents. Ones you'll be sharing with me soon enough. Start talking. This is your last chance."

Elissa worked for him, too? What the hell had Tal gotten himself into? I met Asher's chilling black eyes and pierced him with my own. "It doesn't matter what you demand. You're never going to get what you're asking for."

He let out a humorless laugh. "I always get what I want."

A loud crash sounded at the door, but then the commotion dimmed as whoever it was seemed to move back down the hall.

"Well, you won't get it from me."

The vampire in front of me vibrated with anger. Then he vanished around the corner.

I forced myself to stand and lurched forward. "Talisen!"

An agonized groan filled the room. I struggled to keep moving forward and as I turned the corner to peer into the sitting room, my throat tightened at the sight in front of me. Tal's arms were duct-taped to the armrests of a wooden chair, his head tilted to the side. He was unconscious and turning a stark shade of white as Asher tore into Talisen's neck.

"No!" I thrust with my wings, barely able to move. My hands were outstretched, grappling for Asher. But I couldn't get there. My body turned heavy and I landed with a thud more than a few feet away from Talisen.

"Stop!"

Slowly, Asher lifted his head and looked at me. Blood dribbled down his chin. "Five seconds."

I had no words. I couldn't give up Beau and Tal wouldn't want me to.

Asher snarled and sank his teeth back into Tal's neck.

"David, help!" I cried, desperate for someone, anyone, to tear Asher to shreds. Hot tears of horror streamed down my face as I stood there, trapped in my own personal hell, unable to leave Tal and unable to move any closer to try to help him. Utter pain filled every inch of my being as I strained to move forward, to lash out with my stun gun, to somehow inflict my wrath on the vampire taking away the one person I loved most.

Asher ripped his teeth from Talisen's neck and let go. Tal slumped to the side, blood streaming from his neck. The master vampire moved in a flash past me, and I nearly passed out. I grappled and caught purchase on the nearby wall, barely keeping myself upright.

"You!" an angry, familiar voice growled.

Allcot. He was here. Von and his minions must have talked, thank the Goddess. A surge of relief flooded me and I didn't hesitate to scramble to Tal's side.

"Where's the child?" Asher demanded.

Struggling with the duct tape at Tal's wrists, I whispered, "Tal? Tal, wake up."

"That faery is under my protection," I heard Allcot say.

Asher laughed.

I finally got a piece of the tape up and unwound one of Tal's wrists. As it peeled off his skin, his eyes fluttered. "Wake up, Tal." I grabbed his face with both my hands, "Come on. That's it."

He moaned.

"The boy, Allcot. That's all I ask," Asher said in a reasonable tone. "This can all end right now."

I imagined Allcot leaning back with his feet crossed at the ankle. "And what makes you think I have him?"

"Why else would you be here?" Asher asked.

"The faery. It's not a secret she's important to my son. Keep the fae if you want. But she comes with me."

Shit. What the hell was Allcot up to? I grabbed the tape at Tal's other wrist and yanked hard.

He jerked as the tape peeled away a patch of skin but didn't wake. He was so pale. Asher had taken too much blood already.

"Oh my God." I pulled him forward and wrapped my arms around him. His life force barely pulsed beneath my fingers. I had to do something to help him or we were never getting out of here. I couldn't heal him. Not even with the help of his amethyst. But I did have something else.

I took a deep breath and sucked a tiny bit of his life energy into my being. A spark of what I recognized as his healing magic zinged through my body. It made my head spin and I started to pant.

Whoa.

Adrenaline mixed with Tal's magic made me shake. *Get it together, Wil.* I had to send the magic back into Tal. Now!

I wrapped my hands around Tal's neck and imagined my magic seeping back into him. Immediately the spark reached my fingertips and the world around us faded away. There was nothing—no sound, no fight, no vampires—just Talisen and me as magic swirled inside me. The cool healing force numbed my fingers and flowed freely into his. There wasn't any resistance, only a natural transfer of fae magic.

His breathing evened out immediately and a blush colored his cheeks. Right before my eyes, the marks on his neck healed over.

Whoa again. Our magic healed his wounds. Well, it was likely his magic, but I hadn't taken that much from him. Maybe my magic had given him enough of a boost, and he'd been able to heal himself.

In the adjoining room, the two vampires were oddly silent, but I knew both were there. My vamp-sense didn't lie.

Talisen's eyelids fluttered open.

"Hey," I said.

"Willow?" His voice cracked a bit and he swallowed.

"Welcome back."

"What happened?"

I opened my mouth to answer, but all hell broke loose in the next room. The pair flew past the sitting room opening, locked tightly in a boxer's embrace, and slammed into the outer wall of the house. There was more scrambling, followed by the sounds of fists connecting with flesh.

"We need to go." I tugged Tal up.

He stumbled to his feet, then paused and glanced around. "We can't leave without the professor."

I let out a startled huff. He didn't remember a thing. Dammit. "Yes, we can. I'll explain later."

He planted his feet, not moving an inch as I tugged. "No, Willow. We can't. It's my fault he's here."

I grabbed both his hands. "He isn't who you think he is. Tal, the professor is a vampire. Asher."

"What?" His eyes nearly popped out of his head. Then he narrowed them. "That's impossible. I see him during the day all the time."

I gazed up at him, letting him see the painful truth in my eyes. "He's a daywalker—the vampire who attacked you."

Tal seemed stunned into silence once more.

But when I tugged this time, he followed. We paused at the entry to the main bedroom. Allcot had his hands around Asher's throat and appeared seconds from overpowering him.

Could this really be over soon? Would Allcot really be my savior? He already was He'd stopped Asher from killing Tal. And in that moment, I knew I'd be forever in debt to the master vampire.

The door leading to the hallway swung open with an earsplitting crash and at the same time Asher found purchase, twisted out of Allcot's grasp, and a second later broke Allcot's neck.

"No!" David ran forward as Allcot sank to his knees, holding his head upright, repositioning it on his shoulders. Vamps healed quickly. A neck injury was no different, but the bones did need to be lined up.

Asher lunged for me, grasping me around the waist.

Searing pain shot through my middle. Fire. Everywhere. Someone was screaming. I think it might have been me. But I barely registered the sound. My nerve endings were shouting and drowning out every last thought I had.

And then just as quickly, I was lying in a heap, gasping for breath as the fire fled.

A blur of limbs tangled less than a few feet from me. Talisen's familiar hands grabbed me around the waist. He yanked me to the opposite side of the room and pulled me close in a firm body hug, his healing energy instantly calming me.

I was torn between burying my head in his chest and staring wide-eyed at the vampire fight destroying the room.

The fight won. I twisted so my back was against Tal's chest and clutched his hands as David and Asher landed blow after bone-crushing blow.

Allcot climbed to his feet, his face contorting in obvious pain while his neck healed. The movement distracted David for just a moment. But it was enough for Asher to land a blow that made David fall to his knees and cough up a mouthful of bright red blood.

Holy shitballs. I'd never seen evidence of a vamp bleeding internally before. I knew we should bolt, but I couldn't. I was cemented in place, but this time from sheer fear for David and even Allcot. Asher was going to take them both down right before my eyes.

Asher turned and eyed Allcot. "Finally," he said with a snarl. "You've interfered for the last time."

The last time? When had the two crossed paths before? Or did he know Allcot was protecting Beau Junior?

Allcot smiled a crooked smile. "It must be awful to go through life hating yourself."

Asher regarded Allcot with a stony expression. Then he put his hands in his pants pockets as if the fight was over.

Allcot's grin widened. He glanced at David, who had climbed to his feet. Blood stained his lips, but he didn't appear to be losing any more. Allcot gave David a tiny nod, but before David could react, Asher brandished a black agate.

I screamed, knowing exactly what it was. A sun agate.

He whispered a word I didn't understand and suddenly I was blinded by the brilliant white light. The kind that no vampire could survive.

Chapter 26

I cringed away from the light, my eyes watering. Through my blurring vision, I made out David's prone form, sprawled over Allcot as if he were shielding him. Neither moved. My chest constricted with a bolt of pain.

David!

He shouldn't have been affected by the light. He was a daywalker. I pulled away from Tal to run to his side but was blindsided by the fiery onslaught of Asher's vampire energy as he leaped in front of me and clutched at both of my arms. The fire burned straight into my chest, making my knees buckle.

A buzzing grew in my ears, blocking out all other noise. Then Tal was there, his face contorted with fury. He grabbed for Asher, trying to get him into a headlock, but the vampire sent Tal across the room with one punch, slamming him into the wall. Plaster buckled and rained down on Talisen.

Asher wrapped his hand around my neck and dragged me across the room. My feet twisted under me as I tried to scramble, but my limbs wouldn't cooperate. Far too depleted, my body had started to shut down.

No! I tried to cry, but my mouth stopped working and I couldn't get the word out.

The French doors to the balcony loomed in front of us. Somewhere deep inside, I knew if Asher got me out of this room, I was never going to see my loved ones again.

With almost no feeling left in my fingers, I clung to his arm wrapped around my middle and dug my nails in as hard as I could, but the effort was useless. I wasn't ever going to be strong enough to get away from a vampire. But I sure as hell wasn't going to live the rest of my life in captivity.

So I did the only thing I could think to do. If I was going down, he was going down with me. Magic. It was my only hope. The familiar spark tingled at my fingertips and I forced myself to siphon as much of his vampire energy as I could.

Slashes of pain burned through my veins from the inside out. The room blurred as my vision turned hazy. The agony was beyond words or thought. I ceased to be me and became only the sensation of raw nerves. My entire body shook with the effort, but I couldn't let go. His vampire energy, now consuming me, had turned me into a trembling, immobile statue. I was trapped in my own magic.

And so was he. The vampire stood stock-still, clearly unable to move a muscle. We were trapped together.

The room started to spin and darkness crept into the edges of my vision. I knew siphoning his energy meant I was killing myself. I couldn't take in death and expect to survive. Not as a life faery. But I couldn't let him go, either. It was as if my hands were fused to the master vampire now.

A growl sounded somewhere from the room. One I recognized. Link.

Wham!

Link slammed into us with such force that we collapsed with Asher on top of me. I was past pain, past feeling. Everything had gone cold.

I stared at Link's massive wolf frame, registering only that he was covered in blood.

Why?

Oh. The fight. Right.

Then everything started to burn again. I curled into a ball, realizing Asher was no longer on top of me.

He'd gotten away. I'd failed. And I was going to die because I'd willingly taken in death.

Link's long muzzle nudged me. I cried out in unimaginable pain as my muscles seized and spasmed. I thrashed, trying to get rid of the death swirling inside me. My hand hit something cold, hard, soothing.

The pain in my hand fled. The marbled surface beneath it acted as a balm against the death claiming me. On instinct, I clamped my other hand on the vampire's arm. Instant relief claimed my fingertips.

I squinted, peering into Allcot's blank, unseeing eyes. He appeared to be dead. But was he? The pain in my hand had stopped once I touched him. There had to be some spark inside him still.

I pushed myself up on my knees and focused. Allcot's body was absorbing the foreign vampire energy I'd stolen from Asher. If I could just—

My magic started to flow toward my fingers, dragging the razor-sharp vampire energy with it. I wanted to cry out, to jerk away and curl into a ball, but my sense of self-preservation took over. And inch by inch, I forced my magic and Asher's vampire energy into Allcot.

His stone body warmed beneath my fingers. Bone-deep weariness overtook me and I slumped, my head resting on his chest.

The world passed around us, me lying on Allcot, my body still incredibly raw, but I no longer felt as though Asher's energy was eating away my insides. I was exhausted, battered, but not dead.

A whimper next to my ear made me turn my head. Link's large wolf head dipped and his nose nudged mine. Tears of raw emotion started to slip down my cheeks. I reached up and ran my hand over his soft pointed ear. Link closed his eyes for a moment, then sat on his haunches and pressed his face into my hand.

"Willow?"

Phoebe. She was okay. Slowly, I turned my head and stared into the deep blue eyes of my best friend. "You're alive," I choked out.

A huff of surprised laughter escaped her lips. "So are you."

"Barely." I closed my eyes, taking in deep breaths, trying to steady myself. Then they popped open. "Talisen? Where—"

"I'm here, Wil." His strong, quiet voice came from behind me.

I struggled to sit up and Phoebe helped me. I sat cross-legged on the floor with Allcot at my back, still unmoving. Whatever I'd done to him hadn't seemed to have any effect. My eyes met Tal's. He had blood running down the side of his face and he was cradling his left arm, the one he'd hurt hours ago, with his right. "You're hurt," I said.

He sent me a weak smile. "So are you."

I got my feet under me and tried to stand, but my legs wobbled.

"No. Stay where you are." Tal lifted two of his fingers off his arm, exposing the amethyst healing stone. "This will help until I can get my arm set."

"Willow," Phoebe started in a hesitant tone.

I met her troubled eyes. "What is it?"

"It's Asher, he—"

The door of the destroyed bedroom crashed open again and David appeared in the doorway. Blood covered his mouth and the front of his white button-down shirt. His eyes were wild as he scanned the room. They landed on me and something softened in his expression.

"Is he dead? Asher? Did you get him?" I asked.

That muscle in his jaw pulsed and he shook his head. "No." His entire body was taut with frustration. "I was unconscious for only a few moments, but that was enough time for him to get away."

Son of a...I clamped down on my disappointment, too exhausted to think about it any longer.

Then David noticed Allcot next to me, still unmoving. His face tightened with something I couldn't read. Anger. Pain. Fear. All three perhaps. He crossed the room in long strides and knelt before Allcot.

"Father?" His voice echoed with obvious pain.

I had to glance away as I recalled our conversation from earlier in the day. Eadric Allcot was David's only true family. And coldhearted vampire or not, David loved him. My heart lurched. David and I weren't together, but I'd loved him once. Maybe I still did. How did one turn something like that off? All I knew was I had an almost overwhelming urge to wrap David in my arms and comfort him.

"He's still alive," David said, his voice barely a whisper.

"What?" Phoebe got up and moved to David's side. "How can you tell?"

Allcot still lay motionless on the floor, his eyes fixed on nothing.

"I'm not sure." David raised his gaze to mine. "When I touch him, it just seems like he's still there." David didn't possess any magical abilities. Not beyond his vampire speed and strength and his ability to heal quickly.

"What do you mean?" I asked.

He placed a hand on Allcot's chest. "I'm not sure. But it's almost as if I can still sense his blood."

I frowned. Vampires were sensitive to blood. It drove a lot of what they did, but I'd thought that was human blood, not vampire blood. "Are you saying you can sense when other vamps are around by their blood signature?"

"Not exactly. We usually sense other vampires due to our sensitive hearing. But there's also a sixth sense. Something I can't explain. And that's what's going on right now." He locked eyes with me, his gaze suddenly pleading. "You have to help him."

I jerked back. "What? How?"

He was quiet for a moment, his hand clutching Allcot's. "Save him, Wil. Like you did for me."

"Hell no." Talisen stalked over to my side, limping the entire way.

That had been my initial response. Hell no. No way. Not ever. I'd almost died bringing David back to life after he'd been dusted by Phoebe. And I hadn't been weakened by a vampire fight that night.

But Allcot had burst in and saved not only me, but Tal, too. He'd been watching over me for over a year. And he'd been protecting Carrie and Beau the last four years. This vampire, who hadn't even known me, had been keeping my loved ones and me safe. It didn't matter his reasons. It only mattered that he had. Even when the Void, the magical undercover agency I'd signed my life to, hadn't.

Could I really just let him die, knowing I could do something about it?

The anguished expression on David's face pushed me over the edge. Even if I could walk away from Allcot, I couldn't walk away from David. Not after learning about his childhood. Knowing he'd lost everyone he loved. I couldn't take Allcot from him, too. I just couldn't.

I gave David a tiny nod and inched closer.

"Willow!" Tal moved, blocking my way. "No! You can't risk yourself for Allcot."

The outrage on Tal's face only served to make me more determined. I knew he was worried about me. Of course he was. But Allcot wasn't the enemy. In fact, he'd been one of my very few allies. As crazy as that sounded.

"I have to," I said quietly. "I sort of felt what David's talking about. I do think Allcot is in there somewhere. I can do this." The last line came out a lot more confident than I felt. The only vampire I'd ever saved was David. And that had been pure luck and desperation. And I hadn't been nearly as beaten and battered as I was now. It didn't matter. I had to try.

Tal didn't move.

Phoebe heaved a sigh and stood. She reached out and tugged on his good arm. "You have to let her do this."

"I don't have to let her do anything," he snapped.

She quirked one eyebrow and then laughed. "Right. Because Willow is the kind of girl to take orders from a man. Or anyone, for that matter. If I were you, I'd get the hell out of the way."

I gently pulled Tal to the side and whispered, "I know you don't understand this and I don't expect you to. But this is something I'm going to do. Allcot has kept my family protected when no one else could. I owe him something."

"You don't owe that vampire shit," Tal spat. "And now that Asher is out of the picture—"

"Excuse me," Phoebe cut in. "Asher got away. He's weak and wounded, but he isn't out of the picture. Not by a long shot. You can bet he'll be gunning for us all soon enough."

"Fuck!" Tal ran his right hand through his hair and winced at the movement.

A terrible thought came to me. "Beau!" I cried. "Asher must be going after Beau Junior."

David shook his head. "No. I don't think so. Beau is heavily guarded and so is Carrie. It would take more than one almost-drained vampire to get to either of them."

"Right." I'd drained him before I'd passed out. I squeezed Tal's hand. "Please try to understand why I have to do this."

He scowled and made his way to the open door. "Don't expect me to heal you when you nearly kill yourself this time."

"Tal," I said softly, "you don't mean that."

He turned around, his lips pressed together in a grim line. Then his expression softened and sadness flashed through his darkened green eyes. "I do. I have to take care of myself this time. If you go through with this, you need to find another healer."

I sucked in a breath but didn't say anything. Tal was making me choose. Him or Allcot. I opened my mouth, clamped it shut, and then shook my head. I couldn't. I'd already made up my mind. I wouldn't let Allcot die if I could help it. Not after what he'd done for me. And what he meant to David.

Talisen glared at David as if he were to blame and then gave me a sad shake of his head and disappeared into the hallway.

Phoebe wrapped a hand around my arm. "Are you sure about this?"

I avoided her gaze and nodded. "If this drains me, can you get me to a clinic?"

She squeezed my hand. "Of course."

Link nudged my leg and, still in his wolf form, dropped to lie at my feet. He was a mess. Patches of fur were gone and his tail was bleeding. He needed a healer, too, but his injuries didn't appear to be life threatening. I ran a hand over his head and neck. "Are you okay, buddy?"

He rested his head on his paws and waited.

"We'll get you fixed up as soon as possible."

I sat beside Allcot, thankful I'd at least stopped shaking, and rested one hand over his heart and the other over mine. The only way I'd been able to bring David back was by reaching deep inside myself and pouring love into my magic. I didn't love Allcot, but my love for David was still right where I'd left it. Locked away in the depths of my heart.

"Kneel across from me," I told David. He did as I said and with my hands in place, I studied him, hoping that would help me tap into whatever I'd done before when I'd brought him back. It was tough, because he was all blood and gore. He didn't look at all like himself. Though underneath the blood spatter, he did appear to be pale again, all traces of his sunburn gone. Interesting. Had Asher's blood healed him?

"Willow?" David asked.

"Yeah?"

"You can do this. I know you can."

I nodded, realizing he thought I was hesitant. Well, I was, to a certain extent. But not for the reasons he thought. In order to bring back Allcot, I was certain my feelings for David were going to rise to the surface. I wasn't sure I could handle that on top of everything that had already happened.

Before I could talk myself out of it, I locked eyes with David and got lost in the blue brilliance reflecting back at me. My magic built from deep inside my gut and sparked to life. I shook my head. No. I needed this magic to come from my heart. That felt right. That's what had worked before.

I focused on memories of David. The times we'd curled up on my couch watching movies, late dinners in the French Quarter when he'd been human, the bedroom picnic we'd had just last week. Warmth ignited in the middle of my chest, growing into a small ball of magic.

There. That was it. But I'd need more. I let myself relive the moment David and I had first kissed, the gentle way he'd cuddled Link the night I'd brought him home for the first time, and finally the day he'd told me about his dreams to have a family. The one he'd never have now, because of me.

My heart swelled and I clutched at the memories until the magic pulsed in time with my heartbeat.

Now.

I pressed down on Allcot's chest and imagined pulling his life force from deep inside him. Nothing.

Damn. Allcot still had some spark in him somewhere. He wasn't gone yet. "Stay with me, Eadric," I mumbled and pressed my fingers harder to his marbled chest. I imagined a metaphysical connection to his being, and then after a moment, something flickered. There. I'd found it. A small twinge of his energy connected with my fingers. Coaxing the threads with my mind, his energy reluctantly flowed into me, shooting searing pain straight to the ball of pulsing magic in my chest.

I groaned and slumped over Allcot but didn't break the connection.

"Willow?" Phoebe called, worry clouding her tone.

I shook my head, indicating I didn't want to be interrupted. I didn't remember experiencing pain when I'd changed David. But I'd blacked out, so I couldn't say for sure.

Gasping in deep breaths of air, sweat ran down my back as I used every last bit of my waning strength to force the magic into him. The connection between us pulsed back and forth, almost as if in limbo, trapped between us. "Come on," I mumbled and bore down on the magic, willing it to move. Then something broke loose and suddenly my magic spilled into him, flowing easily from my fingertips into him. "Oh my goodness, it worked," I said in surprise and pulled my hands away, my body swaying from the loss.

When I'd saved David, my magic had kept bouncing back into me. This time was different. Allcot didn't give me a chance to wonder why. He sat straight up and stared at me with wide, stormy gray eyes.

I sent him a weak smile and then let my eyes close as I collapsed in an exhausted heap. I don't know if I lost momentary consciousness or if I fell asleep, but I woke to a cool cloth pressed to my forehead.

"Tal?" I mumbled trying to focus through blurry eyes.

"Shh, relax," a deep, familiar voice said. A voice that was definitely not Talisen's.

No, this was David. And his touch was so gentle and welcome, I closed my eyes again. "Is Eadric all right?" I asked, though I wasn't sure I wanted to know.

"He's fine. Don't worry about any of that right now. We have a healer coming. Then we can talk."

They called a healer. That meant Talisen hadn't been bluffing. I hadn't truly believed his threat. A loss that had nothing to do with magic or life energy materialized and took over until my insides felt empty. It was more painful than the physical fire of a vampire's touch.

David pulled the cool rag from my head. My eyes popped open in protest. He leaned down and pressed a cool kiss to my temple and whispered, "Thank you. You have no idea what you've given me."

He pulled back. I stared up at him, not answering. I had a pretty good idea of what I'd given him and it was exactly why I'd saved Allcot in the first place.

"Can I get you anything?" he asked.

"Water?" I croaked, though I wasn't thirsty at all. I only wanted a moment to myself to process the emotions threatening to overtake me. I wanted Tal. Wanted his healing touch. His kind eyes. And his arms around me, keeping me safe.

"I'll be right back." David retreated. I didn't know how long I'd been out, but it must not have been for long because I recognized the French doors and the four-poster bed. It was the room David and I had broken into. Why were we still here? Wasn't anyone worried Asher or his people would come back? I tried to prop myself up and slip from the bed, but I was too weak.

A few minutes later, footsteps sounded in the hall and the door swung open with a squeak. David was back, though I wasn't ready to face him or anyone. The fact that Talisen wasn't there, that he'd left, hurt me more than anything David had ever done. Even his breakup text. I *needed* Tal. If I hadn't been in my enemy's house, I would've curled into a ball and stayed there.

Instead, I reluctantly rolled over to face David. But then I froze and my heart started to race.

"Agent Rhoswen," the faery said.

I gulped. "Director."

Chapter 27

"I'm glad to see you're awake." Director Halston smiled, but her tone was far from friendly. "The healer will be up in a moment. After she's finished, please join us down on the main floor." She swept back out of the room, leaving me alone once more.

Oh shit. Join us. Who was us? And who had called her? Not Phoebe, surely. How much did she know? A weight of foreboding settled over my chest. Was the Void a part of all this? Had I been their target again? My mind jumbled. Nothing made any sense.

The door squeaked again and this time a tall slender blonde poked her head into the room. "Willow? Is it okay if I come in?"

My gaze flicked to the canvas backpack slung over her shoulder. "Only if you have painkillers in that bag."

She chuckled. "Not exactly, but I think I have something better."

Even in my battered state, I couldn't help but notice her inner light, both peaceful and magnetizing.

She stopped at the edge of the bed and dropped her bag to the floor. "Do you mind if I sit?"

I shook my head, swallowing the lump lodged in my throat. Talisen should've been the one sitting next to me, the one to place his sure and gentle hands on my body. Not this stranger from the Arcane. How could he just leave?

"I understand you used some unusual magic this evening," Blondie said.

"You could say that," I mumbled and stared at the door, willing Talisen to appear. It wasn't that being healed by someone else would be unpleasant, it was that Tal had always been there for me before. I knew he was hurt himself, but he'd been clear he was staying away as a consequence of my choices, not because he couldn't heal us both. I knew him. If he hadn't been so upset with me, he would've never let someone else take his place.

It was the rejection that left me empty and alone, my heart torn in two.

"I'm Sierra. If you don't mind, I'm going to run my hands over your torso and limbs to get an idea of the damage."

I nodded my agreement and stared at the wall.

The second her hands made contact, my back bowed and I nearly flinched right off the mattress. "Ouch! Stop. I can't take it."

She broke the connection. I lay panting, my insides more raw than ever.

"That's never happened before," I choked out between breaths.

Her brows knit together. "It's like you've been charred from the inside out."

That was exactly what it felt like.

"How did this happen?" she asked.

I met her curious hazel eyes. She was a healer, not my superior, and I was under no obligation to divulge any details. "Classified," I said.

Disappointment registered in her slight frown, but she didn't press the issue. Instead, she rummaged through her canvas bag until she found a silver tin and a bottle of water. She flipped the lid and took a pinch of dried herbs, which she held over my mouth. "Swallow these."

I choked the bitter seeds down with the help of the water, gagging in the process. My tongue darted out and I had to fight to keep from scraping it clean of the foul substance. "Ugh, what the hell is that shit?"

She tossed the tin back in her pack and regarded me with a critical stare. "That shit is going to stabilize you so I can put you back together without you coding from shock."

The herb hit my bloodstream, instantly numbing the aches and pains. "Oh my Goddess," I said in a barely audible whisper.

"Amazing isn't it? Hibiscus seeds cured with a healing balm. Tastes like shit, but it works every time." She moved her hands over my body, but I barely felt a thing other than the sweet relief of her magic cooling my charred insides.

Her healing gift was very different from Tal's and for that I was grateful. Any magic that was similar to Tal's would've likely made me break down in tears. That was the last thing I wanted to do in front of the Arcane healer. She trailed her hands over each bruised section, lingering on the worst wounds, and poured her cool magic into me until I was almost buzzing. It was so different than Tal's magic. With her, she was filling me up with magical energy and using her coolness to numb parts of my body.

With Tal, his magic seemed much more natural. Effortless. As if all he had to do was touch me and my wounds were healed. I shut my eyes and tried not to think about him. He wasn't here. Sierra was. After she pulled her hands away, I smiled up at her. "Thank you."

She picked her bag up and slung it over her shoulder. "You're welcome." With a nod, she headed toward the door.

"Wait," I called, sitting up too quickly. My head swam from the sudden movement. She'd cured my aches, but my energy level wasn't even close to normal. Not quite the treatment I would've gotten from Talisen, but at least my insides didn't feel like they'd been filleted with a razor.

She paused at the door with her eyebrows raised. "Did you need something else?"

"Those seeds. If you're interested, I can probably turn them into something that doesn't make you want to cut your tongue out."

"I doubt it," she said.

I shrugged and stood on wobbly feet. "Doesn't hurt to try."

She studied me, a puzzled expression on her flawless porcelain face. "Why?"

"Why what?"

"Why do you care what it tastes like as long as it works?"

I stiffened, feeling ridiculous because of my involuntary physical reaction. "I own a magical bakery. I believe all magical substances should taste good. Who wants to buy a Kiss Me chocolate if it doesn't make your mouth happy?"

She snorted, the wrinkling of her nose messing up her perfect beauty. "My healing seeds aren't for sale."

"So? What does that matter? I'm just saying it might be nice if your patients didn't gag while you were treating them."

Her eyes narrowed. Then she shook her head and left, mumbling under her breath. I thought it sounded something like, "Fucking cupcakes."

For some reason her response made me chuckle. Here I was in Asher's hideout, my friends beaten to a pulp, the director of the Void waiting for me, and I was talking about cupcakes. We all had our coping mechanisms, I guess.

I half expected David or Phoebe or even Talisen to come see if I was all right, but no one appeared. In fact, the entire house was eerily quiet. I steeled myself and went in search of answers.

Once downstairs, I headed into the large living room, carefully stepping over broken glass and splintered furniture. I paused and glanced around at the destruction. Sadness overwhelmed me. All of this was for what? The quest for power? To create superhumans? To make sure no more vampires were turned into daywalkers? I didn't even want to turn anyone else.

"Willow?" Phoebe's voice came from behind me.

I twisted and found her clutching the doorframe. She had bruises on the left side of her face and her leg was bandaged, but she appeared to otherwise be okay. "Yeah."

"In here."

I followed her into the formal dining room.

"Rhoswen," the director said from her spot at the head of the table. "Have a seat."

I started to move to the first available chair but then stopped in my tracks and stared with incomprehension. Against the opposite wall, four people had been restrained, no doubt magically strapped to the chairs they sat in. Three of Asher's humans took up the first three chairs. The forth one was a few feet away from the rest. I locked my gaze on those forest-green eyes. "Tal," I breathed in utter confusion.

He didn't speak, but an array of emotions flashed through those eyes I knew so well: relief, frustration, anger, and maybe even grief.

I tore my gaze away from Tal and rounded on the director. "Let him go," I demanded. "There's no valid reason to have Talisen restrained. He was helping me. This is insane."

"Have a seat, Rhoswen," Director Halston said again.

My wings flared in total frustration. "What's going on?"

She waved a hand toward my chair, her expression grim.

Dammit! No matter what I said, she wasn't going to answer. Reluctantly, I took a seat next to Phoebe. An athletic-looking woman, about my age with dark blond hair was between Phoebe and the director, while David, Allcot, Nicola, and Harrison were seated on the other side of the table. The healer was nowhere to be found. I glanced at Tal one more time and that's when I noticed Link, curled at his feet back in Shih Tzu form. His tail was bandaged in white gauze.

I clamped my hands together in an effort to keep control. I was moments from flying across the room and scratching the director's eyes out. How dare she bind Talisen like that?

"As you can see, Asher has escaped." She glanced at the unfamiliar girl first, then Phoebe. "I must say, I am rather disappointed in you both. Kilsen, I hope you are aware your incompetence has ruined two years of Meyers's undercover work."

My head snapped up. Two years of undercover work? Meyers. That name sounded so familiar. Elissa Meyers. Tal's contact and Asher's assistant. It had to be her. The house in gang territory. The money to afford college. The reason she was sitting at the table now instead of handcuffed to a chair.

Phoebe caught me staring at Elissa and whispered, "She's a witch."

"Yes," Halston chimed in. "An exceptional one who has been working with the master vampire Asher for the last nine months. She's also the one who's been investigating your fae friend."

"And the one who broke into your office," Allcot said to me in a stony voice.

"Yes," the director said. "She did that under my orders to keep her cover. The bird, however, was Asher's doing."

That's why she'd shown up to do the inspection herself. But I was more worried about something else she'd said. "Investigating Tal? Why?"

These people were crazy. Tal was just a fae working for the university. Working for Asher. But he hadn't known he'd been working for the notorious vampire. Surely they had to know that.

The director gave me an incredulous look and then waved at the humans. "He not only made the super drug that allowed Asher's people to almost take out my two strongest witches but he willingly gave it to Asher as well. You're all lucky Allcot and his witch showed up. Otherwise you'd all likely be dead."

"He didn't give the drug to Asher. Asher had access to it because Talisen thought he was a respected researcher. Tal would never give the drug away," I said.

"No? It looks like he gave it to someone." She jabbed her hand toward Allcot. "Seems they had a deal."

Anger built from deep in my chest. "He only—" I stopped, abruptly realizing I was just about to give her solid testimony that Tal was guilty. He'd only given it out to protect me. But hadn't I warned him he'd get in trouble? Distributing unsanctioned enhancements was a crime. Tal could easily be locked up. "So that's it then. You're going to take him into custody?"

She glanced between the two of us and then shrugged. Up until then she'd been the no-nonsense, hard-assed Director. That one movement told me she wanted something. But from who? Me or Tal? I raised one eyebrow and waited.

She stood, placing both palms down on the table. Leaning over, she locked her piercing gaze on mine. "I know everything.

If you'd come to me, you would've had the Void's protection and none of this would've had to happen."

I bit my tongue to keep from blurting out that she had refused to grant Void protection for my store. Or that I had zero reason to trust her.

"From now on, you'll report all your supernatural activity, any unusual abilities, and you'll submit to Void testing and research."

"But—"

"No. I understand you've been exploited in the past. But you put the entire city in danger and the daywalker knows what you can do now. You have not helped your situation. Learn to trust me or you will be put in lockdown."

Phoebe pushed herself to her feet. "Pardon me, Director. But you must have some idea what it's like to have your life on the line and not know who to trust."

Halston nodded. "Yes, one does not rise to my rank without ruffling some major feathers." She tore her gaze from Phoebe and focused on me once more. "That's why we'll consider this a warning instead of taking you to task in front of the Arcane disciplinary board."

Holy fae. The disciplinary board had the power to expel an agent from their contract. And no one walked away from such a fate. They were either sentenced to death or put into servitude for the remainder of the contract. I should have been relieved she'd only issued a warning, but I knew better. Everything came with a price.

And in this case, it meant Void testing. My freedom as I'd known it was over.

"As for Mr. Kavanagh, I would consider putting him on probation if he consents to turning over his notes and research on his new drug to the Void. *All* the research." She turned to Allcot. "Including what your operation has discovered."

I clamped my mouth shut to keep from revealing my surprise. He'd already started testing? He'd just gotten some from Tal the day before. Damn, Allcot didn't waste any time.

Allcot narrowed his eyes and leaned back in his chair. It seemed odd that he remained sitting, letting her dominate the conversation. "Why should I help the Void?"

The director straightened and crossed her arms over her chest. "You and your son are now daywalking vampires. If word were to get out..."

My fingers curled and my nails bit into my thighs. "You can't leak that information." Panic slipped into my tone. "It's too dangerous."

The director shrugged. "For you and the vampires, sure. But not for the Void."

David and Allcot leaped to their feet simultaneously. David's face was contorted in rage. Allcot's was stone-cold. Allcot held up a hand to stop David from ripping the director's head off. Then he turned to the short faery. "What do you hope to gain by threatening us? It's not about information on the drug. It seems you could run any number of tests to find out any information you might need." He cocked his head, studying her. "No. You want something else. I suggest you just ask for whatever it is."

"Or what?" The director seemed more curious than angry or annoyed.

"Or Davidson and I will walk out of here and we'll take Ms. Rhoswen with us."

I glanced at Tal. He was staring at Allcot with murder in his eyes. "And Talisen," I added.

Allcot kept his gaze on the director. "If you wish, Ms. Rhoswen."

Relief swept through me as I realized Allcot would protect me. Then a sinking feeling formed in the pit of my stomach. Allcot acted as if I was one of his people. I didn't want to belong to him. Yet it was better than being a lab rat at the Void.

The director shook her head. "I cannot allow that. Mr. Kavanagh has broken several Arcane laws. Another vampire we've been investigating for over two years knows about the drug and Rhoswen's unique ability. This is going to get out and if there aren't any official repercussions, the entire Arcane is going to be investigating you." She leaned in, locking eyes with Allcot. "And we both know there are certain parts of your business dealings you don't want exposed."

Allcot ground his teeth together, clearly enraged at her insinuation. "What exactly is it you want from Ms. Rhoswen and her friend?"

"Mr. Kavanagh will need to come in and answer our questions. We'll also want to test the effects of the daywalking on either Mr. Laveaux or yourself. And most importantly, we'll want to figure out exactly how Ms. Rhoswen's gift works."

I held my breath, not daring to say anything. When the Arcane wanted something, they went after it full force. The last time they'd wanted me for tests, I'd been locked in the basement…and it hadn't been sanctioned. No one but the old director and his minions had known I was there.

Allcot turned his gaze on me. "I'm also curious about this new gift."

Omigod! The a-hole was turning on me already.

"No," David said. "Absolutely not."

Allcot held up a hand. "How about we make a deal?"

"No," David repeated. "No deals."

"May I remind you that Rhoswen is under a binding contract with the Void? If she breaks it, her life is forfeit." The director pursed her lips. "However, contrary to what everyone here seems to think about me, I do want to come to an agreement. If there is no attempt on your part to work with us, I will do what is in the Void's best interest, whether you take Rhoswen with you or not."

Phoebe swore under her breath and I slumped in my chair. The Void had my signature on a magical document. If I ran, they could and would track me down. They could even force me to turn myself in by having a witch activate the desertion clause.

David glanced at me, a silent question in his eyes. I shook my head. Whatever he was planning was only a temporary solution.

Allcot seemed to understand the predicament. "I see. Well, it looks like a compromise is in order." He stood and waved a hand toward the destroyed living room. "Director, shall we have a private consultation?"

Halston raised a skeptical eyebrow. "My witch will join us as a witness." She pointed an elegant finger at Elissa.

"Certainly." Allcot waved them both ahead of him. David leaned in and whispered something to Allcot. The master vampire nodded and swept out of the room.

I ran to Talisen's side and inspected his bound wrists. Duct tape. How original. It seemed to be the binding of choice today. He hadn't been magically bound as I'd thought. Thank the powers that be. I frantically tugged at the edges, but the tape ripped in two places, not allowing me to unravel it neatly. "Dammit. Phoebs?" I jerked my head up. "Do you have a knife?"

She shook her head. "The director took it."

"Here." David got up and moved to my side. "I got it."

Talisen jerked back. "No. Don't touch me."

"Tal. He's only trying to help," I said, placing a hand on his shoulder.

"I don't want his help." His jaw jutted out in stubborn defiance.

"I've got it," Nicola said quietly. She reached up and pulled a large hair clip from her blond locks. A metal decorative dragonfly was attached to the top. Smiling, she yanked on the tail, revealing a slender silver knife. In two deft movements she had Tal's hands free.

"Thank you," he said, rubbing his red wrists.

I moved in to hug him, but he stiffened and frowned, not meeting my eyes. "What is it?" I asked. "How's your arm?"

"It's fine, Willow." His voice was low and emotionless. "I just need some space right now."

I stared up at him, trying to see into those deep forest-green eyes. Finally he met my gaze and I saw everything I needed to see.

Anger. And it was directed at me.

Chapter 28

After fifteen minutes of sitting in silence, Allcot and the director reappeared with Elissa in tow.

The tension in the room made me jumpy and it was all I could do to stay seated.

Allcot and Halston stood together at the end of the table, providing what appeared to be a united front. Neither looked especially pleased or upset.

"Elissa," Allcot said. "Would you please relay the agreement?"

"Certainly." She pulled out a thick pair of rimless glasses, perched them on her nose, and flipped open a notebook. "The agreement reached decrees that either Mr. Allcot or Mr. Laveaux will volunteer to participate in Arcane-sanctioned testing of their new daywalker abilities. The testing shall consist of no less than eighty hours and shall not exceed one hundred and twenty hours unless a new agreement is reached. In return, the Void will share all relevant findings with the vampires Allcot and Laveaux. In addition, no attempt will be made to restrict reasonable and safe testing of the fae Rhoswen. At the end of one hundred and twenty hours, the Void will cease mandatory testing and must secure an agreement from agent Rhoswen for any additional testing. In regards to the fae Kavanagh, he shall be taken into custody and debriefed but not retained by the Void for more than twenty-four hours unless evidence of intentional harm is recovered."

David stood. "I'll volunteer myself for the Void's experiments."

Allcot nodded, clearly anticipating his reaction.

"Ms. Rhoswen?" Allcot asked.

I nodded mutely. I was terrified of what the Void would put me through, but if I was honest, the idea that David would be with me lessened the fear. And it really was a good thing Allcot had negotiated for me, as the Void did own me. If the orders came down to test me indefinitely, they could find a way to do it without my consent for the next two years. This way we had a contract. One that involved the most powerful vampire in the city. She didn't want war with him. No one did.

No one asked Talisen what he thought.

"Good." The director picked up her phone and hit a button. "The cleanup crew is on their way." She glanced at Phoebe. "Kilsen, I expect you to bring the humans in as well as the fae."

"Davidson," Allcot said. "I've agreed to turn over the vampire and two humans that are presently unconscious in your sunroom. Please see that they make it into Director Halston's care."

"Of course, Father."

Tal stood and moved to stand next to Elissa. "There's no need to apprehend me. I'll go willingly. The sooner this is over, the sooner I can go home where I belong."

Where I belong. Tal wasn't talking about his trashed apartment. He couldn't be. He'd only been there less than two weeks. He meant Eureka. Back to the Northern California coast. My chest started to ache. I stared at Tal, trying to catch his eye, but he refused to look up. Why was he so angry? Because of Allcot? Or was there something else?

"Fine. You can ride with Elissa and me. Rhoswen, Laveaux, report for the first round of testing tomorrow evening. Six p.m. sharp." The director floated out of the room, her wings fluttering with elegant grace. Talisen turned on his heel and followed her with Elissa trailing behind him.

My heart squeezed tighter and I had to swallow back a silent sob. Tal was leaving me.

"Six?" Phoebe asked Allcot.

He nodded. "Ms. Rhoswen runs her bakery and Davidson has his own responsibilities. The testing will happen in the evenings with weekends off."

David nodded. "That's good." He met my gaze. "Can I take you and Link home?"

I glanced at Phoebe.

"Go on. I have to wait for the cleanup crew and deal with these three."

Harrison and Nicola followed Allcot out.

I gave Phoebe a hug. "Thank you."

She hugged me back and whispered, "It'll be all right."

I sighed and picked Link up. He whimpered and tried to lick his injured tail. "I know, bud. We'll get you to the vet first thing in the morning." He settled against me, resting his head on my shoulder.

David placed a hand on the small of my back. And for the first time since he'd turned vampire, I didn't feel the urge to jerk away.

He paused and glanced down at me with a question in his eyes.

I gave him a small shaky smile to hide the turmoil ripping apart my insides. "Take me home."

I sat in my lab, fingering the red hibiscus petal, contemplating recipe experiments for an all-purpose healing treat. The way those seeds had soothed my insides had been remarkable. If I could come up with something even a quarter as effective, I'd have a new best seller on my hands.

A quiet knock sounded on my door, waking me from my near trance. I'd been sitting there, unmoving, for more than forty-five minutes.

"Come in."

Tami poked her head inside. "Sorry to bother you, but it's time for Link's pain medication."

"Thanks." In a mental fog, I rose and headed for my office.

Link raised his head, the cone of shame making him appear even more pitiful than his sad puppy-dog eyes did.

I sat next to him on the floor and ran a hand over his back, holding the meat-flavored anti-inflammatory up to his mouth. "I'm sorry, Link, buddy. It's for your own good."

Link took the medication and flopped down on his stomach, staring at the door as if someone would come in and save him from his utter humiliation.

His tail had been broken, and the vet had needed to amputate three inches. Not only was he stuck wearing the cone of shame, he also couldn't shift into wolf form or he'd rip his stitches out and have to go back to the vet. Though shifters in general do heal faster than non-shifters, it's a myth that they magically heal when they shift. The wounds just show up in their new form.

It had been three days since the showdown with Asher. That night, David had taken me home and sat with me until Phoebe arrived. He'd been sweet and thoughtful, waiting to make sure I was no longer being followed.

He'd picked me up the next day and we'd headed to the Arcane to start testing. So far we'd only been subjected to blood tests and physicals. I knew it wasn't going to be that easy forever, but at least we'd been treated with respect and I was starting to feel as if maybe it wasn't too bad of an idea to really understand the effects of what I could do.

And as much as I hated to admit it, I was glad I had Allcot on my side. They'd think twice before they did anything to piss him off. Not that they wouldn't, but they would consider the consequences first.

The loud shrill of my old-fashioned rotary phone filled the room. Link jerked and his cone got caught on the edge of the area rug he was lying on. He shook and whimpered until I repositioned him.

"I'll be right back." I rubbed his neck and jumped to my feet to grab the phone. "Yeah?"

Silence.

"Hello?" I tried again.

There was a rustling in the background.

I sighed heavily and then yelled into the phone, "Dude! You're butt-dialing again." I went to set the receiver back on the cradle but just as I was about to hang up, I heard "Wil?"

My breath caught and everything went cold. "Tal?"

I'd gone to his apartment right after our testing was done at the Arcane the last two nights, but he hadn't been there. Or if he was, he'd been ignoring me. I hadn't seen or heard from him since he'd walked out of Asher's house with Elissa and the director.

"Tal?" I said again.

He cleared his throat. "Yeah."

"Hey," I said softly. "Where have you been?"

More silence.

I closed my eyes and took a deep breath. "Where are you now?"

"Outside."

That tightening in my chest was back. I had to remember to breathe. "The store?"

"Yes."

I moved to my private entrance and opened the door. "I don't see you."

"I'm across the street."

"Why?"

"I'm not sure I want to come in," he said.

Trepidation coiled in my stomach. He didn't want to see me. He'd stayed away three days and although he was standing outside my store, he didn't know if he could bring himself to come in. Cracks formed in my already-bruised heart, and I clutched at my chest, trying to keep it together. "Tal, please, we need to talk."

There was more silence on his end, and then I saw him crossing the street with a duffle bag slung over his shoulder. His brows were pinched with determination. He slowed when he saw me, arranging his face into a careful, neutral expression.

I stepped away from the door and gently replaced the phone back onto its cradle.

He paused just inside my office, and for a moment I thought he was going to bolt. But then Link bounced to his feet and tried to run to him. He got three steps before his cone crashed into the floor and he tumbled.

Talisen tried to hide a chuckle as he picked my dog up and snuggled his face. "Did you lose something, Link?"

"Part of his tail," I supplied, swallowing the building anguish.

"Oh, that's rough, bud. I'm sorry to hear that."

Would Talisen ever again be as easy with me as he appeared to be with my dog? My heart didn't think so. "He's fine," I said mildly. "He just needs a few days to recover."

"Right." Tal set Link back down on my floor and then shoved his hands in his pockets. He shifted from foot to foot, his mask sliding back in place.

I picked up an empty box sitting on the corner of my desk. "This came in the mail for me the day after the fight with Asher." I pointed to the handwritten address. "You sent this, right?"

He took the box. "Yes. Was there anything in it?"

I shook my head. "No. It had been opened and resealed though. You mailed the extra drugs to me, didn't you? That's why no one could find them."

He looked inside the box and frowned. "Yeah, but what happened to the potions?"

I shrugged, forcing myself to appear as if his aloof demeanor wasn't killing me. "Someone stole them. It would explain why that gang David and I ran into appeared to be hopped up on the drug." I went on to explain our run-in while we'd been looking for Elissa.

"Shit," he mumbled.

"That pretty much sums it up," I said. Those drugs could be in anyone's hands by now.

"I'll inform the director," Tal said almost to himself. "They have the resources to investigate." Then he glanced over my shoulder, not quite looking at me. "I tried my best to keep it out of the hands of criminals. Who better to send it to than you?"

"It was a good plan. Too bad the post office is as corrupt as every other government entity in this town." I glanced at the duffle bag and noted how he couldn't seem to look me in the eye. "You're leaving."

Talisen nodded.

"When?"

This time he did chance a glance in my direction. "Today. I'm on my way now."

Anger bubbled up in the back of my throat and it was hard to talk. "You...you didn't want to discuss it first?"

He shifted his duffle to the other shoulder. "And make it harder?" His voice went soft, almost gentle. "We both know your heart lies with someone else. You're safe for the time being. It's time for me to go home."

I stepped back as if I'd been slapped. "What's that supposed to mean, my heart lies elsewhere? What are you talking about?" A few days ago he'd told me he was all in. Said he wasn't going anywhere. He'd even had a tree put in his bedroom. Now he was running. I wasn't sure if I wanted to scream or cry.

Tal dropped his bag and leaned against my desk. "Come on, Wil. Look at what you did for him. You brought him back to life when you thought he was dead. You nearly killed yourself to save him. And then you did it again to save his father. But you didn't do that for Allcot, you did it for Laveaux."

"I..." How was I supposed to respond to that? Yes, I'd saved them. And yes, I had still loved David when I'd saved him, but shortly after that I'd chosen Tal. Completely.

"You don't have to answer." Tal moved forward and brushed a lock of hair off my forehead, his voice and his touch tender. "I can already see it."

I jerked away, offended he'd taken it upon himself to decide how I felt. "How dare you? Are you claiming you can see into my heart now? That I don't have a mind of my own?"

He shook his head, his expression resigned. "No. I can't see into your heart. If I could, I suspect mine would be more battered than it already is."

There was a sadness about him I'd never seen before. Tal was never sad. And definitely not over a girl. He was broken up about what he was doing. But the determination in his eyes told me he believed he was doing the right thing.

I stepped close and rested my hand over his heart. "I chose you."

His lips formed a sad smile. "I know. That's what makes this so much harder. I'm sorry, Wil. I don't want to be second best. I can't. I love you too much." He pressed a light kiss on my lips and then grabbed his bag and headed for the door.

I stared at him, my vision turning blurry with unshed tears as I stood there in total shock. What just happened? "Tal, wait!"

He turned and gave me a bittersweet, pained smile. "I'll always be there for you if you need me." The door closed with a soft click behind him as he walked out of my life. Back to the one that didn't mean he had to compete with vampires for his girlfriend's affection.

I slammed my hand down on my desk and let out a cry of frustration. A minute later, I sank to the floor, tears streaming as my body rocked with sobs.

Tal had left me.

Chapter 29

My chest ached and my eyes burned from too many shed tears. Every part of me felt hollow as I walked into the Arcane building, preparing for the night's testing.

"Willow?" My aunt Maude emerged from behind security. She frowned and linked her arm through mine. "What happened?"

I sucked in a breath. "Tal left. Went home to California."

"Oh, sweetie. I'm sorry. When will you get to see him again?"

"When I go home for Christmas I guess. Maybe. If he wants to see me." My tone came out flat, almost as if I didn't care.

"Of course he'll want to see you." Maude ran a hand down my arm. "He's not going to forget about you just because he was transferred back to California."

"Transferred?"

"Yeah. Didn't he tell you? About his Void agreement?"

I shook my head. "No." What Void agreement? He was a healer. Not a Void agent. Is that the real reason he'd left? Did he think a long-distance relationship was too much to handle?

"Oh." She led me through security, bypassing the magic neutralizer. I needed to have all my skills for the testing.

"Maude? What agreement?"

She shook her head. "You'll find out soon enough, anyway. He's going to make his drug for the Void. It's going to be tested first, but it will likely be highly controlled. Even more so than Orange Influence."

I didn't like the idea of Tal working for the Void. Not one bit. But I was more focused on the fact that the only thing he had to do was make his drug. He could do that from anywhere. He hadn't needed to go home. The emptiness filling me intensified. The only thing that stopped me from hopping on a plane and dragging him back was the contract I had with the Void. For the next two months, I was chained to them. It was hard to fight for someone when they wouldn't even answer their phone. Tal had made his choices. Now I had to live with them.

We stopped outside a sterile white door. "Is David already here?" I asked.

She nodded. "Yes, but he's being sun tested tonight. You should see the tan he's gotten in just two hours under the rays."

That actually made me smile. He'd already been testing his sun limitations. That's why he'd been sunburned. But a drink of Asher had cured him. How long could he last in full sun? Hours? Days?

"What am I doing while he's tanning?" The image of him lying in a tanning bed with eye protection made me giggle. I got a little warm imagining his chiseled body. Then guilt took over. If Talisen knew what I was thinking, it would only confirm his suspicions. But admiring David's body wasn't the same as being in love with him. Not even close.

"I think they brought in another vampire."

"Crap." That meant I was going to be in a world of pain.

She grimaced. "Sorry."

"Don't worry about it. I already feel like shit. This is the perfect end to a terrible day."

She squeezed my hand. "You'll be okay?"

"I'll live." I took a deep breath and went into my evening torture chamber.

I spent the next three and a half hours hooked up to electrodes while the tech measured my responses to the vamp's proximity.

A buzzing sounded, indicating the use of an intercom. "Ms. Rhoswen, we need to start the physical portion of the testing. Are you up for that tonight? Or would you prefer to start another day?"

I glanced at the clock. Twenty-seven more minutes. I could leave, but then I'd only have to endure whatever they had in store for me the next night. "It's fine to continue."

"Good. Cox, please move closer."

The vampire positioned himself next to me, his heavy vampire aura keeping me rooted to the floor. Whatever he did, I was going to be completely helpless.

"Now, start with her hand and work your way up her arm. Let's see what kind of reading we can get."

Cox sent me a reassuring smile. What did that mean? That he wouldn't be sucking my blood any time soon? That I was reasonably safe with him? I almost laughed at that last thought. Because being beaten and battered by a vamp was really safe.

It didn't take long for Cox to realize his touch was leaving me black and blue. In fact, he noticed the dark bruises instantly and pulled back holding his palms upright.

"Mr. Cox," the researcher chided. "Do not stop until you are instructed to."

The vampire stared at me, his brow wrinkled in what appeared to be concern.

I shrugged. The sooner he got on with it, the sooner we could be done. The Void wasn't going to go easy on me. Not that I was being punished, necessarily. They just wanted their research to be as thorough as possible. And it wasn't as if I had a choice. "Just do as they say," I told him in as strong a voice as I could muster.

"Run your hands from the nape of her neck and down her spine," the administrator ordered.

I sucked in a shallow breath. Yeah, that wouldn't hurt at all. I tensed but turned to give him access.

His touch on my neck caused lightbulbs to pop behind my eyes. Soon enough, darkness began to close in from the constant contact. I pressed my hands to the wall, trying to hold myself up, but when he was ordered to place both hands on the side of my head, my knees buckled and I lost the battle.

I floated in a dream state for what seemed like an eternity. And honestly, I was glad to be there. Whatever they had Cox doing, I couldn't feel it. But all too soon, voices crept into my awareness. My body ached with dull pain from the top of my head to the tips of my toes. I tried to sit up but couldn't. I was trapped against something rock solid.

"Relax. I've got you now." David's voice penetrated my haze.

I stirred unsuccessfully and blinked rapidly, trying to focus. The harsh fluorescent light made my eyes water.

"David?" I whispered.

"Yeah?"

"What happened to the testing?"

"It's over for the evening. I'm taking you home."

My vision finally cleared. I stared up into his concerned face, realizing he was carrying me through the Arcane building. "Thank you."

He gave me a reassuring smile. "There's nothing to thank me for."

A few moments later, we were at my Jeep. He deposited me in the passenger's side and then pulled out his phone. "What's Talisen's number?"

I frowned. "Why?"

He raised both eyebrows. "You need a healer."

"Oh." I slumped down into the seat, wrapping my arms around myself. "Tal went home to California. But don't worry about a healer. All I really need is my oak tree and some anti-inflammatory herbs."

He frowned. "You definitely need a healer."

"No, David." I heard the panic starting to rise in my voice and did my best to tamp it down. I probably did need one, but I still wasn't up for another healer touching me the way Tal would. "I'll be fine. If I'm not better in the morning, I'll go to a clinic."

He stood on the street, appearing to debate with himself. I got tired of waiting and shut the door.

After a moment, he took out his phone, sent a quick text, and then climbed into the car. "Will you really?"

"What? Go to a clinic in the morning?"

"Yeah."

I let out a small laugh. "Probably not."

He started the car and carefully pulled away from the curb. "That's what I thought."

Ten minutes later, David parked in front of my house and before I could raise my arm to grab the handle, he'd already made it to my side of the car and was pulling the door open.

"Thank you," I said again and let him wrap a strong arm around me.

"There's no need to thank me every time I do something for you," he said softly.

"Okay." Muscles I never knew existed complained with each step and as hard as I tried not to wince, I couldn't stop the reflex. David moved slowly, not rushing me, but when we got to the porch and it became obvious I wasn't going to be making it up the stairs without some serious help, he pulled me into his arms again.

"David, let me down. I can do this." I swatted at his arm.

"In a minute." He strode onto the porch, deftly opened the door, and had me upstairs before I could protest further. Once inside my room, he gently lowered me to my feet, but I had the suspicion he'd only done that because my bed was too high off the ground for him to put me in it himself. He ran his thumb ever so lightly over my cheek.

I averted my eyes. He was being so gentle. So caring. It was what I expected from Tal...who wasn't here. The loss of him made my breath hitch.

"Wil?"

"Hmm?"

"You're going to be okay." He gave me a gentle kiss on the top of my head and turned to go.

A yelp, followed by a high-pitched whine, came from across the room. I clutched the edge of my bed and spotted Link under the window, the drapery cords caught around his cone. "Oh my God, Link. How did you do that?" I fluttered toward him, but David beat me to it.

Link started growling and snapping, but with his cone, he couldn't reach David.

"Calm down, boy. I'm going to get you free. That's it. Almost there." David methodically untangled the cord, working Link free of this makeshift noose. Holy cow. How long had he been mixed up in that mess? I shuddered, terrified of what could've happened to him.

As soon as David had him free, Link scurried over to the edge of the bed and leaped onto the old-fashioned elevator I'd gotten just for him. It creaked and groaned. I still needed to oil that darn thing. When it stopped, he jumped and stumbled due to the unwieldy nature of the cone, tumbling with an ungraceful flop onto the edge of the bed. I thrust my wings and settled beside him, scooping him into a tight hug.

"Thanks," I said, my heart beating with gratitude.

"Don't mention it." He turned to leave.

"David?"

He paused inside the doorway and glanced back at me. "You're not going to thank me again, are you?" A smile tugged at his lips.

I smiled back. "No. I just wondered how you're going to get home since your car is at the Arcane building."

"Harrison is picking me up. Now get into bed and let the oak work its magic." His boots hitting the wood stairs echoed through the silent house.

The emptiness in my heart intensified. It's not that I wanted David to stay...okay, maybe I did, a tiny bit. But the truth was I craved Talisen. In the short time he'd been in New Orleans, I'd come to rely on his easy friendship and the fact that he'd always been by my side...except now he wasn't. And it hurt more than I'd ever dreamed. It's exactly what I'd been afraid of when we'd decided to start dating. Not only had I lost my boyfriend, but I'd lost my best friend as well.

Downstairs the door creaked open, and light footsteps sounded on the stairs again. My heart beat faster, praying it was Tal. That he'd changed his mind. But deep down, I knew it must be Phoebe. I sighed, scooted against the trunk of the oak, and closed my eyes, grateful for the trickle of life slowly fortifying my body.

The footsteps stopped near my door. "Phoebs, if you love me at all, you'll get me a cup of hot tea."

"How about some healing balm?"

My eyes flew open. "Mom?"

"Hi, baby." She fluttered her ice-blue wings and landed softly on the edge of the bed, holding a white plastic jar.

I reached over and hugged her fiercely, the heartache consuming me fading a tiny bit. "What are you doing here?"

"Taking care of you." She unscrewed the lid of the jar. With two fingers she scooped out some gel and started smearing it on my bruised arm.

Sweet relief rushed through me. "How did you—"

"David texted me. He didn't want you to be alone."

Whoa. That was thoughtful. But then he always had been, except when he was dumping me to turn vamp. Would I ever get over that? It's not like he didn't have a good reason.

"I'm sorry about Talisen," Mom said softly. "I heard he went home today."

I only nodded. What was there to say?

Mom squeezed my hand. "He'll come around."

Frowning, I glanced away. I wasn't at all sure he would. It was classic Talisen to walk away when things became too complicated, and that's exactly what he'd done. Mom moved to my other arm. The gel wasn't doing much for the bruising, but it was taking the pain away and that was good enough for now. "I thought you were supposed to be hiding out with Allcot?"

"I was." She peeled back my covers and coated my bare calves. "One of Eadric's contacts spotted Asher at the airport.

He got on a plane headed to Argentina. Eadric had someone follow him. Asher is now in Rio. And as far as anyone can tell, all his people have been apprehended. Everyone is safe for now."

A weight seemed to lift off my heart. *Safe for now.* "Does that mean life will be back to normal for a while?"

"That's what it looks like."

I stared up at the lush green leaves of my oak. "You've been here almost a week. When do you have to go back?" There was a tremor in my voice I couldn't quite ignore.

Mom reached over and smoothed a lock of hair behind my ear. "Not until I'm sure you're okay, sweetie."

The unexpected tenderness in her tone made my eyes well with tears. "I've missed you," I choked out.

Mom chuckled. "You spent the summer with me. You can't miss me that much."

I caught her worried gaze and wondered if she was thinking of my physical or mental state. "I meant I miss this interaction. This honesty. It seems...Well, since Beau, it's been too hard to talk."

Mom's eyes misted and she pulled me into a gentle hug. "You're right, baby. It has been hard. But I'm here for you for as long as you need. I can stay. I just have to make a few arrangements back home."

She'd have to get someone to run her nursery. And we both knew that person was likely Talisen. He'd do it, no matter how upset he was with me. "Just for a little while?"

"However long it takes," Mom said. "I'll make the arrangements tomorrow."

Chapter 30

By three o'clock the next day, I was exhausted. I pushed up my long sleeves, no longer caring if any of my employees noticed my bruises, and stood next to the air-conditioner vent in my office. Between the healing ointment and my oak, the pain had all but vanished, but my bruises hadn't gone anywhere.

Link raised his head from his place on the floor and let out a low whine.

"I know, buddy." He was still stuck with the cone of shame. "If you wouldn't chew on your stitches, I could let you out of that thing."

He lowered his head, the cone resting between his paws.

I sat down next to him. "Aren't we a pathetic pair?"

He stared up at me with his amber puppy-dog eyes. His silky hair slipped through my fingers as I pet him.

I was getting ready to head back to my lab when my phone buzzed with a text message. I'd been careful to keep it charged just in case I heard from Talisen. I grabbed the phone and my heart skipped a beat. It *was* from Tal.

I'm sorry.

How was I supposed to answer that? And what exactly was he sorry for? Leaving? Hurting me? Or that our short-lived romance hadn't worked out?

I stared at the readout for a long moment, then typed *Me, too.*

The minutes ticked by. No response. After a half hour passed, I scowled in disgust. *I'm sorry?* That was it? I wasn't doing the text message thing again. I'd had my fill after the Dear Jane text I'd gotten from David last spring. In total frustration, I touched Tal's number and waited for him to pick up.

Voice mail. Dammit.

I sucked in a breath. "Tal, it's Willow. Although I was glad to get your text, I think we need to talk. Please call when you're ready." I hit End and slumped down.

At the mention of Tal's name, Link lifted his head and was now looking at me expectantly.

"Sorry, dude. He abandoned us both."

The office started to close in around me. My chest started to burn as if I couldn't get enough oxygen. The message from Tal had only reopened the wound I'd been nursing since the day he'd left. Silence would've been less cruel. "We've gotta go." I grabbed Link and without letting Tami know, we burst out of my private entrance.

Ten minutes later, we were curled up in my bed under the oak. I took Link's cone off, and clutching my silent phone, I snuggled against his small body. Sadness overwhelmed me, but my eyes stayed dry. All I felt was a sense of loneliness and despair. Tal wasn't coming back. He couldn't even bring himself to talk to me. And even if he did, I wasn't sure I could forgive the fact that he'd run after everything that had happened. He hadn't even given me a chance to explain. There was no way I would've left him. Our relationship had ended before it had really even started. The worst part, the part that made my heart hurt the most, was that he was my best friend. And I was positive I'd just lost him.

Link pressed his little body closer to mine. I buried my face in his silky fur and closed my eyes. I focused on the darkness and prayed for oblivion. It wasn't long before I was pulled under.

"Willow?"

"Hmm?" I rolled over, wincing at the ache in my crooked neck. Link shifted and he vibrated with a low growl.

"It's time to go. We have to be at the Arcane in less than fifteen minutes."

I placed a hand on Link. "Shh, it's okay, Link. It's just David." *David?* What was he doing here? I jerked up into a sitting position and rubbed the sleep from my eyes. "What's going on? How…? I mean why…?"

David grinned at me. "You're really out of it."

"I was asleep."

"I can see that." He held out a hand. "Let me help you down."

Tentatively, I took his hand. "What are you doing here?"

"Picking you up." He pulled me into his arms. "After yesterday, I figured it would be easier if I drove you. That way you won't have to worry about driving home, no matter what tests they run." He set me down on my feet and I felt myself smile.

"That was thoughtful."

His midnight-blue eyes softened, but he didn't say anything.

I glanced at the clock. "Give me five minutes to get Link situated and I'll be right down."

David nodded and retreated down the stairs. How had he gotten in? If Phoebe was home, she would've come to wake me up. I decided it didn't matter. I trusted David and his presence seemed to fill the emptiness inside me.

"Just a few more days," I told Link as I fastened the cone around his head. "Then your tail will be all fixed up." He whimpered and curled up at the foot of the oak tree.

He looked so pathetic I picked him up and flew him to the bed. Then I pushed the button so the makeshift elevator was ready should he need to climb down. I kissed his neck and promised I'd be home soon. Downstairs, David was waiting for me near the front door.

"Thank you," I said.

"Anytime." His eyes lit with humor and my cheeks warmed. If he didn't stop doing nice things for me, I was going to owe him my firstborn.

Over the next two weeks, we fell into the same pattern. I worked in the morning at The Fated Cupcake, came home to take a nap, and then went with David to the Arcane building. Every night I came home bruised, pricked, and utterly battered. The first week Mom had come to check on me each night, bringing the magic ointment. Between the hibiscus cupcakes I'd concocted and the ointment, I was healing well enough. A certified healer still would've been much faster and far more efficient, but my routine was working for me.

Except for the night the Void decided it was time to test what would happen if a vampire fed from me. In my weakened condition, I hadn't lasted more than a few moments once the vampire broke skin. I'd passed out almost immediately.

This particular night, David had been scheduled to feed right after the other vamp, so he'd been in the room. And when I woke up, I'd never heard him sound so angry.

"Look at what you're doing to her," he said, seething. "Do you ever deem it necessary to check on her health?"

"David," I said weakly, holding a palm to my neck. Blood was trickling down my neck from Zac's bite.

He wrapped his arm over my shoulders and pulled me close. "What do you need?"

"Sleep." I hadn't had a decent night's sleep in over two weeks. Not since before we'd started the testing.

"Then let's go." He tugged me toward the door, despite the fact we still had two hours scheduled that evening.

"Mr. Laveaux, may I remind you of the contract?" the director said.

"You can remind me of anything you damned well please. But nothing is going to stop me from taking her to bed."

My cheeks burned. I knew what he meant, but everyone else was already speculating the status of our relationship. His statement had added a lot more fuel to the fire.

"She needs to recover before you do anything else," David continued. And damned if they didn't all back down.

"Let's go." David tugged me close but didn't pick me up, much to my relief. I was weak enough and he was already casting me as a damsel in distress. It wasn't exactly the image I wanted to convey to my colleagues. "She's taking a few days off," David said.

The director eyed us both and I was sure by the hard set of her face she was going to argue. But then she gave us a short nod. "Fine. It's Wednesday today. Take the next two days and the weekend. We'll resume on Monday."

"Really?" I said, not daring to hope she was serious.

"Yes, we need to start compiling results anyway."

"Thank you." I leaned into David for support as he guided me toward the door.

The early-October night air was cool on my skin and I shivered. David ran his hand down my arm as if to warm me. I laughed and smiled up at him. "You're a vampire."

"So?"

"You don't have any body heat."

He chuckled, then his lips morphed into a devilish grin. "I'm pretty sure I could heat you up if I put my mind to it."

"I can't believe you're flirting with me when I'm an inch away from passing out again." My tone was teasing, but my heart skipped a beat. Dammit, if I didn't enjoy the exchange.

He slid his hand to rest on my hip. "Just trying to keep you awake."

His words warmed me all over. The blood loss must've messed with my common sense. Yeah. That was it.

He tucked me into his silver Mercedes, and once I was sitting, my entire body went limp. I slumped against the window and closed my eyes.

The other door shut with a soft click. "Willow?"

"Hmm?"

David reached over and squeezed my hand. "You okay?"

"Just tired." I was exhausted. Physically. Mentally. Emotionally. Between the lab tests and running The Fated Cupcake, my mind and body had turned to mush. But added to that, I'd stayed glued to my iPhone, waiting and praying for a phone call from Talisen. Other than the one text, I hadn't heard from him at all. He'd never returned my call.

I couldn't even say I was mad. Not anymore. No, I was hurt and resigned. My life was too much for him to handle. Or more likely, the decisions I'd made regarding David and Allcot were too much for him to handle. And the thing was, I didn't feel guilt or regret over saving either of them. I'd do it again with no second thoughts. For David. Sure, he was a vampire. But that didn't mean he wasn't a good man. One who would do whatever it took to protect those he loved, including me. And he'd been there for me when no one else was. In fact he was here for me now, when Tal wasn't.

Why did he have to turn vamp? Right. To protect me. Suddenly I didn't care that he'd turned. All that mattered was that he was my friend. And I was his.

"Wake up, sleepyhead," David said.

My eyes popped open. Lights glowed from the living room windows of my house. "Looks like Phoebe's home already."

David jumped out of the car, and like always, he came around and pulled my door open for me. I wobbled as I climbed out.

"Steady there," he said, holding my hand.

"I've got it."

He stepped back, giving me my space.

I had to fight to not let my disappointment take over, because I really wanted to feel his arms around me again. To have him press me against his chest. To feel his lips against...

Shit. Stop it, Willow.

He hadn't tried to carry me since that first night of testing when I'd been too weak to walk. After that, I'd been armed with Mocha in Motion and the ointment my mom had brought me. The combination was enough to keep me moving under my own steam. And when I'd said as much to David, he'd backed off, probably realizing I *needed* to take care of myself to maintain some modicum of self-respect.

"Ready?" David asked.

I pushed away from the car. "Yeah, sure."

We walked slowly up the path, David patiently matching my turtle pace. I didn't even ask if he wanted to come in. He would anyway. He'd insisted every other night and tonight would be no different. He had to see for himself that my house was clear of any intruders and that I'd made it safely to my oak tree.

My feminist side thought I should be annoyed at his overprotectiveness, but really, I was grateful. It was nice to be looked after.

"Phoebs," I called as I walked through the front door.

Link, finally free of his cone, ran forward in excitement, wagging his stubbed tail.

"Hey, buddy." I leaned down and scratched him behind his ears.

David stopped behind me. Link glanced up at him, then acted as if he wasn't even there. Ever since the night David had freed him from the window-covering cords, Link had ceased to growl at him. They weren't best buddies, but the pair had come to some sort of unspoken agreement to get along.

Phoebe poked her head out of her office and pointed to the phone pressed to her ear. I waved and pointed up, indicating we'd be upstairs. She nodded and gestured to David. Her hand froze mid-wave. Her eyes widened as she pulled the phone away from her ear and pointed at me. "Dude, what the fuck is that?"

I clamped my hand over my neck. "More testing."

She narrowed her eyes at David. "You let this happen?"

"Phoebe," I said, exasperated. "He didn't let anything happen and you know it. This is the work of the Void's hired vamp."

She pursed her lips together and then uttered, "Fuck me."

"Yeah," I said.

"Sorry. It's hard to watch this and not be able to do anything about it." She stared at me, her brow crinkled in frustration.

"It'll be over soon."

"She has a reprieve until Monday," David said

Her eyebrows shot up in surprise. "How'd that happen?"

I waved at David and started climbing the stairs. "He insisted."

"Well. Looks like you're good for more than standing around brooding." She smirked at him and ducked back into her office.

I chuckled and kept climbing. David followed, just as he had for the past two weeks.

Once inside my room, I fluttered my wings and perched on the edge of my bed, staring down at David. "I made it."

"I see that." He moved closer and placed both hands on either side of me on the bed.

Warmth spread in my belly. In a soft voice, I asked, "What are you doing?"

His eyes flickered to my neck. "I can't leave until I heal those marks for you."

"Oh," I breathed. He'd healed vampire marks on my neck once before. It had been tender and sensual at the same time and had made me feel things I'd never felt with anyone before.

His hands moved to my waist and ever so gently, he lifted me off the bed and set me down in front of him. I clutched his shoulders and stared up into his deep, midnight-blue eyes.

He met my gaze. A flicker of emotion flashed over his features.

My breath caught with anticipation. Goddess help me, I wanted his lips on me. Wanted to be wrapped in his embrace. Wanted him.

His gaze dropped to my mouth and I couldn't help licking my lips in preparation. His eyes closed as if he were praying for control. Then he leaned in and pressed those cool lips to my neck. He trailed a circle of kisses around the punctured area, soothing with each soft flick of his tongue.

My knees went weak and I clutched at him to keep from falling. His arms wrapped around me, pulling me tight to his statuesque physique.

Holy hell. There was a fire burning from my neck straight to my center that had nothing to do with the vamp bites. And it only intensified when his tongue flicked over the wounds, sending a rush of pleasure straight to my toes. I gasped.

David lapped at my neck until I was almost vibrating, and when he pulled away, the loss was almost too great to bear. I twisted my fist into the front of his shirt and stood on my tiptoes until our lips were inches apart.

"Willow," David said, his voice husky.

"Yeah?"

"Your neck is healed."

"Good." My brain had stopped functioning. All I could think about was kissing him. And the way he was staring back at me said he was consumed with the same thoughts. I closed my eyes and moved in. Our lips touched, slow and gentle at first. Then my lips parted and he tasted me, igniting an inferno between us. We kissed hungrily, deeply, hands everywhere, our bodies molded together. I was lost in his embrace, one that was both familiar and foreign at the same time.

I buried my hands in his thick dark hair and moaned as his lips moved to that sensitive spot right below my ear.

David's arms tightened around me once more, and then he pulled back, running his thumb lightly over my bottom lip.

I was frozen, horrified by what I'd just done. It scared me. But I didn't step back.

David did, instead. "I think now is probably not the time for this."

"You're probably right." Once he wasn't touching me, I could think more clearly. And the thing was, I realized I didn't want him to leave. And not only because my body was humming with desire, but because I liked having him around.

"I should go," he said.

"Okay." Because there was no way I was going to ask him to stay. Not tonight. He was right. This was not the time. I wasn't over Talisen. Not even close. Plus I'd spent two weeks getting battered and then bit by another vamp. I needed time to heal, to mentally put myself together, and he knew that.

He pulled me into one more hug and quickly let me go. "Get some rest, Wil."

"You, too," I called after him, knowing that was going to be next to impossible thanks to the minor make-out session we'd just had.

Twenty minutes later my phone buzzed. David. *We'll talk tomorrow.*

I spent the entire next day whipping up batches of Kiss Me chocolates and Truth Clusters, all the while worrying about what I'd say to David when he called.

By two forty-five, my phone hadn't so much as buzzed once. And mostly I was happy about that. I wasn't sure how I felt about what had happened between us. But one thing was for sure, Tal had been right. I wasn't over David. Now I had a choice to make. Fight for Tal or see what happened with David?

I tossed my phone on the desk and headed to the front of the store. As I walked through the door to the retail area, I came face to face with Tami.

"There you are," she said. "I was just coming to get you. You have a visitor."

"A visitor? Who?"

She shrugged. "No idea. I've never seen him before."

"Did you get a name?" Panic had started to wind its way into my chest. After being followed and subjected to Asher, my tolerance for strangers was nonexistent.

"No, sorry. I was busy with a customer. He's sitting out front, though," She pointed to a tall, tan man, lounging in a metal chair at one of the small tables out front.

I squinted. He wore khaki knee-length shorts, a T-shirt advertising a local pub, and dark sunglasses. A Saints ball cap covered most of his dark hair.

Shrugging, I headed to the front door. I had a store full of witnesses. What could go wrong? I chuckled to myself. Famous last words. However, it was the middle of the day, so at least I didn't have to worry about vampires.

Or did I? The posture of the man waiting for me was entirely too familiar. What was he doing out during the middle of the day? Crap.

I pushed the front door open and strode over to my visitor. "David, what are you doing here?"

He tugged his sunglasses down just far enough to make eye contact and smiled at me from across the table. "Waiting for you. I figured I'd surprise you."

"But it's the middle of the day. What if someone recognizes you?"

He gave a noncommittal shrug and waved a hand at himself. "You really think anyone's going to make the connection?"

Honestly…no. He was tan from his sun experiments and he was dressed like every other student in the city. Heck, Tami hadn't even recognized him and I'd dated him for a year. He'd been in the shop more times that I could count. "Probably not."

He reached into a backpack and pulled out a thick manila envelope. "This is for you."

"What is it?"

"Open it."

More than curious, I pulled the tabs up and peeked inside. I let out a tiny gasp as I recognized the first of many images. They were all the pictures I'd thought I'd lost on my phone, plus a USB drive. "How…"

"I told you I'd get someone to try to recover them. It was stupid to smash your phone without saying anything first."

I wanted to throw my arms around him and hang on until the pressure in my chest disappeared, but since he was sitting down, I hugged the packet instead and smiled down at him. "That was thoughtful."

He shrugged. "It was my fault." Then he grinned and held out his hand. "Hello. My name's David. It's nice to meet you."

Laughing, I let him shake my hand. "What are you doing?"

"Introducing myself."

"I caught that part," I said dryly.

He sat back and regarded me for a moment. "I was hoping we could start over. Maybe put the last few months behind us and get to know each other as the people we are today."

"You already know me. And I know you," I said.

"Sure. But wouldn't it be nice to just start over? This time with complete honesty."

That got me. "Yes, it would. Give me a minute." I ran back into the shop and grabbed two Happy Cookies and a Kiss Me chocolate.

Smiling to myself, I headed back outside and sat across from David. "Here." I handed him one of the cookies and set the Kiss Me chocolate in the middle of the table.

"Is that what I think it is?" he asked, eyeing the bag.

"Yes."

"Why?"

I grinned. "We're starting over."

About the Author

Deanna is a native Californian, transplanted to the slower paced lifestyle of southeastern Louisiana. When she isn't writing, she is often goofing off with her husband in New Orleans, playing with her two Shih Tzu dogs, making glass beads, or out hocking her wares at various bead shows across the country. For more information visit her website at www.deannachase.com.

Book Three of the Crescent City Fae series will be released in June, 2014.

www.ingramcontent.com/pod-product-compliance
Lightning Source LLC
Chambersburg PA
CBHW030319200626
46816CB00006BA/1855